Plaster Saint

by
Addis W. Morgan

PublishAmerica
Baltimore

© 2005 by Addis W. Morgan.
All rights reserved. No part of this book may be reproduced, stored in a retrieval system or transmitted in any form or by any means without the prior written permission of the publishers, except by a reviewer who may quote brief passages in a review to be printed in a newspaper, magazine or journal.

First printing

ISBN: 1-4137-4927-5
PUBLISHED BY PUBLISHAMERICA, LLLP
www.publishamerica.com
Baltimore

Printed in the United States of America

*For my daughter, Jan, and son, Tom,
of whom I have always been proud
and who are, themselves, accomplished writers.*

"Single men in barricks don't grow into plaster saints."

(from "Tommy" by Rudyard Kipling)

Preface

This story is concerned with the experiences of several people, two in particular, who live all or most of their lives in the fictional but typical western Connecticut small town of Newvale.

The central characters are Christopher Drummond Hacker (Hack) and Elizabeth Josephine Pontillo (Libby.) They are of the same generation, know each other from early childhood (in the 1920s,) fall in love, eventually marry, have children and encounter complications not foreseen.

Along the way, Hack decides against college in favor of learning the manufacturing business, while Libby goes off to Middlebury College in Vermont. America's entry into World War 2 occurs while she is there. Hack enlists and has an exciting and dangerous period of service, including experiences which strongly influence his future.

Libby is a paragon. She is beautiful, intelligent and is possessed of a gentle and generous nature, which endears her to virtually everyone with whom she comes in contact. She has, however, an odd and unexplained weakness. On rare occasions, particularly under stress, she becomes momentarily detached from her surroundings and is engulfed by a frightening sense of unreality. It always passes rather quickly. She never mentions this to anyone.

Hack, although a generally upstanding citizen with an excellent reputation for character, ability and ambition, is secretly consumed from childhood by a desire for wealth and the envy of others, and tends always to put his own selfish ends at the head of the list. Although he would not like to admit it to himself, his concern for others, even those near and dear to him, pretty much ends at the point where it conflicts with or threatens his personal agenda. It is this callousness which eventually contributes to his downfall.

Other important characters in the story are:

Christopher Drummond Hacker, Jr. (Chris) Hack and Libby's first born.

Susan Eleanor Hacker, their second and last child.
John and Melody (Drummond) Hacker, Hack's parents.
Anthony and Mary (Mulcahy) Pontillo, Libby's parents.
Sean Mulcahy, Mary's father, Libby's grandfather.
Ingmar Borgeson, Swedish immigrant and mechanical genius. His assistance makes a great contribution to Hack's eventual success.
Sally Finch, English girl who befriends Hack during his short stay in her country while staging for the invasion of Europe. Her parents, Mr. and Mrs. Finch, who welcome him into their home.
Grandma Drummond, Melody's mother.
Spenser Maitland, Sally Finch's son.
Various and sundry others who appear briefly.

The circumstances of the courtship and marriage of Hack's parents require some attention. Melody was the product of a rather strict southern upbringing in Alabama. Her father strove to live up to the image of a southern planter, but unfavorable conditions, such as the arrival of the Mexican boll weevil, and a natural instinct for making wrong business decisions submerged him in such heavy debt that the family struggled to keep their financial heads above water. To do so, Drummond drove his family and a few hired hands and several families of sharecropping blacks, relentlessly. Everyone had to work hard. Even his beloved daughters were required to dig, hoe, plant, spray and pick in order to keep the plantation's perilously teetering finances from total disaster. Melody, schooled in southern charm, regularly had to fight the battle of rapid transition from sweaty and callused field hand to coquetteishly demure and prettily eligible young lady. She vowed to get away from that life and when an opportunity to visit relatives in Newvale, Connecticut occurred, she made her move. She turned her southern accent up a notch and completely bedazzled young John Hacker, freshly graduated from college with an engineer's degree and with a good job in hydraulics, handling the water supply for a fairly large city and for Newvale as well. John never had a chance. He thought it was necessary to bend every effort to win her before other suitors had a chance, and could scarcely believe his good fortune when she agreed to be his wife. What he did not know was that she had assessed him and approved his credentials the minute she saw him. As luck would have it, they were well suited for each other and their marriage was successful from its January 8, 1921 start. Their first child, named Christopher Drummond Hacker, arrived on January 14, 1922.

Libby's parents were somewhat lower on the social ladder. Her father, Tony, arrived in Newvale in 1918 at age 15 as a penniless orphan, his only assets were his strong body, his practical mind and the gifts of tenacity and determination. He came from Bridgeport where his Italian immigrant parents had both succumbed within a month of each other to the influenza epidemic. His only relative in America was his mother's sister, his aunt, Maria Cappozzi, who worked as cook and housekeeper for Doctor Franklin Graham, one of the well-to-do town fathers. The doctor and his pleasant, somewhat corpulent and rather detached wife, Gwen (Monroe, of the Newport, Rhode Island, Monroes) occupied one of the larger Victorian residences on Main Street, which also housed his medical office. He loved his local practice and the townspeople and accepted without bitterness the fact that Gwen had contracted a serious case of scarlet fever while in her first and only pregnancy and had lost the baby. She was left with diminished capacity mentally, which caused a dramatic change in her personality and drastically altered their relationship. She relied completely on the doctor and on Maria, who worshipped her and danced constant attendance on her. The doctor, upon hearing about Tony, insisted upon bringing him into the household where Maria could take care of him. The boy's pride allowed him to accept the kind offer only if he would be permitted to work around the house and grounds when not involved in school or social activities. This arrangement was mutually agreed upon and Tony's industriousness and gratitude resulted in converting the rather shabby grounds into the neatest in the neighborhood.

It was not long before Tony fell for Mary Mulcahy who was in many of his classes at school, where he had been able to earn acceptance as a sophomore. They quickly became a familiar couple at school functions and youth activities. They felt a certain kinship because of their both being children of immigrant parents. Mulcahy was a hearty, outgoing Irishman who had worked many years for breweries and had discovered his wife, Peg, in Boston where he first settled after entering the United States. They looked Tony over carefully when their daughter acknowledged interest in him and registered approval and even admiration. The rest of the way it was all smooth sailing. Tony and Mary laid their plans and were married on January 22, 1921, and enjoyed a wedding trip to Washington, D.C., which they never would have been able to afford, the tab for which was picked up by Dr. Graham.

The happy young couple had both attained jobs which, while not making them rich, did provide for their simple needs and allowed them to exercise their natural frugality by saving a small amount each week. Tony was an exceptional worker and was soon promoted to a foremanship by the contractor for whom he worked. By late in the year, Mary visited Dr. Graham and he confirmed her belief that she was pregnant. She carried the baby with no trouble, except from an overattentive Tony, and on Friday, May 5, 1922, Elizabeth Josephine Pontillo was born, nearly one month premature but perfect in all other respects.

Chapter 1
Christopher Drummond Hacker

Christopher was a healthy baby. His parents showered him with affection and as the only baby in the immediate area of his home, he was also the darling of the neighborhood. By the time he was three years old, he was as secure and well-schooled as one could expect a child that young to be. He was "well-adjusted" as the professionals in child care delight in saying, and he was not terribly upset when his undisputed rule of the home and environs was disturbed by the arrival of a baby sister. She was born on June 30, 1925, and was christened Susan Ruth.

Now, the primary attention of the neighborhood shifted to the cute little baby girl, but all this meant to Christopher was that the had more time to himself. Wisely, his parents had obtained a mongrel puppy as soon as they learned that Melody was pregnant again, because they believed that it would occupy so much of Christopher's attention that the competition from a new sibling would be mitigated. They were correct. There was an immediate mutual adoration between the little male dog and his human counterpart. By the time the baby arrived, Christopher was only casually interested; he was dedicated to being together with "Frosty," so named because of a rim of white hair along the edges of his brown ears. The dog, now nearly a year old, had reached near maturity, physically, and was just large enough to be strong and worthy as a protector, while not being of such proportions as to make him a nuisance or a threat. He was smart and good-natured and he idolized young Christopher, who, in turn, could be blissfully happy on his own as long as Frosty was with him. Although they were too young to be allowed to leave the yard alone, they found countless diversions both inside and outside. When there was nothing else in particular to command their attention, they were perfectly happy with an impromptu wrestling match or a simple race. And when they had exhausted both their repertoire and their energy, they would simply curl up together and have a nap. When a boy has a dog that he loves, there is no such thing as boredom.

As Christopher grew, his world naturally expanded to include other people in the community; people of all ages, sizes and types. He began making friends of his own age through the friendships of their parents and his, as well as through exposure to them in Sunday School and other gatherings. He never felt especially shy or intimidated with other children and was eager to join in their games and experiments. He quickly became one of the favorites because he was intelligent and agile and well-coordinated, and could take a few knocks without having to seek adult sympathy. He entered all contests with the intention of winning, but he soon learned that no one wins all the time and that a loss had to be accepted with reasonably good grace.

Christopher also proved to his friends at an early date that it did not pay to deliberately try to hurt him, or take advantage of him. When someone made such a mistake, Christopher became menacingly quiet and purposeful. He would stalk his tormenter and exact his revenge in a remarkably cold and efficient manner. When he went to school and was exposed to the normal rough and tumble between boys, he had only a few fights because it became immediately apparent that he fought to win. He always entered the fray silently and cold-bloodedly and the battle was quickly over, due more to his total dedication to his purpose and his disregard for the opponent's skills than to any great superiority in strength or technique. These characteristics earned him the respect and rather nervous admiration of his contemporaries and ensured him considerable success in any competition.

They were also responsible to a large extent for his nickname. Most Christophers can expect to find their name shortened to Chris by their friends and acquaintances, but some of the boys who knew of his resoluteness acknowledged it, more appropriately they felt, by cropping his surname instead. To them he became "Hack," and soon that was the manner in which he was addressed throughout the town, by all except his mother, some of the more proper ladies, and one special girl.

In small town Connecticut in the 1920s and 1930s, lasting friendships were molded between youngsters of different ages because there were relatively few children in any particular age group, and this ensured their getting to know each other very well. Toddlers who became acquainted were still coming in contact with each other regularly at high-school age and beyond. They met under all sorts of circumstances and could readily observe any subtle alterations in character caused by whatever influence; physical change, economic situation, family problems, successes or failures. As a result, they knew exactly what to expect from their contemporaries, so friendships were based on almost total understanding.

Hack enjoyed his youth thoroughly. The many material things which were denied to him, and to all children of the Depression era, were more than compensated for by the peace, beauty, cleanliness, honesty, freedom, decency, hope, loyalty and love which were always their's for the taking. They did their schoolwork as best they could. They were responsible for their chores and earned their amusements. They developed their minds and bodies and molded their lives in the manner which they themselves dictated, for there were not a great many outside influences to force them away from what was to each his normal destiny.

Games and sports were pure fun. Children invented, organized and played them self-supervised and with little interference from adults. Youngsters knew their boundaries and parents knew they were nearly always safely within them. The boys played ball or swam in the several "holes" in the shallow Mannisuit River, which meandered its normally peaceful way through the valley floor of Newvale, or tramped the woods or went "bike ridin'." The older ones occasionally rode their bicycles to the adjoining town of Wentworth to attend movies, the nearest available to them. Most of the girls found less strenuous pastimes at or near home, although a few tomboys were sometimes allowed to compete in the rougher sports with the boys; primarily because of the shortage of eligible players.

One of Hack's close neighbors was his friend, Moe Penning, whose father was an Army officer and who was very interested in firearms. Moe was a few months younger than Hack, but their paths crossed constantly as they grew. A common interest in sports enhanced the relationship. Moe introduced Hack to his father's collection of guns, which ranged from a simple .22 caliber rifle through several gauges of shotguns and up to heavy caliber hunting rifles, as well as a few hand guns. Moe had been thoroughly indoctrinated in the care and handling of these weapons practically from infancy. He passed his information and instruction on to Hack, an avid pupil.

One day, Captain Penning asked Hack if he would like to try some shooting, an invitation which was eagerly accepted. They took several weapons and a supply of ammunition and went to the rear of the Penning property where a simple firing range had been constructed. Several sections of old telephone pole, about ten feet in length, had been stacked horizontally one upon the other to form a thick wall about seven feet high. Targets were attached to it and items such as old tin cans placed on wooden blocks in front of it. These could be safely fired at, because the thick wooden backing could absorb any but the most powerful projectiles. A wooded hill rose sharply behind the range, so that even a very badly aimed shot would simply bury itself in the dirt if it managed to miss the wall.

Captain Penning was careful of details and intent on seeing to it that anyone he taught completely understood what he was imparting, and he pounded the safety steps into Hack's mind mercilessly. Then he gave equal care to instructing Hack and demonstrating for him the loading, aiming and firing techniques for each weapon. When all of the basics had been covered, the captain set the boys up with targets and ammunition and allowed them to bang away for an hour or so. Hack was thrilled to think that such a high-ranking soldier would take the time and expend the effort to give him such a marvelous morning of training, and the lessons made a tremendous impression on him. Captain Penning immediately became one of Hack's idols. What he learned in that short outing stuck with him through the years.

Hack and Moe often practiced with ammunition furnished by Captain Penning or purchased by the boys with hard-earned cash. Guns fascinated Hack and he took every opportunity to practice with any that were available. He finally sacrificed a few of the dollars which he so jealously guarded, to buy a .22 caliber Remington pump gun, and for a long time it was his most precious possession. He patiently oiled and rubbed the sleek rifle and religiously cleaned the bore so that it shone. The gun reposed, when not in use, in Hack's bedroom on a wooden rack which Hack had induced his Manual Arts instructor at school to guide him in fashioning. He often lay on his bed and gazed with reverence at the handsome, clean-lined instrument.

Frosty accompanied Hack on treks to the woods and fields and became an eager accomplice in the stalking of varmints, mainly woodchucks, which Hack learned to seek out and destroy with the complete approval of the farmers whose land they were violating. The dog did have one bad experience with a husky, wounded woodchuck which desperately grabbed him by the nose when he rashly dove at the beleaguered animal as it tried to make it into its hole. Hack rushed up to the thrashing pair and managed to dispatch the woodchuck with the muzzle of his rifle against the animal's body. Frosty sustained a nasty, painful wound which was treated by the veterinarian. The dog had to forego violent exercise for several days. He never made the mistake of leaving an opening for a woodchuck's sharp incisors on subsequent expeditions.

Experience, practice and familiarity with various firearms enabled Hack to become an excellent marksman. He learned to show patience and coolness when hunting; how to lead his quarry when it was on the move and how to squeeze off the shots. He learned how to judge distance, the approximate patterns of shotgun pellets, and whether the size pellet being used was practical for the game of the moment. Under the tutelage of Captain Penning, Hack also learned the feel and use of hand guns. He became adept at handling the light .22 calibers and .32s, and found that the heavy, impressive .45 caliber automatic was virtually useless as far as accuracy over much distance was concerned.

Captain Penning said, "Hack, the purpose of the .45 automatic is to throw a lot of lead rapidly in the general direction of a menacing nearby target. It will knock down just about any living thing up to the size of a horse, but if you need accuracy, and time and distance permit, use your rifle."

Chapter 2
Hack's Obsession

Newvale had only a few families that could be accurately classified as wealthy, but those few greatly impressed Hack, even as a child.

The Lamsons were descended from shrewd fur traders; the Jays' ancestors had built a shipping empire. All of this had happened one hundred fifty to two hundred years before Hack was born, so the current editions of these families had known nothing but wealth. The other moneyed clan, the Borgesons, on the other hand, had acquired their fortune only in the past twenty-five years. The superior mechanical ability and inventiveness of their patriarch had enabled him to create and market a carburetor which had rapidly become the standard in the vehicles of one of the leading manufacturers in the automotive industry.

Most of the Lamsons and Jays carefully avoided flaunting their riches. They lived in quiet splendor amid the peaceful beauty of the rural Connecticut countryside and admired the innate decency of most of its inhabitants and the way these people respected their privacy. The Jays and Lamsons and Borgesons lived on large tracts in impressively large homes, tended to perfection by inside and outside servants. Their estates included such extravagances as formal gardens with sculpted hedges, exotic plants and trees, tennis courts and fountains, but their opulence was well hidden behind thick rows of hemlock and cedar trees and high stone walls. They had chauffeured limousines for travel, but the owners themselves drove around in modest little Ford station wagons for their local errands.

Both the Lamsons and the Jays regularly attended services at the local Episcopal church. Mrs. Jay sang in the choir and Mr. Lamson often passed the collection plate. When the old church furnace failed, Mr. Lamson instructed the pastor to have a new one installed and to send him the bill. When the roof leaked and threatened the interior decor, Mr. Jay had it replaced at his own expense. In both cases, the pastor was asked to refrain from announcing the names of the donors, but the parishioners knew that only the Jays and the Lamsons had the funds for such benefactions. Neither family wanted credit for their gifts—they had no need to seek approbation from the community.

When he was ten years old, Hack happened one day to be riding his bicycle on a route which took him past the border of the Jay estate. His youthful curiosity piqued, he stopped, pushed the bike behind a tree, climbed over the high stone wall and cautiously crept along the thick row of cedars which separated the grounds from the rest of the community until he reached a point at which there was a breach in the tightly woven branches. From this vantage point he was able to get a good view of a substantial portion of the grounds. The long garage, capable of housing five vehicles, was clearly visible and as he watched, the doors on one bay swung outward. Soon, an engine started and after a few minutes of idling it was revved, the gears were engaged and the nose of a huge maroon Rolls Royce rolled slowly and majestically out into the drive. A chauffeur, without a jacket, but otherwise in complete uniform, climbed out of the driver's seat and started immediately ministering to fancied needs of the monster. A bit of water for the radiator, a check of the air pressure in each tire, an almost ceremonial lifting of the hood on each side of the cowl, succeeded by a serious examination of the details of the engine, reassured the vehicle's custodian that everything was in perfect order. Just to be sure, he gave everything another going over and followed his inspection by lightly wiping down every bit of exposed paint, glass and plate with an antiseptically clean chamois cloth. Satisfied that his mechanical ward was fit for yet another day of probable inactivity, he gave it another ten minutes of throaty idling and then backed it slowly through the doors to its lair.

All this, Hack watched, fascinated. When the little drama was over, his gaze traveled to other parts of the estate. One hundred yards off to the left, another man was fussily skimming all traces of debris deposited by the breeze, from the surface of the swimming pool. An aged gardener plodded out of a white-trimmed red tool house, pushing a wheelbarrow loaded with bags of fertilizer and lime.

The mistress, Mrs. Jay, was walking about the lawn near the rear of the main house, pointing now and then to its upper portion, obviously discussing some wanted repairs or alterations with one of the local craftsmen, who glided along in her wake, nodding occasionally and jotting notes on a small pad.

In a fairly distant pasture, several horses grazed or trotted around, apparently denizens of a row of stables to be seen some distance from the house.

Everything looked so efficient and well organized, so attractive and perfect, that Hack crouched, immobile, with his mouth hanging slightly open, lost in the magnificence of the picture before him.

"So this is what it is like to be really rich," he said to himself. A gorgeous mansion and grounds and expensive cars, horses and other things which ordinary mortals could only dream of. Money to buy whatever one's heart desired. Servants to dance attendance on one and cater to one's every whim. And the respect and envy of almost everyone. Power—that was the only word for it, he concluded.

Hack could not tear himself away from his hiding place for some time. He watched and he wished and he dreamed. For many months thereafter, he continued to make occasional surreptitious visits to his hideout in the cedars to further fuel his growing obsession with the plutocratic lifestyle.

❖ ❖ ❖

Young Christopher sometimes felt mild resentment when a household chore interfered with some diversion on which he had been about to embark, but he never minded physical labor. The feeling of health and strength which hard work brought out, satisfied that segment of his masculine ego which required such confirmation. As he reached an age at which he could get an occasional job for which he actually received pay, his willingness became even more pronounced. Hack had great respect—almost reverence, for money. He coveted it. At an early age, he decided that he was going to amass all the wealth he possibly could. When he discussed the future with his father, he received mild encouragement. John Hacker believed in doing as well as possible, financially, but not in letting the desire for worldly possessions control and direct his life. He gave Hack the benefit of such knowledge of finance and investment as he could, but tried to impress on him that there were other things.

"It's fine to be ambitious, Hack, and to want some of the nice things in life that money can buy, but health and honesty and decency are much more important."

"But, Dad, there just isn't any way to feel really successful unless you have more money than most people. That's what I want."

John started to rebut this, but quickly thought better of it. "The boy is still young—why get involved in an argument about such a heavy subject," he thought.

"Well, Hack, you have a long time to decide on your aims. Don't let these serious subjects interfere with your enjoyment of your youth."

Hack understood the message, he simply did not agree with his father's philosophy. From that point on, he continued to ask his father's help in answering specific questions about finances, but tried to make his inquiries as casual as possible so that John would not lecture him about greed.

❖ ❖ ❖

Another phenomenon which was just beginning to manifest itself to Hack, was love. During his preschool days and his first three or four years in grade school, he had been too busy adjusting to the routines of life, too interested in all of the other children, too thrilled with discovering and promoting friendships with his male peers and too wrapped up in finding and establishing his proper place in the pecking order to accord girls any interest. Boys were kindred souls who raced, jumped, yelled, wrestled, climbed and swam. They loved dogs and horses and found snakes, frogs, bees and butterflies, fascinating. Girls were somewhat goofy and liked strange things like clothes, dolls and tea sets. They would get together with each other and whisper and cry if anything went wrong. They were hard to understand, and the boys did not bother trying in the early years. But then, one day without warning, an exchange of glances, an accidental contact, a whiff of perfume or fragrant soap on vibrant young skin, or a tinkling laugh or a shy smile would change everything. To a lad's consternation, all of his disregard, his disdain, his presumed superiority and his haughty independence would come crashing down in a shambles of confused signals and disorientation. He would experience a rush of blood to the head, water to the knees and giddiness to the brain, and love would claim another victim. Thus, it happened to young Christopher Hacker.

Elizabeth Pontillo was as familiar to Hack as the street in front of his house or the trees in his yard or any of the other people or things which had been parts of the scenery of Newvale since he was old enough to recognize them. She was only two months younger than he, so it was inevitable that their paths would cross repeatedly. Every social occasion for a girl or boy was certain to bring out most of the other children of like age. Anything to do with schooling, every birthday party and every community get-together were sure to produce encounters with the same youngsters, so they all knew each other very well by the time they were four or five years old. But the little boys kept pretty much to the company of other boys, and the girls gravitated to their own sex, also. Nothing serious occurred between the sexes until about age nine or ten.

Christopher fitted the pattern nicely, for it was at a tenth birthday party for a mutual friend that he suddenly discovered Elizabeth. There were about twenty guests, roughly half girls and half boys, and at some point in the festivities, before the traditional cake and ice cream, the hostess suggested that the children play hide-and-seek. They immediately set the game in motion; one child was selected to be "it," and soon they were flying in all directions looking for likely hiding places.

Hack started first in one direction, then in another and finally ran for the back of the house. As he passed the corner of a side porch, a large wicker sofa caught his eye and he decided that a vault over its back would put him in a strong position to make a quick dash for "home" when the coast appeared clear.

"Oops!" he cried, as his hurdle landed him awkwardly on top of a slight crouching figure. A small squeal blended with his cry as the little girl who had preceded him to the hiding place felt herself being trampled.

Hack immediately recognized his victim and whispered, "Sorry, Libby. Are you okay?"

"I…I guess so, Christopher," she whispered back, "but I was scared for a minute."

"That's too bad. Hope you're all right. Guess I didn't expect to find someone else back here."

They were nestled into a relatively small space, and the combination of the intimacy of the position and the secretive atmosphere of the game, transformed them suddenly into a tiny island of conspiratorial harmony. For several moments there was no further conversation, and in that brief time, Hack experienced a shocking awareness of something entirely new to him— new, and exciting, and almost frightening. His nose was treated to the fresh, clean sweet scent of the young body so still and so close to his. When he looked into the large brown eyes with the long dark lashes, saw the saucy little nose, the perfect mouth with lips slightly apart, showing even white teeth, he temporarily lost his interest in the game. He simply gazed with his mouth somewhat ajar, unable to speak and interested only in freezing this vision for as long as he could.

Composed now, Libby relaxed and briefly returned his stare. She had not experienced quite the same reaction as he, but her budding femininity was curiously stirred and she was not at all upset by the unusual situation which had developed so unexpectedly and so suddenly.

Shortly, the girl who was "it," trotted past the porch—the brief escape from reality was dissipated, and the two came out from behind the sofa.

"Come on—we can get "home free" if we run," giggled Libby. So they dashed toward the goal, but Hack held Libby's hand tightly in his as they ran.

The rest of the party passed in a blur for Hack. He participated in all the games, presented his gift to the celebrant, ate the cake and ice cream, and sang the birthday song, but it was all done by rote, for he was unable to keep his eyes from constantly seeking out Libby and his mind from dwelling on her.

At the end of the party, he risked the derision of his male friends by walking home with Libby. Although there was little conversation during the short walk, they felt comfortable with each other, and both sensed that there was more to come.

Chapter 3
Elizabeth Josephine Pontillo

Naturally, when Elizabeth was born, the young parents were enraptured with her and gave her all the attention possible. They were, however, very practical in their approach to parenthood, as indeed they were in all phases of their lives, and were able to strike a nice balance without overdoing it.

The little girl was bright and healthy and gave them so little trouble that they perhaps got a somewhat too rosy view of child rearing. By the time Libby, the nickname she had almost from birth, was six months old, Mary was able to spend part of each weekday at the clothing store, where she had worked since high school as a seamstress. Mrs. Hanscom, a neighbor, was happy to babysit. When the baby started toddling around, Grandma Mulcahy also started taking care of Libby occasionally. Thus the child was treated to plenty of variety in her daily activities.

Tony, although very much a "man's man," accustomed to handling heavy machinery and equipment and earth materials, was as gentle and patient as a nurse with his little daughter and knew the routine of her care and feeding as well as Mary did. At times he would find himself gazing at this tiny person, so beautiful, so helpless and so innocent, and his heart would swell with love and pride. His world was now so full of marvelous things; his work, which he truly enjoyed, his home, which he and his wife had developed into a thoroughly satisfying haven, his friends, the community, and mainly of course, his wonderful Mary and this little product of their union. "Why am I so lucky?" he wondered.

As the little girl grew, she started showing signs of the features she would carry into maturity. Because her hair was dark, she was obviously going to be a brunette. Her eyes were a rich brown, reflecting the Latin elements of her ancestry, while her skin was light and fair like the Irish. She laughed readily but could also at times exhibit a serious mien, as though she were lost in thought. As she developed, she proved to have a personality of the sort which attracts people, and her openness and generosity of spirit enabled her to make friends with nearly everyone, seemingly without conscious effort.

But no one is quite perfect, of course. If one looked for a weakness in little Libby's makeup, one would probably have to settle for her tendency to be just a trifle standoffish. As she grew and developed her personality, it was this characteristic which occasionally gave pause to those who wanted so badly to become intimate with her. While she related very well to her contemporaries and, indeed, to older people also, there was a line she unconsciously drew which identified her very private thoughts and feelings as an area that was off limits to everyone else. She was happy to share in exchanging school and community information, and later, philosophical or political positions, but when it came to her personal likes and dislikes, or her romantic leanings or her religion, she became inviolably private. This was frustrating to her girlfriends and especially so to her mother. Mary was so uncomplicated and straightforward that it was hard for her to understand why she was unable to break through this intangible but implicitly present barrier. But both mother and friends came to realize that this was simply an inherent part of Libby's makeup and that she would never deliberately project an air of aloofness or any other characteristic that might be offensive to others. And since it was quite natural to her, it actually lent an almost regal quality of which many of her friends and acquaintances were appreciative, if a bit jealous. It seemed to add a final touch of class to an already enviable personality. If she had had any enemies, they would have hated her for it, but she had none.

Libby was fascinated by nature. Even as a small child she liked to drift off occasionally by herself to any of her private spots, under the trees or on an outcropping of rock or even to the sweet hay of a nearby meadow for short interludes, where she could enjoy being alone and could drink in the beauty and peace of her surroundings. At first, it was simply an inexplicable urge that these little escapes satisfied, but as she matured she found that they soothed and filled her with a deep love for her part of the world, enabling her to concentrate completely on any problem or matter of interest to her. Many of the more important decisions which she was obliged to make throughout her life were fashioned during these solitary intervals. When she and young Hacker discovered each other and were drawn in the inexplicable manner of lovers toward one another, Libby found herself more and more often seeking one of her private refuges to try to sort out the mystery of this attraction, and to savor it. Hack's obvious fondness for her, his healthy good looks, his businesslike method of attacking school work, sports and work, contributed to the pleasure she derived from his attentions. But there was something deeper, more elusive, harder to understand, and it was an explanation of this mystery that she sought in many of her lonesome meditations.

Libby was equipped with a healthy body and an obedient practical but inquisitive mind, a combination bound to produce an excellent student. Although the attainment of the highest grades was almost effortless for her, she had an awareness of and consideration for the feelings of others somewhat less gifted which enabled her to accept accolades for her accomplishments in a manner that was never offensive nor smug.

Libby had known for some time that she hoped to attend college. A motor vacation with the family in her early teens had taken her through the upper New England states, and she had fallen completely in love with the setting and general ambiance of Middlebury College. In fact, from then on, no other school would do. Never mind the fact that it was quite exclusive, very expensive—and Protestant. It was her alma mater-to-be from the moment she laid eyes on it, surrounded by the Green Mountains and the breathtakingly beautiful blazing oranges, reds and yellow and the tempering greens of mid-Vermont in autumn. She researched the school thoroughly and she was impressed with the lore she uncovered. Not many colleges' credentials included well over one hundred years of uninterrupted tutelage of young New England ladies or boasted such an impressive list of graduates who had achieved acclaim in many fields.

She refused to be dissuaded by a few negative appraisals she encountered. Her parents were not familiar enough with the intricacies of higher education to recognize the differences in academic philosophies. Their only concerns were for the quality of the food, lodging and medical care. They wanted to be reassured that the school was operated by "nice people" and that the other students were "nice girls." College was college to them; the specifics were unimportant. They had an innocent faith in educational systems in general, allowing them to feel secure and trusting of the environment into which they would deliver their sweet, smart and basically unsullied young daughter. They agreed with her that Middlebury looked exactly the way a real nice temple of learning should. As it turned out, their nescience in matters academic did no harm. Elizabeth was sensible and was must unlikely to accept any radical or exotic ideology simply because it was being promulgated by some "enlightened" faculty and hence attractive to the more rebellious or at least the more adventurous elements of the student body.

In her typical practical but tenacious manner, Libby applied for admission to Middlebury and was accepted long before most of her contemporaries had even decided upon places to apply.

The imminent prospect of the expense of college was of serious concern to her. Although she had saved some money from odd jobs she had worked at, she knew that her savings would only help to cover the cost of incidentals such as clothing and spending money. The bulk of her educational expenses would have to come from her parents. Tony took her aside after one occasion when she seemed quite upset about the problem.

"Look, Libby," he said, "it isn't something for you to worry about. You are our daughter and we'll take care of it somehow. I've been lucky to make a little more than a lot of men nowadays, and we've saved quite a bit. We don't owe anybody money, so if we need to we can borrow from the bank with no problem. If it bothers you, you can pay us back after you finish school. For now, all you have to do is keep on getting your good marks and be happy and enjoy your school days."

She knew that he was completely serious, and having him express his feelings eased her mind. "You and Mom are the best, Dad," she said as she put her arms around him and kissed his chin. "I'll accept what you say on one condition. If there is ever any problem at all as far as the money for my college education is concerned, you have to promise to tell me. I can quit any time and go back to school after I have earned the money for it. And I'll try to get any scholarships I possibly can, too. Okay?"

Tony smiled and hugged her tightly. "Okay, Libby. That's a deal. Now you just forget about it."

Chapter 4
Tony's Surprise

For all of the residents of Newvale, and particularly for the Pontillos, July 4, 1940, was a day designated for celebration, but it turned instead into one of shock, dismay and sadness. When Dr. Graham failed to appear for breakfast at his usual hour, Maria felt at first uneasy, then gradually more and more concerned. She knew that he had retired at the usual time and had had one of those rather rare nights interrupted by no real or imaginary crises among his patients. She could not remember when he had last overslept. Mrs. Graham was happily humming as she wandered around the dining room and kitchen awaiting her husband's arrival for the breakfast they loved to share, unaware, as usual, of the time that was sliding by. When Maria could bring herself to wait no longer, she trotted to the stairway and climbed to the second floor. She hurried down the hallway to the Grahams' bedroom, where she hesitantly rapped softly on the door. There was no response. With her heart starting to beat rapidly, she knocked again, harder this time. Again, no response. What was she to do? She could not call to Mrs. Graham—if there were a real problem, she would be of no use at all, and should not be exposed to one, anyway. Taking a deep breath, Maria slowly turned the doorknob and pushed the door open a few inches. She could see that there was a form under the covers on the large bed, its back to her, but everything was eerily quiet. There was no sound of breathing, nothing. Quaking with fear now, but determined to carry out her duties whatever they involved, she circled around to the far side of the bed. The doctor was lying on his side, motionless, his sightless eyes staring toward the window through which he had always loved to gaze at the peaceful scene of Newvale's Main Street, with the church spire punctuating the greenery of the hills beyond. In spite of herself, Maria screamed.

❖ ❖ ❖

Several months after Dr. Graham's death, Tony received a phone call from the Newvale Savings Bank.

"Tony? This is Elmer Rolinson at Newvale Savings. I wonder if you could stop in tomorrow and see me for a few minutes? I have something to tell you that will interest you, I think."

Tony hesitated. What could this be about? His only connection with the bank, so far, was his savings account. Even the mortgage on their house was held by a private citizen.

"Sure, Mr. Rolinson. How about right after lunch?"

"That will be fine, Tony. See you then."

When Tony told Mary about the mysterious call, they both pondered over it, but neither could come up with any answer that made sense. While they did not exactly worry about it, it was prominent in their thoughts that evening and all of the next morning.

Promptly at 12:30 p.m., Tony arrived at the bank and asked whether Mr. Rolinson had returned from lunch.

"Yes, Mr. Pontillo, he ate in, and he said to send you right in when you came."

Tony walked to the door marked "E. Rolinson, President," and rapped on it.

"Come in," said a man's voice. Tony opened the door and stepped in, and Mr. Rolinson rose from his chair, walked around the desk and grasped his hand warmly.

"Good to see you, Tony. How is everything?"

"Just fine, Mr. Rolinson. How are you?"

"I'm fine, too, thanks. Have a seat, Tony."

They both sat.

"Well now, I called you here to pass along what I believe you will think is very good news. What it boils down to is that there is a large savings account here which you are not aware of, but which is now to be passed over to your control, since it was a survivorship account and the other party is now deceased. The probate and other matters have been completed, making it legally proper that you should now receive it."

Tony looked bewildered. After a few moments he managed to say, "— What?"

"Yes, I am sure it is a bit of a shocker, isn't it? But it is quite true, Tony. You have a benefactor who has been making regular deposits into a joint account for a number of years, with the request that we refrain from disclosing this information until it became necessary. That time has now arrived."

After a brief pause, the banker continued, "I think you may be a bit surprised at the amount. You realize that a savings account, steadily fed, grows nicely under compound interest. Of course, you do—you have one of your own. I have the passbook for this account here, and I am turning it over to you now." He leaned forward and placed the small book in Tony's hand.

Tony was dumbfounded, not yet comprehending what was developing. Finally, he said, "Thank you, Mr. Rolinson. What—who—who did such a thing for me?"

Rolinson just smiled.

"Open the book," he said.

Tony waited a moment and then cautiously opened it. He read the top line, showing the owners of the account. "Franklin P. Graham and Anthony J. Pontillo, as joint tenants, with right of survivorship." He and the doctor? How could that be? Still bewildered, he turned to the final entry. What was that number? Thousands of dollars! His eyes blurred as he tried to concentrate on the final figure. This was unbelievable.

"Mr. Rolinson, I must be crazy. What is that balance, please?"

Rolinson laughed. "No, Tony, you're not crazy. The exact figure is thirty-three thousand, nine hundred ninety-four dollars and seventy-five cents. And it is yours to do with as you see fit. Congratulations, Tony. If you want any advice on how to handle the money, I would be happy to oblige you; otherwise, my duty is completed."

"But—it's crazy! I can't accept such a fortune, which I haven't earned. This is the doctor's money, not mine! I'm not going to take it!"

Rolinson shook his head. "No, Tony, you mustn't feel that way. Doctor Graham thought the world of you—almost as though you were the son he had never been able to have. He deposited twenty dollars each week into this account with the expectation that he would predecease you and that the money would then become yours without any question or any delay in probate. He told me that he could not hope for anything better than that this would accumulate enough to be a real bonus to you and Mary. He didn't miss the twenty dollars a week and this would have been a minor part of his estate, had it simply accumulated in his own name. No, Tony—realize that this is exactly what that good man wanted. Accept the money in the knowledge that the doctor's wishes are now fulfilled and that all of the years of steady deposits are an indication of his steadfast love and admiration. If you weren't such a fine man, he would never have done this."

Still dumbfounded, Tony nodded weakly. "Well, I just don't know what else to say or do. I certainly thank you."

Then the memory of the doctor and his constant kindness and generosity overcame him. Tears streamed down his cheeks. Embarrassed, he tried to brush them away with the back of his hand.

The banker rose and came around the desk. He placed a hand on Tony's shoulder and smiled.

"Take the book home and tell your good wife that someone else loved you as much as she does! Good luck, Tony. And don't forget that I will be glad to help if you need any financial advice."

They shook hands and Tony stumbled his way out of the bank in a daze.

Doctor Graham's thoughtfulness and generosity would easily solve any problem the Pontillos might encounter with the cost of their daughter's education, and then some.

Chapter 5
Mulcahy

Despite his brutally barren early life in Ireland where his family suffered from too little food, too little work, too many children, tyrannical creditors, the disdain of the well-to-do and the threats of a fiery afterlife from the church, young Sean Mulcahy thrived. He seemed able to suck adequate nourishment from the hostile environment and to build muscle and fat from a diet consisting mostly of potatoes, mutton, salt pork, green vegetables and the occasional cod or haddock yielded by the town's small fishing fleet.

Although his family could not afford to buy such a delicacy, he was a sharp-eyed, lightning quick and a determined young lad. As he mingled anonymously with the jostling, bickering citizens along the waterfront fish markets of late nineteenth century Galway, he was sometimes able to pilfer a fish from one of the hawking peddlers and melt into the crowd before anyone noticed. His poor mother learned to accept such unexpected largesse without asking the question which, if answered truthfully, would have soured the flesh of the fish in her mouth.

Every cheerless thatch-roofed hut such as housed the average poor of the city's outskirts contained its quota of salvaged furniture, mostly broken and crudely mended. A chair or two, a table and perhaps a couple of beds was about the extent of it. As the families grew, as they inevitably did under the dual incentive of the people's ignorance of and the church's proscription of contraceptive methods, the number of occupants in the beds increased until the less competitive children surrendered their claims and settled for a corner of the dirt floor with a ragged coat or some other odd piece of cloth as a blanket to help fend off the penetrating chill of the long nights. When, in the short winter months, it became too cold and damp to exist under these conditions, they would creep back into the jumble of bodies on the bed without arousing protest from those already there, for whatever meager heat remained in their bony little bodies was then welcomed. When the very hot nights of summer came, those on the beds joined the others on the cool floor.

No matter how destitute the families might be, there were three things inevitably found in each of these hovels; a devoutly worshipped statuette of the Madonna, a representation of Christ on the cross and a bottle of cheap whiskey. The wives and children drew their moral sustenance from the former two, the husbands from the latter.

Like so many of the city's inhabitants, Sean's father labored in the peat bogs most of the time and supplemented his pittance by a day's or a week's work for one of the farmers whenever he could, usually harvesting vegetables or helping with the shearing of a flock of sheep. The work was hard and when, as happened periodically, the realization of his miserable existence and the unlikelihood of it's improvement overwhelmed him, he succumbed to a bout of heavy drinking which left him completely incapable of pursuing his occupation for a while. At these times, the family suffered greatly, nearly starving for days at a time.

The boys in the family were also required to provide whatever help they might from the time they were big enough to coax water from a well or pull a weed or tend a peat fire, and as they grew, they were pressed into service for the heavier chores as well. They tried to make themselves scarce around home so that they could expend their energy on more enjoyable things such as sports and games or all of the fascinating and exciting waterfront activities which filled their heads with romantic aspirations concerning the lives of seafaring men. Unfortunately, these enterprises were often rudely interrupted by fathers or older brothers who came seeking them out to work at some miserable task.

Sean grew up in this atmosphere; working when necessary, scrounging for food and comfort, sharpening his awareness of what was happening around him and learning to take advantage of every opportunity for benefitting himself. Yet he was also close and loyal to other family members and would rush to the defense of a brother or sister as quickly as to his own. His mother was deeply religious and saw to it that all of her children were steeped in the teachings of Catholicism from their earliest days. There was no surer way for a young Mulcahy to earn a cuff on the ear, or worse, than to be lax in learning his catechism or to be late for church services, or to forget his prayers or to fail in any other way to meet his or her religious obligations. The senior Mulcahy tried his best to be a devout Catholic, but he was so often exhausted or inebriated that he spent more time in the confessional than in the church proper.

What Sean saw of this life as he grew from childhood to adolescence, convinced him that he wanted something better when he reached manhood. Understandably, young fellows had little respect for the examples set by their fathers. There had been a steady egress of Irish poor from much of the country ever since the shock of the great potato famine in the 1840s. The goal of most, Sean included, was to board a ship for America, where everyone knew there was plenty for all. Eventually, he was able to buy passage and he was off to the new world with a light heart and soaring ambition.

Sean was irresistibly drawn to the heavy Irish population of the Boston area, and it was there that he found both a means of livelihood and a sweet young Irish immigrant colleen to be his wife. Sean became a drayman, transporting goods for a hauling company for a few years before landing a coveted job as a teamster with a brewery in Connecticut, at which time he and his little family migrated from Massachusetts to Newvale.

The nature of the new job caused him to join joyfully the fraternity of heavy drinkers. Sean had tradition behind him. He had learned early how to quaff both beer and distilled beverages, the latter less often because of the price. Now, as a husky, hearty, fun-loving young man, he missed very few opportunities to join in drinking bouts. It was a matter of pride to prove that he could stay with the best of them through the drinking and singing and fighting and walk away at the end of the evening, tipsy but functioning. Since the new job placed him in virtually constant contact with the very source of the potables, he accepted it as a challenge and redoubled his efforts to "drink 'em all under the table, begorra!" But regardless of how much he put away in the course of one of these marathons, he showed up for work the following morning, on time and ready to manhandle the massive kegs and control the powerful horses that pulled his rig.

By most standards, he was a good husband and father, with his large and generous Irish heart. He truly loved his hardworking wife and every one of the babies she presented to him. But Sean never did develop the habit of thrift. He received very good pay for his hard work, but whatever money he was given rapidly turned molten in his pocket. It was difficult for him to hold on to enough of it to keep up with the bills.

When the press of progress replaced his beloved team of Belgian horses with a gasoline-powered Mack truck, Sean continued to drive his route, but something romantic had gone out of the job. While the truck did not need the same amount of personal attention as the horses did, it was not responsive to the strength of arm and heart the way they were. A man could love and respect a big, stalwart team of horses and could expect much of these qualities to be returned in kind. But a truck relied entirely on the driver and required him to do all of the thinking. Occasionally, the horses would take him safely around corners or bring him back to the brewery at the end of the day when he happened to doze off. A truck was merely a dumb machine.

When advancing age and the subtle transformation of muscle and sinew into sagging fat made it harder and harder for Sean to maintain his ability to cope with the physical demands of his employment, he was eased out of the delivery end of the business and into an easier but lower-paying inside job. The effect was immediately noticeable in his attitude. In place of his cheerful personality, a slightly bitter mien developed. The consequence of this discontentment manifested itself in aches and ailments he had never before experienced. Reluctantly, he visited a doctor following a rather odd and frightening dyspeptic attack. He was told that he had several incipient health problems, none of which, the doctor assured him, would be at all improved by continued consumption of alcohol. He suggested that Sean should, if at all possible, retire from his occupation and take care of himself, including that he should stop drinking. Sean bristled and stated that he neither could nor would care to exist as a total abstainer after a lifetime of close personal acquaintance with the flowing bowl. The doctor relented slightly, saying that if he would restrict himself to a couple of drinks on weekends or on special occasions, he might get away with it. He added, however, that he would explain to Sean's wife and daughter, Mary, that they were to keep the score, not himself.

Sean resigned himself to a new, less exciting but ultimately more sensible lifestyle. Since the Mulcahys had never been able to save money to support retirement, and it was before the age of pensions, Sean went to work for the parish. He drove the priest and the sisters to various functions, became caretaker of the rectory and its grounds and assumed the responsibility of sexton of the church. Although the wages were nominal, the Mulcahys were able to manage. His wife picked up some money as a seamstress, and often one of the grown children would drop in for dinner, thoughtfully bringing a roast, half a ham or some other dish, the uneaten portion of which would provide another meal the next day.

Sean gradually settled into his new lifestyle with as good grace as possible. He missed the heavy work and the heavy drinking as well as the companionship of his erstwhile contemporaries, but as time went by and he was able more easily to accept the changes, he found that the doctor was right—he actually became a healthier man. The strong constitution with which he had been born responded positively to his new agenda. After a while he found that he was able to skip even the occasional drink, and the plaudits he gathered from family and acquaintances buoyed him up and enhanced his self-esteem.

Sean often relaxed with the crop of bright and lively grandchildren with which he had been presented, in many of whom traces of himself were detectable. Although he would not have dreamed of admitting that any one of them was dearer to him than the others, he was always drawn strongly to Mary's Elizabeth, who seemed to combine a trace of dusky Italian beauty with an unmistakable Irish sparkle. Her personality was such an attractive combination of intelligence, friendliness and consideration for others that Sean came to adore her and relished their times together. Elizabeth, in turn, thought the world of her granddad. He was different than any of the other grownups she knew, so big and strong and full of life and joy and merriment and such fun to listen to with his heavy brogue and quaint expressions.

Chapter 6
Borgeson

Newvale's third wealthy family, the Borgesons, were no more interested in being envied or admired by their fellow citizens than were the Jays and the Lamsons. Their affluence was of much more recent derivation, having resulted from knowledge acquired in a long and difficult European apprenticeship and the natural talent thus released. They were only one generation removed from poverty and had not yet acquired the veneer which coats the old-money people and sets them somewhat apart from their proletarian neighbors.

Ingmar and Veda Borgeson were plain people and were extremely shy and ill-at-ease when exposed to the limelight. Their relatively recently acquired riches were still somewhat of an embarrassment to them. When they easily handled, with cash, the financial settlement for the purchase of their land and the building and furnishing of their large Newvale home, they were actually more apologetic than proud. Their son, Tedor, was an almost exact replica of his father; quietly brilliant and completely absorbed in the family's undertakings. He and his pretty wife, Janice, who was nearly as unhappy in the spotlight as he, had two children who were the first generation to exhibit the beginnings of social aspirations and to feel a bit superior to ordinary citizens because they were blessed with guaranteed financial security.

Ingmar Borgeson was born in the freezing cold of Fagersta, Sweden, on January 9, 1874. His family was very poor and through all of his early years, they struggled to provide adequate food and shelter for themselves. Their lives presented little opportunity for enjoyment. The nearest they came to relaxation and contentment was when they climbed with their children to the hillsides on Sunday afternoons in the all too brief summers to see the green foliage and multicolored wild flowers. Winters for them were very long and brutally cold, and were a test of survival. When work was available in the huge local steel mill, the senior Borgeson took advantage of it and was at least warm for twelve hours a day, because his physically demanding job kept him near the giant metal melting furnaces.

When relatives in Germany wrote that they knew of an opening for a toolmaker's apprentice with a man of their acquaintance, and rued the fact that they had no son of their own to take advantage of this excellent opportunity, young Ingmar begged and pleaded with his parents for a chance to go. Succumbing to the fervor of his pleading, they permitted him, as the most literate member of the family, to write to the relatives, plighting his desperate interest in availing himself of this chance. After an exchange of letters confirmed that he would at least be given an audience, Ingmar packed his meager belongings. At age fourteen, he left his home, family and friends to set out for Germany. He had misgivings as to whether he would be accepted for training in a country where the language was foreign to him, at the knee of a very old and demanding but very fair master toolmaker, Max Rheimer.

Rheimer instantly liked the destitute but serious and willing young Swede. After a rather lengthy interview, prolonged by the language problem, he agreed to take Ingmar on as a probationary apprentice. It was months before Ingmar was permitted to do anything more than oil the equipment, clean up the floor and benches, stoke the forge and the wood stove, sharpen some of the simpler tools, and study, study, study. But Max recognized in the lad a worthy pupil, with the wit and grit to stand up to hard, tedious assignments and the old man was determined to develop the boy's talents methodically and carefully. He was able to furnish Ingmar with only the barest of necessities insofar as food and clothing were concerned, but he generously transferred to the young man, step by painstaking step, his font of knowledge of the craft.

Into Ingmar's brain was drilled every characteristic of each metal, including its granular structure and the way it is affected by varying degrees of heat; every variation in result obtained by different sharpening angles; what alloy to use when durability was more important than tensile strength, or when brittleness was less important than keenness; and how to heat-treat each grade of steel and anneal it, or draw it, or temper it to exactly the condition required in its ultimate use. He was taught how to select the proper metal for each purpose and the secrets of successfully drilling, reaming, tapping, threading swaging or trepanning each of them. He learned how to make molds, how to cast and forge iron, how to design and fashion elements into fixtures, instruments, devices and machines which would produce the special result required, and he had instilled in him the patience to do each job right, so that he could feel pride and confidence in everything he created.

Ten years had passed by the time that old Max sat down beside his protege and said, "Mr. Borgeson, I can teach you nothing more. All that I know, I have passed on to you. I am giving you this paper which I have prepared, telling anyone concerned the extent of your studies and of your abilities, certified by Rheimer, and with my craftsman's seal attached. This will be accepted as proof of your skill by any accredited toolmaker anywhere in the Christian world. Now, I am tired and old and my time is running short, but I am proud of you and what you have learned. You are smart and I know that you will use your skills well and will preserve the tradition of excellence of our craft. I ask nothing more."

The eyes of both men were filled with tears as they embraced, then shook hands and parted, their union dissolved because its mission was complete.

Ingmar returned to Fagersta, where he saw each of his close relatives for the first time in ten years. His parents were still healthy and comfortable, considering their lack of desire for a more exciting or rewarding life, and the same seemed to be true of his two sisters, now married and starting promisingly dull families of their own. Ingmar saw nothing that interested him in staying in Fagersta. He knew what he wanted to do. He wanted to find a way to get to America and put his hard-earned tooling talents to work in the new and very promising automotive industry, about which he had been hearing more and more. But how could he get to America? His family was unable to help, so he spent many hours walking around the town, asking everyone he knew for ideas on how to get passage to the United States. He became frustrated and desperate. Finally, he went to Stockholm, found the hiring offices on the wharves and signed on as an ordinary seaman on a ship laden with products destined for Liverpool. Ironically, fine Fagersta steel was an important part of the cargo, but the only contact Ingmar had with it was to help haul, tug and shove into place the containers in which it was stored.

As soon as the ship docked in Liverpool and the crew was released, Ingmar, unlike the majority of the sailors who fled toward the bars and brothels, headed directly to the hiring offices on the wharf. From his more experienced shipmates, he had learned all he could about lines shipping regularly to America from England and it was to those firms that he hied as soon as his feet left the gangplank. After several disappointments he found a line that had a ship scheduled to sail for America within the week and still needed a few sailors to fill out its complement. He signed on immediately, got all the particulars regarding the sailing, and left to find himself a room for a few nights.

The ship sailed on schedule and arrived in New York harbor on Tuesday, May 3, 1898. As the vessel steamed toward its mooring site, Ingmar could not resist joining the others who had never before visited the New World as they lined the ship's rail and stared at the famous skyline with its closely crowded tall buildings. Of significant beauty was the celebrated Statue of Liberty, recently dedicated, but already recognized and worshipped by immigrants from all over the world as the ultimate symbol of freedom and opportunity.

Once he was released from duty as a member of the crew and had received his pay, Ingmar started for the city, thinking to find himself temporary lodging while he hunted for work. Much to his dismay, he was informed that he was not allowed to leave the dock area. As a new arrival from Europe he was routed through Ellis Island, where he was shocked to learn that unless he had someone to vouch for him, or an employer who agreed to take him on, or relatives who planned to house and feed him, he might be denied entrance to the country. This caused him great consternation. Could he have worked and planned so hard for his goal only to have it snatched away when finally within reach?

Desperately, he tried to locate someone who would listen to his story and help him gain access. It was an almost impossible challenge to try to ferret out someone who had the combination of qualities which would be needed to help him. First, the person had to speak Swedish or German; next, that person had to be compassionate enough to want to help. Finally, such a person had to have enough position, clout or brazenness to make those in authority consider Ingmar's story. What chance had he of finding someone who had those qualifications? None, he feared. The small amount of money he had been able to keep would last only a short time, even if the authorities did not put him back on a boat for Europe. As the hopelessness of his situation bore down on him, he began to feel physically ill. His stomach felt as if it were tied in a knot and he felt a sudden chill as though he was starting to run a fever. He sat down on a wooden bench and held his head in his hands.

He would never know what he would have done next, if left to his own devices. As it happened, a middle-aged blond female immigration worker spotted him. From his appearance, she suspected him of being more than an ignorant, uneducated cheap-labor type of person. She approached him and read the name tag hanging around his neck which identified him as a Swede, like herself. With a smile, she beckoned him to follow her into a room where there were a great many small tables, behind most of which there were people interviewing recent arrivals. She motioned to him to be seated on the opposite side of the little table, and when he had done so, she said, in perfect Swedish, "Herr Borgeson, my name is Gretchen Oleson. How can I help you?"

Relief flooded over Ingmar. In Swedish, he immediately started pouring out his story.

"I come from Fagersta."

"Ya, I am familiar with that area. Very cold winters and very short summers!" she laughed pleasantly.

"My family lived there, but I wanted something better."

He proceeded to tell how he had gone to Germany and served a long apprenticeship.

"My teacher, Mr. Rheimer, was very strict but very thorough. I feel confident that I am qualified for a position as toolmaker in almost any American factory. That is what I trained for and that is what I am determined to get—in the automobile industry, if possible."

Mrs. Oleson was quite pleased. She felt that her initial impression of this young man had been accurate.

"I believe that we can help you, Mr. Borgeson. I will arrange for you to have a temporary permit to stay in this country. I will give your name and the particulars of your training to a committee which handles these matters. Only a small percentage of arrivals from Europe have skills such as yours, which are badly needed in American industry. I feel confident that it will be only a short time until you locate work in your specialty. If you are successful in getting a position and if you prove capable, you will be allowed to apply for permanent residence."

She proceeded to get from him all of the information needed to complete the immigration forms, and after thanking Mrs. Oleson profusely, Ingmar listened carefully to the instructions she gave him and then proceeded to follow them explicitly. Within two days he was directed to the Swedish consulate, where a minor official took charge of his case and soon had made arrangements for him to be interviewed for a job with a company specializing in vehicular development. It was, however, in the railroad field rather than automotive. But Ingmar was desperate and could not afford to be insistent.

The aftermath of the violent strike and subsequent ill feelings between management and labor at the Pullman Palace Car Company in Pullman,

Illinois, left many openings in the work force, and it was to fill one of these that the eager young toolmaker was destined. This talented, enthusiastic young man who had no knowledge of the recent strife, was a potentially ideal employee, and so was quickly hired. The fact that he spoke no English was a serious impediment, but he was fluent in the language of tools and machinery, and it was not difficult for his supervisor to communicate what he was required to do.

Ingmar felt as though he had landed in Heaven, because company policy was to supply their employees with company housing, furnish their wants at company stores and cater to their spiritual needs at company churches. The cost of these goods and services was deducted from their pay, which left precious little, but Ingmar was used to living on a meager income, so he was initially happy. He settled into the routine, enjoying the opportunity to use the excellent equipment and facilities in the shop. Because he was unable to converse with most of his fellow workers and supervisors, he seldom looked up from his work for more than a few seconds at a time, which endeared him to his superiors.

Ingmar soon recognized that the language barrier had to be overcome as quickly as possible, so he listened carefully to the words his fellow workers used. It was not long before he began to understand some of the simpler conversations and to file away certain expressions for use when an opportunity arose. Nights alone in his small quarters were boring and Ingmar formed the habit of taking home newspapers, pamphlets or booklets discarded by others. He pored over them, looking for familiar words, or captions under pictures which he could try to decipher on the basis of the subject illustrated. By this means he managed over a period of several months to accumulate a very small but comfortingly helpful English vocabulary. Using what he read and what he heard, he began to find verbal communication with his fellow workers at least possible, although difficult.

Another young toolmaker in the shop, Jim Barton, often ate his lunch at the same bench as Ingmar. What he at first took for aloofness, he found to be simply a combination of Ingmar's natural shyness and his inability to speak the language. Barton began to make friendly overtures which were eagerly accepted by the lonely young Swede. Having someone of roughly his own age to talk to and to correct his mistakes was a Godsend, and within weeks, Ingmar was able to express his thoughts more fluently. Like so many other immigrants, he assimilated the words and managed to string the right ones together most of the time, however, once he gained the ability to get his thoughts across, he stopped actively trying to learn the proper use of the language. Thus, grammar and syntax remained a mystery which he did not make the effort to solve.

Acquisition of the ability to communicate rapidly broadened all aspects of Ingmar's life. He could ask directions and he could listen to and understand the ideas and beliefs and complaints of his associates. The chief complaint came from dissatisfaction with the net amount of wages. By the time deductions for all the company-furnished goods and services were made, there was little left over.

By now, Ingmar understood Mr. Pullman's iron-fisted and parsimonious policies as well as the demands of the equally adamant American Railway Union, headed by the flamboyant Eugene V. Debs. The more he learned of these stubborn factions, the less interested Ingmar became in remaining with the Pullman company.

Ingmar's thoughts turned often to his original intent to become involved in the business of tooling for automobiles, which was still his goal. He and Jim spent many hours discussing that exciting new field and trying to imagine just how they might obtain jobs connected with it. Jim pointed out that Pullman, Illinois, or even Chicago was not the most likely location for that kind of work. Jim had heard that Detroit, Michigan, was becoming the center for auto development, and so they agreed to cast about for leads to opportunities there.

From what he had heard, Ingmar believed that the new internal combustion gasoline engines were the most practical power sources for the vehicles being developed, because they could furnish the most speed and endurance at the lowest cost. A newspaper article caught Jim's eye, and he excitedly brought it to Ingmar's attention.

"It says here that a company in Detroit by the name of Halburton Motor Works has just developed something new for automobile engines and is planning to expand its plant to handle the anticipated increase in business. What say, Ingmar, let's cash in our chips here and take a chance on getting a job with Halburton? We've got experience and no families to worry about. Let's just risk it! What do you think?"

Ingmar was not inclined to be the precipitate type, but Jim's proposal sounded like the opportunity he had been looking for. And Jim was right—he had no one to worry about but himself. He had certainly gambled more when he headed blindly for the United States with nothing but his training in his pocket. Now, at least, he did have a small amount of savings to carry him for a short time. Slowly, he raised his head, looked at his friend and said, "Ya, Jim—ya. I t'ink you say right. Ve go Detroit!"

The two young men leaped up, danced around the room, singing and shouting, and then collapsed, laughing, across the bed.

Two days later they were on a train bound for Detroit.

Chapter 7
Detroit

After securing a hotel room, Ingmar and Jim immediately went out to investigate their new surroundings. They were surprised to find it a rather large place, with a great many factories involved in production of a wide variety of goods, but wherever they went and with whomever they struck up a conversation, it took only a few moments before the subject swung to automobiles. Everyone seemed charged with excitement and enthusiasm over the promise of these new and wonderful machines. Old line companies were feverishly investigating possibilities for utilizing their existing facilities for some phase of auto production. Every small shop and empty loft was a candidate for use as a proving ground for some gadget or idea or hope by anyone who had ever learned to use a lathe. Although most of them were destined to fail miserably, those that survived because of sound theories and craftsmanship reaped enormous riches.

The Halburton Motor Company was a solid business which had been developing and improving internal combustion engines for many years. A disciple of Carl Benz and Nikolaus Otto, Mr. Halburton had been convinced for some time that the development of the self-propelled carriage was only in its infancy and that "automobiles" would one day be the focus of a huge industry. His studies had convinced him that the four-cycle gasoline engine was the most practical power plant for the vehicles, and it was on the refinement of that theory that he planned to expend as much of the time and energy of his plant as could be spared from the design and production of engines for farm and industrial use, which paid the bills and provided the profit. He was personally interviewing the men who responded to his advertisement for skilled designers and toolmakers, and in Jim Barton and Ingmar Borgeson he found eager young mechanics of the sort he had had in mind.

Both were hired and put to work in the special section of the factory, a working laboratory and development area. They were ushered around the department by the "Head of Research," who showed them what had been accomplished so far and where they were expected to make their contribution to the success Mr. Halburton pursued. At the moment, the main thrust of the department was to develop and improve a water cooling system for a small lightweight four-cycle gasoline engine which would be practical as the power source for an auto. After a quick appraisal of the work which had been done so far, Ingmar felt his pulse quicken with eagerness to get into the project because he had already spotted something in the design which he felt sure he could improve.

Mr. Halburton was one of the most visionary automotive men in the city. He was convinced that his best chance for future success was to gather about him talented and inspired young men who would be given unrestricted opportunity to experiment with ways to improve existing automotive elements and develop new ones. He kept a shrewd, watchful eye on each of his proteges and quickly dismissed anyone who showed little inventiveness or enthusiasm. By this method, he developed a cadre of well-above-average artisans, and he did it the most economical way. He hired young men, most of whom were single and did not have the responsibilities of supporting a home and raising a family.

Jim and Ingmar took to the system enthusiastically. They were impatient to get to work in the morning and often shocked at how quickly the work day sped by. Most evenings they spent reading trade manuals and discussing every aspect of their occupation. They did occasionally take an evening off to relax. Ingmar usually attended a church sponsored entertainment, since he had not taken up drinking or other more boisterous forms of amusement. The church meetings and socials suited his temperament. Eventually, it was at one of these affairs that he met his future wife, Veda Thorsen. His friend Jim, on the other hand, did experiment more and more with the temptations of faster diversions, whereupon his work gradually lost its excellence. This pained Ingmar because he felt as if Jim were like a brother. Ingmar tried hard, in his rather timid way, to talk sense to his friend, but did not succeed in convincing Jim to mend his ways. Within a few months, Jim was dismissed and dropped out of Ingmar's life for good. The sadness which this caused was alleviated by Ingmar's courting of Veda Thorsen, an honest, decent and shy girl who was as Scandinavian as himself. They were a natural match, and both knew it from the moment they met. When Ingmar proposed marriage a year later, Veda happily accepted.

Her family welcomed him like a long lost son. Veda's parents had come to America as early immigrants from the old country. Veda, much to their pride, was born after their arrival and thus was an American citizen. For her to have found such a fine, hardworking and intelligent mate of the same background was more than they could have hoped for. They insisted that the young couple move in with them, because Veda's bedroom would otherwise be empty, and economies would be realized by all. This arrangement worked out very well and continued for several years. When Veda became pregnant, Ingmar located a pleasant, small, affordable apartment nearby.

As time went on, Ingmar became more and more deeply involved in the Halburton Company endeavors. Eventually, he became a foreman. He was well versed in all aspects of automobile motor development, and he had repaid Mr. Halburton's decision to take him on many times over.

And now Ingmar's inventiveness began to assert itself. He had an inspiration for a radical departure from the existing design for the gasoline engine carburetor. He was sure that his idea was sound, but he did not want to try making up a model at the shop using Halburton's equipment, for to do so might jeopardize his rights to the design. When he mentioned this to his father-in-law, Mr. Thorsen suggested that he set up a small shop in their basement, and Ingmar was very appreciative. Although he had some money saved because he was thrifty, he knew that it would take some time and more money to outfit even a very modest shop. He began to look for good used equipment. After about six months, he was able to assemble enough equipment to produce a simple model. He worked during his free time on his invention with a clear conscience, and in another six months he had built it and proved it out.

Through his years with Harlburton, Ingmar had often met engineers and executives for a number of the well-known automotive firms including several from the fast-growing General Motors Corp. Conceived by Mr. William Durant, a carriage manufacturer from Flint, Michigan, this was to be a conglomerate of individual auto makers; Buick, Cadillac, Oldsmobile, Oakland and several smaller firms. The company ran into financial problems in 1910 and was reorganized by a financial syndicate. Hesitantly at first, Ingmar approached one of the gentlemen from General Motors whom he had met and who seemed very friendly toward him, Mr. Albert Beadle. He told Beadle that he had developed a new style carburetor for which he had high hopes, and asked whether he thought he might be able to stir up some interest in it with the big company. Beadle wanted to see the model and made arrangements to visit Ingmar at home to inspect it. When he saw the carefully designed and expertly machined device, he was quite excited. He had liked and admired this quiet young toolmaker from the moment he met him, but he had had no idea how brilliant the man really was. Although Beadle had always been a loyal company man, he felt it would be completely unfair for anyone other than Ingmar to reap the rewards which he was sure would result from the introduction of this product. He made an instant decision.

"Ingmar," he said, "I think you've got a tiger by the tail here. This is a radical departure and it looks to me as though it is destined for great success, assuming it works as well as it should, and as you assure me it will. Have you protected it?"

"You mean patent?" asked Ingmar. "No—no patent, yust drawings and model."

Beadle shook his head. "Ingmar, you must protect your ideas every way possible. You are a talented man, and there are plenty of people around who would jump at the chance to steal your inventions. Before you show me anything more about this, I want you to go to a patent attorney and have him see whether it is patentable. He will tell you what steps you have to take to write up the descriptions and have drawings made. It should only cost you a hundred dollars or so, and if this is as good as I think it is, it might save you a fortune. I'll write out the attorney's name and address, and you must promise me you'll go see him right away."

Ingmar looked a little shocked, but after a moment he nodded. "Whatever you say, Mr. Beadle. An' t'ank you very much."

Beadle asked, "You do have the money, don't you, Ingmar?"

"Ya—you say maybe one hundred dollar? I…I t'ink I can get it."

"Well, you mustn't let the lack of a few dollars keep you from doing as I suggest. Believe me, it is vitally necessary. You can get a loan from the bank, you know. Or perhaps your in-laws would like to help. It isn't important where it comes from—just be sure to get going on this right away. Promise me."

"Ya—I promise."

After Mr. Beadle had left, Ingmar went over the whole situation with Veda. "He t'ink my carburetor look very good, but he vorried someone try to steal idea unless I get lawyer to patent it. Trouble is, expensive."

"Oh? How much he t'ink?"

"Mr. Beadle say maybe hundred dollar. I only got about fifty."

Veda smiled, slyly. "I save a little here and there, Ingmar. If you t'ink is good investment, I give you the rest."

Ingmar looked at her in amazement, then chuckled and put his arms around her.

"You a tricky vun, Veda."

The very next day Ingmar followed Beadle's advice and visited the lawyer's office. Beadle had given him a note to introduce himself, and after reading it the man was very pleasant and helpful. He took some little time getting everything properly set up and giving Ingmar guidance, since he could see that the language problem was going to make it difficult to get all of the required information in presentable form, but eventually it was completed.

"Mr. Borgeson, I will make all of the necessary applications. I will have my secretary type up all of the descriptive information you have furnished and will have a professional mechanical draftsman do a set of drawings from your sketches. Once that is done, you will take the written description and the sketches and seal them in an envelope and mail them to yourself. When you receive them, you must take the envelope, unopened, to your bank and place it in a safe deposit box. Then you are protected whether or not you have received your patent."

This process took a few days, and when everything was completed, Ingmar got in touch with Mr. Beadle again.

"Well, Ingmar, I'm certainly glad that you've taken care of that problem, or potential problem, anyway. Now I can feel at ease in going over the operation of your device without worrying about your losing control of it."

Arrangements were made for Ingmar to bring his carburetor to a factory where he met Mr. Beadle and two other gentlemen. He showed them his model and described, with Mr. Beadle's help, just how it differed from conventional ones and what advantages would be gained. It was turned over to their mechanics, who adapted it to a test engine. It worked flawlessly. There was an air of excitement in the room as the engine purred.

"Can we keep the carburetor here for three days for further tests?" asked the head of the group. "It certainly seems to be everything it was cracked up to be, but we want to see how we compare on gas consumption and extended usage and a few other things. If that is okay with you, Mr. Borgeson, we will give you a receipt and you can return for your model in three days."

"If Mr. Beadle t'ink that okay, okay with me," replied Ingmar.

"That should be fine, Ingmar," Beadle assured him.

It was a long three days for Ingmar, But he survived it. When he came home at noon, Veda excitedly told him that he was to get in touch with Mr.

Beadle as soon as possible. "He stopped here this morning and says he has good news for you," she reported.

Without bothering to stop for lunch, Ingmar set out for the GM plant where Beadle had his office, but was told by a secretary that he was out to lunch.

"Whom shall I say called?" she asked, rather haughtily.

"My name is Ingmar Borgeson."

The secretary's attitude brightened immediately.

"Oh, Mr. Borgeson. I have a message for you from Mr. Beadle. He wonders if you might be able to attend a meeting here at the office at seven this evening?"

"Oh, ya, sure. I be here seven o'clock. T'ank you."

The meeting was attended by Beadle, a lawyer for the firm, and an executive whose title Ingmar did not understand. Something about "Product Development," he thought. They were all very cordial and all expressed enthusiasm over Ingmar's carburetor.

The lawyer brought things in focus by saying, "Mr. Borgeson, let's get down to cases. We are favorably impressed with your model. We believe our company can make use of it by adapting it to some of our engines. Would you be interested in selling your design outright?"

When Ingmar hesitated, the lawyer continued, "Perhaps you would prefer to discuss some other mutually satisfactory arrangement. The company is prepared to make what we feel is a generous offer."

They all peered expectantly at Ingmar, who felt completely out of his depth in this group. It was all very bewildering, but he was shrewd enough to know that it would be foolhardy for him to discuss anything specific under these circumstances.

"Dis very nice of you people," he said. "Ya, I t'ink I vant to do business, but I need help from lawyer or somevun who know much more dan me about such t'ings."

"That is understandable, Mr. Borgeson," said the lawyer. "If it is agreeable to all parties, why don't we arrange for another meeting at as early a date as possible. At that time, the company can present its offer and you will be free to do the same."

"Ya, I like dat," Ingmar nodded. He agreed to be in touch again within one week. Since he and Mr. Beadle were well acquainted, Ingmar was to make the arrangements as to time and place with him.

Ingmar had not been home more than half an hour when the doorbell rang. It was Beadle.

"That was a pretty good session, wasn't it?" he asked.

"Ya, I t'ought it vas kind of exciting," Ingmar replied.

"The reason I stopped by is that I'm having a bit of trouble with my conscience. As a representative of GM, it is a responsibility of mine to see that the company gets as good a deal as it should, but as a friend and admirer of yours, I can't help feeling that without some good advice you may settle for less than you should, and I'm not going to be a party to stealing your work. Do you trust me enough to answer a question about this settlement? Believe me, it will be off the record completely."

Ingmar was puzzled by Beadle's approach, but he felt nothing but friendliness from the man.

"Ya, sure, Mr. Beadle. I trust you good. You have been my friend and I trust you. What question?"

Beadle spoke very seriously. "If you were to give a number right now—understand, this is just between you and me—how much do you think you might take for your design? Make it high. Think about it a minute, and then give me a number. Remember, this is just sort of a game between the two of us, okay?"

Ingmar nodded. After a long pause, he said, "Okay. I got a number, but I don't know why I got it."

"Tell me what it is."

"Vell, I vas t'inking less, but you say to make it high, so I guess, oh, twenty-five t'ousan' dollar!"

There was silence for several seconds, and Ingmar was about to say that he was sorry for being so foolish, when he heard a sigh escape from Mr. Beadle.

"That's about what I thought you would say, Ingmar. Look, I want you to get in touch with a lawyer right away—one whose name I'll give you, as I did before with the patent attorney."

He produced a card and on it he wrote a name, address and telephone number and handed it to Ingmar.

"You see, Ingmar, I couldn't let you make a mistake of that kind. You don't, and of course you couldn't, realize the potential here. You could wind up receiving huge benefits—far beyond the figure you mentioned. Your lawyer will come up with a proper offer once he knows the details. Let him see the drawings and the model, if you like, and tell him how anxious the GM people are to make a deal with you. I can't discuss it with him, ethically, but you can tell him that this carburetor will probably be installed in almost all

GM cars for years to come. He'll get the message, and will do a good job of bargaining for you. Now, my conscience is clear, for I believe a settlement can be reached which will be fair to all parties."

Ingmar was stunned. Far more than he had mentioned? It did not seem possible! All he was able to do was to say, "T'ank you again, Mr. Beadle. T'ank you very much!"

As a direct result of the good offices of Beadle, Ingmar Borgeson was quickly transformed from a modestly paid master toolmaker and designer to a very wealthy inventor. The lawyer recommended by Mr. Beadle did, indeed, see the potential and shrewdly negotiated an extremely lucrative licensing arrangement where Ingmar was paid a handsome sum, including a royalty on every "IB" carburetor placed in nearly every car produced by GM for many years. In addition, Borgeson was to be under contract to them for twenty years as an independent expert in tool design and product development. They were to be given first refusal rights on any of his inventions or designs in the automotive field during that period. And, best of all, to Ingmar's way of thinking, he was to be furnished a small shop area, equipped with the latest in machine tools as his own private laboratory, where he could come and go as he pleased, and where he could put his training and talents to work.

At age 40 he was as happy and successful as a man could be, but he was still having trouble believing all that had happened. It was not long before his income each month was more than he had been willing to sell his whole idea for. And he really owed it all to one unusually honest and decent man by the name of Albert Beadle.

Chapter 8
Ingmar's Home

At first, the neuveaux-riche Borgesons made virtually no changes in their life style. The possibilities of bales of ready money simply had not struck them. The first huge settlement check was rather like a hanging in an art gallery—it was awesome to look at, but nothing that they could consider a part of their lives. For a week after it arrived, Ingmar would occasionally take it out of its hiding place in his father-in-law's old desk, sit and look at it briefly and then tuck it away again. What finally snapped him out of his trance was the receipt of two lawyers' bills—a small one from the patent attorney and a monstrous one from the one who had engineered the deal with General Motors. Now, he had to begin to use the money because he could not have possibly paid them from his previous meager assets. He went to the bank and presented the check, which caused, in a breathlessly quiet way, a buzz of disbelief among the teller, her supervisor and their superior. After a short delay, during which the use of the telephone was much in evidence, Ingmar was politely invited into the office of a vice president, Mr. Farnsworth, who greeted him with considerable deference and assurances of how happy they were to have his business. He asked what sort of account Mr. Borgeson had in mind for the money, and Ingmar was able only to say, "I vant to save it and get interest. That is okay?"

Mr. Farnsworth assured him that it was just fine.

"I got a couple of bills to pay," Ingmar said, producing those from the lawyers. "Can you show me how to do this? Can you make account for me and I pay from that?"

"Oh, certainly, Mr. Borgeson. We will set up an account for you and draft bank checks to cover these obligations. No problem at all." He nodded and smiled happily.

"T'ank you."

"Anything else we can do for you, we will be delighted to do, Mr. Borgeson," said Farnsworth. "If you like , I will have a list of suggestions prepared as to how you might invest these funds, and you can then decide, with your advisors, which will best serve your purposes."

This sounded good to Ingmar.

"Ya, I like dat, Mr. Farnsworth. I need help with money. You good honest people—I glad to hear what you t'ink I should do."

He left the bank quite pleased that he could anticipate some professional assistance in the handling of his funds.

Gradually, the extent of his income dawned upon him, and he worked hard at learning how to handle it. From his lawyer, the banker and his friend, Mr. Beadle, he learned a great deal about investing and within a year or so, he had established a routine by which the money was distributed as it came in; some to purchase common stock, some in government securities and some in liquid savings accounts.

He also began to realize that it was ridiculous to live like a $4,000 a year toolmaker when he was actually receiving an income of six figures. He discussed this pleasant situation with his wife and his in-laws and they agreed that since he had been so fortunate, he should enjoy his affluence. He agreed to pay the mortgage on the Thorsen's home, and he made arrangements through the bank for them to receive a monthly check for $500, which made them cry, but about which he would accept no refusal. He and Veda had long discussions and finally decided that they should find a small house for themselves and their 2-year-old son, Teodor, in the vicinity of Ingmar's work. Later on they would look for a larger place.

Ingmar, Veda and Teodor lived for nearly twenty years in a modest house in a quiet neighborhood. Ingmar went daily to his shop and Teodor, as he grew, went to school. When he graduated from high school, cum laude, he enrolled at the University of Detroit, where his sober and industrious intelligence stood him in good stead. When he graduated, his proud parents and his maternal grandmother were in the audience. Teodor greatly regretted the absence of his grandfather Thorsen, who had passed away two years earlier.

Teodor went to work as an engineer at General Motors, but soon found that he was not happy in industry. He enrolled in graduate school at the University of Detroit and rapidly accumulated the credits necessary to obtain a teaching certificate, whereupon he resigned from his job and went to work as a high school teacher. This he found much more to his liking. He studied constantly and soon had his Master's degree, which spurred him on to further research and writing, and in only a few years, he became Doctor Teodor Borgeson. Now he had the latitude to teach or write or engage in industrial research, whichever interested him most. And in the course of his endless visits to the libraries, he met, fell in love with and married a pretty young librarian, Janice Moreland.

Meanwhile, Ingmar's money piled up. He and Veda were content with their simple lifestyle. They were modest in their material desires, and so did not spend money unnecessarily. After a while, the burgeoning bank account began to weigh on Ingmar's mind. He consulted his good friend, Albert Beadle, who encouraged Ingmar to set up a trust or scholarship fund to be used to reward promising young toolmakers and designers in the automotive community.

"That way," Beadle told him, "you will be directly responsible for promoting the cause of craftsmanship in the field you love." He smiled broadly and added, "Who knows, your help may lead to the discovery of another Henry Ford or—even another Ingmar Borgeson!"

Although he felt embarrassed by Beadle's remarks, Ingmar recognized the value of this suggestion and began immediately to establish such a fund. It was an ideal solution, for it not only did much to improve the quality of automotive products over the years, but it also permitted Borgeson to feel that his wealth was an honorable thing with which he could finally be comfortable.

In 1934, when Ingmar was sixty years of age, he began to have some minor health problems. The rich Scandinavian diet to which the family had clung was gradually creating circulatory problems and his doctor was concerned about damage to his heart. After a thorough examination, he suggested that Ingmar would be well advised to consider retiring and spending his time walking and puttering in his flower beds.

"The automotive business can struggle along without you now, Ingmar," the doctor offered, jokingly. "Don't interpret this as meaning that you are in any serious danger, health-wise, at the moment. You simply get too involved in whatever mechanical marvel you are working on. I know, I have talked to Veda about it. She tells me how you get started on some project and can't get any rest, night or day, until you have seen it through to a conclusion. By the time you have succeeded in completing it, you are worn to a frazzle. Now, you've had your fun with things of that sort all your adult life, but it's time to quit before the pace you set for yourself gets you. You don't need any more money, I'm sure—you just need to realize that it's time to sit back and relax and enjoy the less hectic things in life. Give your good wife a break. Move out of this car-crazy area. Buy a nice home in the country and take time to smell the flowers, as they say."

This was not a suggestion that sat well with Ingmar.

"But, I love my vork!" he argued. "I not ready to quit and act like old man!"

"Of course, you love your work. I love mine, too, but when I'm your age, I'm going to give the old blood pressure a chance to slow down and let someone younger see to the doctoring. Any time they really need me, they'll call, and I can feel like a big shot solving their problems. But it'll be at long distance—not where I've spent my working life. You should do the same. Take my advice, Ingmar—you pay enough for it!"

When Ingmar told Veda what the doctor had said, she was delighted.

"When we took that trip East a couple of years ago, remember how much we liked that little town in Connecticut—what was it—Newvale? Let's go there and see if we can find a nice place. And I'm sure Teodor and Janice and the children would like to live there, too. Could we try that, Ingmar? Please?"

He smiled as he looked at her.

"You had that answer ready pretty qvick, Veda. I t'ink you and the doctor been talkin' ven I didn't know!"

Veda blushed and dropped her eyes. Then she looked up at him, smiling, too.

"I guess you caught me, old man. But you know it is good advice you're getting. Let's go look!"

The idea was beginning to take root in Ingmar's head. Maybe Veda and the doctor had something there. Maybe it would be nice to get out of the routine and try other things in new surroundings. And he certainly owed it to Veda to look at other possibilities if that was what she wanted.

"I have to let company know I vant to close my shop. I can't run avay without giving notice. And ve have to discuss with Teodor and Janice—see what dey t'ink."

"They'll be happy to go, Ingmar. I'll take care of the details. I'll figure out when we should go and get any tickets or reservations we need. Janice will help me if I get stuck. The young ones know more about traveling than we do."

Ingmar eyed his wife and chuckled.

"I guess not only doctor who have this idea, little Flicka. How you know the kids vant dis?"

"Oh, Ingmar, just take my word for it!"

And so it was that arrangements were made for the trip. The whole family, including Veda's mother, Mrs. Thorsen, who now lived with them, made another journey to the east coast. Teodor had talked with a real estate man he knew in Detroit, who referred him to one in northwestern Connecticut. By the time they arrived in Newvale, the realtor had located a couple of possibilities. As it turned out, neither was attractive to the Borgesons and they were about to leave, disappointed, when the realtor mentioned that there was plenty of land available if they would consider building.

"Vy not?" Ingmar asked of no one in particular.

They spent several days riding around town, looking over a number of potential building sites. Finally, they came upon a substantial tract on one of the hills which rose away from the valley floor, and they all seemed to know at once that this was where they would henceforth spend their lives.

"Oo, Papa! This is beautiful," Teodor exclaimed, as his wife, Janice, nodded enthusiastically.

"Oh, Ingmar—what a lovely spot for a house!" Veda chimed in.

Ingmar himself was impressed. The area on which they were standing was elevated enough to provide a nice view of the surrounding wooded hills with much of the town spread out below. Private enough to satisfy the reclusively inclined man, but with easy access to the village. It consisted of well over fifty acres, with at least a ten acre open meadow in the approximate center. After a very short bargaining session, they arrived at a purchase agreement.

The Borgesons all returned to Detroit and spent the next few months happily winding up all of their affairs there.

An architect visited the site and then drew plans for a very large house which reflected suggestions from all of the family. A special ell was included to house a workshop area where Ingmar could satisfy his need for creative expression. After more than a year of construction, landscaping and final touches to their new home, the Borgesons, old and young, moved into their beautiful new house to settle into becoming solid Newvale citizens.

Chapter 9
Hack

In the Spring of 1939, Hartshorn & Company, originally, H & K Mfg. Co., was the only truly industrial operation in Newvale. It had been conceived by Fred Hartshorn and a business acquaintance of his, Albert Kronenberg, as a private enterprise, intended to make and assemble elements of large timepieces such as mantel or Grandfather clocks. They had learned the clock business while employed in nationally known clock factories, of which there were several in the western Connecticut area. With typical Yankee ambition and self-confidence, they were impatient to strike out on their own and make a place for themselves in manufacturing. They were able to convince the management of the large plants that they could produce such elements faster and more economically and provide them with worthwhile savings because of low overhead operation.

They invested what money they had and borrowed more and started in business in 1924. Several power presses, screw machines, gear hobs, milling machines and assembly benches were set up in an old vacant building. Local people were hired and trained and with orders from the big clock companies, the business soon became profitable.

Both men were familiar with production machinery as well as with business management. They hired local men who were talented mechanics and who could fine-tune the equipment and keep it running smoothly.

Unfortunately, in the early thirties, a combination of problems conspired to make life difficult for the young company. The Great Depression was starting to be felt in all businesses, and although clocks were essential and production of them was not hit as hard as was that of many other things, there was a definite slowdown. Added to this was a steadily increasing changeover to electric power for large clocks, which drastically reduced the need for the type of assemblies H & K Mfg. Co. had been designed to supply. As the effects of these problems began to seriously affect the business, Kronenberg became more and more despondent. His efficiency dropped dramatically as he spent more and more time worrying and complaining, while Hartshorn, on the other hand, worked harder and harder and gave much consideration to possible alternative actions which might salvage their once promising enterprise.

Finally, after yet another substantial postponement of delivery was requested by their largest customer, Mr. Kronenberg threw up his hands and said, "It's no use, Fred. Another six months like this and we'll have lost everything we put into this business. And not only that, my family will starve. I've got to get out of here and get a regular job."

"Are you sure that's what you want to do?" asked Hartshorn.

"Not what I *want* to do, Fred - it's what I *have* to do. I've no choice. Let's sit down and figure out what we can do about closing up the place."

Hartshorn's hand went up.

"Hold it, Al—when did we say anything about closing it up? If you want to get out, that's your business, but that doesn't mean that I feel that way. I still look at this little place as having a lot of potential, and I'm damned if I plan to just throw in the towel and quit."

Kronenberg snorted, impatiently.

"You're not being realistic, Fred. Business is going no place but down for the foreseeable future, and that means H & K Mfg. is done. Let's salvage what we can and go to work in a big plant the way we used to."

"Al," Fred said, "I didn't start this shop just to give up as soon as things got a little tough."

A short silence ensued, during which both men stared at the floor, despondently. Then Fred's manner changed. He stood up, turned to Al and said, "Tell you what I'll do, Al. I'll sit down with a lawyer and see what sort of arrangement can be worked out to protect what interest you have, while still allowing me to operate. I'm sure it will mean cutting back on the help and taking home less pay, but I think it could be done."

Kronenberg paced back and forth, head down, hands clasped behind his back.

"Fred," he said, "we've always gotten along well with each other, and I don't want to do anything to spoil that, but you have to understand that I need my week's pay and whatever equity I have left in H & K. If you can set something up that I can live with, okay. When can you do something about it?"

"I'll get hold of a lawyer this afternoon and set up an appointment as soon as he is available. I'll keep you posted on everything as fast as I have any information. Is that okay with you?"

Kronenberg sighed and nodded his head.

"That sounds all right. Meantime, I'm going to see Charlie Campbell. He told me I could come back to work for him anytime I wanted to. If he meant it, it will make the whole deal a lot easier. I'll let you know as soon as I talk to Charlie."

The two men looked at each other silently for a minute, then Kronenberg held out his hand to his partner. They shook hands without a further word, and Kronenberg turned and left the office.

❖ ❖ ❖

A serious but confident Fred Hartshorn arranged an immediate appointment with lawyer Jonathan Cartwright, partner in Brideshead and Cartwright, Newvale's major legal firm. He was shown into the musty second-floor office by the secretary-receptionist. Cartwright rose from his chair behind a large desk, smiled, and offered his hand.

"How are you, Fred? We don't see much of each other, do we, even though we're both in town most of the time." He motioned Hartshorn to a chair.

"That's right, we don't seem to," replied Fred.

"Family okay?"

"Fine, thanks—yours?"

"Fine, too. Well, what can we do for you, Fred?"

"Well, you know business has been hard to come by in recent months. Al and I have been finding it harder and harder to make ends meet, especially when we are trying to support two executive-level salaries. He has decided he wants to go back to his old job with Seth Thomas, which means either I have to buy him out or we close the doors. I think I can make a go of it alone, so what I need from you, Jon, is a workable plan which will permit me to continue to operate the business while gradually paying Al off. I don't want to be strapped completely or repay Al too slowly. And, of course, I want it in the form of a legal agreement which will stand up over the future."

He opened up his brief case, saying, "I brought along a copy of our latest financial report and P & L statement, so you will be able to judge what kind of dollars we are talking about. And, incidentally," he added, with a sardonic smile, "which will disabuse you of any notion you might be able to charge a big fee."

Cartwright took the proffered papers and laid them on his desk.

"Is there any problem between you two, Fred? Is this something that is going to have to be argued out or fought over? I always thought you two had a wonderful arrangement."

"No, there's no problem except the bad economic situation. We have slowed down enough that, as I said, it isn't practical to try taking two executive salaries out of the business, and Al is ready to go back to his old job—assuming he can get it, but I'm more stubborn. I have a few ideas for a somewhat different approach which I think I can make work well enough to see me through the bad times and come out with a solid base for the future. I'll have to cut the work force a little, and reduce my own salary somewhat, but that's just part of the joy of being in business, I guess. One big problem is that I need this agreement right away—like within the next day or two. Can you do it for me?"

"Well," said Cartwright, "I guess I'll have to. Fortunately for you, you caught me in a somewhat slow period—you know, lawyers feel the pinch sometimes, too."

He laughed, but it did not sound sincere. "Thanks, Jon." He rose and headed for the door. "Call me the minute you have anything, please."

Fred left as the lawyer resumed looking over the papers he had provided.

In the next few weeks, there were several meetings with the two principals and the lawyer, as well as a number of phone calls and visits to the local bank. Fred had to sell some lucrative real estate to pay off Kronenberg, who had convinced Campbell to reinstate him in his old supervisory capacity. Finally, a solid agreement was reached and the little manufacturing business became the sole proprietorship of Fred Hartshorn. Fred trimmed his operating personnel and lengthened his own working hours to include most evenings and much of each weekend.

After a few months on this schedule, he began to realize that he would have to have someone to whom he could pass along a lot of the routine work. He was constantly short of the time he needed to determine how he could branch into other kinds of production. He wanted time to research the type, cost and availability of used machinery, the potential customers in the area, the extent of competition to be faced and the need for representatives or advertising to present his capabilities to prospective customers. Unfortunately, he could not afford a person with extensive experience who would command a large salary.

When he realized he was about at a loss as to what to do, a possible solution unexpectedly presented itself. Mr. Christopher Hacker, scheduled to graduate from Newvale High School in June, 1940, applied to Hartshorn & Co. for a job.

From the moment the young man walked through the office door, Hartshorn was impressed with him. Of course, he had known the family for years and was quite friendly with the senior Hackers. They belonged to the same church and he and John Hacker were fellow LIONS and they naturally bumped into each other on a regular basis. He also thought Melody Hacker was one of the most attractive women he knew. He had observed young Christopher casually as he grew up. Chris was a valuable member of most of the varsity teams in high school and was involved in many of the activities of the youth of the town. Also, Fred had often noticed the lad mowing lawns or shoveling sidewalks or doing any sort of work available to growing boys. All of this demonstrated ambition.

"Come in, Christopher—have a seat," Fred said.

"Thank you, Mr. Hartshorn," Hack replied as he sat down. Fred noted approvingly the clean, healthy appearance of the lad, and especially the clear unwavering eyes.

"My dad said you mentioned something about hiring an assistant, and I wondered if you might consider me for the position?"

Hartshorn was rather taken aback. He was not prepared for such a direct approach. After a moment, he answered, "Well, yes, I have been thinking about adding a man to sort of understudy me, but frankly, I had someone a little older in mind. You haven't finished high school yet, have you? And you must be planning to go off to college in the fall. I don't think that would work out very well, would it?"

"I understand what you mean, Mr. Hartshorn, but it isn't like it seems. I will graduate next June, but I have pretty well made up my mind that I am not going to go to college. I want to go to work as soon as I can, and I think I'd be very interested in the manufacturing field."

Hartshorn felt that there was something wrong. Here was a bright, capable young fellow, whom he felt sure must be a good student, from a family obviously capable of giving him assistance with furthering his education. Yet, here he was saying flatly that he did not intend to go on with his schooling.

"Do you mind my asking why you've decided against college? I'm sure it isn't for lack of ability or lack of funds. What is it that looks attractive to you about going to work? Do your parents agree with you on the course you are planning?"

Hack shook his head slowly from side to side. "I haven't told them yet. I know it's a big decision, and I'm sure they will be shocked and disappointed at first, but they'll let me make my own moves because they trust my judgement, believe it or not. I guess I must be a little different than a lot of kids. I've never minded working—in fact, I've always enjoyed it. Most of the kids want to go to college because it means a few more years that they won't have to go to work. To me, it's just the opposite—going to college would mean several more years before I could get started on a career. And maybe I shouldn't tell you this, but ever since I was a little kid, I've wanted to work and earn money. If I can do things the way I want, and I get decent breaks, someday I'm going to be wealthy, and it is going to be because I got started early and got the jump on others my age. I can always pick up specific knowledge that I find I need by taking courses in night school or in other ways, but in the meantime, I'll be learning plenty about the field I'm in by practical experience. By the time my classmates get out of school, I'll be their boss!"

Hartshorn was really surprised.

"You mean you really are that enthusiastic about going to work in a factory? You don't think you'll regret your decision when you're elbow deep in grease and oil, while your contemporaries are sitting around reading books and drinking beer?"

"No, Mr. Hartshorn, I really mean it. All I ask is a chance to show you that I'm sincere." Then he added, with a slight smile, "You can always fire me if I don't work out, can't you?"

Hartshorn nodded. "You're right—I can do that, even though I'd feel badly about it. Tell you what, Christopher. Let me think this over for a day or so. Then I'll call you and either tell you I've decided against it or ask you to come in for further discussion. Does that sound okay to you?"

"That's just fine with me, sir. I sure hope you'll see the possibilities if you decide to give me a chance. And thanks again for talking with me. Oh, and I'd appreciate it if you'd keep what I told you about my plans between you and me. I wouldn't want my parents to hear it from someone else."

"Yes, I will do that. And there is one thing that you can do for me, too. Tell your parents that this is all your idea. I don't want them to think that I had anything to do with your decision to skip college."

"Don't worry about that. For now, all they need to know is that I'm trying to get work for after school and Saturdays. I'll give them the whole story at the proper time."

They rose and shook hands.

Hartshorn gave the matter considerable thought over the next few days. He could not get out of his mind the forthright, even rather audacious manner in which young Hacker had presented his case. Furthermore, he could not seem to find anything wrong with the logic of giving Christopher a try. As the boy had said, he could always fire him if it did not work out. And he certainly was sorely in need of someone to pick up part of the load under which he was laboring.

"I'll bet this kid could handle it," he thought. "Hell, why not?" he said to himself aloud.

He picked up the phone and dialed the Hacker's number.

"Hello," a young voice answered.

"Is this Christopher?"

"Yes, it is. Who's calling, please?"

"This is Fred Hartshorn. I've thought a lot about our discussion and I've decided that I should give you a try, if you are still interested. Could you come to the shop after school tomorrow?"

The elation in Hack's voice was unmistakable. "You bet I can!"

"Fine. Wear clothes that you won't mind getting a little oil on. See you then, Christopher," and he hung up the phone.

Chapter 10
Decision

The months of high school remaining were shrinking fast for Hack. Originally, the question as to whether and where to continue his education after graduation had been a critical issue. He had asked himself a lot of questions. What college? Where? How expensive? What course of study should he choose?

His parents had been after him about it for some time, but recently the tempo of their concern had increased, and the pressure to start making some decisions was steadily mounting. Hack had found, too, that his subconscious had been busy with the question a great deal of the time and that it had irritated him. When he was still thinking of college, he had decided he should try to select a school that would fit into a rather loosely formed mental matrix which included academic reputation, scholarship possibilities, cost and distance from home. He knew from hints which were dropped occasionally that his father would be trying to influence him without seeming to do so, to consider his own alma mater, Benson, but he had heard little about that institution which would make it seem like an attractive choice. And, besides, it was too close to home. Hack had already decided that any school he chose would be far enough away to permit him to be a true college man; living on campus, probably in a fraternity house after a while, with a high degree of independence and without the option of running home every weekend or every holiday. Dad would be disappointed and perhaps somewhat hurt, but that was tough—he'd get over it.

The Ivy League schools had undeniable advantages. For example, he had never heard of a Yale or Harvard or Dartmouth graduate who was unsuccessful. However, he was not sure that his grades would be acceptable to them or that the family would be able to afford the cost of his attending such prestigious institutions. He decided that the state schools were not a good choice because they were looked upon by some as inferior in quality, both academically and socially. He had no intention of wasting years in college only to be snubbed by potential employers or influential people who could help him attain his goal, simply because they felt his choice of college to have been inferior. Perhaps some places like Bates or Bowdoin or Amherst were possibilities. He realized he would have to start getting more and better information if he was going to avoid making a mistake that might haunt him forever.

But suddenly he realized that his indecision was for a different reason altogether—he did not really want to go to college at all! And that was when he went to Hartshorn & Co. and made his bid for a different career. The time was not yet right for him to inform his parents, but he knew that it would be soon.

By February 1940, Hack's parents were very upset over his inability to select a college, or even to select a *type* of college.

"I swear, I just don't know what the boy is thinking of, Melody," John said to his wife. "The only thing he has made perfectly clear is that he won't be attending Benson. He's never been like that, but do you think for some reason he made that decision just to hurt me?"

"You mustn't look at it that way, at all, John. Heaven knows you have been as good a fatha as a boy could have, and Ah do believe he would be the fust to agree. There is somethin' botherin' him. We're goin' to have to sit him down and say, 'All raght, son—what are you goin' to do about schoolin'—this suspense is killin' us!'"

John sat, palms together between his knees, and gazed at the floor, hoping for answers, but none came. After a while, he said, "I guess you're right, hon. It's time we thrashed this out so that we can all relax. Let's corner him after supper and see if we can't get to the bottom of it."

Hack's antennae detected the tension in the atmosphere at the table, but no one seemed about to explain, so he just enjoyed the good food and waited for something or someone to relieve it. His mother and father did not seem to be overly interested in the chops, potatoes, carrots, lima beans and homemade bread, mincing away at first one thing and then another and sipping at their drinks unusually often.

When Hack had eaten all he wanted and asked to be excused, his father said, "Just a minute, son. Your mother and I want to clear up this matter of college. We've been waiting out your decision for quite a while, and now the time is getting impossibly short and we still don't hear anything from you as to where you want to go or what you want to study or any other information. I understand that, for whatever reason, you don't want to go to Benson, and I accept that. Far be it from me to tell you at your age and with your intelligence that you must go to a certain school. You know it's entirely up to you, but your mother and I are losing sleep over the fact that you just don't seem to have made any progress at all. Libby has had her acceptance to Middlebury for months, and I'm sure a number of your male friends are all set with their plans, too. For God's sake, Hack, when are you going to make a move?"

Melody had been sitting on the edge of her chair, looking fixedly at Hack and nodding agreement with everything her husband said. Now, she added, "Please, deah, you must know how difficult this indecision is fo' us. Once you decide, we can get on with the things we will have to do to help you. There will be trips to make, lettahs to write, finances to arrange, shoppin' to do—my heavens, I shuddah to think of it!"

"Okay," Hack said, heaving a big sigh. "Okay, I guess I have been a little unfair to you, but it's because I wasn't sure myself what I wanted to do. Every time I concentrated on it, I seemed to come up with a different answer. There wasn't a single school that I considered that I could honestly say I was enthusiastic about. And then it came through to me that I was looking more for their faults than their strengths. And you know why? It was because it finally dawned upon me the real reason for my inability to decide. You see, I finally realized that I don't want to go to college at all!"

Melody sagged back in her chair.

John's jaw dropped and he stared at his son. "Don't want to go to college? Are you joking? Not go to college when the opportunity is there? You can't be serious!"

Melody had recovered enough to wail, "Oh, Hack, deah—don't say such a thing!"

"Well, it's true," he continued. "I know just what I want to do. I want to graduate from Newvale High and go out and get myself a job that I like in manufacturing and start my future. I've know for a long time that I like to work, and I *love* to make money. If I have my way, I'm going to make a lot of it, and I'm going to enjoy everything it will do for me and my family."

"But, Hack—do you realize what such a decision could have on the rest of your life?" his father asked.

Hack, primed now, plunged ahead. "Just working lately in the shop has changed my whole outlook on the future. There's something about the smell of machine oil and the sound of smooth running machines and the wonderful things they can be made to do that really excites me. I've found out that I'm not much of a mechanic, but I can see the way that machines can be made to do all sorts of things and I've got a pretty good imagination as far as developing methods and systems is concerned. I'm sure that Mr. Hartshorn will take me on full time and will give me all the breaks he can. He likes me and he knows that I'm there to work and to learn and that he'll get his money's worth out of me."

John had his response ready. "That's fine for the moment, but as a life's work, it doesn't seem very appealing."

"But, Dad, Mom—think of it this way. School work doesn't appeal to me at all, because all of the time I would put in trying to get As and Bs or Cs, I would be thinking about all of the 'G's I could be making if I had a good job and hustled my tail off. I know all of the arguments in favor of a college education and against going to work instead, but I don't buy them. I'm no dummy—I'm not going to take some twenty dollar a week job that's going nowhere—I'm going to find one where I can be learning something I really like and be getting paid for doing it. Maybe you don't believe it now, but just you wait and see—by the time the fellows who graduate with me are through with college, I'll have learned as much or more than they have and will have money in the bank and some seniority in my job. I'll leave most of them in the dust, you just wait and see!"

The gist of Hack's totally unexpected news had hit both parents like an anesthetic. They sat, numbly, mouths slightly agape, eyes rather glassy and shoulders drooping. Melody was gradually recovering, at least to the point of articulation.

"Christopher! Wherever did you get such ideas? How can you say you aren't goin' on to school? Why, you've always been one of the top students in yoah class. What will folks in town think? How can Ah face Mrs. Ashburn or Mrs. Sorenson or that snooty Mrs. Smith-Healy when they find out that ouah son is quittin' school an' takin' a job in some smelly factory or somethin', while theah sons are attendin' Williams or Vanderbilt or Notre Dame!?"

Her husband interrupted, "Wait a minute, Mel. You're just giving a gut reaction because you feel hurt by what he has said. I personally don't give a good Goddam what folks in town may think. It isn't as though he'd be doing something dishonest or immoral or anything. This is really quite a bomb you've dropped though, Hack. This is something we've never even considered. How did you come up with this idea? Do you really think what you are saying makes good sense? Don't you realize that the fellows who take four year courses in college are going to start at much higher salaries when they go to work, and that they will always have the advantage of those degree letters after their names? How do you think you will compare with them in ten or fifteen years?"

"I've thought about that a lot, Dad, and I'm convinced that I'm right. I can't say how someone else might make out under the same conditions, but I'm telling you that I'll be ahead of the college guys when they get out and they'll never catch up with me! Hey, if I wanted to be a doctor or a chemist or something that takes special education, I'd be right in line, looking to crack those books and get the necessary degrees, but they don't have courses in college in the sort of thing I'm interested in. You have to get into it and experience it and think about ways to improve it—that's where the money is, and that's where I plan to be!"

Again, Mrs. Hacker spoke up. "What do you think Libby is goin' to do when she heahs about these plans? You don't think a beautiful, smart girl like her is goin' to go to Middlebury fo' foah yeahs and then come back and marry a factory hand, shoahly."

"Mom," Hack answered, "we've talked it out in the past few days and she says it really doesn't make any difference to her what I do, as long as it is what I want to do. If I can't find ways to keep her from throwing me over while I'm working and she's in school, then I probably wouldn't have been able to anyway. After all, we would have been in completely separate places for most of the time if I had decided to go to college, too. At least so far, Lib isn't much impressed with degrees and flashy collegiate types. With luck, she'll stay that way, and if she does, you can bet that we'll be married right after she graduates."

"Well, Ah'm certainly glad to heah that, at least," said Melody.

John Hacker had pretty well recovered by this time. He turned to his wife and said, as jovially as possible under the circumstances, "Well, honey, let's let this young fellow go now. We've got a big new mouthful to digest." To Hack, he said, "You don't know how glad I am that at last we have something to mull over. Whether or not we like your decision, we know where you stand and we can think about it and talk about it and see if anything crops up that we haven't yet had time to consider. Don't assume that we are automatically against your plans just because we were a bit shocked by them. Give us a little time to look at it from your angle. And don't be too concerned about your Mom's reaction. You know that whatever your final route is, she'll be right in there trying to help."

Instinctively, Hack reached out and shook his father's hand, then leaned down and gave his mother a kiss on the cheek.

Chapter 11
Working

It did not take Hack long to discover that production machinery fascinated and excited him. The fact that metal strip or rod could be fed into machinery and be converted into a virtually endless variety of usable items of shapes and sizes limited only by the talents of the designers and craftsmen who controlled it, seemed to him an almost magical process.

Hack found the machines to be less complicated than they at first appeared, once he realized that they were merely an agglomeration of rather standard parts, altered in size and shape and assembled in various ways to bring about certain results. Nearly all production equipment of the early twentieth century was made up of some combination of gears, shafts, cams, feed mechanisms, chains, gaskets, pulleys, spindles, chucks, clutches, collets, springs, latches and pumps, in addition to castings or sheet metal stampings or forgings which made up their frames and skeletons. All of these parts were designed, shaped and fitted so as to properly hold and present to the raw material stock, the tools which were the heart of the machining process. It was the carefully designed and lovingly created cutting, shaping or forming tools and punches and dies which actually yielded the product. And all of the other complex-looking paraphernalia was only there to serve them. The trick was to force the machine to present the creative tools to the work at precisely the right time and place and at exactly the correct angle and speed to accomplish the desired end. To do so required painstaking machine maintenance, thorough and constant lubrication, and scientifically formulated coolants and cutting liquids.

When Hack first started working for Hartshorn, he had had very little exposure to the world of manufacturing, and so it was necessary for him to learn everything from the ground up. Hartshorn was impressed with his interest and eagerness to understand. Therefore, he spent much more time introducing him to all of the equipment and procedures than he would have done with most new employees. Like any teacher who realizes that he has an avid pupil, Hartshorn found himself digging deeply into his own wealth of knowledge in order to furnish Hack with as much information as possible, and he was delighted to find that the young fellow absorbed it, digested it and asked for more. Although it was necessary to restrict Hack to simple tasks in the early stages of his employment, Hartshorn often interrupted Hack's work to impart to him some tidbit of a special nature which, while valueless to an ordinary employee, would mean something to a career man, which he was convinced Hack was destined to be.

By the time Hack had been at Hartshorn & Co. for a year, he had, because of his eagerness to learn and Mr. Hartshorn's willingness to teach, acquired sufficient knowledge to be conversant with the entire operation. He could receive an inquiry, estimate the cost, prepare a quotation, accept an order, visualize and design and order the special tooling for the job, and purchase the necessary raw materials and standard expendable tools. He could then participate in some aspects of the actual production and could handle inspection and finally, shipping and invoicing. It was all becoming quite clear to him. He understood the flow of a job through the various manufacturing steps and the teamwork necessary to accomplish positive results. Mr. Hartshorn had given Hack thorough training in the paperwork involved, but he soon realized that although Hack had the necessary interest in the physical aspects of machining, he lacked that indefinable instinctive talent which sets true artisans apart from others. But what he also realized was that Hack had another equally valuable instinct—that of grasping the difference between what was important and what was not. He could identify energy judiciously expended or energy wasted, and knew immediately whether or not a given procedure would produce profits.

Another quality which added to the growing admiration Hartshorn had for his protege was Hack's personality. He was obviously serious and dedicated to learning and making progress, but he did not project an air of superiority or lack of humor. He looked people straight in the eye and spoke in a straightforward but courteous manner. He could talk to customers on the telephone without making the youthful mistakes of being either obsequious or officious. And he always came through as honest.

Hartshorn, childless and middle-aged, gradually decided that Christopher Hacker was destined to be his next partner and his eventual successor. He could turn a project over to Hack with confidence that it would be taken care of properly, and that the lad would recognize precisely the point at which he had reached the limit of his own training and talent and needed to ask for help from the experts. And he could request such help with no feeling of inadequacy or embarrassment.

Everything proceeded peacefully and smoothly and with a growing mutual feeling of satisfaction between Hack and Hartshorn until December 7, 1941, when the Japanese attacked Pearl Harbor. Nothing would ever be quite the same again, for Hack or for anyone else.

Chapter 12
War Plans

The first few weeks after Pearl Harbor, Hack followed his normal routine as closely as possible, but now everything appeared quite different. The everyday procedures no longer seemed to be of much importance. He found that his thoughts were constantly straying from what he was doing to the far away places where battles were being fought or planned, the outcome of which might critically affect the remainder of his life. It was very hard to concentrate on bookkeeping entries or a customer's orders when the call to distant battles and the stirrings of patriotism kept the young blood inside him coursing at an accelerated pace. Finally, the urge became overpowering, and he sought out his father as a sounding board.

"Dad," he said, "I've just got to talk to you about this war business and find out whether you feel about it the way I do, or the way you would have felt if you were my age."

"Okay, Hack—shoot!"

"I know that I'm starting to do okay at my job, and I still haven't completely given up the idea of college, but I also know that I'm young and healthy and will be getting drafted before too long anyway, and the more I think about it, the more it looks like I'd be happier if I enlisted."

John raised his eyebrows. "Oh?" he said. "What makes you think that that would be a good idea?"

"Well, if I enlisted, I might have a better shot at getting something I want in the service, or at least I'd be in ahead of most of the draftees and should be in line for promotions ahead of the majority of them. What do you think?"

"To tell the truth, Hack, I've been watching you for the last few weeks and I could see exactly what was churning around in your head. The way you are thinking makes a lot of sense, I'll have to admit, although it's not going to please me to see you jump in before you have to, and you know it will tear your mother up. But it's true that you're a cinch to get drafted anyway, and she'll just have to brace herself and face up to it like millions of other moms around the country. Have you talked it over with Libby?"

Hack stood up, turned and looked out of the window. For a few moments, he said nothing, but then, rather softly, he said, "No—we haven't discussed it."

John waited a while to see if anything else was about to follow, but it appeared that that was all Hack planned to say. "None of my business, Hack, but I hope there's no problem between you two."

Hack turned back, shaking his head. "No problem at all. It's just that Libby has been practically in shock ever since Pearl Harbor and just can't seem to bring herself to talk about the war or the draft or anything connected with it. I guess it's because she knows that all of us guys will be in it one way or another before long. It has just changed everyone's plans so drastically. She just hasn't had time to adjust."

John nodded. It was interesting to see how mature these young folks had suddenly become, but he felt it was a shame that they could not have had a few more years without such disruptions in their lives. "If you did enlist, which service branch would you prefer?"

Hack paced slowly around the room as he replied, "Well, I've thought about it a lot. I don't think I'd like being confined on a boat for weeks or months at a time, so I think the Navy is out."

"What about the Marines?" his father asked. "There's lots of adventure there."

Hack slowly shook his head. "No, I don't think so. I'm impressed by the spirit and tradition of the Marines, but I also know they are the first ones in whenever there is a nasty job to do, and I'm not planning on being a hero, particularly. It pretty much boils down to the plain old Army, I guess."

"Well," said John, "there's nothing wrong with the Army."

Hack continued, "From what I have read, though, there are a lot of Army branches and all of them are right up-to-date with the latest technical advances. I don't believe it's just marching and shooting and saluting any more. If I do enlist, I may get to pick the branch I want, and I think that might be either Ordnance or Signal Corps. If I was really lucky, I might get exposed to some pretty good new types of machinery in Ordnance, or some of the latest communications equipment in Signal. You see, Dad, I plan to live through this war, and I want to come out of the service a little bit smarter and a little better prepared for life than I am when I go in."

John looked at his son almost in awe. He thought to himself, "This lad has it in Spades. How he has learned so much and applied it in such a matter-of-fact, practical manner at such a tender age is more than I can fathom." Aloud, he said, "Hack, I don't think you have to ask me any more about your plans. You don't know how happy and proud I am right now. To see that you recognize that you have an obligation to serve the country in this critical situation is very satisfying to me, but to see that you also plan to make it work to your advantage as much as possible tells me that you've got your head on straight, and haven't just got stars and stripes in your eyes and martial music in your ears. You can leave the nest whenever you're ready, without our having to fret about your ability to take good care of yourself."

"Thanks, Dad. I'm still mulling over just what I plan to do, but don't be too surprised if I come home some night soon and tell you I've signed up."

John nodded. "I understand, Hack. If you want, I'll try to catch your mother in the right mood and break it to her as gently as possible. It won't be easy, but she'll accept it better coming from me—I've had to bring her bad news before, and you haven't."

"Appreciate it, Dad."

❖ ❖ ❖

By the middle of March 1942, the pressure of uncertainty became too much for Hack to live with. One morning, he found it impossible to follow his usual routine. He decided that the time had come to make a move. He called Mr. Hartshorn and said that he had to make a trip into Danbury.

"I can't say exactly what time I'll be back, but I'll be here as soon as I can," Hack said.

"Okay, Christopher," the older man replied, feeling that there was something going on.

Hack made a fast trip to Danbury, going directly to the Selective Service office on the second floor of City Hall. When he told them that he was interested in finding out about enlisting, he was told that there was an Army recruiting officer set up in the lobby who would be able to furnish any information needed. Down the stairs he went and he immediately saw a desk set up in one corner of the lobby, and behind it, a much be-striped and be-ribboned Army sergeant. Hack approached him and was soon subjected to the beginning of a canned recruiting speech.

"Excuse me, Sergeant," Hack interrupted. "but you can skip the sales talk.

I've already decided that I want to enlist—I just need to get some information about the different possibilities and the chance I have of getting into the type of specialties I'm interested in."

The sergeant relaxed a bit. "Okay, kid," he said. "You tell me what you think you're looking for and I'll tell you how to go about getting it."

"Well," said Hack, "I've pretty much narrowed it down to Ordnance or Signal, and I think, of those two, I'd prefer Ordnance."

"Shouldn't be any problem," the sergeant said. "Let's get you on record here first. I'll give you a few forms here and you can fill them out and we'll set up the next steps for you so you can move right along."

❖ ❖ ❖

Hack was surprised and pleased to find that the wheels of the military were turning fast. The country had armed forces to build, and the need for haste was obvious. Volunteers, such as Hack, were exactly what was needed because they permitted the machinery of the Selective Service department to skip over much of the paperwork which would have been involved in conscripting them. Men who might otherwise be in the drafting process for months, or even years, before their number came up, were instead rushed into active service. They were either trained for almost immediate duty in a combat theater or developed into teaching cadre to handle the millions of civilian-soldiers coming through the system at a feverish pace.

Hack was directed to the New Haven armory and was hustled through all of the pre-induction processes including various tests and a physical examination. It was late in the day by the time he started back to Newvale. The Army gave him a week to wind up his personal affairs before reporting to the induction center.

The first thing the next morning, he went to Mr. Hartshorn and told him what he had done.

"Really, Mr. Hartshorn, I didn't know I was going right in. I've been kicking it around in my mind for several weeks, and finally it got to the point where I had to do something."

"Well, Hack, you've sort of thrown a monkey wrench into my plans—no, that's not fair. Of course, I realized that you would be virtually certain to be drafted, so I knew I couldn't expect to have you here for much of the war period, but it is a shock and a serious inconvenience to have you leave so soon. On the other hand, I don't know why I shouldn't be inconvenienced—

war does things like that to people. I just hope you are planning to come back to us when the war is over. I have big plans for you, as I'm sure you know."

"Yes, I do know, and I really appreciate it. I told the Army people that I wanted to get into Ordnance if possible, so that I could get to work with the latest machinery. If they don't put me there, I asked for the Signal Corps as second choice, because they have some great equipment, too. I'm hoping to come through the war with some new skills, or at least, with some knowledge about machinery and equipment that I don't have now. And the Army will be footing the bill for what I learn."

Hartshorn smiled. "That's smart, Hack. Any information along that line which you can pick up will be bound to be beneficial to you later. And to the company, too, I might add."

"I'm sure glad that you understand why I'm doing this," Hack said. "I'll write to you whenever I get a chance, and I'll be real anxious to get this over with and get back to work. If you don't mind, I'm going out in the shop now and say goodbye to everyone."

"By all means, Hack. I'm just sorry we didn't have more time so that we could have had a little party and given you a proper send-off."

"Oh, that's okay. You've already done enough for me, Mr. Hartshorn. Well, I'll say goodbye, for now."

Hack left the office after a warm handshake, and made a short visit to his friends in the shop. He explained to them that he had been mulling this move over for some time, and that it had all fallen into place yesterday. He assured them that he had every intention of returning once the war was won.

❖ ❖ ❖

The last few days before Hack had to report were spent in satisfying himself that what few personal affairs he had were put in good order, and in visiting with his friends around town. Moe Penning's father had been activated immediately and sent to a distant Army post, with an instant advancement to the rank of major. Moe was now at a college in Massachusetts and there was no chance that Hack could get together with him before reporting for duty, which was a disappointment to him. Several other friends who had not gone to college or were still in high school, treated Hack to a dinner and bull session one evening.

"So, Hack, you're really about the first of the Newvale gang to take the plunge," said an ex-classmate.

"Yes—I guess so," Hack replied, "but it won't be long before you're all in. I'm just selfish. I figure I may get a better chance at doing something I like by enlisting."

"What did they promise you?" asked one of his friends.

Hack laughed. "They don't promise you anything, except maybe a shot at a branch that you think that you prefer."

A little fellow named Ned, rather scrawny and with very bad eyesight, piped up, "Hey—the whole thing sounds pretty exciting to me! I'm thinking of enlisting too—maybe in the Marines!"

The rest of the gang jeered and hooted.

"Why?" cried one. "You think they need a mascot?"

"You just wait and see," continued the little man. "I may be small, but I've got guts!"

"What will you do if you lose your glasses, Ned?" teased another. "Write home for another pair?"

The laughter resumed, but Ned was undaunted.

"If you get sent to the Pacific, Hack, do you think you can handle those sexy little oriental gals? If you can't, send for me and I'll rush right over to help!" another chimed in.

The rest of the evening passed pleasantly, with more give and take, all centered around the war and their probable involvement in it.

Each evening, Hack picked up Libby, home now for Easter vacation from Middlebury, and they went for a drive in Hack's father's car. Although they pretended to be going to a movie, or to visit some of the other young folks, each evening they drove and talked for a while, until darkness fell, and then drove to a special secret place off one of the back roads, where he could park with very little chance that anyone would discover them, even if they had the desire and the rationed gasoline to do so. And then they would fall into each other's arms passionately and share hugs and kisses until they were out of breath.

Like most curious, hot-blooded and aggressive young men, Hack had experimented with petting on several occasions with some of the more willing, concupiscent young girls in town. His strong, young body and mind reacted instinctively and feverishly to the lure of them. But, somehow, his reaction when he was alone with Libby was different. He thrilled to her looks, her voice and her movements. He desired her completely, but it was a different desire—one which recognized boundaries of time and place. It was a desire coupled with respect which normally satisfied itself with gentle and soft touches and smiles and starry eyes and long, sweet kisses, and the promise of even greater joys to come in the future. Suddenly, with his enlistment and his imminent departure, this no longer seemed enough. Every time he saw her now, his pulse raced and a feeling of panicked urgency engulfed him. He could not wait to get her alone and close, where he could smell the wonderful odor of her, feel the warmth of her body pressed against him, touch the smooth skin of her arms and shoulders, taste her moist lips, kiss the hollow at the base of her neck, and—and?

On the last night before Hack's departure, they broke away to their trysting place as soon as they were able. Once the car was backed into the overhanging brush and the lights extinguished, they came to each other. They exchanged soft, tender kisses and snuggled their bodies against each other. For a long moment, they simply held that position, feeling as though they were one entity, each knowing that the thought of separation was intolerable.

"What are we going to do without each other?" Libby whispered.

"I don't have any answer for that, darling," he whispered back. "It just doesn't seem right that all of this has happened, just when we should be getting married and starting a new life. I never knew it was possible to love anyone the way I love you. I'm not sure I can stand it!"

"I know. It isn't fair, but that's the way life is, I guess. It seems that obstacles just have to be put in front of people, perhaps so that they will appreciate more what they eventually get, if they persevere."

"Well, Libby, they can't put any obstacles in front of me that will keep me from reaching you. I've always wanted to be filthy rich—that's been my big goal in life—but now, I realize that that is secondary. What I want more than anything else is you."

With that, he started showering her with kisses, across her forehead, her cheeks, her nose, her chin and down her neck. then he returned to her lovely mouth and drank from it with a passion they had not previously experienced. After a while, as the tempo and the temperature of their caresses continued to increase, he started making more aggressive moves, but Libby finally resisted.

"Don't, Christopher—please don't," pushing him away slightly.

"But, Lib—this is our last time together before who knows how long a separation. Don't turn me away, for God's sake!"

"Dear, dear Hack. You know I love you beyond words. The thought of you leaving tears my soul and seems almost impossible to bear, but as much as I love you, my conscience and my upbringing and my faith won't allow me to go any further. If I did, I'd feel ashamed and guilty and it will haunt me. You don't want that, I'm sure. Hack, darling, I am completely sure that you will come through the war safely and will return to me and we will be able to continue our beautiful life together. You know that I will be totally faithful to you, however long it takes."

Hack was silent for several moments, and then said, "What can I say, Lib? Right now, I am so revved up it's hard for me to think straight, but I'm also so much in love with you that I wouldn't do anything to risk losing you. I suppose you're right—you usually are—so I've got to accept what you say. But as long as we agree on where to draw the line, let's not waste any more of this evening talking. I want to hug you and kiss you and pet you every minute until we have to go home. I'm afraid it's got to last me a long time."

With that, he clasped her to him again and they resumed their lovemaking, staying always just within the boundaries which Libby had established.

Chapter 13
Off to War

Hack was escorted to the train by his mother and father, his sister and Libby, who had debated with herself long and hard as to whether or not she should go to see him off. Would she be able to maintain her composure? Would her presence perhaps be resented by his family, or would they be more critical if she chose not to go? And most important of all, certainly, was the question of what Christopher's attitude about it would be. She had nearly convinced herself that it would d be better for her to stay away, but the last words out of his mouth when he took her home from their last evening of passionate petting were, "Well, pick you up at 1 p.m. tomorrow, honey," so that settled it.

They had only about fifteen minutes to wait for Hack's train, and that time was filled rather uneasily with small talk and self-conscious glances, with each member of the party wondering whether any of the others were going to break down and create an embarrassing scene. All seemed to go well until the sound of the approaching train's whistle shocked them into nervous activity.

Melody grasped Hack's arm and lifted her face close to his. After a long and ardent kiss, she said, "Goodbye, Christopher, darlin'—I know yo'll be fine. Write every chance you get, and don't you hesitate to phone us, collect, jus' any ol' time at all!" Tears welled up in her eyes, but she fought them back successfully.

"G'bye, Mom."

John stepped closer to his son and offered his hand. As they clasped their strong fingers together, John said, "I'm just not going to worry about you at all, Hack. I trust you to do the right thing and to be in the right place at all times, and that'll bring you through whatever you're faced with. Nobody you meet will have anyone rooting harder for him or wanting him back home more than your family and Libby will be rooting for you and wanting you." He gripped Hack's right biceps with his left hand momentarily, and Hack was startled by the older man's strength.

"I won't let you down, Dad," Hack said, as he and his father looked deeply into each other's eyes. Each knew for certain that the other was speaking straight from his heart, with not the slightest trace of insincerity, as might be displayed in such circumstances.

Now, sister Susan, the typically lighthearted, giddy seventeen-year-old high school girl, who had been nervously pacing around the edge of the group as though she were at a loss to understand the proceedings, suddenly leaped forward and flung her arms around her big brother's waist. She buried her face in the front of his jacket and cried, "Oh, Hack—please don't go! Please! Tell them you changed your mind. Forget about this Army business!"

She sobbed and sobbed as she clung tighter and tighter. Hack was taken aback. This was unexpected. He loved his sister and he knew she loved him, but it was normally in a playful and sometimes exasperating way. they often had rather loud differences of opinion on a number of subjects, and there was just enough disparity in age to prevent them from being able comfortably to confide in one another. But now, it became shockingly clear that Susan did really think a lot of him, and the realization struck him that he would surely miss her!

"Okay, sis," he said, squeezing her tightly and laying the side of his face on the top of her head. "Okay. I'm only going into the Army—I haven't volunteered for any suicide missions or anything! Calm down. Look up here and let me see that ugly puss!"

She did stop the violent crying, but her body continued to be wracked occasionally with huge inadvertent sobs. He planted a hard but affectionate kiss on her forehead and gave her a peck on the lips.

"You be good, Sue. Don't let me hear of you getting into any of your silly scrapes. I'm leaving you in charge of these decrepit elderly folks, so see that you take proper care of them!"

The train stopped for only a few minutes. The conductor stood on the platform with his stepstool placed in front of the entrance of the passenger car.

"B-o-o-ard," he called.

Now, only Libby was left to give and receive farewell. She had cried in her room the night before and most certainly would do so tonight, but for now she was determined to avoid any teary demonstration. She stepped up to Hack and he pulled her to him.

"I love you, Christopher," she whispered. "I really, really do!"

"My darling, Libby, I love you so! I'll call as soon as I can, and I'll write every chance I get." He stepped back and drank in the love flowing from her eyes. He squeezed her hand, picked up his small valise, then turned to the others.

"Bye, Dad, Sue, Mom. Love you all. Bye!"

He turned and jumped up the steps and into the train. As the conductor picked up his stepstool and lantern and followed him, they could see Hack walking down the aisle and selecting a seat. Then, as the train gave its preparatory belches of air and steam and started slowly forward, he looked for them from the window and waved. He continued to do so until he could see them no longer.

❖ ❖ ❖

Now that he was actually on his way, a great many disconnected thoughts tumbled about in Hack's mind. Had he remembered to do this? Should he have done that? How were his folks and Libby reacting now that he was really gone? Would he live to regret that he had enlisted instead of waiting for the draft to take him as most of the fellows did? He might have had many more blissful months with Libby if he had waited. Would Mr. Hartrshorn be able to hold a place for him to fill when he returned? Was he foolish not to have gone to college, or was his plan for getting ahead on his own in manufacturing going to work out eventually?

As the train rolled along, he gazed out of the sooty window and gradually settled into a sort of dazed disengagement from his surroundings, enhanced by the click of the wheels and the swaying of the railroad car. "Well," he thought, "I can't change anything now. I've made my decisions and I'll just have to hope and pray that they turn out okay. Now, I've got to concentrate on finding an acceptable niche in the Army." He settled back in the seat and relaxed for the rest of the short journey.

He disembarked at Hartford and proceeded to the assembly point in the armory. There, he reported to the sergeant herding his group together for the trip to Fort Devens, and within two hours, they were again on a train.

Once they entered the gates of the camp, all civilian niceties were dropped. Their futures and their fortunes were placed in the hands of sergeants who directed the activities of the inductees, and who immediately became implacable tyrants. The sergeants looked for their commands to be enforced by their corporals; self-important underlings who reissued orders with the insolence and ruthlessness of working sheep dogs. The commissioned officers were on a more exalted plane altogether, creating the impression of rather benign inaccessibility. They floated around in the background like shining idols in their crisply creased finery and polished insignia. But they got results.

Hack was assigned to a group with which he would stay throughout the induction process, marching from one phase to another. They were given another thorough physical examination complete with shots and a vaccination, and a battery of tests identified as General Aptitude, Mechanical Aptitude and Radio Aptitude. On the trip through the clothing mill, they received their complete military wardrobe. They also received an orientation lecture, designed to convince them that as long as the country was at war, and as long as they had to be in the service, it only made sense for them to do the very best they could, both for the good of their country and for their own chances of survival. All of these stops along the way were in different sections or different buildings scattered throughout the Reception Center, and they did not all take the same amount of time, so there was a lot of marching between stations, or from a station to a mess hall, or to or from their company area. At the end of each march, there was a fairly long period of standing in line, waiting to enter, waiting to leave or waiting to be fed. The recruits were convinced that "Hurry up and wait," was the Army's motto.

After a couple of days which seemed more like weeks to Hack, he found himself about to be given a fast final interview. The specialist who spoke to him seemed very sharp and much more friendly than most of the induction center personnel. He skimmed through the file which had been building on Christopher Drummond Hacker, nodding his head from time to time, and then said, "Well, Hacker, you certainly have a nice, clean record to start off with. Your physical is perfectly normal, your mechanical and radio aptitudes are normal or slightly above, and your general aptitude is well above average. If the time comes that you want to apply for OCS, (Officer Candidate School) I'm sure you'll have an excellent chance, although some college would have been helpful. I see you are a volunteer, and as such you are to be given your best choice of Army branch, if they are shipping to that branch when you are scheduled to leave."

"Can you tell me when that is?" Hack asked.

The interviewer replied, "No, but since you have completed the induction process and have no apparent physical, psychological or dental problems, you'll be out of here almost immediately, or I miss my guess. They aren't letting any grass grow under their feet when it comes to getting people off to training camps. I'll bet they'll read you off at breakfast formation tomorrow."

"So, what else do we have to do here?"

"Not a thing, Hacker. Interview finished. And good luck to you."

"Thank you."

At the breakfast formation the next morning, the first sergeant produced a long sheet of paper, which he scrutinized closely in the early light. "Listen close as I read off these names. This is the first list of travel assignments for you men who have finished your induction. I'll read off the name of the camp and then the names of the men going to that camp. Be sure you know which camp it was under if you hear your name called. Then the men for each camp will fall in together and each camp detail will be given their instructions.

"Fort Benning, Georgia. Anderson, Fred E., Appleton, Charles F., Eggerton, Alphonse…"

The sergeant continued to call off the names, first for Benning, then for Camp Gruber, Oklahoma, then for Fort Sill—all infantry training camps. Hack stood nervously waiting for his name and hoping against hope it would not be on one of those unless they also had an Ordnance training facility. Next came Fort Monmouth, N.J.

"Dudzinski, Francis P., Gardner, Wallace M., Hacker, Christopher D."

There it was; but what was it? When the formation was dismissed, Hack quickly looked for Dudzinski, who had been in his group all the way.

"Hey, Frank! We're going together, by the looks."

"Yeah, hey, that's all right! We didn't get sent to the infantry—at least, not yet!"

"Do you know if Monmouth is an Ordnance camp?" Hack asked.

"Ordnance? Hell, no. Monmouth is the big Signal Corps center for the eastern part of the country. What made you think it was Ordnance?"

"I just didn't know, but I was kind of hoping for that because I like machinery. But Signal Corps was my second choice, so I guess I can't complain."

"Whaddaya mean, choice? Since when did that matter?"

Hack laughed.

"Hey, Frank—you sound like a draftee. I enlisted. That's why I was supposed to have a chance of getting the branch I wanted. That's one of the carrots they hold out, ya know."

"You bet your ass I'm a draftee. I wouldn't enlist unless the Nazis or the

Japs were about to invade us. O' course, I knew I'd be drafted anyway, and I wouldn't want to sit home once my friends all started goin' in. Hell, I'm a lover, but I can't take care of all the women by myself. But this is the only damned raffle I was ever in where my number came up early!"

The two new friends and the other Monmouth-bound soldier, Gardner, stayed together and were collected shortly, given all the necessary instructions and by afternoon were on their way to New Jersey.

Upon arrival, they were assigned to a basic training company, and proceeded to spend the next eight weeks being instructed in all types of military drill, with the emphasis on the physical aspects. They marched until their feet were ready to drop off, and then they marched some more. And when it seemed that they had reached the limit of their endurance, the drill instructor would fall them out in the middle of the night with full-field equipment and make them hike another ten to twenty miles. If they thought the non-coms were mean at the induction center, they now felt that those guys had been models of sympathy and compassion when compared with these ogres, who punished their aching bodies and insulted their protesting minds with heartless demands on their physiques and violently loud and degrading vocal assaults. They were force-fed a wealth of information about rifles, carbines, tommy-guns and bayonets, explosives, military vehicles, shelter-halves and aircraft identification as well as other subjects, including "Mickey mouse" films warning of the unpleasant results to be realized by unwise and unprotected sex.

Further training included instruction involving double-time, crawling in the mud with machine gun bullets whistling overhead, how to dig foxholes and the cleaning of arms and equipment, the meaning of KP, the boredom and bone-weariness of walking guard duty, and more aircraft identification. Then came the various drills, rifle drill, bayonet drill and close order drill, and close order drill and more close order drill. And when basic was finally over, they all said it was ridiculous, sadistic and a big waste of time, but they knew inside that they were now fairly well prepared for what they might have to face. They knew that being sharp physically was a big advantage for a combat soldier.

Next came the decision as to which men were to be assigned to line outfits and probable imminent overseas duty and which were to be given further training in one of the numerous specialty schools which the Signal Corps conducted. Hack and his friend Dudzinski were tapped for radio school and transferred to a training regiment.

The Army's method of teaching a skill such as radio operation was simple and to the point. Expose trainees to Morse code hour after hour, day after day and week after week. They would then either learn it thoroughly or go "dit-happy" and fail. Hack and his buddy survived the ordeal and found themselves qualified "High-speed, Manual," operators and ready for assignment. They were soon transferred out of the training regiment and into a line outfit, the 2442nd Signal Battalion.

Here, it was implicit in the general attitude that the battalion was on the verge of being shipped out. It was expected that they were soon to go overseas. As yet, the unit had not been given its assignment; that is, they did not know what infantry division they would be attached to, but that it would be one of them was a certainty. Eventually, it evolved that the 2442nd shipped with elements of the U.S. 2nd Corps, but they were still unsure of their exact role or where they were to fit in. When they found themselves in the middle of a huge convoy of ships heading east across the Atlantic Ocean, they were finally informed that their destination was North Africa.

❖ ❖ ❖

After being resoundingly defeated by Montgomery's British Eighth Army at El Alamein, General Erwin Rommel, also known as "The Desert Fox," and Hitler's ace, collected his battered legions and on November 2, 1942, retreated westward all the way to Tripoli.

But another massive Allied attack was in the making. Operation Torch was a huge amphibious operation comprised of more than 75,000 American and over 30,000 British troops. They stormed in from the sea on November 8, 1942, to attack Casablanca, Morocco; Oran, and Algiers, Algeria. The American infantry and armor fought savagely before subduing the defenders of Oran, who surrendered on November 10. Immediately before the scheduled start of a bombardment of Casablanca by air and naval forces, Admiral Darlan, commander-in-chief of Vichy French forces, ordered a cease-fire.

It was hoped, particularly in view of the success of these landings, that the Allies could dash all the way to Tunis and Bizerte in a couple of weeks. However, this was not to be. The first clash of American and German armor at Chouigui sobered the Allies considerably. Their light M3 tanks could not compete with the German Panzer IV and its heavy armor. Also, the Allied supply lines were getting thin, and the weather was worsening.

Reluctantly, General Eisenhower was forced to delay the big push until Spring.

Adding to the problems was the fact that the major force in this theater, the U.S. 2nd Corps, was not battle tested and its ability to deal with a serious Axis onslaught was questionable. Proof of their shortcomings arrived shortly. Axis General Arnim attacked and drove the Americans back across Tunisia, all the way to the mountain range know as the "Western Dorsal." There, they dug in to defend their position at Kasserine Pass. The Afrika Korps attacked and were repulsed, but on their second attempt, they overran the Allied outposts at dusk and had seized the critical pass by midnight. Here, most military historians agree, Rommel made a crucial miscalculation. Had he continued to drive forward, he could probably have altered the course of the African campaign and delayed the eventual Allied victory for quite some time. Apparently, he was afraid of outrunning his supply lines, as well as being awed by the wealth of equipment and supplies abandoned by the retreating Americans. Therefore, rather than pressing forward, he pulled back through the Kasserine Pass and marched east again to meet his old nemesis, the British Eighth.

Hack's unit, the 2442nd Signal Battalion, had been assigned to serve with the U.S. 2nd Army Corps, and he had therefore been involved in much of this action. They had crossed the Atlantic in a stream of convoys consisting of more than 500 American and British ships, miraculously without contest from German submarines, and all had made their amphibious landings on the African coast. Hack's outfit went in at Oran, where they experienced heavy resistance. After Oran, they continued to move east and were among those badly defeated at Kasserine Pass.

Hack received his baptism of fire around Oran. As is often the case, particularly with inexperienced units, his infantry regiment became somewhat disorganized and he had to duck from building to building as he tried to reach a point in the distance where he could see American armored vehicles. He was more excited than frightened. His every sense was keyed to the highest degree as he planned each leg of his route. His sharp eyes darted everywhere. Suddenly he saw an enemy soldier's head rise cautiously above a shattered masonry wall. Immediately, it popped into his mind that this was just like the old days, when he and Frosty lay silently waiting for a woodchuck to stick his head up. He brought his carbine up and took quick aim at the man's ear, just below the edge of his helmet.

"Crack," went the carbine. The man's arms flew up, his rifle flying out of his grip, and he disappeared.

Hack waited a moment, watching the place where the soldier had been. "Funny," he thought, "just like shooting a woodchuck." Instead of the revulsion and nausea that many soldiers experience upon killing for the first time, Hack felt a sense of exhilaration and satisfaction. "Hey," he reasoned, "isn't this what they taught us to do? Just another woodchuck, that's all."

He had plenty of chances to employ his skill later, when they were fighting desperately but unsuccessfully to hold the Kasserine Pass. He had no way of knowing how many Germans he dispatched there, but he had sufficient confidence in his marksmanship to be satisfied that his tally increased.

After the assault at Oran, Hack's commanding officer, noting his purposeful air and his obvious ability, promoted him from "T-5" to sergeant. The C.O. wisely wanted to see Hack with a line rating, rather than a technician's, as he knew that most GIs, subconsciously, at least, fail to recognize "T" ratings as people to follow when the bullets start flying.

Chapter 14
North Africa, 1943

The weapons carrier bounced and rattled its way over the rocks and ruts of the primitive roadway, used more for herding goats and cattle than for motorized vehicles. Actually, it was merely a seldom used shortcut between the Gafsa-Maknassy and the Gafsa-El Guettar roads. The private first class driver had the advantage of having the steering wheel to anchor him, but Sergeant Hacker, in the seat beside him, found himself hanging on determinedly as the open vehicle plunged doggedly onward, eating up as rapidly as possible the miles of desolate countryside. The two passengers were uneasy because the territory they were traversing was so unfamiliar that it could have been under Axis as well as Allied control. Things were definitely in a state of flux so any solo trip was subject to sudden and disastrous interruption.

General George Patton's crack First Infantry Division had dashed all the way from Tebessa, Algeria, and had entered and left Feriana, Tunisia, without Axis opposition and had stopped at Gafsa to evaluate the situation. The terrain at the next little town, El Guettar, suddenly became much more hazardous, with numerous steep and rocky hills flanking the main thoroughfare. It was obvious to Patton that this was ideal country for the Germans to deploy their tanks and artillery and that they could doubtless just lie in wait for the Americans to land in their trap. In fact, he was developing his strategy with this in mind.

The minor mission on which Sgt. Hacker had been dispatched by his captain was hazardous. Because there were no road signs, the trip had to be made mainly by instinct. Hack felt they should find the spotting position which he was looking for among the rocky prominences looming a short distance ahead. He believed he was far enough north of El Guettar to be relatively safe from any of the main concentrations of German strength and, if he had followed his map correctly, he was enough out of the way to be alone. His main fear was that a prowling Stukka or Messerschmitt might spot his lonesome vehicle and attack.

"Pour it on, Jim," Hack yelled to his driver. "We'll be in those hills in a couple of minutes and won't feel like such sitting ducks. We'll find a good place for an O.P. fast and then get the hell out of here."

The PFC hunched a little lower over the wheel and pressed his foot harder on the accelerator. The hard working motor whined in a little higher key.

"Christ, I hope so," he said. "This ain't my idea of a drive in the park!"

The German tank commander was convinced that there would be another engagement between his armor and the British or the Americans very soon. He was, in general, satisfied with the performance of his men and his machinery in recent encounters, but the new "Tiger" tank which he was commanding, with its 700hp engine and a capability of 40 kilometers per hour, was somewhat more machine than the Mark IVs which had, until now, been the standard heavy tank issue in the North African campaign. He was flattered that he had been singled out to introduce the marvelous weapon in this theater and with his usual thoroughness, he decided to do a little extra road testing between skirmishes. In particular, he was drooling in anticipation of having an opportunity soon to see what that vicious-looking long-barreled .88mm cannon projecting menacingly from the turret might do. He assembled his crew and took off to the north and west from his battalion's location at El Guettar to get better acquainted with his new charge.

The commander was sure that the enemy would be seeking likely spots for observation posts somewhere in the vicinity of the road from Gafsa to Maknassy and decided that he could accomplish two goals simultaneously by identifying likely locations onto which he could direct artillery fire or bombing runs once the battle started, while at the same time testing out the maneuverability and response of his powerful new weapon. He and his men went up progressively higher hills, one elevation after another striking him as unsatisfactory. Caught up in his search, he probed several miles further than he had originally intended. Finally, he directed his vehicle into a secluded little gully behind high rocks and fairly heavy brush and called a halt, thinking to give his crew a short break before retracing his tracks.

They had hardly had time to crawl out on top of the machine and light cigarettes when a cloud of dust appeared about a mile south of them. A quick look through the binoculars told the commander that the lonely machine approaching was a small American Army vehicle. Quickly, he ordered his men back inside the tank. The engine came to life and the turret swung into position to track the unsuspecting approaching vehicle. When preliminary commands were completed, the commander waited only for optimum range as the sleek but vicious .88 silently tracked its prey. Closer and closer it came. When, in his opinion, it had reached the perfect distance, he shouted, "Fire!"

❖ ❖ ❖

Scarcely had the driver of the American vehicle finished expressing his apprehensiveness when there was a sudden tremendous jolt. The weapons carrier was lifted completely off the ground, split into several large and many small twisted and burning pieces, and deposited over a wide section of the countryside. Immediately, the German tank, its extremely effective long-barreled weapon protruding from its turret with smoke rising from the recoil vents, churned into view from its hiding place behind the rocks and headed toward the scene of destruction.

As the tank approached its victim, the commander braced his arms on the cowling before him and smiled with satisfaction as he surveyed the proof of his excellent marksmanship, the new machine, its armament and its crew. Upon reaching the site of the explosion, he called a halt, jumped down from the big vehicle and strode purposefully about, briefly examining the scattered remains. He was mildly amazed at the disintegration which had resulted from his shell's detonation, but soon realized that it was even more than that. "Ah,"—he thought, "a direct hit on the petrol tank." He paused for a moment beside a mound of human flesh in the tattered and smoking remnants of an American uniform. Some echo of decency from his upbringing caused him to deliver a quiet salute in its direction. After striding briskly around the immediate area of the hit and seeing nothing else of importance, he climbed agilely back into his iron monster, barked out commands and, like a successful spider, dashed back to his cover among the rocks to analyze and gloat over his small victory before journeying back to his encampment.

Some time later, about fifty yards away, in a small depression behind a scraggly bit of vegetation, consciousness slowly began to return to Hack, the other passenger. His first shreds of awareness came in the form of an unbearable, throbbing headache. It hurt so much that he just lay still and hoped that it would pass. As he opened his eyes a tiny slit, he discovered that he could see nothing except flashing lights of many hues.

"My God, I'm blind!"

The sickening thought filled every cell of his tortured brain, and obviated any further effort to examine his injuries. Instinctively, he started to get to his feet, and another shock struck him—he was unable to move his limbs. An overwhelming sense of terror wracked his now feebly functioning brain, and the adrenaline which this released induced a few blood vessels and nerves to resume operation. In a few moments, he glimpsed something on the ground ahead of his previously sightless eyes. Soon, he was aware of some feeling returning to his arms, and gradually to other parts of his anatomy. Now, the realization of what had happened struck him. His vehicle must have received a direct hit from a powerful shell. Cautiously, he turned his pulsing head from side to side, then slowly, up and down. It did not hurt any worse than when he held it still.

As his eyesight improved, and with great anxiety, almost hating to do it, he made himself look at his arms, then his legs. He hesitantly wiggled the toes on one foot, then the other. There seemed to be some blood staining his right pant leg, and he was suddenly aware of something amiss with his left hand—it looked wrong, somehow. With a conscious effort, he focused his gaze on it. He remembered that he should have five fingers, but now he could see only four. The pinky was missing, sheared off as neatly as though by a surgeon's knife. Oddly, there seemed to be only a modest amount of blood connected with the amputation, and as yet he felt no pain associated with it. The fragment of hot metal which had so efficiently clipped off the finger had also partially cauterized the wound.

Gingerly, he felt his way through the process of standing up. Left leg first—slowly, left arm pushing up gently, then right arm braced against the ground, and finally, right leg pulled ever so slowly up into place. Then he carefully flexed his knees and bent his still numb back and—he was up!

He stood there, weaving slightly, trying his best to clear his brain and steady his body. When he decided that he was fairly stable, he believed that he could maintain his balance well enough to try a few steps. Mustering all of his will power, he thrust his left foot hesitantly forward a few inches, ignoring the stabbing pain in the hip which this move evoked. As he moved his right foot forward, it suddenly felt as though a knife had been thrust through the calf of his leg—a knife which had first been heated to about 500 degrees. His mind had cleared enough to permit the full force of this assault to register, and the agony of it made his stomach turn over. He fell on his knees in the sand as he retched and heaved. The terrible waves of nausea came again and again.

He did not have the strength to hold himself upright. Soon he fell forward helplessly into his own disgorged mess, and passed once more into unconsciousness.

❖ ❖ ❖

How long Hack lay there he did not know, but when perception finally returned, night had set in. Again, he slowly assessed his situation and shuddered. He instinctively pulled back when he realized that he had been lying in his own vomit, but even that slight movement brought a searing reminder of his still uninvestigated injuries. With great care and numerous pauses to replenish his short supply of strength, he managed to get himself into a position which allowed him to examine the source of the shocking pain in his leg. He fumbled in his pocket, brought out his cigarette lighter, and flicked it on. The light revealed a chunk of metal imbedded deeply into the calf muscle. He realized this was the source of both the terrible pain and the blood he had noticed earlier on his trousers. However, because the large piece of metal had buried itself so solidly, it effectively prevented any large amount of blood from escaping. The shock and distress he had already suffered, and the mounting anger they had engendered, suddenly crested. He grasped the offending invader of his person and wrenched it cleanly from its lodging. Doing so caused a substantial amount of blood to flow. He quickly realized that he had better stanch it immediately or he would bleed to death. He fumbled, finally extracting a handkerchief from his pocket and stuffed it into the wound. He pulled off his belt and wound it around the leg, over the piece of cloth, and then fell back on the sand, exhausted and gasping. When normal breathing returned, he picked up from the sand the package of sulfanilamide-bearing dressing which had fallen from his belt when he ripped it off. He patted it gently against the joint where his left little finger had been, then loosened the belt around his calf, pulled out the sodden handkerchief, and applied the sulfa dressing directly to the open wound. He wrapped the belt around it fairly tightly and lay back again, totally spent. "Well," he thought, "it will either hold or it won't. That's the best I can do," and with that he lapsed into a deep sleep.

When he awoke, he became aware of the much colder air temperature. He shivered and gazed at the sky and the horizon around him. Far off in the distance he could see occasional flashes of pink and orange against the sky and could hear, faintly, the sounds of artillery. Hesitantly, he felt around the dressing he had applied to his calf and gave a sigh of relief when his fingers came away dry. Gentle movement of the leg revealed that there was a lot of stiffness present, and in the process of examining his lower limbs he was reminded of his missing finger, in the vicinity of which he was now experiencing a dull but throbbing ache. The terrible headache seemed to have abated substantially. He decided that, despite his wounds, he was amazingly lucky. Suddenly the thought struck him that he had no idea of what had happened to his driver, Jim. There was enough light in the sky to permit cautious movement, so Hack decided to try shuffling around if he could. Some slow, painful dragging steps brought him back to where he thought he could distinguish the outlines of the road, and at about that time he suddenly became aware of a smell which shocked and sickened him. He strongly suspected it was the smell of roasted flesh—one which he had smelled before and which, once exposed to, was impossible to forget.

Gritting his teeth, he forced himself to creep along in the direction from which it seemed to come. Along the way, he encountered several large and small distorted chunks of what must once have been his weapons carrier. Abruptly, he stumbled against a softer mass. He knew immediately that he had found the source of the odor. Fighting the urge to vomit, he made himself drop down in the sand and feel about on the corpse. He located the neck and groped for the chain which held the dogtags, required of all soldiers. When he found them, he isolated the short bead chain from the long one, felt for its connecting link, and after several unsuccessful attempts to unhook it, felt it pop loose. The identification tag dropped into his palm. He clutched it and began withdrawing from the charred remains as rapidly as he possibly could. He moved about seventy-five yards away to rest behind some bushes.

Hack knew that his chances of being rescued were very slim, but he also reasoned that if both he and his attacker had been in this area there was a good chance that others might also be there from time to time. He realized that whether they would be American, German, British or Tunisian, was a matter for fate to decide. By this time, he was feeling considerably better and was beginning to notice hunger pangs. Groping in his pockets, he found the remains of a K ration chocolate bar. He popped it into his mouth and sucked at it greedily, and he seemed to feel some restoration of strength as a result. He did another inventory of his effects and found again his cigarette lighter and, in a small holster beneath his field jacket, the little .32 caliber Walther automatic which he had taken to carrying, despite its being a violation of regulations. In his outfit, enlisted men beneath the rank of staff sergeant were not issued sidearms, but had to rely on either M1s or carbines for firepower. He thought, "God only knows what happened to my carbine when the shell landed." The feel of the little Walther snuggled against his side was reassuring.

He spent the remaining time before daybreak trying to devise a plan to get back to his outfit, but no matter what solutions he considered, none made any sense. He knew he was not well enough to try to walk back to his base and knew he would not move fast enough to hide if he saw an enemy vehicle or aircraft approaching. Finally, he decided that all he could do was to try starting back and pray that the first people he encountered would be friends. Now that daybreak had arrived, Hack pulled the retrieved dogtag from his pocket and looked closely at it. Stamped into the metal was the information, "Thompson, James R., 30269905, T-42." Near the right edge was the letter "O" and below that, the letter "P"." It was Jim, all right. The fact that he had been immunized against tetanus in 1942 was pretty unimportant now. At least, Hack could turn in the tag and give the general location of Jim's remains to the Graves Registration people and hope that they might be able to find enough of him still wearing the other tag to bring him in for proper burial.

Another inspection of his right calf and the stub of his little finger showed that there was very little bleeding, and the slight exercise he had already had made it a little easier to move the stiff muscles. With a sigh of resignation, he started painfully shuffling his way back toward Gafsa.

Hack covered a distance of perhaps a couple of hundred yards before weakness and trembling forced him to call a halt. "Damn," he said, "I am not ever going to make it several miles if a tenth of a mile exhausted me. Someone had better show up to help me before long or I am really in big trouble." He sat on the ground, cursing his situation, but after a while he found the frustration of doing nothing worse than the agony of action. He forced himself up again and continued dragging himself along, sweating and cursing, now bent forward, which seemed somehow to ease a few of the aches and pains created by the effort to walk.

He gritted it out for another fifteen or twenty minutes, but was about to have to stop again when he heard, faintly, the sound of a motor coming from behind him. From that direction it was pretty certain that any motorized visitor could only be of one breed—German!

It was not yet close enough for its occupants to have spotted him. His mind raced. If he looked in bad shape, perhaps they would be thrown off guard and he might gain a momentary advantage. He slipped the Walther from its holster, flipped the safety, racked a cartridge into the chamber and palmed the small weapon in his good right hand. He allowed himself to remain bent forward and to lurch and totter and his foot to drag. This action, added to the disarray of his uniform, his reeking, vomit-covered tunic, his lack of a cap and his dirt-smudged face, were enough to give momentary pause to anyone coming upon him unexpectedly.

The approaching vehicle was, in fact, a German command car, carrying the Tiger tank commander, a major. Ever since the encounter, it had bothered him that only one corpse had been found among the wreckage of the American vehicle he had destroyed, and finally he decided that he had to return to the scene for another more exhaustive search. Now he had accomplished this, and he had been rewarded with clues which convinced him that there had, indeed, been another occupant of the vehicle. Furthermore, signs indicated that that person had treated his wounds and had dragged himself painfully away from the scene in the direction of Gafsa. The evidence told him that the wounded enemy soldier would not have been able to cover much ground. He instructed his driver to run toward Gafsa until they overtook the escapee or until the major decided to abandon the search.

As the command car hove in sight, Hack partially turned toward it and weakly waved his left hand. Riding stiffly erect in the back seat, the German officer spotted him and snapped out a brisk order. His driver jammed on the brakes, and the car slid to a halt near where Hack stood, wobbling slightly.

By now, the major had unfastened his holster and drawn a large, ugly Luger automatic. However, the bedraggled and obviously badly injured soldier beside the road appeared on the verge of collapse. The officer jumped down to the ground and took a few quick steps toward the tottering American. He was convinced that this man was no threat; therefore, as he moved forward, he slipped the weapon back into its holster, leaving the flap open. The distance between them was now reduced to about eight feet.

Suddenly, Hack's right arm came up, his finger squeezed the Walther's trigger and a .32 slug tore its way into the German officer's chest. The force of the bullet stopped him in mid-stride. His jaw dropped open, his body sagged, and he collapsed onto the ground like a deflated balloon.

The speed with which this unexpected attack had occurred caused a moment of shock and confusion in the mind of the vehicle's other occupant, the driver. As he scratched, frantically, but too late, for his weapon on the seat beside him, Hack emptied the remainder of the Walther's clip into his chest and stomach, then slipped the spent weapon back into its holster. Satisfied that the man was dead, Hack again turned his attention to the major, who lay twitching and groveling on the ground. Swiftly, Hack plucked the Luger from the still unfastened holster on the man's belt, pointed it at the writhing figure, and squeezed off two rounds. All motion ceased, except for a slight flattening and spreading of the major's body against the sand as his muscles lost their tension.

Hack unbuckled the officer's belt and slid off both the leather holster and a sheathed dagger. He pulled the dagger from its scabbard and inspected it. It was a beautiful piece of work; primarily a perquisite of rank, but deadly nonetheless. The rosewood haft had contoured metal guards on the top and bottom, and an inlaid insignia—the German eagle perched on a wreath, inside of which was a swastika. Near the top of the haft, another small inset of metal showed the lightning bolt of the dreaded "S.S." "Alles fur Deutschland" was engraved in large letters along the shining blade.

A wry smile creased Hack's haggard face as he read the inscription.

"Up yours, Fritz," he said.

He stuffed both weapons under his belt. Coolly, he shuffled to the side of the car, reached up with his right hand, and grasping the shoulder of the driver's tunic, pulled the body out of the open vehicle and onto the ground in a heap. He tossed the holster onto the floor of the car, then dragged himself painfully up into the driver's seat. After resting for a few moments to gather strength, and without another glance at the fallen foes, he put the still running engine in gear and set off for Gafsa.

Chapter 15
Casablanca

Hack urged the German command car along as fast as he dared in his weakened condition. He was sure that he and Jim had only been driving for about ten minutes when disaster struck them, so he thought he had a very good chance of making it back to his outfit, or at least to friendly territory, before being interrupted by another crisis.

Suddenly, it dawned upon him that he was barreling toward the American lines in a German vehicle. This could be disastrous. He braked to a halt and took a quick look in both front and back seats for anything he could use as a truce flag. There was nothing. In desperation, and with much difficulty because of his condition, he removed his outer clothing and stripped off his undershirt, which, fortunately, was one of the white ones such as were issued prior to the change to olive drab. Lacking anything to use as a staff, he tied the shoulder straps of the garment to the top of the windshield post, from where he hoped it would unfurl in the breeze when the car was in motion. Having done this, he replaced his outer clothing and resumed his journey.

In a matter of only a few minutes, he saw ahead, a truck blocking the road, and in front of it, a squad of American MPs, running a check point. They had already recognized the command car for what it was, but the curious flapping white cloth at the top right side of the windshield had them somewhat unsure what to expect. Hack had reduced his speed to a crawl and was waving his arm to assure the MPs that he was in no way belligerent. As he neared them, they halted him and a sergeant stepped forward to investigate. By this time, Hack had used up all of the energy he possessed, and he simply slumped forward against the steering wheel, too weak even to explain either his appearance or the incongruity of his mode of transportation. Sizing up the situation rapidly, the MP sergeant ordered two of his men to help Hack into one of their jeeps and to deliver him to the nearest area where medics could be found.

The medical corpsmen who were the first to examine Hack, did what few simple things they could to help make him more comfortable, and then transported him by GI ambulance to the nearest field hospital, some twenty miles west. There, he was examined thoroughly by a doctor, his wounds were dressed, he was sedated, and put to bed. When he awoke after having slept soundly for twelve hours, he was allowed to eat. He was just finishing his meal when Captain Lindemann, his C.O. who had dispatched him on the ill-fated mission, walked up to his cot.

"Well, Hacker," he said, "what the hell happened to you?"

"Hello, sir," Hack replied, "I guess we were in the wrong place at the right time. I'm sorry we didn't accomplish our mission, but somebody dropped a shell on our weapons carrier and blew everything to hell, including my driver, Private Jim Thompson."

"That was rough, Hacker. We'll be able to set up OPs anyway, so don't worry about that part. It's just tough that you had to go through what you did and that poor Thompson was killed. What's the story on the German command car? How did you come by that?"

Hack suddenly remembered that he had not spoken to anyone about that episode. Had he done right? He wondered if what he had done would be accepted as all right. Would he be subject to criticism, or worse, if it were revealed that he had shot the two Germans without giving them a chance? Should he have tried to capture the Germans and have them drive him back to his own lines? Or could the old saying, "Everything's fair in love and war" be taken literally? He decided that perhaps it would be wise for him to make some slight alterations in the story to avoid any possible repercussions. After all, who would there be to dispute his version of what had occurred?

"Well, sir, I was pretty sick during the night. I slept off and on, and in between, I managed to patch myself up enough to keep from bleeding to death. I crawled back to the spot where we got hit and finally found what was left of Thompson. I brought back one of his dogtags—it's in one of my pockets. I decided that I had to try to make it back to the outfit after daylight came, so I dragged myself a ways and then rested, several times. Then I heard a vehicle. I knew it had to be Germans, coming from that direction. I guess what happened was that they came looking for us because they had blown up our weapons carrier and were wondering about survivors. I don't know any other reason why that car would have come along, heading toward our lines.

I was too weak to even try to hide. I had a little Walther pistol, so I palmed it and tried to look pathetic and harmless, which I guess I did, all right. I was covered with dirt and blood and puke, and hardly able to stand up. They stopped, and the German officer jumped down and came toward me with his Luger pointed at me, while his driver just sat in the car with the motor running. The officer jabbered something at me in German. I didn't know whether he would shoot me or take me prisoner, but I wasn't ready for either of those choices. He couldn't see my gun, and when he got within a few feet, I put one shot into him before he could do anything about it. Then I unloaded the pistol into the driver before he could get this rifle off the seat. He was dead, but the officer was still flopping around, so I took his pistol out of his hand and finished him off with it. Then I got into the vehicle and came on here. It's really kind of hard to get the details straight. The explosion left me pretty shocked and confused, but that's about it."

The officer sat quietly, gazing at the floor as he painted a mental picture of Hack's ordeal. Finally, he raised his eyes to the recumbent sergeant.

"God, that's quite a hairy experience you've had, Sergeant. It's amazing that you got out of it alive. Of course, you'll be getting a Purple Heart for your wounds, anyway, but the way you overcame the Germans and took their vehicle, and the fact that you returned to the scene to try to locate your comrade, deserves some special recognition. I'm going to recommend you for a Bronze Star, if the Major agrees. For now, just get rested and healed and we'll look forward to seeing you back at the outfit after they release you."

"Thank you very much, Captain. Will you do me a favor and make sure that someone holds that Major's Luger and dagger for me? I worked had to get them."

"Sure will, Hacker," the officer said, smiling. He turned and walked away and Hack sank back against the pillows, feeling somewhat proud, somewhat guilty, but rather self-satisfied and very relieved.

❖ ❖ ❖

A week passed, with Hack's wounds being attended to several times a day. The staff of the field hospital was by design, small. It was not equipped to do more than a minimal job of analyzing and treating battle wounds and illnesses. The doctor who had assumed the responsibility for Hack's treatment sat down beside his cot one morning and said, "Well, Hacker, you seem to be healing very well. You've pretty much passed the critical point as far as infection or complications from your injuries and your battlefield first aid procedures are concerned, but it appears to me that you have a bit more of a problem with that leg wound than we had hoped. Whatever it was that entered your calf did a bit of a job on a couple of the muscles there. Even though you are healing fast, I believe you are going to need muscle surgery or you run a serious risk of having a nasty limp the rest of your life. I want to ship you to a full scale hospital, perhaps in Oran, or back in England, where they have the facilities and the specialists to confirm my diagnosis and perform the surgery, if they agree that it's necessary. You have to get out of here anyway, because Patton is pushing hell out of the Germans and we've got to keep moving along behind him as fast as we can."

Hack shrugged his shoulders and then said, "Whatever you say, Doc. Thanks for what you've done."

"It was a pleasure, Hacker. Good luck."

The next day, the hospital unit packed up and pulled out to stay close to the front. All patients who were not desperately in need of a doctor's attention were signed out—some to return to duty, others to a Corps hospital, and a few, like Hack, had to await orders and transportation to health facilities of a more complex nature far away from the action.

After numerous delays, waits, cancelled orders and other frustrations, Hack found himself traveling west until finally, he was admitted to a large, well-staffed, efficient general hospital in Casablanca. There were a large number of physicians and surgeons from African countries, a number from France and Spain, a few from India and a couple from England. It was one of these British medics, Major Phelps, who eventually inherited Hack's case. Although he was not very friendly, the fact that he spoke a language Hack understood made him an oasis of relaxation.

Dr. Jonathan Phelps was a specialist in muscle surgery. He performed a very thorough examination, including some minor probing and snipping under a local anesthetic. The following day, he stood stiffly beside the bed and explained to Hack, "Some of the damage which has been done to your leg has prevented proper restoration to full mobility without some reconstructive surgery."

He drew little sketches to illustrate how the muscles should be formed and layered. He continued, "In their present damaged condition, they will try to reform themselves into an awkward and restricted pattern unless corrective surgery is performed."

"How much of an operation are we talking about, sir?" Hack asked.

In his rather haughty manner, the doctor replied, "In a case such as this, it is impossible to ascertain precisely how extensive the corrective surgery must be until one can lay open the area and observe the extent of mutilation with which one must deal. It is, however, my opinion, on the basis of the degree of impairment of mobility evident, that full restoration can be anticipated. Recovery from surgery and completion of basic therapy would, I expect, be a matter of two or three months. There are no guarantees, you understand."

"Oh, no, sir. I just wondered how long it would be before I can get back to my outfit."

"A commendable attitude, I am sure. Assuming no surprises and no complications, three to four months subsequent to surgery, which I shall schedule within the week, should suffice to return you to the fray."

The operation was performed in accordance with Dr. Phelps' arrangements and in less than a week, Hack was gingerly testing the leg with short and hesitant steps. He then began a regimen of exercise and manipulative therapy. It looked as if he would be released and returned to duty on the schedule the surgeon had predicted.

While Hack had been incapacitated, the American II Corps under General Patton had driven the Germans back relentlessly from the west, while Montgomery's and Alexander's British 8th Army were squeezing them from east and south. On May 12, 1943, the last German armor surrendered, and the African campaign was, for all practical purposes, ended. It would be only a matter of days before the troops were freed to be redeployed to their next assignment, which was purported to be the invasion of Italy.

Hack still had six to eight weeks of recuperation to undergo before he would be certified for active involvement in another campaign. For him, the long, boring days in the hospital were impossibly frustrating. He had been receiving mail from home fairly regularly before his injuries, but no mail had yet reached him in Casablanca. He knew that his parents would write regularly, but the letters he longed for were those from his beautiful Libby. To know that they were being written every day but were stagnating somewhere was driving him crazy. When it seemed that he could no longer stand the enforced inactivity, the non-delivery of his mail, and the separation from the friends he had made in his outfit; when he was about convinced that he was going to go AWOL and accept the consequences, he suddenly received a package of letters. The Army post office had tracked him down.

First, he separated out the letters from his family, ripped them open, and dutifully and gratefully read them through. He was relieved to find that there was nothing to indicate that anyone was sick or that there were any unusual problems, and he appreciated the obvious concern for his safety evident between the lines of each letter. The family was great, and he knew he was lucky to have them and their love.

Next, he carefully sorted all of Libby's letters according to postmark dates and then opened them and savored their contents slowly, absorbing every sweet syllable, every delicious word and every succulent phrase. Libby told him of all of the little events occurring in her life and all of the newsy tidbits about friends and acquaintances in Newvale. She discussed her experiences at school, the subjects she loved and those she struggled through, and the friendships she had formed with girls from distant places. She mentioned that the unavailability of gasoline had eliminated joyriding and that, instead, she and her friends had been hiking the surrounding countryside. She had come to love the beautiful, peaceful scenic Vermont. One of the training areas offered at Middlebury was equitation. She had always loved animals and found herself drawn strongly to these large handsome creatures. Now, she spent as much of her free time as possible happily perched on the back of one of the school's mounts. She also related the stories being passed around concerning the experiences of other servicemen from home—but only the ones of a positive nature. She did not mention the names on the casualty lists, as though by omitting them she eliminated the existence of such problems. And at some point near the end of each letter, she professed her deep and abiding love for him, simply, gracefully and with unmistakable sincerity. These he reread until he could close his eyes and still see each precious word.

Another two boring weeks dragged by. The uplift provided by the mail bonanza was just about exhausted when Hack was informed that he was to report to the American liaison officer in the hospital's administration section. Wondering what was about to happen, he asked an orderly to guide him to the proper office. Down stairways, through corridors, and around corners they went, the recuperating sergeant looking very unmilitary in his hospital pajamas and bathrobe, until they eventually reached their destination. There, he was surprised to find a rather old-looking American Army WAAC corporal ensconced behind a desk, busily juggling papers. Efficiency fairly dripped from her. He gave her his name, rank and serial number.

"Oh, yes, Sergeant Hacker. Captain Mason has orders for you, I believe."

"Shipping orders, Corporal?" Hack asked hopefully.

"That would be up to the Captain to reveal, not I. I will tell the Captain you are out here. Just a moment," and she whisked herself through the door of the inner office.

Although it seemed like hours, it was actually only a couple of minutes until she reappeared. "You may go in, Sergeant," she announced, crisply.

Hack entered the office. A middle-aged captain with the insignia of the Adjutant General branch on his collar sat behind an old, beat-up wooden desk, looking forlorn and weary. Hack thought, "What a lousy gig this must be!" but he stepped to the front of the desk, saluted, and said, "Sergeant Hacker reporting as ordered, sir."

The captain returned his salute, desultorily. "At ease, Sergeant," he said. "I have just received orders instructing you to ship out of here at 0600 tomorrow morning."

Hack stifled, with difficulty, an impulse to shout, "Hurrah!"

"Now," the officer continued, "I'll have to try to locate some medical person with enough authority to sign you out. In the meantime, you'll have to gather whatever uniforms, gear and belongings you have and report back here. By then, with luck, I'll know where you are to meet your transportation in the morning. You'd better get cracking—sometimes these things get snafued, and I have an idea you'd hate to miss this trip, am I right?"

"Right on the money, sir," Hack grinned. "May I ask were I'm being sent?"

"Oh, yes—I guess that would be rather important to you, too. Well, it looks as though you're being sent to jolly old England." Then, rather dejectedly, "I wish I were going with you."

He looked up again at Hack and, in a marked departure from the usual commerce between unacquainted officer and enlisted man, he added, "When I found out I was being sent to North Africa, I thought I might be getting into the action, but they stuck me here behind this desk and forgot me. The only excitement I get is passing along shipping orders to other GIs like you, who have really done something they can be proud of. That lady soldier out there could handle this job easily without any help from me—better, in fact. She's the one who knows all the routine. I'm just here to sign my name when and where she tells me to. Hell of a way to spend the war!"

He looked so despondent and lonely that Hack almost felt like patting him on the shoulder in sympathy. "It must really be getting to him if he's ready to unload his problems to an enlisted man," he mused.

"Yes, sir. I sympathize with you, sir, but I guess that's the way the ball bounces." He saluted again, did an about-face, and hurriedly left the small room.

It did not take Hack long to assemble the limited amount of gear and clothing which had accompanied him to the hospital. It had been so long since he had been with his own outfit that he had only an odd assortment of uniform parts, some of which had been given to him by understanding soldiers along the way. Not since his encounter with the tank had he been at any sort of station where there was a quartermaster or a supply room where he might replenish his wardrobe, and he had none of the incidental paraphernalia normally accompanying GIs in their travels. But he had jealously guarded his two souvenirs, the German Major's Luger and dagger, which his C.O. had retrieved for him, and he checked often to be sure they were securely tucked away near the bottom of his one sparsely stocked barracks bag.

Hack returned to the captain's office, now dressed in his piecemeal uniform, and was instructed rather officiously by the bestriped WAAC to "take a seat and wait." He decided that no purpose would be served by replying, so he simply sat down on the one wooden chair and occupied his time by inventorying the office. No pictures adorned the dull, yellowed walls, but there was an official-looking map of North Africa, dutifully studded with colored pushpins, describing the progress of Allied forces in the campaign. Hack stood up and stepped close enough to examine the map, half expecting the corporal to order him back to his chair, but she did not make that mistake.

He was quite absorbed in tracing his own route through the upper continent when the door swung open and Captain Mason entered. He did not bother to follow correct military procedure by going into his office, taking up his position of authority behind the shabby desk, and waiting for his crusty secretary to escort Hack into his presence. Instead, he simply said, "Okay, Sergeant Hacker. I've got it straightened out, I think. You and three other mended fellows are to be in the driveway near the emergency room entrance at the rear of the hospital at 0600 hours. You'll be picked up there and taken to our airfield, west of the city. There, you will board a C-47 which is flying back to England for supplies. They'll drop you off at a field near Winchester. From there, you will be transported to a Replacement Depot. That's all I can tell you. Except, Good Luck."

Then, with a wry smile, he added, "Oh, yes—and when you get there, see if they could possibly find a little more exciting spot for a virtually unused Captain!"

To Hack's surprise, and to the shocked disapproval of the WAAC corporal, the officer held out his hand and shook Hack's, warmly, then he quickly turned and entered his office, obviously to let Hack understand that he did not want a parting salute, which would have reinstated the officer-enlisted man demarcation he had gone to some length to relax. As Hack left, he thought, " A real nice guy. Too bad the poor bastard's got himself stuck in this swamp."

Chapter 16
England

On August 10, 1943, Hack and three other American soldiers who had been released from the hospital at Casablanca, and half a dozen other military and non-military travelers, as well as a limited miscellaneous assortment of inanimate cargo were loaded into the yawning hatch of a C-47 transport, know as a rugged workhorse of the air. The logistics of the trip were such that any unusually strong headwind or even any deviation from the planned course could deplete its fuel and cause it to ditch in the inhospitable sea. Nevertheless, it took off and headed sharply northwest, flying out over the Atlantic Ocean and widely west of the Iberian Peninsula and France, in order to risk no encounters with Axis aircraft. Finally, it swung east again over the Bristol Channel and across much of lower Britain to its destination near Winchester.

Although the flight was uneventful, it was tedious, boring and uncomfortable. Hack and his three fellow GI passengers conversed occasionally to pass the time. Two were privates, Herman and Moskus, who had been involved in a freak accident when they were bringing gear ashore at Oran. One had broken his ankle, the other, a foot. The third, Talbot, was a big, heavy PFC who smelled of sweat. He had had an allergic reaction which caused him to be hospitalized. By the time the medics were able to isolate the problem, his outfit had moved on.

Upon arrival at Winchester, they reported to American Air Corps headquarters, where they were detained for several hours. Finally, they were collected by an Air Corps corporal, who led them to a waiting jeep. They bounced along out of the airport and down the road for several miles until they reached a rather shabby, temporary-looking military installation, a replacement depot, or "repple-depple." They were assigned to barracks, drew their bedding, and went out to locate their quarters. They quickly spotted the barracks with a big #6 painted on its front, and entered. It was deserted. After a quick look around, they selected cots, unrolled the mattresses and made up the cots and stowed their gear behind them. There was nothing to do then but await further orders.

"Looks like more 'hurry up and wait,' Sarge," Moskus offered.

"Yeah," Herman chipped in.

"That's the way it looks, all right," Hack agreed. "But we haven't been doing much else lately, anyway."

"Yeah. Anything's better than that crappy hospital, I guess," Moskus said, nodding.

After another fifteen minutes slipped by with no indication that they would be summoned, Hack stood up, stretched, and said, "Well, as long as we are apparently not going to do anything right away, I'm going to go see what the shower facilities are." He opened his barracks bag and groped around inside for a towel and soap. Finding them, he stripped off his clothes, stepped back into his shoes, draped the towel over his shoulder and headed for the rear of the barracks. As he passed Talbot, hunkered down on his bunk, he could not resist saying in a low voice, "You could stand a shower, too."

Hack found the latrine, complete with shower room. He laid his towel on a bench, kicked out of his shoes and stepped in. After some adjusting, he managed to get a fairly satisfactory stream of warm water and proceeded to lather up. As he was working at it, Talbot stepped in.

"You had a good idea, Sarge," he said. "Mind if I join you?"

"It's a free war—anybody can get in," Hack replied.

The big PFC laughed loudly. Hack did not think he was so funny.

"This guy's a jerk," he thought, "and a dirty one, at that."

Talbot busied himself with the water adjustment, watching Hack out of the corner of his eye.

"How did you get that nasty looking scar on your calf, Sarge?" he asked. "Did you get shot?"

Hack did not want to engage in conversation with him, so he said, sarcastically, "No, a shark bit me."

"What? Oh c'mon—what was it?" Talbot asked again, and he bent down to give the leg a closer inspection.

"Just a piece of metal—don't worry about it, okay."

"Gee, it's too bad. It sort of spoils that nice calf," Talbot persisted. He reached down and gently ran his fingers over the wound. He straightened up and added, "You've got such a nice, strong body, it would be a shame to harm it." He stepped closer, and in a low, simpering tone said, "It looks terrific, all wet and shiny," as he placed his hand on Hack's buttock.

When the fingers touched his calf, Hack felt his blood turn cold, and an icy spot formed in his belly. He had not suspected Talbot of being a pervert, but here the jerk was, aroused and trying to make up to him. Talbot must have thought that Hack was hinting for him to follow him into the deserted shower room. Hack looked at Talbot standing there with a sickening grin on his face, obviously hoping for a positive response. Hack took a quick step out of the shower room, reached down and grasped the bail of a heavy mop bucket. He turned, stepped back into the shower room and swung the pail, hard, crashing it against Talbot's arm. The hardware on the bucket rattled loudly, and one of the wringer-rollers flew off and bounced across the room as the noise blended with Talbot's howl of pain. He sagged to the floor, the color draining out of his face. The injured arm swung limply, the bone obviously broken.

Mouth quivering and eyes tearing, he choked out, "You bitch—you didn't have to do that!"

Hack looked at him, eyes glinting coldly. "You wanted action, you creep, I gave you some. You ever touch me again, I won't just break your arm, I'll take it off! You got that straight, shithead?"

"You'll get busted for this, Hacker. You'll be Private Hacker now. I'll see to that!" sobbed the wounded hulk.

Hack's voice dropped even lower, "Your mouth is working, but not your brain, you goddamned queer. Are you going to tell them that you're a fag, and get discharged on a Section 8? Fat chance! Just keep your goddamned mouth shut. You slipped, that's all."

Despite the pain which was coursing through him, Talbot had a feeling that it would indeed be unwise to pursue any idea of reporting what had actually happened. There was something in the cold manner of this sergeant that created fear in him which was greater than the hatred which the attack had fostered.

By this time, the other two soldiers were clumping down the length of the barracks to investigate the noise. They ran into the latrine and could see Talbot on the floor of the shower room, with Hack standing nearby.

"What happened?" they chorused.

"Talbot slipped on a piece of soap, kicked the mop bucket and fell on his arm. Looks like he broke it," explained Hack.

"Jeez," said Herman, "it sure does!"

"Give him his towel and help him up," Hack instructed Moskus. "As long as you're dressed, Herman, go find out where to take him to get the arm looked at."

"Okay, Sarge," Herman replied, as he hurried out.

Moskus helped the whimpering Talbot to his feet, without help from Hack, who could not bring himself to touch the man. Moskus draped a towel around him, and helped him make his way gingerly back to the area of his bunk, and then helped him get into some clothes before departing for medical assistance.

Hack stepped back into the shower room, readjusted the water and proceeded to take another shower. He felt much cleaner and refreshed when he was finished. He put Talbot and his problems completely out of his mind.

An hour later, Hack, Moskus and Herman were summoned to the orderly room and told to report to the motor sergeant for transportation to the air base. Upon arriving at that installation, they were advised by a first sergeant that they had been assigned for temporary duty, or "Detached Service" with the Air Corps.

The first sergeant referred to folders on his desk containing all of their duty records, known as their 201 files. He skimmed through each one rapidly, saying as he did so, "Nobody knows how long you'll be in this classification, but for now, you'll be reporting to Major Hammelberg, or, more accurately, to me. I'm First Sergeant Skoronski. Any of you guys had any connection with the Air Corps?"

They all shook their heads or said, "No."

"No, I see you haven't. Well, we won't hold that against you, but you may find things a little different than they were in your former outfits."

As he looked from one to the other, he said, "This is an air maintenance company, attached to a long range bomber group. There are a bunch of outfits just like us scattered around England, all part of the total effort being made against the Axis. Just keep your eyes open and do whatever you're assigned to do, without any crap, and we'll get along just fine. Chances are that someone like you, Hacker," he looked up and interrupted himself, "which one of you is Hacker?"

Hack raised his right hand slightly.

"Okay, someone like you, with a specialty and with some combat experience may get reassigned to his own or some other ground branch eventually. You other birds may discover that you've found a home."

Skoronski walked across to a window, stood looking out and clasped his hands behind his back.

"You'd better take whatever job you're given here very seriously," he instructed, as he lowered his voice. "This is the greatest chance you'll have of getting a whack at the enemy. We'll win this war by knocking Hitler out from the air, and our pilots and crews here will have as big a part in it as anyone, anywhere."

"Oh, boy—here comes the Air Corps commercial!" Hack thought. But Skoronski did not pursue the subject. He gazed out at the airfield a few moments more, then turned back to his charges and said, "I'll get someone to give you a quick tour of the installation so you'll know where things are. You can settle into the barracks where you were taken at the repple-depple for now. Within a day or two, you'll move up to one of the barracks here at the base. You'll be assigned to your duty at reveille tomorrow and the others will show you the ropes. Good luck. Dismissed."

As they started out of the orderly room, a PFC fell in beside them.

"Hi," he greeted them. "I'm Jack Prentice. I'm supposed to give you guys the ten-cent tour of the base. Jump in my jeep, there," indicating a vehicle which stood at the end of the gravel walk.

By now, a light, steady rain had started. Despite the fact that it was summer, it was uncomfortably chilly. Hack wished he had his raincoat. Prentice sensed that the newcomers were uncomfortable. He chuckled and said, "You'll get used to this weather after a while. It seems that the only time it doesn't rain around here is when the fog is so thick it can't get through!"

For the next half hour, Prentice pointed out numerous buildings: the mess hall, enlisted men's barracks, motor pool, supply room, recreation hall, chapel, officer's quarters and officers' club. Finally, they got into the interesting part, the operational sections of the bomber base. Since none of the men were Air Corps, they were fascinated by the great planes, the extensive maintenance facilities, the ammunition sheds with their impressive stacks of various types of bombs and cases full of machine gun cartridges, and the long runways, showing clear evidence of having been repaired in numerous places.

"How come the runways are patched up so much?" Moskus asked.

"That's where the Nazi calling cards hit. This bombing business is a two way operation, y'know. You can't believe how lucky we've been so far. Not one of the buildings has gone up, but we do have those pock marks on the runways, and we've lost a few planes."

"Don't you have any protection against bombing?" Herman inquired.

"We sure do. The RAF—that's the Royal Air Force—does an

unbelievable job of chasing off the German bombers. Also, we're far enough inland here that they usually unload before they get to us. There's plenty of other targets nearer the Channel that really catch hell."

"Are there any planes out now?" one of the men asked.

"No. You hit the only day in the past two weeks that we don't have any missions out. By this time tomorrow afternoon, this place will look deserted."

Much to Hack's delight, the guide pulled up near one of the huge planes, jumped out of the jeep, and shouted to a staff sergeant in coveralls who had obviously been working on one of the plane's engines, "Hey, Shotzy, okay if I give these guys a quick tour of your baby? They're groundlings and dumb as horseshit."

The sergeant grinned and said, "Sure, Jack. Show 'em anything you want—just don't let 'em touch anything. She's all set to go tomorrow."

"You got it, Shotzy."

They climbed up inside the plane and Jack proceeded to give them a surprisingly thorough explanation of everything. He pointed out where each member of the crew was stationed during a mission and what his duties were. By the time they climbed back out, they knew a lot more about the operation of these death-dealing machines than they had ever expected to learn. Then he gave them a description of the entire procedure, from the briefing of the flight officers to the loading of the planes, the taxiing out onto the strip, and the signal from the tower which sent the great planes racing down the runway and into the air. When a plane returned from a bombing mission, the ground crew members were feverishly put to work, doing such repairs as were necessary, or possible, inspecting the plane from stem to stern because they had to be extremely careful to examine everything for hidden damage. Control cables might have received glancing hits from flak or machine gun bullets, thereby weakening them so that they might fail in the next mission. The ground crew's responsibility was to replace and patch.

"How do you know so much about all this, Jack. Are you a ground crew man, or what?" Hack asked.

Prentice grinned and said, "Yeah—something like that."

"Okay," said Hack to himself. "It's your business, not mine."

"Well, if you guys have seen enough, it's almost chow time, so let's head back for the barracks, okay?"

"Fine. That was a hell of a good tour. We'll know who to ask for if we need more information," Hack said.

At reveille the next morning, the first sergeant read off assignments, including instructions for Hack to report to Lieutenant Jamison at the radio shack. He did so, and found that since his spec number indicated that he was a high speed radio operator, he was to be put to work sharpening up the code proficiency of many of the newer arrivals who had trained in that field. This sounded awfully dull to Hack, but he knew that all he could do was to make the best of it. He was supplied with the necessary equipment and a room in which to operate, and began teaching radio operation.

By late morning, it became apparent to Hack that he was in a fully operational installation. Everyone directly connected with the planes, whether air or ground crew, turned very serious. They went about their tasks with an air of dedication, and the intricate and varied jobs of those who crewed each plane gradually blended into an end product; a composite war monster, rumbling down the airstrip on its way to destroy or be destroyed.

Hack's first impression of the Air Corps personnel had been unfavorable. He was shocked at the lack of military protocol, the informality, the sloppiness of dress, and the generally nonchalant air about them. Even in combat zones, he was used to seeing the rules of discipline and attire much more closely observed. But the first time he watched the faces of ground crew members as they strained to pick out their own plane from among those straggling back from a bombing mission, and the flood of relief when they spotted it, or of shocked disbelief and abject grief when it failed to appear, he began to understand. The highs and lows were nowhere greater than with these people. Except for occasional German air raids, there was no physical involvement in the war for most of them, but every time their plane or the plane of their friends and comrades took off, they flew the mission vicariously and there was no peace of mind until its safe return.

And for the air crews, Hack realized it was an even stranger war. While at the field, it was much like being on a base at home. Eat, sleep, jump into a vehicle to get a ride to town, drink the booze, chase the women, and be ready to fly the next day. But here, it was not just to be ready to fly but to fly into hell. It was war on a time clock. Punch in for a few hours, then punch out and go home. Maybe you make it, but your plane gets whacked and pelted with scorching lead and iron and some of the guys in there with you die, or are maimed or blinded, or go raving mad from the tension and fear and shock. Maybe you make it, but the plane beside you, or behind you, or ahead of you gets hit hard and slides off, trailing black smoke, taking a couple of your close buddies on a horrifying ride to a fiery end. So you fly back to England, land, go to town, drink the booze, and chase the women. And at some point in the evening, there is a solemn moment where you and your buddy have one for the guys in that plane, and then try to put it out of your minds.

It did not take long for Hack to fall into the routine of the base. Although his working hours were not very long, the job was boring. He would get his pupils set up and copying code tapes according to the speeds they could individually handle, and then, if the weather was good, he would step outside the building and have a smoke. There were always a few other Permanent Party men on similar schedules, so there was always someone to talk with. He made friends with several other non-coms and gradually began spending much of his spare time with them.

Those who worked on the base were given permanent passes, so that they were able to go into Winchester or anywhere else within a range which would enable them to get back in time for taps, or for reveille if they made an overnight connection. For many of these fellows, the main purpose of off the base excursions was to pursue females. The English countryside had its share of young ladies, most of them wholesome and decent girls who were not about to surrender their virginity, or, in the case of those where it was too late, their respect and reputations, to every dashing young GI who came along. On the other hand, there were a surprising number who had adopted the oldest profession and who made themselves readily available to the open-fisted, open-hearted if rather brash young Americans.

Time, circumstances and hormone activity were working away quietly at Hack. It was easy enough for him to eschew the favors of other women during his relatively short training period in the States, because the memories of his trysts with his beloved Libby were fresh in his mind and heart. During his rapid trip through North Africa, he had been much too involved in the fighting, or traveling much too fast to spend time on such diversions, even if they had been in evidence. England, however, presented an entirely different picture. Here, he had settled into a routine, and at times he felt very lonely and depressed. He missed Libby very much, and sometimes his fantasies seemed grossly inadequate to satisfy him. He found an outlet for some of the emotion, by talking at length about Libby to an English girl he had met, who lived within two miles of the base.

Her name was Sally Finch, and he met her at a dance given for the troops by a local church group. She was cute and pert and was doing her very best to entertain the foreign lads in a respectable manner. She reminded Hack of the girls back home in Newvale, and he enjoyed a dance with her. When the music stopped, he was reluctant to let her go, so he said, "How about a cup of punch, Sally? I'd like to get you one."

With only a brief hesitation, she nodded, "Very well,—Hank, is it?"

"No," he laughed, "but I can see why you thought it was. They call me Hack, from my last name, Hacker."

"Oh, I'm so sorry—Hack," and she smiled sweetly.

Hack led her to a seat and assured her he would be right back. He collected two cups of punch and made his way back to her. They looked at each other over the cups and both felt more at ease than the situation would have led them to expect.

"So, Sally, do you live in Winchester?"

"On the verge, actually," she said. "We—my parents and I—have a home out Damien Road, which leads directly past the airbase from here."

"Oh, sure. I know the road. I see your wild English drivers zipping past the base on it all the time."

"Wild, is it?" asked Sally, looking surprised.

"They sure seem to barrel around these little narrow roads a lot faster than I'd want to—especially on the wrong side! Oh, I shouldn't have said that, should I? I'll bet you folks are awfully tired of hearing us say that, aren't you?"

She laughed again. "Well, perhaps it does seem somewhat overdone. But I'm sure we would feel the same, in the circumstances."

They found it easy to talk to each other, and time slipped by quite rapidly. After about twenty minutes, Sally exclaimed, "My word! I've missed three dances! I'll be having to explain this to the chairlady, if I don't mend my ways! We are instructed to keep dancing; preferably with an assortment of partners, as they don't wish to give the impression that the purpose of the evening is the formation of 'entangling foreign alliances.'" She stood up, inferring that she was about to leave.

"But, Sally, I am enjoying talking to you so much—can I see you home? Or can we make a date so that we can get together again? I'd really like to," he implored quite earnestly.

The expression on her face suddenly became much more serious. She said, reluctantly, "I don't wish to misjudge you, Hack, and I have truly enjoyed our dance and our chat, too, but I hope I haven't given you any improper signals. I feel very badly about you Yanks having to come all these miles from home, and I should like very much to help alleviate your loneliness and boredom. However, I have a soldier boy of my own, fighting somewhere with Monty, and it is my firm intention to be true to him, however long it takes."

Hack realized that Sally had misinterpreted his suggestion as an attempt to become more intimate, so he quickly said, "No, no, Sally. Don't misread me, please. I am engaged to a beautiful girl back home, and I agree with you—I don't plan to try making any other conquests. But it would be great to have someone to talk to and compare notes with. Don't you think that might be arranged? I promise, I won't make any physical demands of you."

"Oh, Hack. I feel awfully rum about this! I surely wasn't accusing you—merely trying to set the record straight. I expect we can make a date, as you call it. Why don't we compare schedules and see what can be done?"

They set a mutually agreeable time and place to meet. Thus began a most pleasant and rewarding friendship. Over the next few months, Hack and Sally met regularly, sometimes in the park in town, sometimes at her home, from where they strolled through the fields and down the lanes, and where he learned to enjoy the custom of taking tea with her and her parents. He and Sally were like twin brother and sister—they confided in each other with complete frankness. They were able to communicate innermost feelings and always seemed to come away from their exchanges refreshed and relaxed. Hack was pleasantly surprised at the attitude of Mr. and Mrs. Finch toward their friendship. Sally had explained to them that it was a match of empathy, not a romance, and the elder Finches accepted this without suspicion or reservation. Hack was not so sure that his parents would be quite that civilized, if the tables were reversed.

This relationship helped get Hack over a relatively long and patience-trying period between the autumn of 1943 and spring of 1944. However, there was one brief interval where the combination of the uncertainties of war, the frustration of being separated from Libby, and the incessant hormonal pounding convinced him that he needed more intimacy. He had become very friendly with Jack Prentice, who was smart, full of fun and had lots of savvy. Jack always knew what was going on and what to do to get in on it. Although no one could get Jack to talk about it, the story finally came out that he had been a staff sergeant tail gunner and had survived nearly twenty missions when his plane one day limped home, shot nearly to pieces, and practically disintegrated upon landing. Miraculously, the tail section broke off and tumbled to a halt, and Prentice climbed out, unscathed. But the remainder of the plane, as it skidded crazily along, suddenly caught fire, and all the other members of the crew perished. Prentice raced to it and had to be restrained from diving into the blazing wreckage in a frantic attempt to save his buddies. He felt that the captain in charge of fire control had responded too slowly and had given up too soon, and when it was all over, he bellowed his opinion of him in his face, in front of many witnesses. Jack threatened to do the captain bodily harm. What was the captain to do? This flagrant violation of military rules could not go unpunished, despite the circumstances. So the captain, very wisely and compassionately, wrote in his report that the sergeant had shown severe disrespect for a commissioned officer, and it was his recommendation that the man be broken to the rank of PFC and grounded. And that was why Jack was a tour guide and errand boy when Hack met him.

Chapter 17
London

After a monotonous three or four months of teaching had passed, Jack suggested that Hack accompany him to London on a weekend pass, which he was sure he could arrange.

"Why not ?" thought Hack. "It's about time I got out of this rut."

So they made plans to go the next Friday evening.

Since it was Hack's first trip to London, Jack made sure that he saw as many as possible of the essential points of interest that they could cover during the weekend. He arranged for them to bed down at the Red Cross, and then hailed a cab to take them to a section where he was acquainted with the proprietors of a couple of English pubs. Hack was impressed with the warm welcome accorded them by the first publican, who was much more fondly disposed toward Jack than was routinely to be expected among such people toward visiting GIs.

"Any friend of Jack's," he said, with what passed for a smile. "One on the 'ouse to get yer started," and he poured a shot of whiskey and placed it in front of Hack.

"Thank you, sir," said Hack.

"Sir, is it?" the surprised barman asked. "I don't get that, often. I knew Jack's friend would be a gentleman. E's the salt o' the earth, 'e is, Yank or no!"

They lounged at their small table for about an hour, drinking steadily, until Hack began to feel drunk. He was not used to drinking much, and as he drank, he wondered why he was doing it. Subconsciously, he knew that he had been abstemious for, perhaps, too long, and alcohol was a way to release some of his pent-up emotions. Shortly, the volume of liquid he had been absorbing manifested itself. He rose just a bit unsteadily to his feet and said to Jack, "Where's the latrine?"

Jack pointed, and Hack picked his way through the bar's patrons in the smoke-drenched dimness until he reached his goal. After relieving himself, he walked back to the table somewhat more normally, only to find that a woman was now sitting with Jack, and they were chatting happily. He felt a little awkward, but Jack said, "Come on, Hack, old buddy. Sit down. I want you to meet Brenda, an old friend of mine—right, Brenda?"

"Right, indeed," the woman responded, "and a very good friend, as well. Sit close by me, 'ack—may I call you that?"

He nodded.

"I want to become a very good friend to you, too."

"Sounds good to me," Hack smiled. The liquor made him feel warm and relaxed inside, and he thought, "She isn't half bad looking."

She was wearing a dress, cut square across the chest, exposing her shoulders and arms, and accenting the bust line. Her mouth, although painted perhaps too much, was pleasantly shaped, and her smile seemed genuine. Hack slid a chair close to hers and sat down. The heat which radiated from her body felt pleasant against his thigh. It was a long time since he had been physically close to a woman.

"So, Brenda, what do you think of having all us Americans cluttering up your city—your whole country, for that matter? Bet you wish we'd all get the hell out of here, eh?"

She looked astonished. "You must be orf yer track, sweetie. You lads 'ave finally put some life into 'bally old.' Aven't ever 'ad the fun before, and never again, I'd judge."

Hack looked at his nearly empty glass. "I need another drink. Waiter! Bring us another round here. What are you drinking, Brenda?"

"'E knows my drink, don't yer, luv?" she said to the waiter with a grin.

"How about you, Jack?" Hack asked.

"Not right now. I've got to meet somebody up the street. I'll take off and be back here at, say, eleven-thirty, okay, Hack?"

Although Hack was surprised at this, he was not averse to having some time to himself with Brenda, so he said, "Okay, if you're sure that's what you want to do. Brenda and I will do all right, won't we, Brenda?"

"Better than all right, I expect," she replied, with a laugh.

"See you at eleven-thirty then," said Jack, and he rose and made his way to the door.

The waiter was back with the drinks, and Hack paid him, then lifted his glass to Brenda.

"Mud in your eye," he said.

"Right back at you, 'Ack!"

They continued to talk as the drinks came steadily, with a new one arriving every ten or fifteen minutes. Hack was finding it difficult to maintain a clear head. He checked his reflexes occasionally to be sure he was sober enough to continue. He did not want to embarrass himself in front of Brenda. He would turn quickly to focus on someone across the crowded, dingy room, or beat out the rhythm of a familiar tune on the table with his fingers. Hack noticed that Brenda seemed able to handle her drinks without outward signs of being affected, except that she became increasingly amorous as she drank each drink. At some point, she dropped her hand casually into Hack's lap and gripped his leg lightly. While this surprised him, it felt good, so he did not object.

Gradually, through the liquor-induced haze that enveloped him, the thought stole into Hack's mind that he could talk this girl into going to bed if he wanted to. Fleetingly, he thought of his promise to himself that he was not going to cheat on Libby. But the proximity of Brenda's warm body stimulated him and pushed that resolution to the back of his mind. They continued to talk and laugh. After one particularly funny remark, the girl tilted her head back and howled, then boldly slid her hand up to his crotch and groped him.

Now, Hack finally realized that he had been deliberately planning to carry this situation further than he had pretended. His head was muddled and fuzzy, but his body was sending clear signals. The pent-up longing for Libby, the months of denying his virility, the frustration of being separated from his home and his love, and the pounding in his loins, all marshaled their forces against his resolve, and the anesthetizing effect of the liquor completed the job. He leaned over and whispered in Brenda's ear, "Is there any place around here that we can go to be alone?"

With a lascivious smirk and an extra little squeeze of her exploring hand, she replied, "Of course, luv—my digs are only a 'op and a jump from 'ere."

"Well, let's go!" cried Hack.

He dropped and extra bill on the table, took Brenda by the elbow, and proceeded to walk to the exit as rapidly as his uncooperative legs would allow.

Once they were out in the cold, clammy air of the London December, Hack sobered up enough to avoid tripping or falling, but he still weaved considerably as Brenda led the way to the end of the block and around the corner. She continued down the dingy, shabby cobbled street past several doors, then said, "'Ere we are, luv," and climbed up several steps to an entrance. In a moment, she had inserted a key and the door gave way to a drab, uncarpeted foyer. They crossed it and started up a long flight of rickety stairs. Gaining the top, she turned left, down another dimly lit hallway, the lack of illumination of which helped to mask its faded and flaking paint. There was nothing to camouflage a most unpleasant and foul smell which seemed to permeate the whole structure.

"Now, then!" she sang, as another key gave access to their destination. Hack stood a moment in the semidarkness while Brenda turned up a gas lamp on the wall just a little. Its feeble rays revealed a small room almost bare of furnishings. He could make out two chairs, a small table, and a dry sink, on which a battered pitcher and wash bowl stood, and a large bed with brass-spindled head and foot.

"'Ere's my digs, 'Ack. No palace, but I calls it 'ome! You can throw your clothes over the chair there," she said indicating an old wooden relic with pieces of the rush seat sticking out at crazy angles.

"I'll be with you in 'alf a mo'," and she gave him a playful goose and tripped into what was evidently an adjoining bath or dressing room.

Hack stood, dumbfounded. The liquor was to blame for some of his confusion, but the shock of what he had gotten himself into was mainly responsible for his immobility. He reached over and turned the gas light up some more, which made the hovel look even worse. The light disclosed that every nook and corner was layered with dust and dirt. A small two-burner hotplate sat on the floor against one wall, and on it was a battered aluminum pot containing a large spoon and the crusted remains of a frugal meal. A dilapidated fiberboard wardrobe was crowded in the corner beside the bed. It bulged with gaudy dresses, blouses, skirts and jackets, and several pairs of cheap high-heeled shoes cluttered the bottom. A framed print from a magazine, depicting a young boy and girl running hand in hand through a field of daisies, incongruously adorned one wall. By the time Hack's liquor-numbed senses had inventoried the room, the door to the other room opened and Brenda emerged. She was attired only in a garter belt and a skimpy bra. She wore a large and suggestive smile. With a slinking step or two, she approached him and as she did so, a wave of cheap perfume scent washed over him. The brighter light was not kind to her. It revealed a lot of subtle puckers about her face, upper arms and chest. Even the exposed tops of the tightly harnessed and boosted breasts showed wrinkle lines. The smile, which had seemed quite pretty in the smoky murkiness of the pub, now exposed teeth of a yellow hue, with areas badly in need of dental work. Hack fought back an urgent desire to vomit.

"Ow comes it you 'aven't undressed, darlin'? Are you ashamed of wot you've got? No need to worry on that score—Brenda will be nice to you, whatever the equipment! But, before we start, let's get business out of the way, eh? Always best to. One pound will do nicely, unless you've ideas about some special attention. There's a luv!"

Quickly, Hack reached into his pocket and pulled out his wallet. He fumbled out a pound note from among the unfamiliar currency and handed it to her.

"Okay, Brenda, thanks a lot. I've lost my desire for action. Too much booze, I guess. But you've earned your pound, so don't worry about it."

Quite sober now, he turned on his heel and stepped out, leaving her standing there, gripping the pound note, but with a startled expression on her face.

He hurried down the hall, down the stairs and out the door. Fortunately, Brenda's flat was so close to the pub that he had no trouble finding his way back, and soon he was again seated at a table inside. He ordered a glass of seltzer and sat sipping it, the disgust in his gut gradually subsiding. "What a jerk I am," he thought. "How could I have failed to spot her as a prostitute? Am I really that naive?" It must have been the fact that Jack had introduced her as a friend that had thrown him off. That, and the fact that he was subconsciously aching for sex and was susceptible to practically any suggestions along that line. Well, now he was sober in more ways than one, although not as he had anticipated he would be.

Hack struggled through the remaining hour of Jack's absence; an hour made no easier by the almost immediate reappearance of Brenda. She ignored him completely, and had seduced another GI within fifteen minutes of her return. Before Jack arrived, she had left, snuggled up adoringly to her new friend. Hack silently raised his glass of seltzer in the direction of her retreating back. What a way to make a living!

In due time, Jack returned, spotted Hack and worked his way through the crowd to his table.

"Trust you made out with your friend, Hack," he laughed. "She was a hot one, wasn't she?"

Hack smiled wryly.

"She was a hot one, all right. I must have been pretty dumb not to have spotted her for a pro, but I didn't. How did she get to be a friend of yours?"

Jack gave a surprised laugh.

"Friend of mine!? Where did you get that idea?"

"You introduced her to me as 'your good friend', didn't you? What else was I supposed to think?"

"Oh, Geez—I'm sorry, buddy. That just rolled off my tongue. I figured you'd know she was a hooker. What happened—anything?"

"Well, I had more than I needed to drink and we went to her place. I turned up the light when she went into the next room to get ready, and I realized what a situation I'd gotten myself into. So I paid her and said, 'Thanks, but no thanks!' and came back here."

Jack rocked back and forth with laughter.

"Wait 'til I spread this around the base! They'll be calling you 'second thought Hack.' Instead of 'love 'em and leave 'em,' you'll be known as 'pay 'em and leave 'em!"

Despite himself, Hack had to smile.

"You know, you got a mean streak, you bastard!" he chuckled. "You'd better be kidding!"

"No, I wouldn't do that to you," Jack promised. "Not if you're nice to me and do little things for me—like loaning me money when I need it. A little blackmail never hurts, right?"

"Right," Hack replied. "But a little punch in the nose does!"

They laughed again and ordered another drink.

Chapter 18
Reassigned

The Allies' campaign in Italy was progressing; not rapidly, but satisfactorily. A beachhead had been established at Anzio on January 22, 1944, but did not really accomplish its purpose; that of relieving the stalled offensive at Casino. It would not be until early April, when the Eighth Army and the Fifth Army attacked ferociously around Lake Comacchio and Bologna, respectively, that it could be said that the end of the Italian campaign was in sight.
Of course, since before the end of 1943, the buildup of troops and equipment had been increasingly evident in Britain. Many new and temporary camps had sprung up throughout the countryside, and the roads were jammed with an increasing avalanche of military vehicles. Training sites for specialists in various areas were in operation, and a strong effort was being made to maintain an air of imminent action and sharp readiness among the hundreds of thousands of troops.

It was after lunch on a Tuesday late in April that Hack was summoned to the orderly room by Sergeant Skoronski.

"Orders for you, Sergeant Hacker," he said. "You will report immediately to Commanding Officer, 2886th Signal Battalion, attached to US 4th Infantry Division, 8th Regiment, for assignment in your specialty. Collect your gear and report back here at 1600 hours. I'll have your papers ready, and transportation will be furnished."

"Where is the outfit located?" Hack asked.

"Let's see—they are at Sherborne. that's about 40 - 50 miles southwest of here. Good luck, Hacker. Give 'em hell!"

Since he had about three hours to wait for his transportation, Hack decided that this would be a good time to make a quick trip out to see Sally and the Finches to let them know that he was being transferred. He dashed back to the barracks, emptied his foot locker and rack, and stowed everything in his duffel bag. He ripped the blankets off his cot, rolled up the mattress, and turned the blankets in at the supply room. Then he carried his duffel bag down to the pebble path in front of the orderly room. He stepped inside and told the company clerk that he was leaving his gear and suggested he take a peek at it once in a while.

"I'll be back before 1600," he said. And, with that, he ran down the path and out to the gate.

"Anything going west that I can hook a ride with?" he asked one of the off-duty MPs whose unit was guarding the gate.

"All the time, Sarge. Hang on a minute."

The soldier turned to the sentry box and yelled, "Hey, Baker. Flag down the next vehicle going west. Sarge, here, wants a ride."

The sentry nodded. Within a couple of minutes, he halted an exiting vehicle and exchanged words with the driver. Then he turned to Hack and signaled him to climb into the waiting truck. Hack held up his pass for the sentry to see, then jumped in. He waved to the MPs and shouted, "Thanks a lot."

The truck's route took him right to the end of Robin Lane, on which sat the Finch cottage. After thanking the driver, he jumped down. A quick walk and he was at the front door, and he rapped on it.

Mrs. Finch opened the door and immediately Hack sensed trouble. She did not give him her usual broad smile of welcome; instead, she said, in a hushed tone, "Oh—dear, Hack, do come in."

"Have I come at a bad time, Mrs. Finch?"

"On the contrary, perhaps your visit is extremely *well* timed," she replied, softly. "Step into the kitchen, please, Hack."

He followed behind her, wondering what could have produced such a change from the usual happy atmosphere. He did not have long to wait for the answer. In the small, bright kitchen, Mrs. Finch turned to him and said, as her head shook gently from side to side,

"I'm afraid our Sally has had shocking news. We've just learned that her young man has been killed on the Italian front."

Involuntarily, Hack let a deep breath escape. After a moment, he said, "Oh, my God! I'm so sorry to hear that! Poor Sally! She must feel just terrible! When did she get the word?"

"His name was on the casualty list in Winchester this morning. Unfortunately, one of her acquaintances rang her up and informed her in a rather tactless manner. She fainted dead away at the telephone. We revived her and helped her to her bed, where she sobbed out the dreadful news to us when she regained her senses. Then she simply cried herself to sleep. I am afraid she is a bit under the weather still. But perhaps having you call may be just what is needed to bring her 'round. Would you like to see her, if she agrees? Of course, she'll look a fright!"

"Certainly—I'll do anything I possibly can to comfort her, poor kid!"

"I have the kettle on and there's milk in the fridge," said Mrs. Finch. "Why not have a hot cup of tea whilst I peep in at her and test the waters, so to speak?"

"Thank you, but I'll wait and see how she reacts. Maybe she will be up to having a cup with me."

Mrs. Finch moved quietly out of the kitchen. Several minutes elapsed in silence as Hack simply stood, feet apart, staring blindly out of the window, the appetizing fragrant odors and warmth of the cozy room making no impression on him in his preoccupation. "This is the way it happens," he said to himself. "One day, a man with a lovely young girl eagerly awaiting his return—the next, just a memory."

He heard soft footsteps in the hallway, and turned to see Mrs. Finch returning, shaking her head apologetically. She was embarrassed.

"Sally simply isn't up to seeing anyone, Hack, dear. She just lies there and cries softly and refuses to eat or to speak with anyone. I am positive that when this shock wears off, you will be the first she will wish to see, you've been such a dear friend. Since we can't call you at the base, will you keep in touch?"

"I certainly will. I'll call as soon as possible, and as often as necessary, until she gets over this initial reaction."

After a moment's hesitation, he continued, "But I am afraid that I have news that she won't care for also. My purpose in coming today was to tell you folks that I've received shipping orders. I am being transferred to a signal battalion attached to the infantry. You can understand what that probably means, as far as our eventual destination is concerned. Fortunately, I am only moving about forty miles from here for now, so I hope to be able to visit at least a few more times. Whenever we are permitted to call, I will phone you."

Mrs. Finch appeared crestfallen upon receiving this news.

"Goodness," she said, "this will deepen her misery, I fear. If I have your permission, Hack, I shall delay giving her your message until I feel she is strong enough to handle it. In fact, it would be much better if you could come to see her and tell her in person. Do you suppose that will be possible?"

Hack hesitated, then nodded. "Oh, I am quite sure I will still be getting passes at my new unit, at least for a little while. And you can be sure I will come here as quickly as I am able. I will check with you by phone before coming, to be sure Sally is ready to see me. Don't you think that is best?"

"Without doubt."

Mrs. Finch looked so sad, so much older somehow, that Hack's heart went out to her. She spoke softly again.

"Oh, it does seem hard that we have to continue under such wretched conditions, Hack. Whatever possesses we humans to be forever bent on killing one another? Oh, how I pray that these troubles will pass and that you young folk will have many bright and happy future years to enjoy." She then added, "Though for poor Sally, it appears that those times are rather far away."

Hack turned and started toward the front door, with Mrs. Finch close behind. At the door, he bent and brushed her soft cheek with a light kiss.

"Take care of our girl. I am sure she will be fine after a while, despite the rotten shock she has had. I will be in touch regularly. Give my regards to Mr. Finch, please."

He walked down the path and back to the road, where he stood awaiting any vehicle in which he might get a ride back to the base. "What a lousy break for Sally," he mused. "Why is it always the nice ones who get shafted?"

Back at the base, the promised transportation picked Hack up promptly at 1600 and a little over an hour later, delivered him to his new billet with the 8th Regiment, 4th US Infantry in Sherborne. The differences between this and his Air Corps berth were plain to see. The off-duty ease and relaxation of the former were not evident here. He was quickly assigned to a barracks of Company A of the 2886th Signal Battalion and found himself a bunk, with the assistance of the barracks orderly. His instructions were to report to Captain Rudman, so he made his way to the orderly room. He told the company clerk who he was and why he was there, and was told to wait while the clerk checked on whether the captain could see him. He returned in a minute and said, "Go right in, Sergeant Hacker."

He stepped into the captain's office, came front and center, and saluted. The captain returned his salute.

"Sergeant Christopher Hacker, reporting as ordered, sir."

"At ease, Hacker. Glad to have you aboard. I see from your 201 file that you are a qualified high-speed radio operator and have been familiarized with various types of radio equipment, including the SCR191 and SCR299, which we will be utilizing."

"That's correct, sir."

"Also, I believe you participated in maneuvers in a joint Signal Corps-Infantry operation during your training, and then worked with the infantry during the North African campaign. Correct?"

"All correct, sir."

"Well, Sergeant, I am personally damned glad to have you with us. No secret about where we're going, I guess, and the more experienced people we can have with us, the better our chances will be of getting through okay."

"Thank you, sir. I hope that is true," Hack replied.

"I'm damned sure of it," said the captain. "I read and reread your personnel file. With your training, your battle experience, your being wounded and all, I can't understand why you are still a buck sergeant. Is there anything that should be in the record that doesn't show up?"

"If there is, sir, it's something I've never heard about. I've just never been in an outfit where the TO had room for a higher rank for me, I guess."

"Well, by God, we're going to take care of that in a hurry. I know we've got an open slot for a Tech Sergeant, so as of now, you're it! Better get the stripes on right away, so not too many of the guys see you've just been boosted two grades, or everybody will be looking for a promotion. Also, I see that you've earned a Purple Heart and a Bronze Star, but haven't been awarded them yet. Consider that corrected, too. I'll have the company clerk finish the paperwork and get you the ribbons. I want you to put them on your Class A jacket and wear 'em."

Hack was nonplussed at this sudden recognition. "May I ask why you are doing so much for me so soon, sir?" he asked.

"Sure, Sergeant," the captain replied. "Two reasons. First, I admire and respect men who have shown courage and have been wounded in combat and who have come back for more without complaining, and I like to see them get the honors due them. But, second, and even more important; since you are new in this outfit, and are going to be called upon for some very important duty, it will gain you a lot of respect. Very few of our people have seen action, and the guys around you will feel more confident with a blooded veteran beside them when things start to get rough. That's plain talk, Sergeant, but that's the way I like to do business. No secrets, no bullshit and no chickenshit.

And that's the way I want my non-coms to operate. Any problems?

Hack couldn't resist a smile. He thought, "Here is a guy you just have to like, assuming that what he says is straight." And Hack believed himself a good enough judge of people to accept it completely.

"No problem at all, Captain. Thank you for the promotion. I'll do my best to live up to your expectations, but I'm going to need some direction about what my job is supposed to be. Who do I see?"

"Well," said the captain, "your platoon leader will be Lieutenant Kelsey. He's going to be a good man, but he's green as grass right now. I'll tell him, off the record, to not be afraid to let you sort of run things in the field, and I am telling you, right now, not to embarrass him in front of the men. Of course, if I thought you would, I'd never have given you the stripes or this kind of inside information. I think you and Kelsey are going to make a hell of a good team, once you get a chance to work together. That's about it. Tell the clerk to round up Kelsey and send him in here. I'll explain the setup to him. Good luck, and do a job for me, Hacker. Dismissed."

Kelsey proved to be a nice guy, not the sort one would at first pick out as a dashing, daring military type, but upon closer acquaintance, a person whom one knew could be trusted to do his part when things got tough. He was of average weight and height, but his carriage indicated some athleticism, and it was obvious that he was not interested in playing the heavy officer. He told Hack that he had discussed their situation with the captain and agreed wholeheartedly that the two of them would be able to work well together.

"I am not so proud that I can't learn from a guy with less rank but more experience and knowledge," the Lieutenant said. "We'll get along fine, Hacker."

"I'm sure we will, sir," Hack responded.

"The first thing you can do, is knock off the 'sir' business. When we are talking alone, call me, 'Kip.' I'm going to call you Chris, if that's okay with you," said Kelsey, consulting the copy of Hack's orders in his hand.

Hack laughed.

"Don't do that, please. I wouldn't know who you were talking to! Everyone calls me 'Hack'—from my last name, you see."

"Oh, okay, fine. Hack it is. Now let me arrange a nickel tour for you. I'll go over the TO with you and explain how our deal with the 8th Regiment is supposed to work. Basically, we're supposed to be their eyes and ears, and to set up and run the signal network. We'll have various mobile stations in operation, from Regimental headquarters all the way down to platoon. We should have all the operators we need. Your job will be general overseer of the network—seeing to it that they are all doing their jobs properly and that all of the equipment is functioning. Sound familiar?"

Hack nodded. "Yeah. that's basically what I was doing before on the company level. Now, I'll just have a bigger department, I guess. I'll want to get together with all the team chiefs and operators, so I know who I'll be working with."

Lieutenant Kelsey made the arrangements, and over the next few weeks Hack got to know very well the people he would be working with. Most of them were young and confused and scared, but for the most part, they responded well to the level-headed, low-key sergeant, who had tasted contact with the enemy. It gave them a feeling of security to know that he would be involved right along with them, whatever was destined to come their way.

Hack waited three days after his visit to the Finches, then he made a phone call to them. Mrs. Finch answered. She sounded even more tired and frail than she had at his last visit.

"Are you all right?" Hack asked.

"Oh, yes, quite," she replied.

"And Mr. Finch?"

"Yes, fine, as well."

"Well then, how about our girl? Has she recovered somewhat?"

The answer did not come immediately, as though Mrs. Finch was trying to decide how best to describe the situation.

"Sally is all right, I believe. It is just that she is behaving rather oddly, it seems. Perhaps that is not an accurate appraisal—more unusual than odd, I suppose."

"How do you mean?"

"She is still confining herself to her room, but now she seems to be on a mission of sorts. She cries occasionally, but most of the time, she plays, over and over again, a few recordings which were, apparently, favourites of her young man and herself. She refuses to come to the table with us, but does seem to be getting sufficient nourishment from trays which I take to her. Communication is still meager, but she appears to be in command of all her senses."

"Do you think it is time for me to visit her?"

After a moment, Mrs. Finch replied, "No, I think not, Hack. I have been trying to insinuate suggestions that she should step out of doors and that she should talk with some close friend, but her response has been such a firm negative that I feel we must give her more time. I would suggest you call again in one more week. Is that satisfactory? And do you think that will be convenient to your schedule?"

"Oh, sure," Hack replied. "I'll leave it at that for the moment, then. You will hear from me again in about a week. Are you sure there is nothing I can do for you folks?"

"Thank you very kindly, but no. You are very good to offer, Hack, but the mister and I are up to the task. Until later, then."

They hung up and Hack started walking back toward his barracks. "Too bad Sally is finding it so hard to take," he thought.

Hack's duties in the new outfit were beginning to fall into place, as he became more and more familiar with the personnel and with the role the battalion, as a whole, and his company, in particular, would be required to play in the upcoming action. They were starting to have drills designed to sharpen up their cooperative efforts with the rest of the regiment, and to make their jobs as clear as possible. Not only his mobile radio people, but also the wire men with the field telephone equipment and all the other communications specialists were doing their best to blend into the infantry modus operandi with as little friction as possible.

Hack's mail was arriving quite regularly now, and he spent much of his free time reading and rereading the letters from home, especially those from Libby. She was doing an excellent job of keeping him informed about her personal activities at Middlebury as well as of the news back in Newvale, about which she obviously kept very close watch. Although it hardly seemed possible that she had only another couple of months until her college graduation. "I suppose I will have to bow to her superior knowledge now that she'll have letters after her signature," he smiled to himself. "Anyone but Libby. No way is her education going to give her a swelled head," he mused. "If anyone is less self-important because of such things, I've yet to meet her. What a doll!" God, how he wished they would suddenly announce that the war was over and he could return to her.

A feeling of guilt came over Hack when he suddenly realized that it had been about ten days since his last communication with the Finches. As soon as he had free time, he took his place in line at the bank of telephones and when it was his turn, he rang them again. After several rings, the connection was made and the voice of Mrs. Finch came faintly over the line.

"This is Hack, Mrs. Finch. How are you all, and how are things progressing?"

"Oh, hello, Hack," she said quietly. "I am so relieved to hear from you. Sally is somewhat improved—at least she is up and about, though she is not communicating very much. She just stepped out for a breath of air, which is a good sign, don't you think?"

"Yes," he replied. "That sounds encouraging. Have you told her anything about my situation?"

"Oh, no. I fear she has not yet decided to break her isolation, and I daren't mention anything which might upset her further. She no longer plays the music constantly, but now has entered a period marked by long meditation and occasional bursts of writing. I managed to steal a peek at her compositions and was relieved to find that she is simply trying to record all that she can recall about Richard's poor, short life. If you will stay in touch, I shall certainly ask you to visit the moment I feel she is ready."

"Very well," said Hack. "I'm sure you know best, Mrs. Finch. Good-bye for now."

Chapter 19
Sally

Another ten days slipped by before Hack felt that it was time to call the Finches again. He was beginning to be a little impatient with Sally. She was certainly entitled to be miserable for a while, he thought, but continuing to keep the full burden of her loss to herself was neither logical nor healthy. So it was in a mood bordering on ultimatum that Hack placed a call.

As usual, it was Mrs. Finch who answered.

"Hack, again, Mrs. Finch. Has the situation changed yet?"

"So very glad you phoned, Hack. Yes, I think that we can now safely say that our girl is mending. It is clear that even she is becoming a bit bored with the long isolation. In fact, she actually said, out of a clear sky yesterday evening, 'I wish I might speak with Hack. It has been so long since we've seen him!'"

"Oh, that is great news! I'd better try to get right up there and see her, then."

"Are you able to get away?" Mrs. Finch asked.

"Yes, I should be free after Retreat tomorrow, since it is Saturday. I've made a few friends here, and my Lieutenant tells me he can get me a ride to your place whenever I'm ready. Are you sure that it is not too soon for me to come?"

"Oh, not at all," answered Mrs. Finch. "The sooner the better, I believe. She so desperately needs bucking up, and you are the one to do it, we're convinced. May I tell her, then, that you will try to be here tomorrow? I think prudence dictates that I shall wait until the morning to tell her, however."

"All right—fine," said Hack. "I can't give you an exact time, but probably between six and seven tomorrow evening. See you then."

"Wonderful, Hack. Bye-bye for now."

Kelsey came through with a jeep and a trip ticket for Hack for the next Saturday evening. "I'm sorry, Hack, but it's only good until midnight. Hope that'll work out okay for you."

"That's fine. It will give me a couple of hours at the Finches'. I probably shouldn't stay longer than that, anyway. Thanks for your help."

He left immediately after Retreat formation and made the trip without incident. He pulled into the short drive beside Finches' cottage on Robin Lane, got out, and went up to the front door. Before he could knock, the door opened, and Mr. Finch was there, smiling and extending his hand.

"So very nice to see you again, Hack," he said with obvious sincerity. "Our Sally is somewhat improved, though she's a long way to go. We're expecting big things from your visit. Do come into the parlor. I'll see she's out directly," and he left the room to fetch his wife and daughter.

Soon, the two women entered the parlor where Hack was standing a bit uneasily. Sally seemed to hang back for a moment. Then, realizing that her reticence was perhaps unfair to Hack, she stepped forward, held out her arms toward him, and said, "I am so happy you've come, Hack. Really, so happy."

"She doesn't look happy," he thought. She looked unhappy—very unhappy, indeed. Her hair was not combed as neatly as usual, she had given little or no thought to her selection of clothes, and her poor little face looked pale and drawn. The eyes were red-rimmed and listless.

Hack stepped forward and took her in his arms and gave her a long, tender hug, saying, "Poor Sally—what a blow you've had." He could feel the tenseness in her slender figure, even a slight trembling. Softly, he murmured, "Don't put up a front, Sally—we're certainly good enough friends that you can let yourself go with me."

He could sense that she was listening. He heard a small sigh escape from her, and her muscles seemed to relax. But she kept her face buried in the hollow between his chin and shoulder for several seconds as he gently rocked back and forth, soothing her as one would a child who had skinned her knee. The senior Finches hovered close by, but after a few moments, obviously began to feel somewhat embarrassed. Mr. Finch cleared an imaginary obstruction from his throat, while his wife fidgeted, patting her hair and straightening phantom wrinkles in her dress. Still, Sally gave no sign of any intention to alter her position. "She isn't going to open up to me in front of her parents," Hack realized. "I think I'd better try to get her out of here."

"Sally, it's an unusually nice evening for this early in the spring, and you haven't been away from the yard for some time. I've got a jeep outside—let's take a little ride, what say?"

In the background, the parents nodded animatedly.

"What say, Sally?" Hack repeated.

They waited expectantly. Finally, Sally slowly raised her head, leaned back, and said, "All right. Let me collect myself and freshen up a bit, first."

"Fine," Hack agreed. "Take as much time as you wish. I have at least two or three hours."

She smiled rather wanly, turned, and went to her room.

Mrs. Finch was plainly delighted, and her husband seemed to be, as well. "This will do her a world of good," she enthused. "She needs badly to escape these four walls."

Shortly, Sally returned, looking a little more relaxed. She had recombed her hair so that it more nearly resembled its normal neatness. A large, light shawl was draped across her shoulders to ward off any chilliness in the evening air.

"All set," cried Hack. "We'll be back sometime," he added, laughing.

The Finches watched, beaming, as the young couple climbed into the jeep and started down the road.

They rode in silence for several minutes. Then Sally put a hand on Hack's arm, saying, "Let's go down to the lane where we often walk. I think I would feel better there."

"Sounds good to me," Hack said, nodding. "We're lucky to have picked such a nice warm evening, and one with no rain."

When they reached the lane, Hack pulled the jeep out of sight behind a thicket.

"Don't want someone to relieve me of this vehicle while we're off walking," he said, jokingly.

"No, indeed," Sally replied, and she showed almost a glimmer of a smile.

"Well, that's encouraging," Hack thought.

Sally slipped her small hand into his. They walked a hundred yards or so, neither seeming to want to break the spell of the pleasant twilight, the occasional calling of the birds and the sounds of other forms of life eagerly striving to commence another warm season.

Suddenly, like a dam bursting, Sally cried out, "Oh, Hack! Whatever am I to do? My Richard—my poor, poor Richard, is gone—gone! How can it be? Where is the fairness? He was only a lad! He hadn't tasted much of life. And he had such plans! Such marvelous plans! It isn't right—not right at all!"

She threw herself against him, pounding his chest with her small fists. Hack gathered her to him, effectively halting the pummeling, and stroked her hair, as he said, soothingly,

"I know, honey, I know. It isn't right and it isn't fair. It's just the way things are, unfortunately. We are all like puppets on strings. All that we can do is dance to the tune of whomever is pulling the cords. Sometimes the cords get pretty tangled, and the puppets get hurt. You've had a rotten break, Sally, but before this war is over, I'm afraid there will be millions of girls who will be in the same boat. Maybe that isn't much comfort, but you have to look at it that way. Richard is gone, and that's terrible, but what you have to do now is love the people you have left just that much more. That is what he would have wanted. Life goes on."

Sally stood for some time, pressed against him, sobbing gently. Finally, she pulled away a bit and looked up at him. "Oh, Hack—you are so good. I don't know how I could ever get by without you! Please come to me often and help me with your strength, will you please, Hack, dear?"

Hack took a deep breath. He had his own bad news and he knew that he had to give it to her now, regardless of how much it would hurt her.

"Sally, I am afraid that I have more bad news for you. You might as well have it all in a bunch and get it over with."

"Whatever do you mean?" she asked, as the trembling started again.

"Sally, honey, I am no longer stationed at the air base. I've been transferred to a signal battalion down in Sherborne."

It took a few seconds for the information to sink in, but when it did, she cried, "Oh, no! Why would you be sent way down there?"

He hated to continue, but knew that he had to tell her everything, now that he had started. "The battalion is attached to the US 4th Infantry division, Sally. I guess I will be going with them when the big drive on the continent begins.

She gave no verbal response, but the trembling increased alarmingly. Hack feared that she might be about to become hysterical. Instead, she suddenly turned completely calm. The trembling ceased abruptly, as though a switch had been thrown. Still, she gave no indication that she had heard and digested what he had told her. He continued to hold her to his chest. In the silence, he now realized that he could feel faintly the rapid beating of her heart.

Slowly, she turned her face up to his and said, simply, "Kiss me, Hack."

The evening shadows fell across the sweet, sad little face, tilted expectantly beneath his chin. The small, warm body molded itself against his. The clean, sweet fragrance of her assailed his senses. Really, for the first time, he became thoroughly conscious of her as a woman; lovely, desirable, tragically wounded but an exciting woman.

"Kiss me!" she repeated, insistently.

He hesitated only another moment or two, then, knowing deep down that he should push her away, but unable to resist, he bent his head to hers and placed his mouth over the soft, warm lips. She responded instantly and with startling ferocity, crushing her mouth upward against his, then opening her lips and forcing her small moist tongue between his teeth. She wrapped her arms more tightly around him and slowly slid her lower body up and down against his. Thoughts started rushing through Hack's mind. This was a Sally that he had never known. This was not what he had planned. Or was it perhaps exactly what he had planned, but had not admitted to himself? What about his unspoken promise to Libby? But what about his own prospects for the next few months? What about his part in the coming invasion? What chance would he have of ever seeing Libby again? "Probably in a few months I'll be just another name on a list, like Sally's Richard, and Libby will be crying on some other guy's shoulder," he rationalized, as his senses responded to the stimuli.

The tempo of Sally's assault was increasing and whatever desire he had had to resist it was rapidly diminishing.

"What are you doing, honey?" he whispered, disengaging his mouth from hers momentarily, as his hands automatically started to explore.

"Don't talk, Hack—please!" she purred, sliding the shawl from her shoulders. She freed herself from his grasp and stepped back, spreading the cloth on the spring-cold ground. Quickly, she dropped on it and stretched her arms up enticingly to Hack. Any trace of reluctance now gone, he immediately started ripping off garments, surprised to find how rapidly he was breathing in his eagerness to satisfy their sudden mutual lust.

Some time later, their passion spent, they walked slowly back up the lane, climbed into the jeep and sat, saying nothing. After several silent minutes had passed, Hack turned to Sally and asked, "Are you sorry?"

"Not one bit!" she replied, softly but convincingly.

Then, in a moment, much more loudly, "Not one damned bit! No matter what happens now, they can't take that away from us, can they!"

Hack thought about it, briefly. She was right. Why feel guilty? What good were all the wonderful, romantic rules and solemn promises and noble loyalty, when nobody could say whether they would turn out to be all in vain, as had poor Sally's?

After a few more quiet moments, Hack started the jeep and drove slowly back to Robin Lane.

Chapter 20
Invasion

With the Allied forces in England, events were beginning to move rapidly toward a climax. Individual units were having up-tempo run-throughs of some of their specialties—dry runs, in military parlance—and everyone was catching the fever. Even men who had always been noted for avoiding the drill at every opportunity—the goldbricks—were now evincing a new interest in learning. One of the exercises which brought the imminence of action home to them was cargo net drill. It was these oversized rope and float nets which would be the means by which most of the invaders would transfer from transport to landing craft, and after that there was nowhere to go but to "hit the beach."

All through May, there was a new rumor of departure almost hourly. Men who had not been particularly nervous or concerned were now worried. Passes were cancelled and telephone calls were restricted. Junior officers were kept busy clipping potentially revealing passages from outgoing mail. Weapons were cleaned, recleaned, and then cleaned again, just to be sure.

At the end of the month, Hack's outfit was moved from its Sherborne camp to a staging area just outside of Portsmouth. Everywhere one looked, in any direction, the roads and fields were filled with men and materials.

The rain and fog visited them all regularly. In Supreme Headquarters, the various commanders were anxious about weather forecasts, as bad weather was the only thing which could impede, even temporarily, the embarkation of this vast conglomeration of men and equipment for the enemy-occupied mainland. General Eisenhower, Supreme Commander of all Allied forces, worried more than anyone. He knew that his troops were as ready as they could get, and that every delay because of inclement weather would tend to dull the edge of their resolve.

Finally, the long awaited, and also the long dreaded day arrived. Eisenhower pushed the "Go" button and the expedition was under way. Shortly after dawn on the fifth of June 1944, huge numbers of the attack force, including the US 4th Infantry Division, sailed from Portsmouth harbor. And, attached to its 8th Regiment, the green but nervously willing 2886th Signal Battalion rode with them. The crossing was fairly rough, and this, in combination with the anxiety over what lay ahead, emptied a great many stomachs long before the trip was finished. By the time "H hour" arrived on June 6, a numb resignation had enveloped the minds of thousands of troops so that they clambered down the nets, rode the bouncing, heaving landing craft, and splashed into the water and onto the beach in an almost total daze, legs and arms operating entirely by rote.

Compared to the landing at other preassigned beaches, particularly that of their brother Americans at "Omaha," Hack's division had it fairly easy. They were assigned to storm "Utah" beach, the westernmost of the five Allied landing points, on the Cherbourg Peninsula, and this turned out to be the one which offered the least resistance from the German defenders. Their installations had been hit hard by the offshore naval batteries, leaving the survivors too stunned to react as savagely as would normally have been expected. In addition, the heavy tides had pushed the Utah assault over a mile south of the intended landing area to a point where the coast was somewhat less heavily defended.

The circumstances of this operation were entirely different from Hack's combat experience in North Africa. For the first time, he knew the gut-wrenching fear that grips any intelligent soldier in a beach-storming situation. By its very nature, such an attack exposes the invaders to murderous fire, with no opportunity to return it. There is usually no place to hide. The only possible relief lies in the direction of the enemy rather than away from it. Therefore, it is essential to reach the beach quickly to attain whatever cover presents itself. The few minutes, which seem hours long, spent in wading desperately through what seems like twenty miles of water, is probably as agonizing as any time anyone will ever spend. It is, for all the world, like the nightmare encounters everyone has had. The water thwarts all efforts to hurry through it exactly as some unseen force locks the legs in an immobilizing grip in a bad dream, permitting only feeble and agonizingly slow progress. The difference is that in a nightmare, one is running *away* from ones attacker—here, one is forced to move *toward* him!

Because Hack was busy urging on some of the petrified members of his communications teams, he did hot have time to dwell on his own fear. As he helped a T5 burdened with a field radio to struggle through the waves, another of his men, Corporal Henley, a wire man from Oklahoma, received a fatal wound within a few feet of them. But they were in the second wave of invaders, about ten minutes behind the first wave, and the defenders' fire was concentrated primarily on those already ashore.

With the exception of Henley, all of Hack's men reached the shelter of the dunes beyond the beach with no worse than a few minor wounds, and they immediately proceeded to try to establish communications according to a preassigned Standard Operating Procedure (SOP). The 8th Regiment continued to press forward with the rest of the Division, units of which continued to come ashore for some time. By midday, three exits from the beach were in their hands. The Atlantic Wall had been breached along a two-mile front by tanks and infantry by 9 a.m., and the rest was just hard fighting which steadily pushed the Germans away from the shoreline.

For the next few hours, Hack's outfit continued to advance slowly, moving from one area of shelter to another, and trying to maintain contact with other elements of the Division. The next day, the invaders from the sea linked up with units of the 82nd Airborne, which had landed further inland. By this time, Allied air power had taken control of the skies over a wide band inward from the coastline and was wreaking havoc on motorized columns of Germans belatedly endeavoring to come to the aid of the defenders above the beaches.

Each day that passed brought more and more supplies and men and equipment to the landing areas and bolstered and solidified the Allied claim to an ever-increasing area of France. There were many skirmishes and some full-fledged battles, such as occurred when German and British or German and American armor clashed, with the Germans claiming victory in some and the Allies in others. However, regardless of the importance of the tanks and artillery, it always befell the long-suffering foot soldiers to follow up and consolidate the gains made, and often to do it all on their own.

The hedgerows of the French villages were the trenches of World War 2 France, hiding a defending or retreating German unit until the Allied infantrymen could rout them out through surrender or annihilation. As elements of the 2886th moved forward with the 8th Regiment, they often found themselves temporarily separated from others. Occasionally, they were isolated for short periods of time. The GIs usually knew toward what city they were advancing, but the names of the villages all sort of ran together in their minds, if, indeed, they were even told their names. Signposts were mostly useless. The retreating Germans either destroyed them or altered the direction in which they pointed, in an effort to confuse and delay their pursuers. It was thus that Hack and one of his signalmen, Private Shortt, found themselves alone on a road one day, rapidly moving east in a 6 x 6 truck which carried needed wire, hoping and expecting to make contact with G Company of the 8th, which should have been advancing on a route parallel to their own. As they moved forward, Hack caught a glimpse of motion on the other side of a hedgerow ahead and to their left. He quickly grabbed the arm of the driver, Shortt, saying, "Hold it! There's someone behind that row, and it's got to be Germans. Hit the deck!"

Shortt jammed on the brakes and dove for the ditch, all in one motion, while Hack dove for the ditch on his side. He slid under the truck on his belly and joined the driver.

"Lay low," Hack whispered. "They had to hear the truck, so they're playing possum, waiting for us to present a target. Work your way back in this ditch for about fifty yards—quiet! I'm right behind you. Let's go!"

They wormed their way back as rapidly as possible until Hack finally whispered, "Okay—hold it."

"What now, Sarge?" whispered the driver, trembling with fright.

"Now, we wait for them to make the next move. I expect to see some grenades come flying over pretty quick, since they didn't get a chance to shoot at us as we went by. They'll try for the truck, I think, figuring that we're still in it or under it. Can't be more than two or three of them, or they would have come out shooting. Keep under cover here the best you can. If they throw grenades, they'll wait a minute after they explode and then come through to be sure they got us. Be ready with your carbine, and *don't miss*! If nothing happens, I'm going to sneak up and try to get a peek under the hedgerow."

Shortt, hands trembling, pushed his carbine into firing position. Sweat stood out on his forehead and ran down his nose. Hack looked at him.

"You got a problem, buddy?" he asked.

The driver cringed. Then, he said, his voice shaky, "I don't know if I can do it, Sarge. I don't think I can shoot a man!"

At that moment, two hand grenades came sailing over the hedgerow. One landed on the truck's canvas canopy and bounced off, exploding as it hit the ground. The other bounced on the ground ahead of the truck and then exploded. The two men in the ditch had flattened themselves as much as possible with their heads down. The shrapnel from the grenades whistled overhead, through the branches of the hedge and against the metal body of the truck. Nothing hit them.

"Lie still," Hack ordered, "but shoot when they come through."

After a long five or ten seconds, a helmeted head poked through, peering at the truck, and shortly, another followed. Then they stepped out, rifles at the ready, and moved cautiously toward the silent vehicle.

"Now!" cried Hack, and his own piece barked. Down went one of the soldiers. The other instantly started to swing toward the recumbent Americans, but before he could fire, Hack's carbine cracked again. The rifle flew out of the German's hands and he toppled backward over his fallen comrade.

All was quiet in the ditch for ten or fifteen seconds.

"You realize you almost got us killed?" asked Hack calmly. "Why the hell didn't you fire?"

"I—I'm sorry, Sarge! I tried to, but I just couldn't pull that trigger back!"

Hack grabbed Shortt's carbine and glanced at it.

"Maybe it would have helped if you had released the safety," he snarled sarcastically.

"Oh, Jesus!" Shortt breathed.

Hack looked him straight in the eye and said, "You're going to wait while I take a peek through that hedge to make sure there aren't any more of those birds. When I tell you it's all clear, go up carefully and shoot that second one again in the chest. I don't think I killed him."

Shortt gasped, and a look of consternation widened his eyes.

"And that, my friend, is an order," Hack added coldly.

Then, he turned and slithered up out of the gutter and was soon out of sight under the hedge. In a few moments, the shivering driver heard him call, "Okay—all clear over here."

Shortt wondered what he was to do. His heart was beating like a triphammer, and it was hard for him to breathe. He had dreaded the moment when he might have to kill an enemy soldier, and he had failed to do so at a critical moment. But to do what the sergeant was asking seemed infinitely worse—it was murder! But then, what was all of this killing and slaughtering? Wasn't it all murder? he asked himself. And what had the two Germans tried to do to them? Worst of all, what would this cold-blooded sergeant do if he failed to carry out the order? Turn him in? Have him court-martialed? The bastard probably would! A wave of hatred for the sergeant welled up in him, bringing bile up into his throat and tears of rage to his eyes. He scrambled to his feet and trotted the fifty yards to where the Germans lay. Eyes streaming, expletives tumbling from his mouth, he snapped off the safety, pointed the carbine down at the chest of the victim and pulled the trigger. Then he spun around and ran back to the ditch, where he fell on his knees, retching.

When the spasm subsided he returned to the truck and started inspecting the damage done by the grenades. Hack returned and did the same. Miraculously, none of the tires were punctured. There were lots of holes in the doors and fenders, but when they climbed in and hit the starter, the vehicle responded as though nothing had happened.

"That's a relief. Let's get going," Hack ordered. They rode silently for a little while, eyes and ears tuned for more enemy troops, but they encountered none, and shortly at a crossroad they joined up with the infantry unit they had been expecting. They stayed with them for the remainder of the afternoon and stopped to rest, reconnoiter and partake of a makeshift meal at dusk. If all went well, they would pick up the main road and the rest of their regiment in the morning.

Hack sought out his driver, who was making a point of avoiding him.

"Look, kid, you don't know it, but you didn't kill anyone. I hit that Kraut right in the forehead—he was dead before he hit the ground. All you did was put a meaningless bullet into a dead man. The point is, you aimed your carbine at him and pulled the trigger, which you didn't think you would be able to do. Next time, you'll find it's not that hard. They're going to try their damnedest to kill you, and if you hesitate like you did back there, you're going home in a box. Now, do you understand why I had you do that, or not?"

The lad spent a few long moments letting what Hack had said sink in, then he nodded. Finally, he said, "You knew I'd be pissed off at you, didn't you, Sarge? Enough so that I'd go up and shoot that guy. I see what you mean. I won't make that mistake again, believe me. Thanks. And thanks for killing the one I should have shot!"

"Okay, kid. Chalk it up to experience. Nobody in his right mind wants to kill anyone, but now it's them or us—we don't have any choice. I want you and all my men to finish this war alive. Just stay loose, that's all."

Shortt watched Hack as he walked away, thinking to himself, "What a hard-boiled guy! The fact that he snuffed out two lives this afternoon isn't a burden on his conscience, at all. And he's right—it's us or them. It'll be different next time I'm in that kind of a fix!"

Chapter 21
Survival

Once the initial frantic, hectic operations of the invading forces were over and it was apparent that the Allies were in France to stay, the battle of strategies between generals began to take shape. Availability of troops, equipment and supplies was assessed. Objectives at all levels were defined; arrangements for naval and air support were laid out, and commanders at various levels were notified as to what was expected of them and what they could expect from others. Finally, when all the plans were set and all the orders were issued, everyone crossed his fingers and hoped that at least some of the desired results would actually come to pass.

Unfortunately, things seldom work out according to plan, especially in the military. Here, a road shown on the map turns up missing, there an instruction is misinterpreted, elsewhere, an essential vehicle breaks down, and in another sector, the vital air or artillery cover fails to materialize. The logistics of propelling hundreds of thousands of men forward as rapidly as possible against a bitterly resisting, well trained and well equipped enemy are overwhelming. And the task is made no less difficult when the attacking forces are made up of armies from a number of countries whose moves must be carefully coordinated, and the jealousies and egos of whose commanders must be evaluated and catered to, so that each is convinced that his is the most important role in the operation.

Throughout the summer of 1944, the British, Americans and Canadians advanced, fought, fell back and advanced again. Although they won some battles and lost others, on balance they continued to build their advantage. Steadily, the Allies gained superiority in the air, and as they did so, the armies on the ground found their missions more manageable.

When the Allied columns broke out of the hedgerows of Normandy and into the more open countryside of Brittany, they often moved forward so fast that they lost contact with their counterparts. The backpack-toted or low-powered vehicular-carried radios of units such as Hack's were useful only over short distances, and unless they had time to stop and set up one of the larger transmitters, it was easy to outrun the signaling range. The danger of encountering and engaging in battle with friends rather than foes was always present. All too often, the speed of the advance caused tragic mistakes, such as the bombing mission during which Lieutenant General Lesley McNair and 110 other American soldiers were killed when the bombs ticketed for the Germans fell on American troops instead.

On August 25, 1944, one of the main objectives, at least psychologically, was realized with the liberation of Paris. The leaders arranged that the French 2nd Armored Division led the way into the city, thereby permitting their countrymen to pretend that French forces were largely responsible for the victory. Early in September 1944, the Allies drove into Belgium, liberated Brussels on the 3rd, and one day later captured the vital port city of Antwerp, sorely needed as a point of entry for ships laden with the vast quantities of supplies and men destined for the advancing armies.

The juggernaut continued to gain momentum through the fall months. The air assaults on Germany were taking a huge toll, and everyone began to realize who was winning the war. Everyone, that is, except Hitler, who still clung stubbornly to a pretended belief in the invincibility of the Wehrmacht and the Luftwaffe.

From mid-December through mid-January, the famous Battle of the Bulge, around Bastogne, Belgium, was the center of everyone's attention. While it exacted a terrible toll of lives on both sides, its successful conclusion by the Allies was a mortal blow to the Germans.

Following this battle, the push was on to carry the war to the Nazi homeland. The offensive designed to reach the Rhine river, symbol of German security, began in February 1945, and was hard fought through mid-March. On March 22, General Patton crossed the Rhine at Oppenheim, beating the British under Montgomery, who crossed north of Ruhr on the 23rd, by one day, much to the satisfaction of the former, who, in addition to being a tremendous warrior, was perhaps the largest ego in the entire war zone, probably outdone in that respect only by Montgomery himself.

April saw many events of historical significance. On the 12th, President Roosevelt died and was succeeded by Harry Truman. On the 23rd, the Russians entered Berlin; on the 26th, the Allies captured Bremen. On the

28th, Mussolini was executed by Italian partisans, and on the 30th, Hitler committed suicide in his secret bunker in Berlin. Thus, within the space of three weeks, the lives of the leaders of the United States, Italy and Germany, all of whom had played major roles in the war, came to an end, and none of them would witness the actual cessation of hostilities.

On May 7, 1945, Germany formally surrendered, and May 8th was declared VE Day.

Throughout the drive from Utah Beach through Normandy, Brittany, Belgium, Eastern France and deep into Germany, Hack's signal unit managed to hold together, although it sustained many casualties and shrunk in size as the campaigns wore on. Replacements arrived periodically and were absorbed into the battalion and quickly picked up the routines established by the battle-seasoned veterans. "Old-timers," like Hack, reached the point where they did not worry too much about being killed during relatively limited-sized firefights and skirmishes with similar units of Axis soldiers. They became expert at moving from building to building, wall to wall and cellar to cellar in town and city engagements. They knew how to be shrewd and crafty—how to make the best possible use of whatever cover was available, when to attack and when it was wiser to lie low; in short, they knew how to be survivors. It was the shelling by artillery and the bombing and strafing by aircraft which they dreaded most, for there was little that could be done then but to get behind or under something substantial and hope that they would not be victims of a direct hit. They suffered along, eating cold canned rations much of the time. At night, they curled up in a shell hole or a foxhole which they had dug, or in a deserted or bombed out building. At times, they slept in the back of a vehicle or on top of a tank where the warmth from the recently run engine lingered, or occasionally in the luxury of a barn with hay or straw for a mattress. But the discomforts and inconveniences any GI experienced were softened to a degree by the fact that they were shared by so many others.

When the announcement came that Germany had surrendered, it seemed almost too good to be true. Celebrations began immediately. Any thing which could be found with an alcoholic content was consumed, everyone hugged everyone else, and many tears of joy and thankfulness were shed. After years of apprehension and doubt, it was at last possible to stand up and walk or drive a vehicle without having to expect to be shot at or bombed.

The sense of relief would have been complete were it not for the fact that there was still a war being fought on the other side of the world, and some GIs would probably be transferred to that theater.

But for Hack, the war was really over. He had accumulated enough "points" through time served and battle stars and decorations won to qualify for return to the United States. He was notified of his good fortune shortly after VE Day, and by the second week in June, he was on his way back to home and family. Nothing in his later life would ever move him as much as did the sight of the Statue of Liberty with the New York skyline behind it as his ship sailed into the harbor. At last, it was really, honestly and completely over.

Chapter 22
Home Again

The day all veterans of World War 2 longed for finally arrived for Hack. After two short days of processing at Fort Devens and an unsuccessful attempt to convince him to reenlist or, if not that, to sign up for the reserves, Hack accepted his discharge and his "Ruptured Duck" emblem for his lapel, shook the dust of Army life from him, and headed for home.

His return to Newvale was welcomed by friends and acquaintances. When he alighted from the bus, all of his family and friends and a number of other townspeople, including the first selectman, were there to greet him. The selectman and a disabled veteran of World War 1, now commander of the local American Legion post, gave brief welcoming speeches. A gift of money was presented to him, and everyone joined in a loud three cheers for the returning hero. Hack waved and smiled and pretended to be appreciative, but he really was impatient to go home, change into civilian clothes, and relax with Libby and the family. When the brief ceremony was over and he was seated inside his father's car, he heaved a long sigh of relief. He pulled Libby over close to him and just let her nearness and the unbelievably good smell of her drive away the tension.

At home, he excused himself and ran up the stairs to his room. His mother had everything in place, just as he had left it, as he knew she would. He sat on the bed and drank in all of the familiar appointments—the dresser, the easy chair, the wallpaper depicting baseball players in various action situations, the curled snapshots stuck in the frame of the mirror, the high school and college banners on the wall, the framed graduation picture of Libby, and the rack with his beloved .22 pump gun. How delicate and graceful it looked after years of handling Army weapons. And how he loved this room! It took him only five minutes to steep himself again in its ambience. It worked like the reassuring touch of a mother on a toddler's head. He was surprised and almost a little ashamed that he had needed this confirming revival of the dormant memories of his past life.

Down in the living room, everyone waited expectantly, and Hack soon joined them. Melody was fairly bursting with love, pride and happiness. Only a mother could understand the cold, clammy depths of fear and dread engendered by having a son thousands of miles away for years in the middle of a violent conflict. Now that he had survived and returned to them, delight and thankfulness lifted her to equally exaggerated heights.

"Christopher, deah, you can't possibly know how eternally grateful we ah to God that you have come home to us safely. Ah've longed fo' this day so much, an' Ah've fairly worn the skin off ma po' knees prayin' that you would come home again. Ah think we should all bow ouah heads fo' jus' a few moments and give thanks fo' yoah deliverance."

And so they did.

"Now," Melody continued, "why don't you jus' tell us anything at all about yoah adventures that you'd like to shaah with us? Ah'm suah—jus' whatevah you want to get off yoah chest."

Hack hesitated. Then he said, very seriously, "If you don't mind, Mom, I'd rather not get started on that right now. I'm just so damned happy to be home and to see all you folks, I'm much more interested in what's happening around here. I do have a few little souvenirs to pass out to you, but aside from that, how about just letting the war stories come out when something reminds me of them, okay? And, how about us grabbing some chow? I'm dying for some of Mom's cooking. Didn't I smell pie when we came in?"

Everyone laughed and Melody cried, "You sho'ly did, darlin'—I baked the biggest ol' pecan pie you evah saw, an' it's sittin' out in the kitchen jus' waitin' fo' you! An' nobody else gets a piece until you've had all you can eat!"

They all jumped up and headed for the kitchen where the huge pie sat resplendent on the counter. John stepped forward, picked up a knife, and said, "Well, since my wife is the clever one who concocts these delicious things, I'm at least going to get in on the glory by serving it to you, Hack!"

And he proceeded to cut out a wedge which reduced the pie by one-third.

"Wait a minute, deah," Melody piped, "theah's whipped cream in the fridge," and she took it out and deposited a huge dollop on top of the pie.

While Hack quickly reduced it to crumbs, everyone else seemed to be talking at once. The slight embarrassed restraint which had hung in the air when they first assembled in the living room, gradually dissipated. By the time they had chided Hack for taking a second piece, things seemed to be back to normal. However, it would be months before any of them felt totally at ease with him, because they knew that he had seen an aspect of life that was beyond their imaginations, and that there would always be an area of his life which they could not share with him on an equal footing.

The days following Hack's discharge and his return to Newvale were almost a blur. There was so much to do—so many really important threads to be picked up and so many new ones to be set into the pattern, that it was difficult to know what to do first. It was most important, first of all, to reestablish his relationship with Libby. Then, with her, he needed to start organizing his marital, social and financial aspirations for the future. Next, it was important for him to reclaim his job, and while all of these were occupying him, he needed to work at readjusting to civilian life.

The top of the list proved to be no problem at all. Libby was right there eagerly waiting for him, just as she had promised to be, and his heart swelled with love and thankfulness every time he saw her or heard her voice. It took only one meeting away from the rest of the doting family and friends to confirm beyond any doubt that their mutual devotion was secure.

Libby had graduated with honors from Middlebury College. Although her main ambition was to be married and start a family, she realized that she was not willing to drop the academic scene completely. The possibility of becoming involved as an instructor, even if only as a substitute, struck her as a logical compromise. To accomplish this, she was taking the courses which would be required to obtain certification to teach at the elementary level.

Hack had not been home two days before he felt an urgent need to confirm his position with Hartshorn & Co. Although he had a date to meet Libby downtown, he could not resist stopping at the factory to say hello.

From the window, Fred Hartshorn saw him coming and hurried to meet him at the door.

"Christopher!" he shouted. "What a sight for sore eyes! I knew you were home and hoped you would be along to see me, but I really didn't expect you quite this soon. Terrific to see you! You look pretty fine to me—I expected to see you pale and thin and limping, but here you are, looking fit as a fiddle! This is wonderful!"

"Gee, it's great to see you, too, Fred! You wouldn't believe how much I've missed this place. Newvale is a pretty small spot on the map, I've discovered, but that doesn't make it any less attractive. Man, am I glad to be home!"

"Come in and sit down, Hack, and I'll fill you in on what we've been doing since you left. Or, it can wait, if you have a lot of other things on your schedule."

"I'm anxious to hear about the shop and what has been going on, but I am due to meet someone in fifteen minutes. I just couldn't stay away from here any longer, so I stole a few minutes to see you and to make sure my job is still available. I sure hope it is," said Hack questioningly.

"Oh, yes—by all means! I promised to let you pick up where you left off, and I certainly plan to do so. I wouldn't feel very patriotic if I failed to offer a returning hero the job he left to defend the country, and in your case, I'd be stupid, as well! You're still my boy, Hack, and the job is waiting for you whenever you're ready."

"That's great," said Hack. "How about Monday?"

It was now Friday.

Mr. Hartshorn's mouth started to drop open, but then he laughed and said, "Are you serious?"

"Why?" asked Hack, with a slight frown. "Is that too soon?"

Hartshorn, still smiling, shook his head and clapped his hand on Hack's shoulder. "Not a damned bit too soon, Hack—not a damned bit!"

"Great," said Hack. "I'll be here by 7:30 Monday morning, rarin' to go!"

With that, he turned and left without stepping into the plant or exchanging greetings with anyone else.

Hartshorn stepped to the window and gazed at the retreating figure. He mused about Hack. It was hard to believe that this young fellow had left only a few short years ago for the greatest of all wars, had learned how to kill, had been sent into an active theater, exposed to the unthinkable trials of modern warfare, had been seriously wounded and had doubtless wounded or killed some of the enemy, and was now back, acting as though the only thing of importance to him was the operation of this little hole-in-the-wall factory. It appeared to Hartshorn that none of Hack's experiences seemed to be worthy of discussion—not the training nor the travel nor the friends he had made nor the horrors he had witnessed. Hack simply wanted to get back to work. The four years at war were merely an aggravating interruption of Hack's career, like a two week bout with poison ivy or a bad case of the flu. Hartshorn shrugged his shoulders and slowly shook his head from side to side.

"Youth," he thought. "What a wonderful thing it is!"

Chapter 23
Nuptials

Hack met Libby at the drug store. After placing their order for milkshakes, they walked back and sat down in the area where there were a few little tables and chairs with twisted wire legs and backs.

"You know, hon, it probably sounds simple and silly, but you wouldn't believe how many times in the past couple of years I have daydreamed about walking in here with you for a milkshake or a banana split. I could close my eyes and almost smell the place and taste that good cold, sweet ice cream on my tongue. Dumb, huh?"

Libby reached over and clasped his hand—an unusually forward move for her in a public place—and said, softly, "I think that's beautiful, Christopher. Those are the sorts of little things that mean so much to sensitive people."

Her bottom lip quivered as she looked into his eyes. "I love you, and I missed you so much. I prayed so hard for this day, and now it's here! No matter what happens now, I'll be eternally grateful that you were able to come back to me. We mustn't let any of this happiness slip away."

"You're absolutely right, Lib. Now that I'm back and Mr. Hartshorn says I can go right back to work, let's not waste any time about getting married. How about working out all the details right away, can you?"

Libby looked startled. She laughed and said, "Why, Mr. Hacker, is that a proposal?"

Hack smiled back and then said, soberly, "It sure is, Libby. I thought it was already understood, but now I'm making it official. How about it?"

"Well, first, just to confirm things, the answer to your unstated question is, 'Yes, I will marry you.' As to when; well, I don't really know how long it will take to make all the preparations. How about some time around the end of September? Do you think that would be okay with everyone?"

"September! That's three months away! What's the matter with next week?"

Now, Libby threw back her head and laughed gaily. "Christopher, don't you know that women have all kinds of things to do to prepare for a wedding? Do you think it's just a matter of saying, 'Meet me at the church at seven and we'll get married'?"

Hack replied, impatiently, "Well, if it isn't, it should be. Let's put it this way. If you rush it just as fast as you possibly can, how soon could it be?"

Libby pondered for a few moments. "I really don't know. But I'll get right at finding out. Let me talk to my mother and Biddy Marshall. Biddy knows I want her for my main attendant, so she's probably got some ideas already, and we have to make sure any date we fix doesn't conflict with her schedule. And we will have to talk to the priest and clear up the religious end of it, since you are not Catholic. Does that part bother you, dear?"

"Nothing bothers me except anything that delays our getting married. I've waited for you too long already, and I'm not about to wait any longer than absolutely necessary. You must realize that, honey."

"Of course, Christopher. I am as anxious as you are. Let me get busy right away—like, tonight!"

They turned their attention to the milkshakes. Hack never remembered anything tasting so delicious.

Because of Hack's status as one of the town's leading heroes and the popularity and admiration which Libby had always enjoyed, everyone was thrilled with the announcement of their engagement. Everyone who was asked to make any preparations for the wedding was happy to give it first priority. As a result, they were able to set a very early date, six weeks later, on August 10. Moe Penning, whose asthma had kept him from being sent overseas, was able to get leave for the occasion to serve as best man. Two other friends from high school, Charlie Davis and Walt Stanevich, were available as ushers. Libby's cortege consisted of her best friend, Biddy, as maid of honor, her college roommate, Suzie Pemberton, and her cousin, Kate O'Connor, as bridesmaids, and her little six-year-old cousin, Debbie Mulcahy, as flower girl.

August 10, 1945, was sunny, although very warm, and the priest performed the marriage ceremony with the practiced air of borderline reluctance proper for indicating that he did not really approve of Libby's choice of a Protestant as a mate. The ceremony went smoothly; no one fainted and the best man did not lose the ring.

The reception was a gala affair. Because it was only three months after the German surrender and the war in the Pacific appeared to be nearly over, everyone was in a festive mood. Many of the guests overdid the celebrating. Foremost among them was the bride's grandfather, the patriarch Mulcahy himself, who exhibited remarkable stamina and capacity for a man of his advanced years. At first, both Libby and her mother were concerned and embarrassed by his behavior, but his Irish good humor and whiskey tenor charmed and entertained more of the guests than were put off by his antics. Seeing this, the ladies relaxed and enjoyed his shenanigans with the rest.

"Who'll jine me in a toast to me darlin' and bee-ootiful granddaughter, Mrs. Christopher Hacker?" he bellowed, after the more formal toasts and obligatory remarks of the best man had been presented. He waved his glass above his head and everyone drank and cheered.

"And now, a toast to the lucky fella himself, Christopher. May he live and prosper and make me a great-granddad soon!"

At short intervals for the next hour, Mulcahy popped up with toasts for the parents, the attendants, individually, the Army, the Navy, the poor departed President Roosevelt, President Truman, this glorious country, and even the priest. And, to cap the performance, he toasted, tearfully, the hand of the master distiller "who blended this darlin', darlin' whiskey," following which he sat down and quietly went to sleep.

After the dinner was eaten and the drinks were drunk, the dances were danced, and the hugging and kissing and the crying were over, the young couple dashed for their car through a shower of rice and confetti and shouts and laughter, and left to a chorus of jumping and bouncing and dragging old shoes and tin cans and paper streamers and auto horns, with the traditional words, "Just Married," scrawled across the luggage compartment. And one by one, as the distance from the scene of the celebration increased, the cars in their wake stopped blowing their horns and dropped out of the chase, until the newlyweds were finally on the road alone.

As soon as Hack could find an appropriate spot, he pulled off the road and he and Libby removed as much of the junk as they could. Then they climbed back in the car, laughed, and fell into each other's arms for a long embrace before starting their honeymoon journey.

Chapter 24
Settling Down

The early days of Hack's and Libby's marriage were packed with excitement, discovery and joy. The thrill of living together and managing their own affairs was a challenge they savored. There were so many details to be taken care of, including the arrangement of furnishings and establishment of workable routines, that each day seemed to end shortly after it began.

It was delightful to realize that they no longer had to be apart from each other at the end of the day. They were now a unit. One's concern was the other's; their bliss was fully shared. In the physical expressions of love to which Libby would not consent during their courtship, she now cooperated graciously and openly, and Hack, although gentle, availed himself of them greedily and reveled in them. For both, it was a time of teaching and of learning. Although it was impossible for Libby to eliminate completely all of her guilty feelings, Hack was able sometimes to coax her gradually into brief repudiation of her inhibitions and so to experience the ecstatic pinnacles of passion. At such times, her religion and her respect for her parents' morality seemed to hover over her like disembodied censors. Although she had been thoroughly exposed to frank and explicit discussions of sex while she was away at college, her inbred Puritanism lurked always in the background, whispering subtle suggestions that the act of sex was basically dirty.

Hack was smugly satisfied with himself because he had been able to resist the temptation of premarital promiscuity. He was proud that he had successfully withstood the wiles of Brenda, the London prostitute. He seemed to forget that it was the shock of the squalid apartment and the revelation of her personal unattractiveness in the harsh light of the gas lamp which had altered his plans for her. As for the episode with Sally Finch, he rationalized that it was actually not his fault, but merely a rebellious and capricious reaction, inaugurated by her and justified by their mutually miserable situation. So, in his mind, he had entered the nuptial chamber as virginal as was his bride. No pangs of conscience diluted the purity he was able to convince himself that he had brought to the union.

Although the early stages of their marriage were as steeped in sensuality as might be expected of newlyweds, the lust after money which had haunted Hack since childhood, was still foremost in his mind. He threw himself into his work at the plant with such enthusiasm and dedication that Fred Hartshorn was amazed. No facet of the business was drab or uninspiring to Hack; if there was a reason for an operation to be performed, he wanted to know that reason and understand it. If it was of a relatively complex mechanical nature, he would study it over and over until he thoroughly understood it. If it was mathematical or literal, he addressed it briefly and locked it away in his excellent memory.

In one of their talk sessions, Hack told Hartshorn frankly that his goal in life was to become extremely rich.

"Well, Hack, I'm not sure you picked the right field if that is your ambition. There must be lots of other ways to make money easier than this, and faster, too."

"Oh, I'm not so sure about that," Hack said. "Not just producing a few million parts that someone else designed and will sell as part of his product-- that isn't what I mean. It's the chance to develop new methods or new products that makes manufacturing exciting. Do you know Mr. Borgeson, Mr. Ingmar Borgeson, who has the big place up on Brown's hill?"

"Yes, I know him. Real nice old fellow, but not much of a talker. His son, Teodor, too. He's just like him. I understand they really hit it big in the automotive field."

"Well, it was the old gent who made the money," Hack went on. "He came over here from Sweden as a young fellow. He learned the toolmaker's trade in Germany. When he was working out in Detroit, he developed a carburetor with some unusual features that he was able to patent and he sold it to General Motors for a fortune. That's the way to do it—develop something that the big boys need and make them pay you for the rest of your natural!"

Hartshorn smiled.

"Lots of luck, Hack. How did you happen to find this out about Borgeson?"

"I did some research. I looked into the backgrounds of all the rich families in town, especially the Borgesons, the Jays and the Lamsons. The Jays made their money in shipping and the Lamsons in trading with the Indians. That sort of thing would be kind of hard to do nowadays, so I'm more interested in the Borgesons. I don't see why I couldn't do as well as they did. At least, I can sort of think along those lines. Can't do any harm, can it?"

"No," answered Fred, "I guess it can't do any harm at all. But aren't you interested in running a plant like this? I thought that was your ambition at one time."

Hack did a bit of rapid backpedaling. He did not want to give Mr. Hartshorn reason to think he was looking for something else.

"Oh, I'm just dreaming. I figure it can't do any harm to see how some of the wealthy people got where they are. I don't mean that I wouldn't want to operate a nice business like this—I sure would, and I hope some day I can. That's another way to be successful—get into a proven business that you can handle and run it right, so you can make a good living, and if it grows, you can get rich at that, too. But you've got to keep your eyes open just in case that big break comes along. Can't be sleeping at the switch, right?"

"That's right, Hack." Hartshorn chuckled. "And if I know you, I very much doubt they'll ever catch you asleep!"

"Well, got to get back to work," Hack said, as he rose from the chair and stretched. "I want to be sure that order for Hammond Company gets off the platform tonight. I'm sure Hammond will give us more business when they see that job. It's perfect."

He left the office and headed for the shipping department. "Got to watch my mouth," he thought.

Chapter 25
The Letters

When Hack arrived home from work one evening, he followed his normal routine of picking up the daily newspaper and the mail from the corner of the kitchen counter where Libby always deposited them after sorting out the letters, bills and magazines.

"How's everything tonight, hon?" he asked, giving her a hug and a kiss, and starting to riffle through the several envelopes.

"Fine, dear," Libby replied. Then as he started toward the living room where he could peruse the mail and newspaper at his leisure, she added, with a smile, "I see you have a letter from England. One of your old girl friends, perhaps?"

A premonitory chill ran up the middle of his back, and he felt the blood rising to his face. "Christ!" he thought, "who could that be from, except Sally, and if Sally, why would she be writing after all this time?" He forced a laugh, and replied, "Oh, really? Probably one of that long string of sweethearts I had."

He spotted the letter. It was from Winchester and bore, in the upper left hand corner, the return address, Finch, 10 Robin Lane, Damien Road, Winchester, G.B. He said to himself, "Sally, for sure. Shit!" Aloud, his voice carefully under control, he said, "Oh, that's nice. It's from the Finches—you know—the ones I told you about that were so good to me while I was stationed over there. Hope it's not bad news about Mr. Finch, or anything like that."

He dropped into his easy chair, pulled out his pocket knife, and nervously slit the envelope open. He had a feeling that it was not going to be good news.

My Dear Hack, the letter began.

It seems a very long time since we last saw you, though, actually, it is a matter of only a few years.

You must think it strange that I should write you now, but it will come clear to you shortly. I had wanted to write you earlier, but at Sally's insistence, I forebore.

You see, after you had left with the invasion forces, our Sally made the shocking discovery that she had become pregnant. She withheld the truth from us for as long as she was able, but eventually had no choice but to confess. She assured us that only you, in whom we had had such faith and trust, could be the father.

Of course, the whole matter was rather like a lightning bolt to Mr. Finch and myself, and just another hard blow of fate for poor Sally. After our initial shock, and when she had explained the circumstances, in all fairness, we were forced to agree that we understood how this had occurred. The shock of losing poor Richard and then the added blow of your imminent departure, when she needed you to buoy her up, caused her to rebel against her sea of troubles in the completely untypical way that she did. And, Hack, although we might have hoped that you would be strong enough h to dissuade her (she insists that the decision was her initiative) on honest reflection, we came to realize that your position, too, was rather desperate and one of perhaps little hope, which argues that your complicity is understandable, even if not, strictly speaking, forgivable.

The birth of the child, an event of February 20, 1945, drove any bitterness from us, for he (yes, it is a boy) immediately captured our hearts in the way that lovely infants will. Sally christened him Spenser Joseph Finch. He weighed well over half a stone (eight and one half pounds, by your reckoning.) He is quite fair, with light brown hair and blue eyes, and is handsome and bright by any measure. Now, at nearly four years, he is dashing about the cottage, bringing joy and light to every corner.

Dear Hack, please do not misunderstand my purpose in sending you this letter. We are quite at peace with the situation here as it is at present, and you certainly mustn't interpret this as a request for aid in any form. Sally has returned to work and we have, between us, sufficient wherewithal. As our only grandchild, the lamb will benefit, through Sally, from whatever we are able to leave, and though it is modest, it will be adequate at least until he is on his own. It is simply that I can't feel that it is right for you not to know, despite Sally's stubborn insistence that she prefers that you not be informed.

I can only hope that I have done right; if not, I pray that I may be forgiven.

No doubt, I should have explained how we knew that you had survived the invasion and subsequent fighting (for which we are all very thankful.) We have a friend who is fairly well placed in the military. He assured us that he could readily discover your fate, as they are still sorting out information on the Allied servicemen and have access to a great many records, including mustering out lists of the American army. We were greatly relieved when he informed us that your record was quite complete. Addresses at the time of discharge are included, and, knowing of your love for your native city, I trust that this will find you without difficulty.

Again, I sincerely hope that I have not done wrong in revealing this to you, Hack, but it seemed to me only proper, and now I am at peace with myself and my conscience is clear.

Please accept the good wishes of the Finches, with thanks for the pleasant times we had with you, and do not let this message prey heavily on your heart.

Fondly,

(signed) *Ethyl Spenser Finch.*

Hack sat numbly in his chair, the bombshell having temporarily deprived him of his senses. He thought to himself, "Sally, pregnant!? No—Sally, delivered of a child—his child! He, a father for several years without knowing it? He, with a little bastard boy toddling around in England? How the hell could this have happened!? Christ, he had resisted the urge all those months and the one and only time he slipped, he had to ring the damned bell! What kind of shitty luck was that? And, despite the tone of resignation in Mrs. Finch's letter, who knew that they might not change their minds and decide to shake him down in the future? What the hell was he supposed to do?"

Suddenly, Libby's voice came from the kitchen. "Was it an interesting letter from those English people, dear? It isn't any kind of trouble, is it?"

To himself, he lamented, "Oh, it was interesting, all right. Damned women, anyway!" Struggling to keep his voice steady, he replied, "Yeah, very nice. No, no trouble." He almost said, aloud, "What the hell trouble could it be to learn that you have a little bastard son?" then he did say, aloud, "It was from Mrs. Finch, just trying to get in touch for old times' sake. They all came through the rest of the war okay, and wanted to be sure I did, too."

"That is certainly very thoughtful of them, isn't it?" Libby asked. "They must have been really fine people. You'll have to write back and tell them what has been happening with you since you came home, won't you?"

"Oh, sure. I'll get around to it one of these days soon." To himself, "Don't hold your breath!"

But the more he thought about it, the more he was convinced that Libby was going to keep bringing the subject up until he did something about it. It would be better to have her think that he had taken care of it, so later in the evening, he sat down at the table and composed a letter. After it was finished, he asked Libby if she would like to hear what he had had to say, and of course, she said that she would.

"Okay, he said, "here goes." He started reading.

It was a real pleasure to receive your letter. It brought back many happy memories of the time I was fortunate enough to have spent with your family. Your hospitality to a lonesome soldier was something I shall never forget.

I am very thankful to learn that all of you came through the war unscathed. We were all surely very lucky.

You will be pleased to know that I found my family in good shape when I returned, and that my sweetheart, Libby, was waiting for me as she had promised. We wasted little time, and were married in August 1945. (I was discharged in June of that year.) We are very happy and are looking forward to settling down permanently here in Newvale and raising little Hackers, of which there are two, so far.

If by any chance, any of your family ever visit the United States, we shall insist that they stay with us for as long as they wish; we will never be able to repay your contribution to my welfare while in your country.

Give my very best to Sally and to Mr. Finch and my other friends in your neighborhood, and God bless you all,

Sincerely,
Hack

"Well, what do you think?"

"That is really very nice, dear," she said. "Very brief, but fine. You men never believe in wasting too many words, do you? No—I'm just kidding. I'm sure they will be thrilled to receive it."

"What more was I to say? I told them I'm back, I'm married, and I appreciate what they did for me during the war. What else should I have said?"

Libby laughed. "Not a thing. Of course, you never were the gushy type. That's one of the things that attracted me to you, I suppose. I'm sure it is just fine. And I am glad you decided not to postpone writing—you probably wouldn't have thought about it again for months, if I know you."

"Okay, hon. Well, it's done. I just wanted your seal of approval."

Libby said, "Just leave it on the kitchen table and I'll mail it when I go downtown in the morning, if you like."

"Oh, that's all right," Hack quickly responded. "I have to go to the post office early for something we're expecting at the shop, anyway, so I'll just take it along."

"Fine."

He carefully folded the letter, put it in the envelope, sealed it, and made a ceremony of being sure to get the foreign address correct, and to wonder out loud about how much postage it would require. Then he took both letters and secreted them in the pages of a book, where he was sure Libby would not accidentally run across them before he left in the morning.

The next day, after he had dressed and breakfasted and was ready to leave for work, he kissed Libby goodbye and started for the door.

"Did you remember your letter?" she asked.

"Yeah—got it right here in my pocket," he replied, patting his jacket.

He drove to the shop, walked through to the rear and out through the back door and to the incinerator, still smoldering with the previous day's trash, which the janitor had just carried out and burned.

He took both letters from his pocket, dropped them in, and watched until they were completely consumed by the fire.

Chapter 26
The Children

Although Libby and Hack wanted a family, they agreed that they would try to avoid starting one too soon, because they preferred to adjust to married life first. They had also decided, however, that they would not go to any great lengths to avoid having a child.

Within six months, Libby discovered that she was pregnant. Their first child was a boy, born on November 12, 1946. They named him Christopher Drummond Hacker Jr., to please Hack's family.

Chris Jr. was a bright, attractive youngster, quietly inquisitive about the world around him and quite shy. His mother, in particular, was very pleased when he gave evidence, even before reaching school age, of an unusual interest in and talent for music. As a toddler, he would pause in his play and listen intently whenever music issued from the radio. By age five, he was familiar with many songs and was able to sing them on key and in proper time. Hack was impressed when Libby pointed this out, but was more interested in little Chris' long fingers, which enabled him to grip and throw a ball with ease.

"This guy's going to be a pitcher and a quarterback," Hack told Libby with a smile. "I had the arm, but my fingers were too stubby. I couldn't hold a football comfortably without plenty of rosin on my fingers. Chris is going to have no trouble like that by the time he is in junior high!"

Libby laughed. "That's nice, dear, but I was thinking more along the lines of the music he loves so much. With his ear and those fingers, he'd be a natural for the piano."

Hack absorbed this thought and then said, "Well, guys tend to think of their sons first as athletes, not as musicians, but you're right—I'll bet he would do well at the piano."

The more Libby thought about this, the more she wondered if their appraisal was valid, so the next time she and Chris were at the church parish house, she led him over to the piano and tapped out a simple tune. It was his first direct contact with the instrument and he was enraptured. As soon as the notes began to flow out, he seemed to forget everything else and to concentrate his whole attention on them. His mother allowed him to touch the keys himself, which obviously delighted him. Rather than banging his way up and down the keyboard as most children would have done, he touched them softly, almost reverently, and coaxed rather than wrenched the tones from them. As each new note was produced, he drank it in and moved to the next. Libby was amazed at the love and respect he showed for the instrument. It was a toy beyond all other toys he had ever known. She let him fondle the keys for a few minutes and then eased him away, pleading that she needed to go home. He obeyed, but looked longingly over his shoulder as they left the room.

"You really enjoyed that, didn't you, Chris?" Libby asked as they were driving home.

The little boy's eyes lit up again as he replied, "Oh, yes, Mama! You can play any song you want if you have a piano, can't you?"

"Well, yes—if you know how to play it, you can," his mother answered, "but people who can play the piano have to take many, many lessons before they are able to make the music come out right. Do you think you might like to learn how to play, Chris?"

He bounced up and down on the car seat. "Would I! I don't think there's anything in the world I'd like more! Why don't we have a piano, Mama? Can we, please? Can I ask Daddy to buy one? Please!?"

Libby's first reaction was to say that pianos were too expensive and that they took up an inordinate amount of space in a small house such as theirs. But instead, she followed her normal practice of letting him down easy when he demanded something that he could not have.

"Perhaps some day, Chris. Right now, we have so many expenses and we are rather short of room at home. I promise that if and when it is practical, we will look into the possibility of having a piano."

While it was obvious that Chris was not happy with this, he was not the type of child to throw tantrums or pout every time he was frustrated in his imagined needs. He settled back in the seat of the car and let the memory of the sounds from the instrument fill his mind.

After Chris had gone to bed that evening, Libby said to Hack, "You know, dear, I had Chris with me downtown today, and when we stopped at the parish house, I showed him the piano. You wouldn't believe how fascinated he was by it! He obviously has some sort of strong musical appetite. He seems to just get carried away whenever he is exposed to music, and the piano seems to strike him as the greatest thing that ever existed. Do you suppose we could even consider getting one sometime?"

Hack gave it a little thought, and then replied, "Well, if he is really all that interested, maybe we should find out if he actually has some latent talent. Guys like Eddy Duchin and Jose Iturbi don't do too badly, you know! If you think we could squeeze an old upright into the corner of the living room, they're always being advertised. I'll bet we could pick one up for fifty bucks. Another ten bucks to get it tuned and we'd have something he could fool around with. If it didn't work out, we could always take it to the dump. To tell the truth, I always liked piano myself. We could get fifty or sixty dollars' worth of fun out of it ourselves, even if the kids got tired of it. Shall I look around?"

Libby was surprised and pleased.

"Why, yes, dear—that would be great! I'm sure we can make the room, at least for a while."

As Hack had expected, it did not take long to locate an acceptable old upright piano in his price range. He enlisted the aid of Moe Penning and a couple of other friends and together they struggled to get the unwieldy instrument into the desired location. The tuner came, and when he was finished, the sounds from the old piano were satisfying.

"That was a fine, expensive instrument in its day, Mr. Hacker," the tuner said. "It should serve you well for quite a few years. Do you play?"

"Not I!" Hack laughed. "We got it for my son, Chris, just to see if he develops an interest in playing, and to fool around with when we have people in."

"Well, it's a good machine. Don't let children pound on it—they'll upset my work if they do."

"We'll take good care of it," Hack promised.

Chris was thrilled to have the piano right there in the house where he could manipulate it. His mother worked with him on it for a little while, but it soon became evident that he needed no other amateur assistance. Within two or three days he had found how to pick out with one finger some of the tunes he knew, and he was delighted when he discovered a few simple chords. Libby heard him playing them and thought it must have been simply by chance, but when she peeked around the corner and watched him, she found that he was deliberately fitting two-finger chords into the melodies. She could scarcely believe it, and was very impatient until Hack came home from work to share the news with him.

"Christopher! You are never going to believe what I found little Chris doing today!"

"Nothing dirty, I hope," Hack answered with a grin.

Libby ignored the attempt at humor. "He is actually picking out chords that fit into the little songs he has learned to play on the piano! Do you realize how improbable that is? For a five-year-old with no training?"

"Yes," Hack replied, "I'm sure it is. Well, you're the one with the fancy education—what does it mean to you?"

"It means that we should get him to an accomplished instructor right away and see if he is some sort of prodigy. A child with no training and only a couple of day's exposure to the piano shouldn't be able to do anything like that!"

"Well, okay," Hack responded. "Find out who you should take him to, and let's do it."

Libby telephoned some of her acquaintances with musical interests, explaining what she had discovered and soliciting advice as to whom she should approach for help. As a result, she was able to make arrangements for Chris to be examined by a renowned professor of music at Yale University. The professor spent several hours with little Chris, at the end of which he proffered his opinion that the boy had a remarkable gift for music and might have a very rewarding future if permitted to pursue it with the right instructors. He said that he would be interested in being involved in the boy's education, but realized that it would not be very practical for the Hackers to travel between Newvale and New Haven regularly, at least during the child's early years. He contacted a colleague in Litchfield whom he thought might be able to teach Chris, but that man's schedule would not permit it either. Finally, they settled on a promising young female teacher in Wentworth for Chris' early instruction, but both men asked to be kept informed of his progress.

Young Chris now had a start in the direction which would prove to be his most absorbing interest. He started lessons with Mary Ellen Fenton before his sixth birthday.

Meanwhile, his little sister, Susan, who was born on February 9, 1949, was developing with more normal instincts. She was full of energy and deviltry which more than made up for young Chris' lack of some of the usual childhood peskiness. She could easily find ways to vex or worry her mother without trying. She was so naturally inquisitive that nothing short of a locked door could keep her from investigating every box, bag, trunk, closet or dresser which might, to her mind, hide something interesting or pretty or exciting. The piano, which was such an important part of Chris' life, was only a momentary stop-off for Susan. She might pass it dozens of times a day without giving it a glance, and then on her next lightning trip through the living room, reach up and give the old instrument a few hearty jabs and then be off again in pursuit of something else. She was particularly fond of rushing up and injecting several discordant clouts any time that she caught her brother seriously immersed in practicing, which was very often. This disgusted him completely; her whole objective, of course. She was cute, but she was annoying to Chris.

"God, it's a good thing we don't have two like that," Hack exclaimed, after dissuading Susan from pouring water into his empty boot.

Despite her precociousness, Susan was a good girl, and as she grew up she learned to behave and became more manageable. Both children were very good students, and Susan, at least, was very, very popular with her peers. A party, a game or an outing was not completely satisfying to her friends unless Susie Hacker was there. Although Chris was popular, he was so absorbed with his music that his participation in many of the usual childhood activities suffered to a considerable degree. His father deliberately spent many hours in the back yard with him, teaching him how to handle a ball and bat and a football, and encouraging him to shoot baskets at the hoop attached to the end of the garage.

It was not that Chris did not like sports. In fact, he did, but he resented the time they took away from his beloved piano. He was not forced, but his parents encouraged him to get onto ball teams. He acceded gracefully, being sensitive enough to avoid displeasing his mother and father, whom he loved deeply.

As his father had predicted, Chris was a good pitcher almost from his first experiences with team baseball, because his hands were large and long-fingered and it was easy for him to control the ball. But to him, the thrill of striking out an opposing batter in a critical situation was nothing compared to the fulfillment he realized by conquering a difficult passage in a Handel fugue.

Chapter 27
The Luger

    Between Hack's work, establishing a smooth running home and the development of a regular routine, the days flew rapidly by. The young Hackers enjoyed lots of social engagements around the town, some with their peers, but much of their free time was spent with their own families.
    Libby was in demand for church affairs as well as various lady's organizations, some of which she did not feel she could refuse, even though she would have preferred to. She also acted occasionally as a substitute teacher in the local schools, and thereby was able to put her college training to use. Hack played in informal sports groups in season to relax. He was an excellent softball player, particularly as an outfielder, for he had a very strong throwing arm and was fleet enough of foot to cover his area adequately. He was sometimes called upon to play third base, where the strong arm was also an asset. His fielding of ground balls was never better than average, but he was often able to make up for a mishandled grounder with the second chance offered by his arm. When it came to hitting, he was above average, but his tendency to pull the ball violently to the left enabled the opposition to load that side of the field and often turn one of his hard smashes, which would otherwise have dropped in safely, into an out. But he enjoyed the game and found it a good way to unwind after a hard day's work. At basketball, he was also adequate. Although he was of only medium height, his strong body and unwillingness to give in to anyone made him an outstanding rebounder. A shoulder or elbow in Hack's face could be counted on to earn early and intense reciprocation, so the rebounding game tended to become rough but clean when he was involved.
    The enjoyment of handling guns, which he had known as a boy, stayed with him as an adult. The fact that he had often fired a gun at another human

while in the service, and had in fact dispatched a number of the enemy in that manner, did not detract from his enjoyment of shooting. He actually felt little connection between the two. To fire a gun at a target or at a varmint, bore no resemblance to firing at an enemy soldier. To Hack, the latter was business, the former was pleasure. The carefully preserved Luger pistol which he had taken from the German Major was tucked away with his other war mementos. He took it out and admired it occasionally. One day, while so doing, the thought struck him that it would be fun to do some practice shooting. He went down to the hardware store and purchased a box of .9mm ammunition. He took the weapon to a nearby gravel bank and began practicing. After an hour, he was satisfied with both the Luger and his ability to use it, and went home. Libby looked up from her kitchen chores when he entered and said, conversationally, "Well, where have you been, Christopher?"

"I've just had some fun popping away at tin cans with my Luger."

"My goodness—I should think that you would never want to see or hear of a gun again, after your experiences in the war. They're such hateful things—it's a shame they were ever invented!"

"What makes you say that? Guns are beautifully made pieces of machinery. They don't have to be used for killing, you know. They are excellent examples of the art of some very skillful, patient, dedicated men. Haven' t you ever fired a gun, hon? I mean, never?"

Libby cringed at the thought. "No, I certainly haven't, and, what's more, I'm sure I wouldn't ever want to!"

This attitude was difficult for Hack to accept, even from Libby.

"Hold the phone, Lib—that's a big mistake on your part, and I'm going to tell you why. There will always be a gun or guns around my house. They're a part of my experience, and of my heritage, and, what's more, I love them. I know how to use a gun, and I know *when* to use it. Handled properly, guns can be completely safe and a source of real enjoyment. And they are capable of providing a large measure of protection against intruders or anyone who might try to threaten the family."

"Oh, that make's a good excuse, dear, but look at the number of accidental deaths there are because of guns in people's homes," argued Libby.

Hack continued, "Sure, if people leave loaded guns around where children or unqualified individuals can get at them, they are a menace, but only fools allow things like that to happen;. Your problem, Lib, is that you are unfamiliar with guns and so you're ready to accept the assumption that they're terribly dangerous and to write them off as the Devil's playthings. Well, that's not like you."

"Whether it is like me or not, I am very much afraid of guns."

"Generally," said Hack, "you want to take a good look at both sides of every argument before reaching a conclusion. If you haven't ever handled guns or learned anything about them, how can you condemn them, wholesale?"

"Oh, Christopher, aren't you overdoing it a bit? Aren't you dramatizing the situation just because you happen to think guns are wonderful? They frighten me terribly, and I hate to think there is such a thing around the house. Don't you think I am entitled to my view of guns?"

"Sure," Hack replied. "Sure you are. But I don't think you're being fair to yourself if you're not willing to learn a little about them."

Suddenly, he was struck with a bright idea. "Look, Lib—you haven't got all that much to do right now of any importance. The kids won't be back from your folks' until after supper. You're coming with me for a half hour or so. Just drop what you're doing and come with me."

Her first reaction was to say, "No," but she knew from the tone of his voice that she would have trouble making it stick.

"Oh, Christopher," she repeated. "I want to finish up my housework so that I can relax. Just what do you have in mind?"

Taking her by the arm and guiding her toward the back door, he said, "Just come along. We're going to take a short trip."

He was obviously not going to allow her to argue the point, but hustled her out to the car and backed out of the driveway.

"Where are we going?" Libby asked.

"You'll find out in a couple of minutes."

Hack drove back to the gravel bank, pulled in, and turned off the engine.

"Okay," he said, "come around here with me. We're going to give you a little instruction in the use of firearms."

"Whether I want it or not?"

"Whether you want it or not!" he said firmly.

Libby could see that Hack was in one of his determined moods, and that trying to dissuade him from his suddenly concocted plan would be useless. She sighed, shrugged her shoulders, and walked along behind him, deeper into the large excavated area until he reached the point at which he had previously practiced.

"Okay, Lib," he said, "you are about to learn what a gun can do and how it can be a trusted friend."

She looked at him with doubting eyes, but he continued like a school teacher with a reluctant pupil.

"If you'll just forget that you are afraid of weapons and replace that fear with respect, you'll have made an important stride in your education."

He proceeded to give her a solid lecture on the handling of guns, and when that was finished, he instructed her patiently and carefully in the process of loading and firing the Luger. At first, she was very nervous and hesitant with the heavy pistol in her hand, but his insistent encouragement and reassurance gradually made her comfortable, and she began to relax. He drilled her over and over on the method of loading the weapon, and of setting the safety, and then of unloading without firing. Finally, he felt that she was ready to try her first shot.

"Okay, Lib, hold the gun out in front of you—better use your left hand to steady your right, it's a pretty heavy weapon for a gal—and sight down the top of the barrel until you have it lined up with the can on that block."

She braced her feet, extended her arm toward the target, steadied it with her left hand and said, "Now what?"

"Now," he said, "you blow the can away. Squeeze the trigger until the gun fires. Try to do it without letting the gun wobble around, or you'll destroy your aim. Whenever you're ready."

Libby gritted her teeth and squeezed the trigger.

Bang!! The Luger discharged, Libby's hands jerked upward, and the tin can went flying!

Hack's jaw dropped in disbelief.

"Nice going, hon!" he cried. "I would have bet anything that you would need dozens of tries before you came close to hitting the can! What kind of prodigy are you, anyway?"

Libby's shock at having the weapon actually fire, rapidly dissipated.

"Just beginner's luck, I guess," she said.

Hack continued with his instructing, showing her how to load cartridges into the clip and slide the clip into the gun, and having her take quite a number of shots. Some found the mark and some did not, but on balance, she did much better than he had expected. When she had emptied the weapon for the last time, she raised the barrel straight up as he had instructed her, and Hack took it from her. She stepped back, fighting an impulse to gloat over her success. She was inwardly delighted to think that she had outperformed Hack's expectations. She could hardly wait for the encomiums which she fully expected Christopher to heap on her, but they did not come immediately.

Hack double-checked the weapon and then said, "Okay, that's it—let's go."

By the time they reached the car, Libby was beginning to build up a sizable resentment at what appeared to be Hack's inability to make himself show any enthusiasm or at least amazement over her surely unexpected success, but he finally turned to her and said,

"—that was really quite an exhibition. Are you sure you haven't been taking secret lessons and target practice? Or, is it simply that I am such an outstanding teacher?" He chuckled and shook his head.

Somewhat mollified now, Libby replied, "Whatever the reason, I don't find shooting that gun to be particularly difficult. It's noisy and dangerous, but not difficult."

"Well, I want you to know, I'm impressed. I thought you'd be so afraid of firing the pistol that I'd have a tough time getting you to get off even one shot, and instead, you come on like Annie Oakley. You really kind of liked it, didn't you?"

"You want me to tell you the truth, don't you?"

"Certainly."

"I hated it! I went through with it because I knew you really wanted me to, and I thought I might as well do the best I could, as long as I was going to have to do it. I learned what you wanted me to learn and I proved that I could handle it. Now, I hope I never have to shoot a gun again as long as I live!"

Hack was disappointed. He had thought that, because she had done so well, her distaste for weapons would have been somewhat reduced, but apparently that was not to be.

"Okay," he snapped. "If that's the way you feel, I'm sure I can't change you. But I really didn't bring you out here to sell you on the joys of shooting. I simply decided that it was about time for you to learn how to handle a gun so that you would be able to in case of emergency. Suppose someone broke into the house when I was away. I'd like to think that you would know how to use a weapon—it might mean the difference between life and death. I'm going to have a place for this Luger that only you and I know about, and another place to keep a supply of ammunition. That way, you could grab the gun and a clip and be ready if you had to use it, but the gun would never be kept loaded. Only idiots keep loaded weapons around. Am I making sense to you, Lib?"

Resignedly, Libby said, "Oh, I suppose so, Christopher. I know that what you're saying is logical, and I guess that I'm actually glad that I do know how to use the gun now, much as I hate the things. You put the gun and the bullets away and tell me where they are, and I'll just put them out of my mind until there's an emergency, God forbid!"

Chapter 28
The Late '40s

At Nuremberg, Germany, in 1946, Nazi leaders were tried for war crimes. and many of them were found guilty and were executed.

The limits of man's environment were beginning to be pushed back. American rockets probed previously untested reaches, as much as 100 miles into space, while on earth, new avenues of trouble were being explored.

America's erstwhile ally, Russia, dropped a veil of secrecy, which Winston Churchill dubbed an "Iron Curtain," between Eastern Europe, which it dominated, and the rest of the world.

The toothless United Nations General Assembly sought a permanent home in New York City, and on July 4th, the United States granted the Philippines independence.

On Broadway, Ethel Merman belted out the score of "Annie Get Your Gun," and long-suffering Boston Red Sox fans watched helplessly as their dreams of a world championship were dashed in the World Series with the St. Louis Cardinals.

In 1947, the Marshall Plan was inaugurated to furnish American aid to rebuild war-devastated Europe.

Financier and presidential advisor, Bernard Baruch, coined the phrase, "Cold War" to describe Russian-American relations.

Captain Chuck Yeager became the first man to break the sound barrier in a Bell X-1 rocket plane.

Two famous Americans' deaths were recorded; Henry Ford's, too soon; Al Capone's, too late.

Eccentric millionaire Howard Hughes' mammoth all-wooden experimental airplane, dubbed the "Spruce Goose," combined its maiden *flight and its swan song, as it took off successfully, flew one mile, landed, and went into storage, never to fly again. "See? I told you it would work!" was the inferred message.*

The quality level of the American world of entertainment broke even, as the enhancement it derived from the opening of the Tennessee Williams play, **A Streetcar Named Desire**, *was counterbalanced by the set-back it suffered with the singing debut of Margaret Truman.*

Under the unflinching aegis of Branch Rickey of the Brooklyn Dodgers, Jackie Robinson became the first black man to play Major League baseball.

The year 1948 saw the signing of the charter of the Organization of American States by most western hemisphere nations, including the United States.

The western Allies started an "airlift" of food and other essentials to West Berlin to bypass a Soviet blockade.

"Hairbreadth Harry" Truman surprised the country and shocked the Republicans by defeating the assumed "shoo-in," Thomas E. Dewey, for the presidency of the United States.

The first successful transistor was created at Bell Laboratories.

The first Polaroid camera was introduced.

The first "McDonald's" opened in California.

In 1949, The United States, together with Canada, Great Britain, France, Belgium, Italy, the Netherlands, Luxembourg, Norway, Sweden, Ireland and Iceland, signed a mutual defense pact to be known as NATO (North Atlantic Treaty Organization.)

For the first time, Russia exploded a "nuclear device."

U.S. Air Force investigators declared UFOs to be nonexistent.

American manufacturers turned out a record six million automobiles.

Joe Louis retired after a popular eleven year reign as World Heavyweight Champion.

The new Rogers and Hammerstein musical, **South Pacific**, *based on a book by the exciting new novelist, James Michener, broke box-office records.*

The New York Yankees (yawn) won yet another World Series by defeating the Brooklyn Dodgers, ("Dem Bums") four games to one.

For the young married Hackers, as for most of the busy and vibrant Americans of that era, the years immediately following the end of World War

2 passed in a constantly accelerating and increasingly complex welter of activities. The world, the country and individuals were moving at a pace never before known. Opportunities abounded—it was difficult to know in what direction one should move, because there were so many good choices available.

By 1949, Hack was making great progress at the plant, having assimilated enough knowledge about every angle of the business to be capable of directing operations efficiently on those occasions when Fred Hartshorn found it necessary or desirable to be absent. Hartshorn recognized that the reins were gradually being transferred to Hack's hands, because it was increasingly often that customers, suppliers and employees came to the younger man for instructions or explanations. Hartshorn accepted this without rancor; it followed the pattern he had hoped would develop, but he was surprised that it was happening so soon.

At Hack's urging, the company had gradually added other types of production machinery so that it was now possible for them to satisfy the needs of a broader spectrum of customers, and to furnish more thoroughly those of their old clients. This fed upon itself because as Hack had pointed out, it gave their sales representatives more to offer and consequently earned them larger commission checks, without really having to broaden their customer base. Hack had realized early that keeping the salesmen happy was one of the fundamental needs of a growing business. His philosophy was, "Never begrudge a salesman his commission. If he gets rich, the company will, too."

In the late Summer of 1951, Melody received word that her father had passed away rather suddenly. Actually, he had been failing for quite some time. The never-ending struggle against nature and the banks was still tilting heavily against him. Over the past few years, he had been trying harder and harder to drown the realization of his own stubbornness and incompetence in nightly bouts with alcohol. Finally, the combined assaults of time, worry and bourbon became too much for him and he simply laid down his arms and died.

Mrs. Drummond Sr. was unable to cope with the overwhelming problems of trying to earn a living from the cotton crop, and her other daughters, true to the fate Melody had anticipated, had married men who had neither the talent nor the ambition to salvage the business. In desperation, she begged Melody for help. Melody discussed the problem with her husband John. He was very sympathetic but was in the midst of overseeing the final phases of construction of a new dam and could not afford to devote the time which it would doubtless take to travel to Alabama to see what could be done.

The family was sitting in the kitchen of the senior Hackers' home, casting about for a solution to the problem when, on a sudden inspiration, Melody said to Hack,

"You'ah a bright young businessman, darlin'—why don't you take Libby an' the children down fo' a week or two and see if you can do anythin'? Grandma Drummond has nevah seen her two beautiful great-grandchildren. She'd be thrilled to death."

The suggestion stopped all conversation short. Why would that not be a real good idea? Hack's first reaction was to say, no, but it was obvious that Libby was ready to give the idea serious consideration. And it was true that his maternal grandmother had never seen the children. As a matter of fact, he had seen her only a few times himself.

"That really does have possibilities, Hack," said his father. "You've got a good business head and might be able to work something out that would help her out of their difficulties. And it would be great for Libby and the kids. You know, you haven't showed them, any of the rest of the country. You haven't even taken a vacation this year, have you?"

Libby smiled. "Nor last year, for that matter," she said quietly.

It was true. Hack kept himself so busy at the factory that he often failed to notice the speed with which the calendar moved. Fred had mentioned to him a couple of times that he had not taken any time off, and that he should do so.

"Well, I don't know," he said. "Actually, things are running pretty smooth right at the moment. If Libby thinks it's a good idea, and if you folks think I could really help, maybe we should give it some serious thought."

It was plain from everyone's reaction that it was a popular suggestion. He promised that they would sit down that evening and try to see if a schedule could be worked out.

When they started to do so, he was surprised to find that Libby was quite enthusiastic.

"This could be an important trip, Christopher. Not only will it be the first time we have been more than a few miles from home since we've been married, but it will also be exciting for Chris and Susan. I'm sure your Grandma Drummond will be thrilled, and it will give you a chance to think about something other than the plant for a little while. And you're so clever, I'll bet you will figure out a way to help her."

"Okay, honey. You don't have to flatter me into going. I'm beginning to get a little excited about it myself. It would be a bit of a different challenge. Why don't you check up on the train schedules tomorrow, and see what you can work out. Right now, I'm pretty flexible, so whatever you come up with will be okay. Talk to Mom and have her call Grandma Drummond and clear the time with her. We can stay with her, or we can go to a hotel, if she doesn't feel she can have us there. Anyway, clear up all the details and we'll go as soon as possible, before something comes up to prevent it."

Libby nodded. "I'll get right on it in the morning, dear," she said.

Chapter 29
Alabama

The trip South was relaxing for Hack and Libby and exciting for young Christopher. Susan was a little too young to care that much about where she was. As long as her basic needs of attention and play were provided, she was content. They went by cab from the station to the Drummond place where a tearful welcome awaited them.

At first, everyone was ill-at-ease because they were practically strangers. Melody's sisters, Hope and Polly, had done what they could to make themselves and their broods presentable with some traces of the old South in evidence, but even their best efforts could not completely hide the wretched economic state of the clan. While everything was neat and clean, buildings and furnishings showed unmistakable ravages of age, and the sisters themselves bore mute but quite visible testimony to the physically and mentally hard lives they had lived for so long. Their husbands were uncomfortable in the presence of the "rich Yankee" relatives, and their greetings were perfunctory. They excused themselves quickly. Hack was actually relieved because he felt that whatever good qualities were to be uncovered, would be found in the ladies, not in their husbands.

Although his encounters with Grandma Drummond had been rare, Hack had always been drawn toward her. He recognized traits in her which had been passed on to his mother, and which endeared her to him. He discovered that she was intelligent and decent and capable of exhibiting a surprisingly sharp wit. She would probably have been a much more popular and socially active person had she not been chained to her obligations at home as wife, housekeeper, mother, strawboss, field laborer and housekeeper. She had been forced to assume these and other duties because her husband was so inept.

Hack took his grandmother aside and asked if they could sit down and discuss the financial problems that were plaguing her.

"I don't want to pry, Grandma, but I guess the main reason for our coming down was to see if there was anything I could suggest that would help you with your money situation. I'm not posing as any kind of expert, you understand, but, speaking frankly, I guess you don't have anyone else in the family to turn to. Mother says you and Aunt Polly and Aunt Hope don't feel you've had enough experience with finances to decide what route to take, and you're afraid that your local bankers might be somewhat more helpful to themselves than to you. Is that right, so far?"

Yes, Christopha', that is jus' about the whole story. Ah have all of the books and papahs, and Ah've tried to keep them up to date. Why don't we set you up in a room by yo'self with all the recawds, close the doah, and let yo' go ovah everythin'. Whenevah yo' need ansahs, yo' can jus' call me, and Ah will come a-runnin'! When yo'ah finished, we'll go ovah it all togetha."

"That certainly sounds like the way to do it, Grandma," Hack said, smiling.

Hack was sequestered with a stack of books and papers and immediately went to work. He discovered that Grandpa Drummond had put all of the property in Grandma's name, a sensible move, Hack thought. And he was pleasantly surprised to find that his grandmother had done a nice, neat job of record keeping, which made his task simpler than it could have been. She had recorded every expense in its correct chronological place with a file of corresponding receipts to match. He was able to quickly trace what had happened over the past few years and how the events had affected the financial situation of the Drummonds.

It was not good. Although there had been some years in which good weather and a favorable market had produced enough modest profit, these were offset by years in which the elements, or the market, or disintegrating machinery, or some other minor disaster sent Drummond disconsolately back to the bank requesting an increase in his loan. The bankers accommodated him at unusually high interest rates because of the relatively poor condition of his collateral. Because the real estate was desirable, they felt it would not be long before they would foreclose. In the meantime, they were making a profit.

But real estate prices had been climbing steadily ever since the end of World War 2. Hack believed that there should be more than enough value in the plantation to cover all of the outstanding debts. Grandfather Drummond had stubbornly refused to liquidate the property as long as he could be a cotton planter, despite his impending ruin. He had always said to anyone who would listen that that was what he had set out to be, and, "by God, that is what Ah will be until Ah dah!" And to that resolve he had managed to be true.

Now, however, was the time to sell. Hack had spent three days going over the books. He felt sure that he could advise Grandma on the situation. First, however, he needed to know what the real estate market was like so that he could try to line up the best possible deal, if, indeed, sale of the property appeared practical. Then he would have to convince Grandma.

Hack's examination of the finances showed that the business was in debt one hundred thousand dollars. He read all of the newspaper ads he could, but he was not able to find anything comparable for sale in the area. Most of the offers were for single family homes on relatively small lots. From his discussion with his grandmother, he felt that approaching the bankers would be the wrong move because she had been shrewd enough to have detected the larceny in their hearts. Therefore, she did not want to trust any advice they might offer. Hack visited real estate dealers in the area, posing as an interested buyer, checking out the market on multi-acre plots and ferreting out land use regulations that were in effect. He found nothing that would interfere with his plan for the Drummond plantation. It was time to move.

Through his contacts at work, Hack knew of a thriving small company which needed expanded quarters. It had developed a timely product which required assembly of a number of components which it was buying from other manufacturers, Hartshorn & Co. included. The company was interested in building a plant in the South to avoid the high taxes and high labor costs in Connecticut. Although the company needed to expand, it had not done anything about it. To Hack, this looked like a perfect setup. He knew that the plantation's acreage was more than adequate for the type of plant the manufacturer had in mind. He also knew that he could ask for a price far below what a similar-sized site in Connecticut would cost. The local untrained labor force would be ideal for an assembly operation. Hack also had a reason to believe that the local property tax officials would consider giving a tax break to a substantial new business. He himself might even make some money on the deal.

"Grandma, what would you say if I told you that the only sensible way out seems to be for you to sell the place, pay off all your debts, and put a nice chunk of money in your pocket?"

Grandma Drummond looked surprised.

"That sounds too good to be true, Christopha'. I sho'ly hate to think of sellin' this place aftah all ouah yeahs of haad work, but Ah've sho'ly got to do somethin' befoah the bankahs take it, which would make me feel a whole lot worse!"

"Right," he said. "That's the point. If you try to hang on much longer, you're going to lose it all, and we sure don't want to see that happen. The point is, I don't think you realize how valuable all real estate has become since the war. A few years ago, you would have been lucky to get enough for the place to pay off your debts, but if I can swing a deal of the type I have in mind, you should come out with a pretty nice nest egg after all the bills are paid. The trouble is, so far it's just pie in the sky. Don't hate me if my idea falls through, but I honestly think I can set up something you'll like."

Grandma Drummond leaned forward and patted Hack's hand. "You know, Hack, Ah could nevah hate yo.'"

Hack continued, "It involves arranging a sale to a businessman I know back in Connecticut who is looking for a place to start a new plant. I think this is ideal for his purposes. There's even a good chance that he might eventually be able to hire some of the people who have worked for you for so long. What do you think?"

"That sounds wondaful. That maaght solve problems fo' a lot of folks aroun' heah, includin' ma sons- in-law!"

"Do you want me to see if I can work it out, or would you rather have me see what I can do with the local bankers?"

"Heavens, no! Don't mention those bloodsudkahs to me! Yo' go raht ahead and try youah idea, Christopha'; jus' keep ol' Grandma infoamed."

"Don't worry, Grandma. I'll do some telephoning, and if I have any luck, we may have a potential customer down here to look the place over before long."

Hack called Arnold Jamison, his business friend in Connecticut.

"Arnold? How are you? This is Christopher Hacker. I'm on a little trip down here in Alabama and I uncovered something I thought you might be interested in hearing about. You're still looking for a site for that new plant, right?"

Jamison replied, "Well, yes we are. We've had nothing but frustration so far, though. What have you found?"

"I've got a place here that has been operating for years as a cotton plantation, but they're throwing in the sponge. There's plenty of acreage, no regulatory restrictions to speak of, and I think you'd find the price right. It's in Ashford, Alabama, right on U.S. 84. If you're planning on mostly assembly in your new plant, you've even got a good labor supply right here. Shall I go on?"

"Tell me more," Jamison said eagerly. "So far, I'm all ears."

On inspiration, Hack said, "Wait a minute—on second thought, why waste time on the phone? Why don't you jump on a plane and fly down here and see it for yourself? If you can get away for a couple of days, I'll still be here and I can show you the place and get you any information you may need. What do you say?"

"By God, Christopher, I don't know any reason why I couldn't do just that, if you're sure it's available and if it's as good as it sounds."

Hack laughed. "Believe me, it's available and it's good. I ought to know—it's my grandmother's place! My grandfather tried all his life to make this a successful cotton plantation, but he never had quite enough luck or talent to make it go. He just struggled to keep his head above water and it finally got to him. He died recently, and Grandma just wants to sell out, pay off her debts, and relax a little for whatever time she has left. I'm sure we can work out a mutually satisfactory deal if you find it to be as good a solution to your problem as I think it is."

"Tell you what, Christopher—I'll check things out here and see if I can get on a plane tomorrow, or Thursday at the latest. Give me your number and I'll call you back later today."

Hack gave him the number. "Call that anytime; it's my grandmother's home phone, and I expect to be here most of the time. Real nice to talk to you, Arnold. Hope we can work something out that will make us all happy. Do you want me to get you a hotel room?"

"No, thanks. I'm not sure which day it will be. I'll get something near the airport after I arrive. I don't imagine it's that crowded around those parts, is it?"

"No. You won't have any trouble getting a room. And if you did, we could put you up at Grandma's, anyway. Okay—sounds good, and I'll be waiting for your call. So long, Arnold."

Early the next day, Jamison called to say he would be arriving that evening. He sounded quite excited.

Chapter 30
The Sale

Now, Hack had to make his presentation ready for Jamison. From his talks with local real estate dealers, Hack felt that their price for the plantation would be less than two hundred thousand. After much consideration, he decided that he could start bargaining at $225,000. Anything higher would probably be dangerous, even though a similar property in Connecticut could not be touched for $300,000.

Hack met Jamison at the little airport in Dothan and took him to breakfast. During the meal and the ride to Ashford, he learned that Jamison was more frustrated than he had realized about trying to get his building program under way.

"Hack, you wouldn't believe the roadblocks that get thrown in your way if you mention building a factory back home. Most of the towns are developing all sorts of boards and commissions designed to keep businesses out."

"That's sort of stupid, isn't it?" Hack asked.

"It certainly is, but that's the way things are. Every town that isn't already committed to manufacturing is trying to prevent any plants from being built. They don't even want to know what sort of buildings you plan to put up. Once you say 'factory' the game is over. The best property deal I have been able to uncover would cost half a million, and then we'd have to meet a whole laundry list of regulations. It's simply impractical."

Hack realized that he had been very lucky in his timing—Jamison was half sold already.

The morning sun of a lovely day did its part in making Jamison's first sight of the plantation a positive one. Good businessman though he usually was, he had trouble containing his enthusiasm.

"Nice level land, isn't it?" Jamison commented.

"Yes, it is. And easy to build on. No trouble hauling in whatever you need. You're only a few hundred yards off U.S. 84, so deliveries and shipments are duck soup. Would you like to walk around the perimeter?"

Jamison said that he would like to, so they took a leisurely stroll and Hack pointed out each of the markers indicating the boundaries.

At the rear of the property, Hack said, "If you take a look back to the main house, you'll see that this is a very large piece of land."

Jamison stopped and looked back. He nodded his head, clearly impressed with the dimensions.

"I don't know what you would expect to do with the main building, Arnold. My grandparents tried hard, but they always seemed to have just enough bad luck to keep them from making any real money, and as a result, the place wasn't kept up the way they would have liked it to be. But Grandpa was always a stickler about maintenance, so you won't find anything basically wrong with the buildings, they just need to be gussied up, painted and so forth. You wouldn't plan on moving down here yourself, would you?"

"Well, not at present, anyway. But I can see possibilities in that plantation house. What I would probably do is to have my manager move his brood down here—he's got a bunch of kids, and they'd love this kind of rural setting. It looks as though there would be plenty of room to put up a twenty or thirty thousand foot plant without disturbing the residential area."

"Hell, yes—and all kinds of room left over. If business booms, you could handle an expansion or two here before you'd have to worry about space."

Jamison nodded. "How is the atmosphere around here as far as manufacturing businesses are concerned Do they try to throw a lot of stumbling blocks in your way if you want to build a factory?"

Hack shook his head.

"No, no. According to the people I've talked to, including some of the officials, they're ready to lay out the welcome mat. They need business in the area. The agricultural process seems to be gradually drying up. Too difficult to get people who want to work that hard for so little money. I understand that there are a lot of people around here who would like nothing better than to have a nice 'settin' down' job in an air-conditioned building, after all the years they've sweated out in the sun, which does get sort of murderous in the summer."

They continued their tour of inspection, and as the noon hour approached, Hack invited Jamison to lunch at his grandmother's. She was expecting them,

Hack explained. Grandma had put out her best linen and china, and Polly, her daughter, served a tempting assortment of dishes. During lunch, Grandma exhumed from her past, some of the charm with which all southern ladies seem to have been endowed. Libby ate with them and provided an added touch of beauty and refinement, which did not go unappreciated by Jamison.

Once lunch was finished, the ladies excused themselves.

"Well, Hack, I guess we've covered everything except price. You know I'm definitely interested—I like what I see—— but the dollars are very important. What's the best you can do?" Jamison asked.

Hack had been very carefully appraising every word and every move that Jamison had made all morning. Because of Jamison's enthusiasm, Hack believed he could inflate his original figure somewhat. As matter-of-factly as he could, he said, "Well, we think the right price is $275,000, but if we can make the deal direct between us, without any dealer in between, we'll make it $250,000. The dealer would get around eight or ten percent, as I understand it.

Jamison was elated, but tried not to let it show. He had been expecting a price of over $300,000, based on real estate values in Connecticut. He knew this amount of acreage, all cleared and ready for construction, and on a main highway, would actually cost more than $300,000. He felt that serviceable outbuildings were added value.

"Tell you what, Hack. I don't think your price sounds too bad. Two seventy-five would be pushing it, I think, but at two fifty, I'd be inclined to go with it. Of course, I'd want to make a few inquiries first—got to test the waters as far as availability of dependable builders, probable labor force, and a few other things are concerned. My inclination is to stay here a couple more days, check these things out, and if I don't run into anything that might queer the deal, we can get our lawyers going on a contract of sale. What say?"

"That's fine with us, Arnold. We'll stay here and wait for you to do what you have to. Just keep in touch, will you?"

Jamison left after promising to call a couple of times a day.

When he was gone, Hack found his grandmother and said, "Well, Grandma, it looks like we may have a deal going. Mr. Jamison is very interested.. He is going to check up on a few things to be sure he can build what he wants here, and if it looks okay, he's ready to sign. What do you think of that?"

"My, that's wondaful, Christopha! Y'all northerners move pretty fast, don't yo'? If it had been two southan men, they wouldn't have gotten aroun' to talkin' bidness yet! What soat of a prahce did yo' come up with?"

Hack could not resist building up the moment a little.

"Would you be satisfied with $175,000, Grandma?"

"Lordy, yes! " she cried. "We don't owe neahly that much. Did you really get him to agree to that?"

Hack threw back his head and laughed.

"Oh, Grandma—it's a good thing you didn't try to handle the sale yourself—they'd have robbed you blind. I could see that Jamison was taken with the place, so I raised the ante a little. I was originally going to ask $225,000 and be ready to back down to $200,000 if I had to, but something told me he would go higher, so I gambled. I told him we felt the price should be $275,000, but that if we could make the deal between ourselves and save a real estate dealer's fee, we'd take $250,000. He feels that's fine, and that's what he'll pay if we finalize the deal. How about that!"

Grandma Drummond was flabbergasted. While she really had no way of knowing much about the real estate market, she would never have guessed that she had been sitting on that kind of value. And she knew she would never have gotten it if it were not for Hack.

"Christopha'! Ah jus' cahn't believe it! Yo' mean to tell me that we maht get a quahtah of a million dollahs fo' this ol' place? That's unbelievable! What kind of magician are yo', anyway!?"

He laughed again, savoring her delight and amazement. "That's not magic, Grandma—that's business! I take it it's all right for me to go ahead then, if Jamison comes back ready to sign?"

Mrs. Drummond hesitated for a long moment, then looked Hack straight in the eye and said, "Only on one condition, Christopha', deah."

"And what is that?" he asked.

"That you take twenty-fave thousan' as yoah commission!"

Hack held up his hands and replied, "Oh, Grandma—I couldn't do that. That's your money. I'm just trying to help out!"

"Christopha', theah's no one else in the world who would have done this fo' me. Aside from maybe yoah fatha, none of the relatives would know what to do or how to do it, and no mattah who Ah had handlin' the sale, he would have chaaged at least ten percent. An' even then, none of 'em would've got such a prahce. Yo' jus' have to take it, or Ah won't sign!"

She sounded very much as though she meant it. Hack thought of agreeing, but he knew he would look greedy if he did, even though Grandma was obviously sincere.

"I'm pleased that you feel that way, Grandma, but let's cool it for a bit, at least until Jamison comes back with his final approval. Unfortunately, the deal could still fall through. Let's just sit tight and wait for word from him."

During the next two days, there was little to do but to wait. True to his word, Jamison called morning and evening, reporting that so far, everything looked good, so Hack packed Libby and the children into Grandma's old car and spent the middle hours just driving slowly around the area, soaking up the atmosphere of the southern countryside, different in so many ways from New England. When it became too hot for the children to enjoy riding around, they returned to the plantation and sat on the shaded veranda and sipped lemonade and iced tea.

Finally, Jamison called to say that he had done all the checking that seemed important. "Hack, I haven't run into anything that looks bad. Unless the lawyers find something wrong, I'm ready to commit."

Hack released a silent sigh. "Fine, Arnold—just fine. Let's set up a meeting. Grandma doesn't care for the local lawyers. She wants to hire a man in Dothan."

"I'll get my lawyer at home to recommend someone in Dothan. They have a referral system for the whole country."

When all of the legal necessities were covered, a contract was drawn up and the sale was accomplished at a price of $250,000. This was sufficient to leave Grandma Drummond a net amount, after paying her debts and all expenses and taxes, of approximately $125,000 to see her comfortably through her remaining years.

Jamison insisted on taking the whole family out to dinner to celebrate the closing of the transaction.

On the train back to Connecticut, Libby breathed a sigh of relief. "Well, dear, I guess there isn't any doubt that our trip was quite a success, is there?"

"Not in the slightest, as far as I'm concerned," Hack said smugly.

"Your Grandma thinks you're pretty special, you know. I don't believe I've ever seen anyone more pleased than she was. I think that is marvelous. And I'll have to admit, you are sort of special. You did a lot for her, and I'm pretty proud of you." She rewarded him with a warm kiss.

"Yeah," he replied. "It really was a pretty smooth operation. Jamison's happy, Grandma's thrilled, and we didn't do too bad ourselves."

"Yes," Libby said. "We had a lovely trip, got away from the routine for a while, showed the children something different, met a lot of relatives we didn't even know—I'd say it was really nice."

Hack leaned back against the seat, fingers laced behind his head. He chuckled knowingly and said, "And you haven't even mentioned the best part."

Libby looked confused. "What do you mean—the best part?"

"I mean the year's pay I picked up for a few days' work!"

Libby was dumbfounded. "Whatever are you talking about?" she asked, waiting for an explanation.

"You know that I set the deal up without going through any real estate people, don't you? Well, on a land and buildings sale like that, a dealer would have made about eight percent—maybe even ten. That's twenty-five thousand bucks! Number one, Grandma couldn't believe I could get that kind of money for the place, and then to find out that there was no dealer's commission, well, she couldn't get over it. She insisted she wouldn't go through with the sale unless I took the twenty-five thou. Naturally, I told her I wouldn't accept it, even though I was itching to, but as soon as the money changed hands and she paid off her debts, she handed me a check for $10,000 and insisted there was no way she'd let me refuse it. I argued sort of half-heartedly for a while, and then graciously accepted it. Add one more happy party to the whole picture—me!"

Libby just sat and stared at him numbly. She was seeing a person she had never really understood before. She knew that Hack was possessed with a desire for money, but she would never have believed that he could enjoy milking away part of his grandmother's return for her property. Libby's pride and satisfaction in Hack's successful solution of the elderly relative's financial problems were dashed by the revelation that he was willing to profit from it at her expense. Her first inclination was to shout, "How could you!?" but she stifled the impulse and said nothing. It was his business—it was between him and his grandmother. Obviously, his delight in making money on the deal overshadowed any tendency toward guilt he might have been expected to have about taking away some of his grandmother's newly acquired nest egg.

For the first time, Libby detected a tarnished spot on the husband she had thought had no blemishes.

Chapter 31
Momentum

The money from his grandmother quickened the tempo of Hack's eagerness for riches. He could play with it to grow his garden of opulence. Although he had played the stock market modestly, he had had so little to invest that it almost did not count. He had, however, purchased some shares of IBM common stock on the advice of a casual acquaintance in the Army, one of a group sitting around drinking beer while awaiting shipping orders back to the States. The soldier had remarked, during a discussion of what they planned to do when they got home, that he was "going to scrape up every dime I can beg, borrow or steal and buy IBM stock with it." He was convinced that this relatively new company "was about to take off like a rocket and reward its investors beyond their wildest dreams." While Hack was not ready to accept this philosophy entirely, he was impressed enough by the man's enthusiasm to risk investing a few dollars. After doubling his money on the stock, Hack sold out and invested the proceeds in Aeronautics Unlimited, which promptly failed. When he could afford to do so, he bought some IBM again. This time, he held on to the few shares of stock and watched as the price rose and rose, the shares split, and the price rose again and again.

Hack wanted desperately to meet the senior Mr. Borgeson, who represented the legendary concept of rags to riches with which he was so impressed. He mentioned it to Mr. Hartshorn, who was well acquainted with the old gentleman and promised to introduce them when the opportunity arose. Finally, it happened. They were attending a church-sponsored picnic, when Mr. Hartshorn encountered Borgeson.

"Nice to see you, Ingmar," he offered. "Haven't spoken with you for some time. How've you been?"

The naturally reticent Swede was pleased to see Hartshorn; one of the few local people with whom he felt comfortable.

"Nice to see you too, Mr. Hartshorn. I been feeling good, t'anks."

"You don't get around town much, do you?"

"Not wery much. I stay home mostly, but I like to support church t'ings ven I can. Veda's better vid people den me—she has lot of friends in Newvale now. She vorkin' vid the vimmin on dis party."

"Yes, I know. Everybody loves Veda, she's always so pleasant and kind to everyone. She's a great ambassador for you. But you should try to get acquainted with more of the townspeople. You'd like most of them, once you got to know them. They are really a pretty decent bunch."

"Ya, I know. It yust harder for me. I don't speak English good, so I yust got in habit early to not talk too much." He chuckled. "Stay out of trouble dat vey, too."

Hartshorn laughed and said, "You speak better English than you give yourself credit for, Ingmar. By the way, speaking of getting acquainted, I have a bright young fellow who works with me who is a great admirer of yours and would like to meet you. Would you have any objection if I brought him over? He's right over there in the lunch line."

Ingmar hesitated a moment, then nodded and said, "Sure. I meet him if you vant."

"Oh, good—he'll be very pleased."

Hartshorn rose and called to Hack. "Could you come over here a minute, Hack?"

Hack surrendered his place in line and walked over to his boss.

"Hack, I want to have you meet Mr. Ingmar Borgeson, whose work I know you admire. Ingmar, this is young Christopher Hacker, better known as 'Hack'."

Hack reached across the picnic table and enthusiastically shook Mr. Borgeson's hand. "How do you do, sir! I'm very glad to meet you."

"Pleased to meet you, young fella."

Hartshorn continued, "Hack has worked for me ever since he got out of high school. He volunteered for the service and fought through the African campaign, where he was wounded, and then landed in France on D-Day and was in the thick of it right through till the end of the war. He's probably our number one local war hero."

Hack felt uneasy with the build-up, but Borgeson was obviously favorably impressed.

"By golly," he said, "I proud to know you. Dem Germans I knew many years ago was pretty nice, but dat Hitler fella ruin dem. He vaste de country and spoil de young people. You boys ver vonderful—I very happy you come back okay."

"That's very nice of you, Mr. Borgeson, thank you."

Hack felt that he must capitalize on the introduction. He wondered what to say next to this man who was not forthcoming with words. Hack knew Borgeson was hard to get to know. All he really knew about him was that he was the father of the famous "IB" carburetor.

"I really admire your work in automotive manufacturing. It was inspiring to read about the way you worked so hard when you were just a boy and then eventually developed some of the finest fuel and ignition systems once you had a chance to show what you could do. You are a living example of the way this country gives people the opportunity to make use of their talents."

Now it was Ingmar's turn to be somewhat embarrassed.

"Vell, I alvays had ideas—I yust had to vork long and hard to get a chance to use dem. And I vouldn't have make out den if it vasn't for a nice man named Beadle, who showed me how to sell dat carburetor. I learned dat yust inventing somet'ing not enough—got to get right people interested."

Oh, boy! He was opening the door that Hack wanted so badly to enter. How lucky could he get!

"That was really great, Mr. Borgeson. Lots of us have good ideas, but we don't know how to market them to the best advantage. Even simple little things can be worth an awful lot, but, just as you say, most of us don't have any connections with the big outfits." He continued, "Would you be offended if I asked to see that beautiful home of yours sometime? I've lived here all my life and I've always loved that hill. There must be a great view of the town from your place."

"Glad to have you," Ingmar replied. "Yust call me on telephone and ve make date. You like machines, ya? I show you my little shop, too."

Hack was delighted and showed it. The old man was almost a recluse, but something about the young war veteran appealed to him and he stepped out of character to invite him into private areas where few others had ever been welcomed.

Two days after the introduction, Hack phoned Mr. Borgeson, who seemed happy to hear from him. A date for the visit was made. However, when Veda Borgeson heard that Hack was to call on them, she insisted that Ingmar ask Hack to bring his pretty young wife and come to dinner.

A pleasant evening ensued, with the elderly couple and the young one finding it easy to relax and just let conversation flow. Veda was a naturally friendly and hospitable hostess, and Libby was her usual amiable self. Ingmar seemed delighted to have an appreciative young man with whom he could talk in a relaxed manner and who was interested in both their beautiful home and the work at which he had spent most of his life. The small but expertly and expensively appointed shop in a small building made Hack drool. He had enough knowledge of tools and machinery to ask sensible questions.

"What is this, Mr. Borgeson?" he asked, indicating a small machined assembly on a work bench. "It looks like a jig of some sort."

"Ya, you right. I machine dat out a few days ago to hold dis, (indicating another metal part) vhile I bore it. Got to be dead straight, so I have to make precision jig."

"Is that part of some new invention of yours?"

Borgeson chuckled. "No, not inwention. Veda need a part for old sewing machine. Can't buy, so I make the part."

Hack didn't want Borgeson to think that he was too nosy, so he said, apologetically, "I don't want to pry into your work, Mr. Borgeson. Tell me if I ask things that are none of my business."

"No, no," Ingmar assured him. "I glad to have someone to show t'ings to who understand vat dey are. You get ideas for t'ings and vant place to experiment, or make samples, you velcome to use this shop anytime, Christopher."

"That is so nice of you, Mr. Borgeson—I don't know how to thank you. If you'd really trust me with your beautiful equipment, I'd sure like to take you up on it."

Hack was so anxious to plant himself firmly with Ingmar, he seldom let more than a couple of weeks go by without finding a reason to either call or visit. And Ingmar loved it. Jim Barton, his only real friend, had not been in contact in many years. Mr. Beadle, his other friend, was more an advisor and mentor than a comrade. He was pleased to welcome visits and phone calls from the smart and ambitious young Mr. Hacker, and to dabble with new ideas which the young man came up with from time to time. They spent many happy hours together in Ingmar's shop, and often strolled around the spacious Borgeson property or sat under a tree and discussed the changing face of American industry and what would likely be needed in its future.

As time went by, Hack felt more and more impatient about the state of his finances. He felt confident enough with Ingmar so that he could get him to use his good offices to promote any sharp idea for the automotive trade. However, Hack had not thought of anything new. And then, almost by accident, it happened. He mentioned that the upholstery on the seat of his car was coming loose from the springs.

"They only attach it here and there with a piece of twisted wire, which has got to be a pain in the neck to put together, and then it doesn't hold satisfactorily, anyway," Hack explained.

There was silence for a few moments. Then Ingmar mused, "It vouldn't be much of a yob to improve on dat, Christopher."

Hack felt a warm sensation pulse through his body.

"Oh—how do you mean?"

"Vell, I don't know, yust yet, but I t'ink it would be pretty easy."

Hack was eager. Imagine what would be involved if he could sell General Motors a better method of securing the upholstery on the seats of all their cars! He tried to sound calm as he said, "Why don't we look into it? Maybe between us we can develop a better design. Let's pull the seat out of my car and look it over—what say?"

Ingmar chuckled. "You sound like me ven I vas young. Got to hurry up! But okay, if you vant to, you get seat from your car and ve take a look."

Soon the two men were studying the system by which the fabric was secured to the springs. Hack rapidly became disgusted with himself because he could not think of a solution. But the still fertile mind of the older man was making a methodical assessment of the problem and had not yet clicked over to the next phase. The twisted wire did, indeed, seem to be a poor method of holding the fabric on the springs. It made a small hole which became larger when pressure was applied to anchor it to the frame which held the springs. Borgeson thought, instead of wire, why not a broader fastener, which would grip the fabric tighter and would not concentrate the strain on such a tiny area? A stamping instead of a strip of wire. Yes, that would be better. He picked up a pencil and started to sketch something on a piece of scrap paper. Hack peered eagerly over his shoulder.

"What have you got, Ingmar?" he asked tentatively.

"Not'ing, really. Yust idea. I t'ink you right—vire not good. Need vider grip on fabric. I t'ink should be stamping, not vire."

Immediately, Hack understood. He nodded in agreement.

"Yeah—I see what you mean." Then an exciting thought struck him. "Why couldn't we design a stamping that would be easy to crimp around the metal of the frame with a small press or pressure tool of some sort so that they would not only get a much better anchoring system, but would make the operation much faster!"

Ingmar thought about it briefly, then nodded. "Vouldn't be hard to do. Let's vork on it a little."

Like children with a new toy, the two men busied themselves with pencils and paper, each coming up with suggestions. After an hour of brainstorming, they had a good idea of how their proposed method would work, and they were both convinced that it would be a great improvement over the present method. The crowning achievement came when the talented old toolmaker hit upon a configuration for a fastener which would utilize steel strip and which would produce no scrap. The top of each fastener would conform to the bottom of its predecessor. It could be produced on a simple light power press at a high rate of speed.

During the next couple of months, Hack spent all of his spare time at the shop with Ingmar, who dived into the project with great enthusiasm and produced the necessary prototypes for both the fasteners and the crimping tool which would be used to attach them. When these preparations were completed, Ingmar explained to Hack how to proceed with protection of the device, based on his own experience with the carburetor and subsequent inventions of his.

"Who should we go to?" Hack asked.

Ingmar looked at him with fatherly affection.

"You go, Christopher. Dis your idea, not mine. I yust help you get it ready."

Although Hack had hoped that Ingmar would feel this way, he had not believed that he could be so fortunate.

"But, Ingmar, I wouldn't have been able to do anything about it without your guidance. I'll feel guilty if I just take all the credit."

"No, no, Christopher. People help Borgeson when he vas young—now Borgeson do what he can to help you. Ve don't know for sure that car people vill vant this, but I going to talk to my friend, Mr. Beadle. I know the big shots vill look at it if Mr. Beadle tell them. He retired now, but they still respect his yudgement. But first, you protect idea like I show you."

Hack left for home with his heart racing. He wondered if Ingmar had really imagined a scenario similar to what Hack thought. Suppose Hack went ahead with the project and it was successful. His financial future would be guaranteed! But how would Ingmar's family feel about it? Hack admitted to himself that practically all of the design of both the fastener and the applicator had been created by the old Swede, with only a few suggestions from him. It was obvious to him that Ingmar would never claim to have been the inventor.

He knew that Ingmar had taken such pleasure from their relationship that he would be pleased to see Hack reap the rewards of the invention. He knew that neither Ingmar's finances nor his pride needed further aggrandizement. Hack also admitted that his intention had always been to get in Ingmar's good graces, and to use his friendship however he could to promote his own prosperity. Hack knew his campaign had been cold-blooded all the way, and now it appeared that it might be successful. He felt no guilt. To Hack, the old man had served his purpose, and with just a little more of his help, he might be on the threshold of achieving the goal he had sought since childhood. If he carried it off and Ingmar's family suspected the truth, why should he let it bother him?

With uncharacteristic joviality, he broke into song as he cruised down the road toward home.

Chapter 32
Success

Hack had planned well. The instinct which had told him that Ingmar Borgeson could be the key to his financial plans had proven correct. The respect in which Borgeson was held by the Detroit powers opened all of the necessary doors for Hack and permitted him to bypass all of the roadblocks which would normally have impeded an unknown man with a good idea. Even though the major components of the proposal were primarily Borgeson's, Hack had so successfully gained the old man's favor that Ingmar was delighted to maintain the illusion that his protege was its source. A few words dropped in the right places by his old friend, Albert Beadle, mentioning that Borgeson was involved, resulted in having those in manufacturing engineering eagerly accept the sample fasteners and model applicators for a thorough trial. They remembered many of the gifted old Swede's contributions over the years that had become standards in GM automobiles.

Once tested, the sample fasteners and model applicators proved able to save substantial amounts of money and time in the installation of automobile upholstery. It was in GM's interest to buy up the rights from Mr. Hacker to be sure that the method would be denied to their competition.

During the few days between the presentation of the procedure and notification that GM was interested and ready to talk price, Hack got very little sleep. When the news arrived, he could hardly contain himself. He and his lawyer went to meet with GM officials in Philadelphia. Hack's attorney and the GM lawyers engaged in hard negotiating, even though Hack and his attorney knew GM wanted the invention. Hack was satisfied with the terms; a large payment up front, plus a monthly royalty on every thousand clips used. They negotiated a limited license for exclusive rights to the use of the applicators, of which they would need hundreds at first and thousands eventually to supply all of the assembly stations in all of their plants. Both clips and applicators would be supplied exclusively by Mr. Hacker, who was at liberty to manufacture them himself or to have them produced for him elsewhere, so long as they passed a rigid inspection upon receipt and were received in timely fashion. A tentative price for the initial million fasteners and one hundred applicators was established, with provision for review of the price every six months. GM also agreed to a stipulated minimum annual usage for the ensuing ten years, and to a penalty clause which would pay Mr. Hacker a very large amount in the event they decided against renewing their options at that time.

Hack floated out of the session. He had actually put it over! The agreement was fantastic! He did not have to wait any longer for the success he had been dreaming about since his youth. He had achieved it!

He grabbed the phone in his hotel room and called Libby. When she answered, he said, in a disguised voice, "Is this Mrs. C. D. Hacker?"

When she replied that it was, he said, "Is this the *rich* Mrs. Hacker? The one with the brilliant husband who just beat General Motors into the dust? Because, if it is, get ready to celebrate like you never have before!"

Libby felt her throat tighten. "What happened, dear? It sounds as though you had good luck."

"We're in, honey—in the big money! Start picking out clothes and cars and building lots and whatever—we can afford it! I'm not even going to stay overnight here like I planned. If I can't get a bus right away, I'll hire a limousine to bring me right to the door!"

And without waiting for a response, he hung up, called for a cab, and threw the few clothes he had brought, into his suitcase. In a few hours, he was home.

Libby had never seen Hack in exactly the mood he exhibited after his triumphant return from Philadelphia. There had been, she supposed, some transformation when he came back from the war, but that was hardly remarkable. No basically innocent country boy could have survived his experiences in the army and returned without having indelible marks etched on his character. He had become far more mature, much more worldly, and if possible even more determined to drive for his goals of wealth and success—synonymous terms in his lexicon. But now it was as though he saw himself as the complete man, convinced of his superiority and rather condescending toward others, including her. He demonstrated arrogance not previously apparent.

"Lib," he said, a few days after returning, "have you started making your list of things you want—clothes, furnishings, anything? Have you given some thought to the type of home you would like, or to potential sites? Gotta get going, you know. We've waited for this a long time, now we're not going to let a lot of grass grow under our feet. That big, fat check should arrive at the bank today or tomorrow, and once it does, we're going to start opening some eyes around town."

Libby sensed that he was not merely being facetious, but quite seriously expected her to begin a wholesale overhaul of their way of life. She felt a little resentful.

"I haven't gotten over the shock yet, dear," she said. "It's going to take some time to readjust my thinking from poor to rich. You don't expect to uproot us from our home here immediately, I hope."

Hack bristled a little. "Well, I should hope that you would appreciate what I've accomplished enough to share in my elation and to help me take advantage of it. So far, it strikes me that you've really been pretty lukewarm about the whole thing."

"I don't think that's very fair, Christopher. I think I've been very supportive of the things you have tried to do, always—I've certainly tried. I think the problem may be more that our wishes for the future aren't exactly the same. You've always been more success oriented than I. You can't be satisfied with a moderate amount—you always want more. And that's all right, I suppose—I admire your ambition and determination, but I guess I just don't have that insatiable appetite for achievement that you do."

"Well, I have it, and don't expect me to apologize for it!" he said, his voice rising. "It was people like me, with impatience and maybe a little greed, who made this country what it is. I've always wanted to have the means to do whatever I wanted, and it begins to look like I'm going to have it!"

"Oh, yes," Libby interrupted. "Now that you've had this stroke of luck, you're going to throw money around like a drunken sailor, is that it? Because, I think you'd better go into some of your big adventures a little slowly. This may not turn out to be the bonanza you expect."

"Are you kidding?" Hack came back sarcastically. "This is only the beginning, you know. This deal is going to provide me with enough funds so that I can get into some of the really big money projects. Don't give me any bullshit about how its not nice to let money rule you, and about all the good things in life that money can't buy. That's loser talk. Anyone who is completely honest will have to admit that money is the key to everything."

Libby shook her head in disgust.

"You can't believe that, Christopher—that money is the most important thing there is."

"Oh, yeah? Well, you'll have to admit that if you have an unlimited amount of it, there's practically nothing beyond your reach, but if you haven't much and you don't have the brains or the guts to get it, then you tell anyone who will listen that 'money isn't really all that important.' I don't want to hear you talking like that. We're going to have all kinds of money from now on, and you'd better get used to the idea and appreciate it, understand?"

Libby's heart sank lower and lower as she listened, astonished, to his diatribe. She could see that he actually expected her to respond to it, but she just did not know what to say. Although they had had some small disagreements over the years, they had not been at all vicious and had been smoothed over quickly. Somehow, she knew that this was a different Christopher altogether. He saw himself as being completely in command now, and he was demanding that she obey.

"Do you understand me, Libby?" he repeated menacingly.

Despite her calm and peaceful nature, she felt the blood rise to her face and the chords of her neck and throat tighten. Without raising her voice, she replied, "No, Christopher, I don't think I understand you at all." And with that, she turned on her heel and walked out of the room.

Libby had never abandoned her childhood habit of going to one of her favorite places whenever she had a problem which she felt required serious thought in solitude, and she went to one of them now. Briefly, as she hurried along, she was aware of a peculiar feeling of unreality—as though her mind were separated from her body. Although she could see everything sharply, nothing seemed normal and she had an almost panicky sensation that she might be losing her sanity. The feeling passed almost as quickly as it had come, and she soon arrived at a little grove of pines into which she stepped and in whose confines she was immediately hidden from the view of outsiders, while still being able to peer out if she so desired. She sat down on the pine needles and tried to relax. She had never known Christopher to be so imperious before. She recognized that he was a strong-willed, virile person and did occasionally get bossy or insistent, but he knew it when it happened and always retreated a little before the conversation was over. This time, however, it had been unmistakably apparent that he was serious. He was stating his demands and she was expected to obey. What was she to do? It was wonderful that he had been so fortunate in the transaction with General

Motors and that the Hackers apparently would soon be affluent, but to her, this meant only that she would not have to be so careful with every penny and would be able to provide more and nicer things for her family, particularly the children. She could not imagine herself gloating over the acquisition of wealth or flaunting it, as it seemed Christopher was interested in doing. She knew that he had always had this abnormal fascination with success, but it really was not until some time after they were married that she recognized how deep inside him the craving smoldered. She now realized that she should doubtless have analyzed more carefully his often repeated desire to be rich. But when she was a young girl, infatuated with one of the town's more attractive young fellows, or a young bride very much in love with her ambitious, capable and attentive young husband, such traits appeared as positive attributes rather than as flaws.

The more she thought about it, the more she realized that Christopher's attentions had for some time been slipping more and more away from her and toward his business interests. He had been trying feverishly to expand and improve the position of Hartshorn & Co., to the extent of spending many evening and weekend hours either at the plant or in the company of Fred Hartshorn or some of their customers, and by so doing had made impressive headway. Hartshorn acknowledged, at least to himself, that the young fellow was gradually turning the business into a larger, better, more versatile and more profitable enterprise, and he had shown his appreciation by steadily increasing Hack's paycheck. Also, she though, since Hack's introduction to the elder Mr. Borgeson, all the rest of his spare time had been spent at the mansion on the hill. Now that the upholstery clip bonanza had materialized, would he let up a little and spend more time with her and the children? Would he fulfill his potential of being a loving and thoughtful husband and father, or would the habits into which he had fallen keep him more business than family oriented? She would have to try to find out, and soon. If his attitude today was indicative of what she could expect in the future, there would be serious problems ahead.

After a while, she stood up, brushed off her skirt, and walked home.

There was an unmistakable coolness in the atmosphere of the Hacker household that evening. Once supper was eaten and the traces cleared away, Libby went into the living room and sat down to listen as little Chris played his current lessons on the old piano. She never failed to thrill to his amazing ability, and he played even more beautifully than usual tonight, it seemed, perhaps sensing his mother's unhappiness and applying the soothing music flawlessly as balm to her discontent.

No words passed between the adults, but there could perhaps have been a suggestion of apology read into a remark made by Hack as he rose, laid down his newspaper, and left the room.

"You won't have to struggle along with that old beat-up piano much longer, Chris. I'm going to buy you a big, shiny concert grand as soon as we get our new house built," he said.

Chris looked at his mother after Hack disappeared. "Are we going to build a new house, Mama?"

"Well, Daddy means 'sometime,' darling. We'll probably try to build a new house sometime, but not right away. And when we do, we would hope to get a better piano for you, because you play so well and like it so much."

"Gee—that's good! I hope it will be before long."

"All right now, Chris. Time for bed. Go get washed up and ready and I'll be up to tuck you in."

Chapter 33
Progress

1962. Adlai Stevenson, Democrat, and Dwight Eisenhower, Republican, were nominated for the presidency.

Following the demise of her father, King George VI, Queen Elizabeth II succeeded to the British throne.

The United States successfully tested the hydrogen bomb at Eniwetok atoll in the Pacific Ocean.

Richard Nixon presented his famous "Checkers" speech, in defense of his integrity.

Actor John Garfield, sister Elizabeth Kenny and character actress, Hattie McDaniel, died.

The Dow Jones index hit a high of 252.

A fifth of Haig & Haig retailed for $4.99.

Steinbeck's **East of Eden** *and Wouk's* **The Caine Mutiny** *headed for the bestseller list.*

Dr. Jonas Salk tested his promising new polio vaccine.

The New York Yankees (yawn) beat the Brooklyn Dodgers four games to three in baseball's World Series.

On Robin Lane, off Damien Road on the outskirts of Winchester, England, Spenser Finch celebrated his seventh birthday with his mother, Sally, his Grandma and Granddad Finch, and his mother's attentive new friend, Gordon Maitland.

Until recently, Sally had resisted all attempts by young gentlemen to break through the protective wall which she had built around her after she learned of her pregnancy, but there was something about Maitland that she found appealing in a touching way. He had never tried to force his attentions on her, but had done every quiet thing in his power to advertise to her how very much he yearned for her acceptance. And when, more through pity than attraction, she finally allowed him to approach her, she was pleased to find him a charming companion.

Maitland was an intelligent man, and one who had really never before been particularly concerned with the other sex. Girls were all right, but he was so busy building his career in pharmacy that he had never really taken the time to study them. When he spotted Sally, however, something clicked inside him and he immediately began making up for all the lost time. No one had to tell him that she was the one for him; he knew it beyond doubt. Once he had succeeded in breaking through her defenses, they found a relaxed, peaceful contentment in each other's company which neither had previously experienced. It took only a few months for him to convince her that they could build a very pleasant life together, and when she hesitantly broke the news to her parents that she was considering marriage, they were delighted. Gordon was exactly the kind of man whom they had prayed might come along to rescue Sally from her rather drab, monotonous existence. Were it not for her intense love for little Spenser, she would have had nothing in life to really enjoy. Gordon could afford her a chance for happiness.

They agreed to a simple wedding, and Gordon pleaded to be permitted to adopt Spenser, whom he found to be a never-ending source of interest and amusement. He felt he would be very proud to call him his son. And so Spenser's seventh birthday was his last as Master Spenser Finch. Henceforth, he was officially Spenser Joseph Maitland.

How to explain the circumstances of his birth to Spenser had been a problem, but after much discussion, Sally and the elder Finches had decided it would be best to tell him that Spenser's father was Richard Abernathy, his mother's fiancé, who had been killed in the service. They did not worry about nosy townspeople who wished to audit the difference between Richard's last trip home and Spenser's birth. Since his parents had been unable to marry before the tragedy, it had been agreed long ago that he be known as Spenser Finch, and he knew this before starting school. He never questioned the explanation. Spenser did not object to his new father, because he knew and liked Maitland. Taking his name gave the boy a sense of security he had not previously enjoyed.

❖ ❖ ❖

In Newvale, Connecticut, Christopher Hacker was bursting with energy. He had so many things to do, but first he needed to line up sources of supply for the product he had contracted to provide to the huge auto maker. The day after returning from Philadelphia, he strode into Hartshorn's office with a large grin, stuck out his hand and said, "Congratulate me, Fred—I've just completed a deal that will make me very rich!"

Hartshorn's mouth dropped open. He knew that Hack had been spending a lot of time with Brogeson recently, but he did not know why. When Hack had notified him that he was taking a couple of days off to go to Philadelphia, he had not included an explanation of the purpose of the trip. Because Fred trusted Hack, he did not mind Hack notifying him rather than asking for the time off. Fred's instinct and his understanding of Hack told him that whatever had inspired this announcement, all or part of it could be traced back to Ingmar's talents and influence.

"Well," he said, "are you going to tell me what is going on, or do I have to guess?"

So Hack gave him a brief but thorough sketch of what he had developed and how he and his lawyer had sold the whole package to GM.

"So, now," he told Fred, "you've got to line up some presses in a hurry, if you want to be one of my suppliers. The fastener itself is so simple it's beautiful." He produced a sample from his jacket pocket. "I can get the tools made Rush-Rush, but you'll have to get a lot of presses set up. I know what I'll pay for the parts—you can make a decent profit on them—but I'll have to have one or two additional suppliers. No way I can risk interrupted delivery—that's the only thing that could lose me the contract."

Fred was not ready for this. He thought a lot of Hack, and if he had made himself a good deal, that was fine. However, he did not care too much for Hack's tone and the assumption that Hartshorn & Co. was about to immediately retool for a rush job about which he knew nothing, as yet. He also wondered if he had perhaps made a mistake in introducing Hack to Ingmar.

"Look here, Hack—you know I've tried to do my best for you, and you've always given me back at least my money's worth or a little more. I've no complaint on that score, but I like to think we are pretty good friends and virtually partners in this firm, even though you have no financial investment in it, so let's be fair—suppose I decide I'm not ready or able to handle this business? Don't I get a choice in the matter?"

Hack's arrogant manner disappeared.

"You're right, Fred. I did come on a little strong. But I know it won't be any problem for you to start up some presses to do this job, and it's a cream puff, believe me! The machines won't cost you much, and two operators can take care of the whole thing."

But Fred needed the answer to another question.

"The way you are talking, Hack, it sounds as though you are just a potential customer. Don't you work here anymore? I haven't heard you say anything about quitting, but you aren't saying 'we can do this or that'—you're saying, 'you can.' What's the story?"

Now it was Hack's turn to look surprised. Did Fred really think that he was going to stay in this little job when he could buy and sell the place with the money he was about to make?

"Well, hell, Fred—I've got so much to do to get things rolling, there's no way I'd be of much use to you. If I kept my job, you'd just get disgusted, because I'd be out of here more than I'd be in. You understand, don't you?"

The older man looked him straight in the eye.

"Hack," he said, "I do congratulate you on whatever it is you've got started, but I want you to know that I'm very disappointed in you. It's perfectly all right for an ambitious young fellow like you to scratch and claw his way up, but you apparently haven't learned that it doesn't pay to step on people who have been trying to help you. Believe me, I can get along without you, but I do feel that you could have found a much better way to break the news. And any employer is entitled to some notice when a valued employee is moving on, just as the employee is entitled to some notice before being laid off. It's just common decency. I though we were much closer than this, Hack. Frankly, I'm surprised at you!"

Hack acted subdued, but did not sound sincere when he replied, "Ok, Fred. If I owe you some sort of apology, consider you've got it. But that doesn't alter the fact that I'm going to need action fast on this fastener project. You do want to make them, don't you?"

Fred shook his head slowly from side to side. He felt his blood rushing to his face, but he had had years of practice in maintaining his composure in trying situations, and that training enabled him to keep his more vitriolic thoughts to himself now. He merely said, "No, Hack—I don't believe I want to get involved with you as a supplier. You're a little too tough for my taste. I think it will be better for both of us if you line up other people." He stood up, indicating that the discussion was over. "Good luck, Hack. You'd better clean out your desk and pick up anything that's yours around here. I'll have Mary send you a check immediately for whatever wages you have coming."

Hack stood and stared at him for a few moments. He almost wanted to tell him to go to hell and take his shop with him, but he restrained himself.

"Okay, Fred. Goodbye then, and thanks for everything. See ya," he said, and he walked out of the door.

The next few weeks were extremely busy for Hack. After receiving his large check from GM, he arranged for production of the upholstery clips with factories in Danbury and Bridgeport. Until he could prove personal responsibility for the financing, no one would commit to do the work because he had not taken the time to incorporate or establish a business identity.

Within his three month deadline, Hack had overcome this obstacle, had started delivering parts, and also had a dozen handmade applicators in his customer's hands. These would be sufficient for now. The mass-produced models were on order for delivery within the next ten weeks. He pressured manufacturers mercilessly and dashed back and forth from Newvale to Bridgeport, to New York, to Tarrytown, Cleveland and even Detroit, to make sure that the clips and applicators arrived on time and that GM employees were instructed in their proper installation.

Libby and the children saw little of him for months, and the encounters they did have were not very enjoyable. He was so wrapped up in the clip project that his nerves were frayed and his temper was short and during his brief visits home, his main interest was in having a few good meals and getting some sleep.

In a relatively short period of time, Hack had everything running smoothly and was receiving a sizable and steadily increasing income. He still had to pinch himself every so often to be sure that all of this had really happened, and when he was convinced that he was not dreaming, his exhilaration knew no bounds.

He had already started formulating further plans for building his fortune. Sleepy little Newvale, now seeing greatly increased traffic due to being in the "corridor" between New York, Boston and other bustling cities in New England, had very few business establishments for the benefit of its growing number of citizens. For instance, it sported but one automobile dealer, and its neighbor, Wentworth, had only two. Everyone seemed now to be in the market for a new car, which caused Hack to investigate the method of obtaining a franchise for one of the leading GM brands. He also recognized that with business booming, people becoming more mobile and the baby boom in full swing, the real estate market was the next logical target. He planned to get into it as quickly as possible by obtaining a real estate dealer's license to sell other people's property and also to buy as much attractive unimproved land in Newvale and surrounding towns as he could.

He was immediately successful in real estate, because he was convinced that no matter what people asked for their land now, it would look like a bargain in a few short years. Therefore, he negotiated briefly whenever he went after a tract, and then agreed to a price and closed the deal. His growing affluence and his ability to show that he had a large and burgeoning contract with GM enabled him to obtain, easily, a substantial portion of the financing for these projects, rather than having to use his own money.

Chapter 34
Building

As one of his early deals, Hack purchased a tract of over 100 acres on Henderson Mountain. It was actually only one of the many rolling hills in the area, but it had always been called Henderson Mountain by the locals. It was mostly wooded, with an assortment of oaks, maples, birches, beeches and evergreens. Hack knew that it would be the ideal place to build his mansion. Once a large area was cleared, it afforded a spectacular view. He was determined that his estate would outdo Newvale's other wealthy families.

In the fashion which had become typical of him, Hack slammed into designing and constructing his dream house. He sought out the best known architect in western Connecticut. After a session in which Hack evaluated the architect's plans of many homes he had previously designed, he found that none of them were large enough or impressive enough for him. They decided that the architect would start immediately to design a plan incorporating the features which Hack wanted. Within a month, a tentative agreement had been reached on the general style and size and in another three weeks, working drawings sufficient to allow the excavating contractor to begin work were completed.

After dinner one evening, Hack sat at a table in the small living room with plans spread out everywhere. He worked feverishly at them for a while and then called Libby to join him He had been pushing poor Libby relentlessly to review plans, select styles, design indoor and outdoor areas, and decide decor. He insisted that she work closely with the architect and supervise the entire project from beginning to end. He would be the authority whose stamp of approval had to be granted for everything. He refused to consider her protestations that what he was proposing was far more than they needed and far more than she wanted. She wanted to approach the project in a slow, methodical manner, but he insisted on moving quickly.

"I've waited long enough—now, I intend to see some action! Just humor me in this, Lib, you'll be surprised at how well it will all turn out if you work with me. And remember, the sky's the limit. We are building for the future. I don't want to leave Newvale, and I don't believe you do either, so this has to be looked at as our permanent home. And it's going to be the best and the biggest in these parts."

Libby sighed. "Christopher, I can see that you are so keyed up about building this palace that you really don't want my input. I would love a new home, but my choice wouldn't even resemble this sprawling complex that you insist on. Don't you think it's a bit ostentatious? After all, I am expected to follow the plans and supervise everything and I don't even know how many rooms there are! This is more like a hotel than a home. Why couldn't we at least start small and add to it as needed, or wanted?"

"On the surface, it appears that we could do that, yes," he replied. "As long as we have an overall plan that can be followed, it would seem logical that the actual building could be done sort of piecemeal."

He pointed to the architect's rendering and said, "However, everything revolves around this grand entrance and the adjacent rooms—the wings are mainly sleeping quarters and maintenance facilities. Now which of these do you suggest we give up for a while? You can't have the wings without the main complex, and the main complex will be useless until such time as you have the support facilities and rooms for family and guests to live in, and you can't have family or guests in a place this size without provision for a staff to furnish the necessary service. Now, what does that leave that you want to try doing without?" He looked at her with an expression which said, "Why don't you stop making silly objections and just do as I tell you?"

Libby, frustrated, could think of no counter argument. She sighed again, deeply, threw up her hands and said, "All right, Christopher, I give up. We'll just do it your way. Give me my orders and I'll try my best to carry them out like a good little soldier. But that doesn't mean that I have to approve."

His first impulse was to refute her, but he thought better of it. After all, he was going to have to depend on her to oversee the construction—he could not afford to alienate her now.

"Look, Lib—I know that you feel this is too much too soon, but it's going to take quite a while to get the whole thing shaped up and put together. By then you will have started thinking more like a wealthy woman with big responsibilities, because that's what you'll be. I can understand that you would be just as happy with a lot less, but I wouldn't, and neither would the kids nor the rest of the family. When you begin to realize how much good you can do with plenty of funds, you'll stop feeling guilty or embarrassed about being rich and start being thankful for it. All of us, especially me, realize how clever you are at organizing things and at handling people, and you'll do a terrific job of masterminding this project once you get into it, I know that."

He rose and stepped behind her chair. He leaned down and put his arms around her, gave her a hug, and kissed her cheek. "We're a team, Lib, and a damned good one. Lately I've been sort of a bastard to live with, I know, but I've had so much on my mind and so many balloons in the air at once that it's made me pretty edgy. I apologize for that. If there is one person in the world whom I need and want on my side, it's you. You know I love you, even though it's probably hard to tell sometimes. If you want, we'll take a break right here and go away for a few days, just the two of us. What do you think?"

This change of tactics calmed Libby. At least, he realized that he had not been easy to live with lately. Probably his seeming indifference toward her in recent months could be explained by the tremendous pressure he had put on himself to complete the admittedly big deals he had been working on with such notable success. Her naturally forgiving nature told her to back down and help make things smoother.

"I know the strain you've been under, Christopher, and I'm really happy that you would stop in the middle of things and go away with me, but I can't ask you to do that. We'll both stick to our jobs for now and perhaps later on we can do something along that line.

He hugged her again—a hard hug this time. Then he helped her out of her chair, held her away and really looked at her for the first time in a long while. He wondered how he could have virtually ignored this beautiful, desirable woman for so long!

She was gazing back at him in a way that said, "I love you very much, Christopher, but I am confused by the signals you send." He read the message and realized that this was the moment to reassure her of his love and, incidentally, to lock her solidly into his program. He drew her back to him and kissed her long and hard.

"We've done enough for tonight, Lib. Let's just forget about everything but each other until tomorrow." He took her willing hand and led her toward the stairs.

❖ ❖ ❖

In the spring of 1954, bulldozers, trucks and workmen attacked Henderson Mountain like an invading army. Trees were felled and stumps dug out, rocks were exhumed and moved into piles and rows as potential elements of wall. Soon, a winding drive took shape, leading from the town road at the base of the hill all the way to the spot far above which had been selected as the site of the new Hacker mansion. Then the power-shovel, bulldozers, trucks and men began to prepare the excavation to accommodate the foundation. Huge cement trucks started churning their way up and down the approach and rivers of their contents were poured, load after load, into the waiting forms. When they were finished and the new walls were sufficiently cured, construction of the building began in earnest. Trucks loaded with lumber, door and window frames, bricks, furnaces, pipes, shingles and other materials beat an almost constant path up and down the hillside, providing an ongoing pageant to entertain interested townspeople. Days became weeks, and weeks turned into months, and still the construction continued. Slowly but steadily, the walls rose, brick on brick, and eventually the skeleton of the numerous roofs took shape and were covered with underlayment, shingles and/or tiles. Windows and doors were set in place and four great columns were installed across the front of the main entrance, lending an added air of elegance to the edifice.

Once the roofs, doors and windows were in place, the plumbers, electricians and carpenters proceeded with the long process of finishing the interior. Libby and the architect were kept busy making inspections and implementing changes. For one who had never undertaken this kind of work before, Libby impressed both the architect and the contractors with her quick assimilation of knowledge about materials, dimensions and practicality. Unlike many picky and woefully ignorant owners, she seldom made a suggestion which they found to be frivolous or unworkable, and her pleasant manner and fairness had them all anxious to please her and carry out her wishes.

All of the winter was spent completing the interior, and when spring of 1955 arrived, Libby immediately became involved with the landscapers, laying out lawns and gardens, approving needed outbuildings, designing a swimming pool and cabana area, a stable and tack room, providing for screening hedges and decorative plantings, and selecting the many types and varieties of shrubs and flowers to be grown in so many places. Since she felt her knowledge of horticulture to be inadequate, she took a course through the agricultural extension service of the state university. For her, it was worthwhile.

All the while that the building project was underway, the lord and master of the budding kingdom was busily engaged in other enterprises by which to provide the required wherewithal. Hack's real estate ventures were booming, and the new Hacker Motors Chevrolet-Oldsmobile dealership, for which he had promoted a franchise through his GM contacts, began immediately to do a fine business. Through a combination of shrewdness and good fortune, Hack had acquired the services of his old friend, Walt Stanevich, to spearhead the operation. Walt had all of the qualities needed to assure the business' success. He was a big, friendly, unquestionably honest man who had been in love with automobiles since childhood and knew them inside and out. He was well known and liked throughout the Newvale-Wentworth area, and he was devoted to his lifelong friend, Hack. Walt had acquired a business degree under the GI Bill of Rights which gave him the expertise needed to operate the business.

Whatever Hack turned his attention and appetites to, prospered. While luck played a part in his achievements, it was also apparent that he had a knack for snooping out promising ventures and the boldness as well as the capital and credit to wade into them, not recklessly but unhesitatingly. Much of his success was due to the fact that he had an almost uncanny feel for the quality of the people with whom he dealt. Some, he knew instinctively that he could trust. Any about whom he felt the slightest doubt were investigated from all angles before even a nickel of his funds was invested. If any thing whatsoever of a negative nature was exposed regarding either their business or their personal lives, Hack dropped them abruptly. His theory on associates was simple. "With all the sharp, honest and capable people there are out there, anxious to get on the bandwagon, why should I settle for anyone who doesn't measure up?" And he instructed those whom he installed in managerial positions to adhere strictly to the same criteria.

Libby, he realized, was a prime example of his ability to choose outstanding people. In addition to being a wonderful wife and mother, she proved that she had few peers when it came to supervising a building project. As the Hacker estate took form and shape, Hack marveled at the smooth job she was doing. He was seldom asked for advice, decisions or to settle disputes and differences of opinion among the architect, contractors and family. Libby took care of everything in her quiet, logical, matter-of-fact way, leaving Hack with nothing to do but to nod his head in approval. All of the changes that were made, and some of them were rather drastic, were at her suggestion, and she was able to explain the reasons for them to Hack's complete satisfaction.

"Lib," he said, "you amaze me, you really do. No one else would have kept those contractors and the architect working so well together. You're a magician! Just in heading off arguments between the various contractors and convincing them to stick to a schedule, you've undoubtedly saved us thousands of dollars. When this is all done, I know what I'm going to do with you."

"Oh? she said. "And just what might that be?"

He grinned and said, "I'm going to make you the construction supervisor for a couple of housing developments I'm planning. I couldn't hire anyone with your talent for $50,000!"

Libby shook her head. "I hate to disappoint you, Christopher, but you couldn't hire me for twice that! I'm doing this because it's ours and it had to be done. Believe me, when this is finished, I'm out of the building business, period!"

"Oh, I'll bet you'll change your mind later, when you get bored and remember how much you've enjoyed running this show. Being the big boss gets into your blood after you've had a little taste of it."

"Yours, maybe—not mine. I'm doing my best here, but it isn't me. No one will be as happy as I the day the last workman drives out, with the architect right behind him. Then I'll get back to being a mother and wife and enjoying my friends and church and community work. This has just been a necessary interruption."

"We'll see," he laughed. But she certainly did sound as though she meant what she said.

When Libby's hopes materialized and the huge building project was finally completed, two years had passed. It was now 1956. The mansion itself was built, the long garage, the stables and other outbuildings were completed. The swimming pool was ready to be filled, and the gardens were ready for warm weather plantings. Many shrubs and small trees were already in the ground, and many more would be as soon as the ground thawed. Acres of lawn had been prepared and seeded the previous fall and awaited only the heat of the spring sun and warm showers to burst into life.

But, if Libby had believed she would be able to return to her prior life, it was not to be. She found that operating the large establishment could be nearly as time consuming as building it was. A large staff was necessary to keep everything cleaned, washed, mowed, trimmed as well as to cook and launder. These people had to be interviewed, hired, instructed, overseen and sometimes replaced. Hack, of course, suggested that a housekeeper should be employed, but Libby wanted to be in control.

"It's bad enough that I can't do my own housework," she complained. "I'm certainly going to at least decide what is to be done and who is to do it, and what and when we will eat! *I'll* be the housekeeper, thank you!"

As it turned out, Libby later found that the job was just too much for her, when coupled with her obligations to the family and to the guests whom her husband was constantly bringing or sending with little or no notice. Reluctantly, she started delegating one job or another to some of the staff who had impressed her as being conscientious workers.

One of the extravagances in building the new place was the inclusion of a large music room. Hack had told Libby to enlist the aid of the Yale music professor who was monitoring young Christopher's progress, as well as that of his instructor and technicians who knew who could help them to properly design and construct the room for maximum acoustical quality. The result was a superior setting in which young Chris could perfect his talent. The Yale professor had also found a family who owned an excellent grand piano which they wished to see in the hands of a promising student because the pianist in the family had passed away. The professor assured the Hackers that this piano could not be matched for quality by a new one. The piano became the centerpiece of the room, and young Chris' pride and joy.

He was nine years old when the family moved into the new home and was eager about his music. With the added incentive of the marvelous piano and the technically correct acoustics, he spent even more hours at the keyboard than before. His command of the instrument improved rapidly. Libby had carefully explained to him that although music was the major interest of his life, it must not become so dominant that other important elements suffered. His schooling, his physical recreation, his religious training, and particularly his interaction with other people must not suffer or else he would find himself unhappily isolated by the time he reached maturity. Chris understood what she was trying to teach him and honestly tried to not resent the time spent on these other facets of his life. But his hours at the keyboard remained by far his favorites.

Chapter 35
Interlude

As the late 1950s and '60s slipped by, the Hacker family fell into routines which insidiously ate up time in large chunks. The children were assimilated into the patterns of all youngsters; studying, attending church and social functions and participating in sports.

Hack and Libby were submerged in multiple duties and enterprises. For Hack, life revolved around his many and growing business interests. He was expanding into areas hitherto unknown to him, but his intense desire for ever greater financial triumphs spurred him on and was responsible for his success in competing with professionals. This success fed upon itself, one victory providing the springboard for the next, his first million dollars becoming seed for more millions to follow. Unfortunately, he was so wrapped up in these enterprises that he found little time to devote to his wife and children. Although he continued to operate out of his small original office on Main Street, he gradually developed larger and more sophisticated headquarters in the east wing of his home. He let himself and others believe that this was an indication of his affection for his family and his need to be near them, but he actually spent little time in residence. His presence seemed always to be needed elsewhere. He was now involved in several manufacturing ventures, and although he had no direct connection with the production facilities, he was the contact man who flew all over the world arranging contracts, entertaining influential people, or sizing up potential licensees for the various products he, as factor, controlled. On such rare occasions as he did find time to be at "Mount Hacker," as it was now being referred to, Hack talked to young Chris and Susan about school, friends, recreation and the future. Both were doing well academically, and much to his surprise, neither was enthusiastic when he suggested that they might like to enroll in private school. Although Libby had told him that she felt they were really better off staying in Newvale schools, he had assumed that the excitement of a change to new surroundings would appeal to them, and might stimulate them to higher achievements. Chris was not willing to go anywhere that he could not take his beloved piano with him. He said he wanted to stay home until it was time for college. He was not very interested in sports, but stayed involved in them to satisfy his father. In most sports he was reasonably proficient, but not outstanding. He might have been better at them had he not secretly worried about his hands. He shied away from hot ground balls or hard passes for fear that injuries might result. His hands were invaluable to him.

Susan was as happy and enthusiastic about school as she was about life. Her nature was to enjoy the present moment and look forward to the next. She did not worry because she had confidence in herself and in the ultimate good in everything and everyone. In fact, she felt sorry for people who felt otherwise. As a result, she was very popular and had many friends. She loved to sit in the music room and listen to her brother play, and she raved about his talent, although she had no desire to follow his example.

"I'm no Chris," she said. "I just love his music, and his ability absolutely amazes me, but I haven't either the talent or the patience to play an instrument. They tell me I have a fairly good voice, and I love to sing, so that's the extent of my involvement in music. Except to listen to Chris, that is."

Both Hacker children participated in social activities. Chris did not care to dance, but was always prevailed upon to play piano, so he was always a welcome addition to parties and dances. Several girls had their eyes on him and flirted whenever they had an opportunity, but his policy was to be impartially friendly with all of them. When he had to escort girls to social events, he made it a point to invite a different one each time. Similarly, Susan had many boyfriends. At various times she was convinced that she was in love with one or another of them, but these juvenile amours usually lasted only a few months before she became smitten with another one.

As for Libby, she was perhaps the busiest of them all. She was mistress of the manor and ran it efficiently. Her only concession was to admit that she had been mistaken regarding the need for a housekeeper. She hired a woman whom her mother knew well and who bonded with Libby immediately. Mary Chaplin proved to be as valuable as she was devoted. Libby soon came to depend on Mary to handle details she was too busy to take care of. Although Libby was sometimes uncomfortable delegating responsibility, she came to accept graciously the personal attentions which Mary bestowed out of deep respect and admiration.

Libby had to assume almost total responsibility for the upbringing of Chris and Susan because Hack was away so much. When he was home, he was usually in his office with papers piled high in front of him or with a telephone glued to his ear. He also often entertained important clients on the tennis courts, at the pool, in the billiard room, at dinner or on the patio for cocktails or a barbecue. He expected Libby to provide hospitality to these visitors, too, often on very short notice. Because of her desire to be sure that Hack's best interests were served, she was always the enthusiastic hostess.

Libby was determined that Hack should contribute to the raising of the children, and she pressed him for assistance in making decisions about them. Often he was short-tempered and impatient with her when she insisted that he help her do so, but she reminded him that they were his children, too. He could not argue against her logic.

The lifestyle which Hack and Libby had developed had one glaring omission. They seldom found themselves with free time to spend together in a relaxed and romantic mood, with the result that marital relations between them became less and less frequent. At first, this scarcely registered with Libby, for her method of expressing love did not rely heavily upon physical contact. However, one day she realized that she had trouble remembering the last time they had made love or had a romantic evening. She began to have gnawing doubts as to her husband's loyalty. Since she hated the idea of jealousy or mistrust, she decided to ignore these possibilities. But, as time passed, she found the subject creeping back into her consciousness at odd moments, and after a few more weeks slipped by,. she felt she had to ask Hack for an explanation.

"Christopher, I need to ask you about something that has bothered me a bit lately."

"Oh? Well, what is that?"

"I—I don't know just how to put this," she said awkwardly, "and I don't want you to misunderstand why I am asking, but—well, I've been wondering if there is some reason why we haven't—why you haven't been suggesting sex much, lately."

A look of surprise crossed Hack's face, quickly replaced by a broad smile.

"Why, honey, I'm surprised at your brazenness! This is really out of character for you! How about tonight? I'm sorry if you feel that I've been lax in my duties as a husband. Will you forgive me?"

Libby felt her face getting hot. "No, no," she stammered. "You're not listening to me. Don't let your male ego take right over. I'm asking a question because I think it deserves an answer—I'm not proposing anything, I just want to know if there's some secret reason why you've changed your ways. You do spend an awful lot of nights away from here, you know. I haven't even thought about you being unfaithful before, and I don't want to now, but you must admit that the degree of your attentiveness toward me has changed drastically. Just give me a satisfactory answer and I'll consider the subject closed."

Now her concern was clear to Hack. It dawned on him that she was right. His mind had been so occupied with several deals at once that he did not notice how much time slid by without him acting the part of husband or lover—or father. The figures that danced before his eyes were financial, not feminine.

"Libby, honey," he said, earnestly, "you can't be blamed for having your doubts, I guess. The days fly off the calendar so fast that I hardly realize that the months change—that the seasons change, even. I have so much going on, and so many places to be, and so many people to see, that time doesn't mean much, except the time that I have to be in certain places. There is no way that I can prove to you that I don't mess around with women. All I can do is tell you that I don't. And I mean, not ever. The closest I ever come to cheating on you is when I have to sit and eat dinner with some woman who's involved in one of my deals. You're all the woman I want or need, Lib. Maybe some day things will slow down enough for me to prove that to you. I certainly hope so."

Libby felt sure that she could believe what he said, If he was cheating, he would doubtless have become angry when she questioned him, or have pretended to be hurt that she could even ask. She put it all out of her mind as a closed subject.

Chapter 36
Mulcahy's Suite

Because of the mutual affection which existed between old Sean and his favorite granddaughter, it was only natural that when his wife, Peggy, died suddenly in 1962, he found his greatest solace in the sympathy and understanding offered by the now adult Libby. She quietly insisted that Grandpa move in to one of the spacious empty suites at the mansion, and in his bereft and bewildered state he reluctantly allowed himself to be persuaded to do so. She had his clothing and personal possessions collected from the little house in town and moved into bureaus and closets in his new quarters. She supervised his settling in and made sure that he had everything that he could possibly need or want. Then she hovered nearby for several days until she was satisfied that her grandfather had overcome the shock.

As the weeks passed and the numbness gradually wore off, the old man realized more clearly the depth of his loss. He remembered his Peggy as a jewel. From the day he found her until the day of her death, she had been his lover, his most loyal supporter, and his helpmate. Whatever happened, Peg was right there seeing to it that Sean's best interests were being served. She seldom raised her voice, but she was straight, strong and constant. And now, he was conscience-stricken with the belief that perhaps he had not adequately demonstrated to her how much he loved her. He had always assumed that it would be he who would go first and pave the way to Heaven for the two of them. Now, he feared he might be unable to find her trail in order to join her when he died.

The more he thought, the more he pined. He suddenly felt completely out of place in the spacious, expensively furnished bedroom-sitting room. What was he, a hard-bitten old relic, doing in these fancy surroundings? He felt that he should be in a thatch-roofed shanty with a dirt floor, not in a hilltop mansion with thick rugs, marble bathrooms and servants everywhere. He belonged with his brewery friends, shouting, laughing, cursing and fighting. He should have a stein of beer or a bottle of whiskey in his hand, competing with the other swaggering strong men when the workday was finished, punctuating every playful, boastful statement with a long swig and ready at all times to bawl or to brawl, as the circumstances dictated. And then he would reel home to Peggy, and she would patch up the cuts and bruises without comment and feed him and love him or tuck him in bed. She had understood that his heritage and his pride demanded that he deport himself in this manner and she had had neither the means nor the desire to change him.

For the first time in years, an overwhelming thirst for liquor assailed him.

"Bejabbers, 'tis time the Mulcahy had himself a drink of whiskey ," he thought. "My poor darlin' Peggy is gone, and 'tis time I drank a farewell toast to her lovin' memory."

Mulcahy rose from his easy chair and tiptoed to the door. He knew exactly where to go. He peered up and down the corridor and, seeing no one, stepped quickly out of the room and turned right. He passed several rooms and then turned right again into an alcove, across the end of which a complete wet bar was set up. He swung open the bar door, slipped behind it and opened the long cupboard. Inside, there was a selection of liquor of all sorts. He quickly slipped two bottles of Irish whiskey into his trouser pockets and stepped back outside the bar. Luck was with him. No one saw him as he retraced his steps back to his suite. He stepped inside and closed the door, then made for the bathroom, where he lifted the heavy lid off the toilet tank. He flushed the toilet and set his two pilfered bottles inside the tank, then replaced the lid. His heart was pounding from the excitement. He walked back into the sitting room and dropped into his chair, feeling rather like a little boy who had stolen cigarettes from his father's untended pack.

Sean knew that Libby would soon be calling him to come to dinner, so he waited patiently until that happened. After the meal, he stayed with the family for an hour to be polite. Then he told Libby that he wanted to take a bath before going to bed. Goodnights were said and he walked slowly back to his quarters. He knew no one would bother him until morning. Sean took off his shoes and his shirt, put on his slippers, and rubbed his hands together in anticipation as he walked to the bathroom. He lifted the tank lid, removed the bottles, replaced the lid and returned to his chair, carrying the hoard of whiskey. With practiced expertise, he ran his thumbnail around the crease beneath the top of the first bottle, cutting the revenue seal, then twisted the cap off. Memories of old times welled up inside him as he sniffed at the open bottle.

"One to start the ceremonies," he said, and he put it to his lips and took the swallow he had been anticipating. His throat and stomach, no longer accustomed to liquor, constricted violently. He gasped for breath. The spasm quickly passed, and the old man laughed.

"'Tis out of practice, y'are, ye old softy! Better have another. Don't mind if I do!" And he tilted the bottle again. This time, the fiery liquid slid down easier. He smacked his lips and exclaimed, "Ah-h-h, tis good to meet you again, old friend!"

He waited a minute and then drank again. Already he was beginning to feel the alcoholic warmth creeping through his body. His brain responded to this new stimulus, rapidly sorting through its files for procedures previously learned. All of the cells dedicated to the handling of strong spirits started clicking into place; the monitors for laughing, singing, fighting and crying stepped to the fore, ready for immediate service. And now that the alterations necessary to transform him from a teetotaler to a toper were accomplished, Sean remembered his need to mourn his lost love. Immediately, tears came to his eyes as he envisioned his dear Peg, alone, lost and wandering through the firmament, seeking him and needing him. A sob escaped his lips and he quickly stifled it with another long draft from the bottle.

"Peg, my darlin', don't be afraid. I'll come for ye soon, and we'll climb thim golden stairs together."

The priest had assured him that Peg would be fine, but that was because she had led an exemplary life. Did the priest know how much they relied upon each other? He was only a man, after all. How could the priest know what plans God had in store for his Peggy? Mulcahy sat quietly and let the tears run down his cheeks. Fragments of some of the old songs were playing around in his mind. Softly, he hummed the tunes and sang such of the words as he could remember. His sorrow deepened. He returned to the bottle again and again, and finally he tilted it only to find that it was empty. He held it out in front of him in disbelief. He had only been drinking for a short time—how could he have consumed a full fifth of whiskey that quickly? He laughed derisively.

"Ye've got yer drinkin' shoes on tonight, Sean!" he mumbled. Without hesitation, he pawed around until he located and opened the second bottle. With a deep sigh, he lifted it to his mouth.

During his several years of abstinence, two important changes had occurred. First, his body and its organs had accustomed themselves to living without having to battle the poison, and second, he and all of his parts had grown older and consequently less able to combat such incursions. When the shock of the raw liquor delivered the message to the heart, the lungs and the liver to gird themselves for battle, the response was neither as rapid nor as robust as in earlier years. Each succeeding dose of whiskey made the labor of these organs more and more exhausting. He had been drinking so fast that he had built up a reservoir of whiskey in his stomach. It was being digested and pumped into his bloodstream at a much too high rate.

Abruptly, his heart ceased functioning. Sight drained from his eyes, his head dropped to his chest, and the bottle slipped from his hand and thumped on the floor, gurgling out the remainder of its contents.

Libby arose at her usual time the next morning. She showered, dressed casually, and went to the kitchen where she had her usual toast and a cup of coffee. As she poured her drink, she asked the cook, "Has my grandfather gone for his walk?" Since he had taken up residence here, he had developed the habit of rising very early, having coffee, and then taking a stroll around the grounds before returning for a heartier breakfast.

"No, ma'am. He hasn't been in here this morning."

"Hasn't been around at all?"

"No, ma'am. I've been here since five-thirty and I haven't seen him."

Libby felt a cold shiver pass over her. She turned and left the kitchen quickly and hurried to the nearest telephone. She dialed the intercom number for her grandfather's suite and waited breathlessly for a response, but none came. Now her heart was beating rapidly and fear mounted as she ran the length of the mansion to his room. By the time she reached his door, she was sweating and panting far more than the exercise warranted. She rapped hard on the door, calling, "Grandpa, Grandpa!"

Hearing nothing, she pounded harder. She twisted the doorknob and the door swung in.

Although the chair in which he sat faced away from her, she could see enough to know that he was dead. The rug was wet from the spilled whiskey, and the bottle which had caused the stain lay on its side next to it. An empty bottle stood upright on the floor beside his chair. The room reeked of liquor.

The top of the old man's head was visible and was skewed over at an odd angle. His right hand hung down, the fingers bent under awkwardly against the rug. Libby instinctively reached out to touch his face, which was so cold that she shuddered.

"Oh, Grandpa, dear, dear Grandpa—whatever have you done!"

She went to the phone by the bed and called the doctor. Then she tried calling Hack at his office in town, but was informed that he was not in. She hurried to Chris' room and woke him up. As gently as possible, she told him what she had found. He immediately recognized the trauma which the discovery had caused his mother. He got out of bed quickly, put on a robe, and led her out onto the balcony, where he insisted she sit down and stay quiet. Suddenly, Libby cried, "My God! It's my fault! It's my fault that Grandpa's dead! I should have known that he would be tempted sooner or later by all of the liquor around this house! If I had only had the sense to have all of it locked up, he would never have been able to do this!"

"Now, now, Mother," Chris said soothingly. "It isn't your fault at all. When Grandpa was ready to drink, he would have found a way. You mustn't blame yourself."

He moved his chair close to hers and placed an arm around her shoulders. But once it struck her that she might be responsible, the strange feeling which she had experienced once or twice before started creeping over her again. She saw everything quite distinctly, yet recognized hardly anything. It was as though she were separated from her own existence and as if she were looking at her life and its events from a distance, as a spectator rather than as the central character. Was this really happening? Was she really the mistress of this huge house? Could this handsome young man really be her son? Was it really true that she had just discovered the grandfather whom she loved so dearly, dead from guzzling down a great quantity of liquor—liquor which she had allowed to be within his reach for the taking? None of this could be true, could it? Desperately, she clung to Chris' robe as he gently rubbed her back to soothe her.

After some long and terrifying minutes, she was able to fight down the horrible sense of unreality and to face facts. But the sense of guilt, she could not erase.

Chapter 37
Chris

Chris finished high school in a blaze of glory. Although he did not lead his class academically, he did attain honors status and could qualify for college acceptance. But, it was in music that he excelled. He had long since outstripped the teaching capabilities of local area instructors, and he had gradually moved to associate with other talented artists in western Connecticut. They congregated in various halls from time to time to experiment and to draw inspiration and "entente cordiale" from each other. Most of Chris' continuing music education and increasing skills were the result of constant daily practice. He also continued his periodic visits to Professor Ludwig at Yale, from which he invariably came away refreshed and with a renewed sense of confidence.

"Christopher," the professor would say, "you are my favorite musician. There is no limit to what you can accomplish. Do not let anything or anybody interfere with your search for perfection in the mechanics and the expression of your music. You will never achieve perfection, as no one ever has nor ever will, but in pursuit of it you will find unending satisfaction. Once an artist reaches the plane at which you now find yourself, each tiny improvement is exquisitely rewarding. Unfortunately, only another serious musician can fully appreciate this, but that does not matter—ultimately, we play only to ourselves, anyway."

Professor Ludwig knew gifted musicians throughout the world. He offered, therefore, to advise Chris regarding his musical education after high school. At first, he had hoped Chris would come to Yale to pursue his studies so that he could shepherd and coach him. However, on reflection the professor decided that it might be better if Chris were exposed to other instructors and mentors who would give him a broader spectrum of counsel and guidance.

"Where do you expect to go for your college training, Christopher?" he asked one day. "Have you picked out a school?"

"Not really. I've thought about it a lot, and I've had suggestions from several of the people I play with, but mostly they just push the schools they attended, which is natural, I suppose. The only thing I have definitely decided is that I'd like it to be away from New England. Not that I don't love it here, but I think it would do me a lot of good and would permit me to concentrate better on my music if I were not too close to home and friends and family. Actually, California sort of intrigues me. From what I hear and read, there are lots of areas out there which are pretty much dedicated to the arts, and they also have that great climate. It sounds pretty romantic and exciting. Do you know of any possibilities in that area?"

Professor Ludwig nodded. "As a matter of fact, Christopher, I do. I have a dear friend out there who would welcome a young talent like you with open arms and would do his level best to help out in any way that he could. His name is Herman Gottfried, and he is a professor of political science at Pepperdine University in Malibu. It's a relatively new school, but it is building an excellent reputation. He assures me that it is destined to be a leader in the arts, and that music is one of the areas in which the trustees have a special interest. And if the ocean and the warm climate and the relaxed life style appeal to you, it would be difficult to find a more attractive place than Malibu."

"That sounds wonderful," Chris said, his face lighting up. "Could he furnish some literature that I could show my parents? I haven't really discussed it much with them, but I'm pretty sure they are open to any suggestions, especially if they come from someone like you."

"I'm sure I can get you a catalog, Christopher. I'll write Herman tonight. Better yet, I'll call him. I haven't spoken with him for some time. He'll be excited about the possibility, I know."

Within a week, Christopher received a call from the professor who told him that the catalog had arrived and that he would send it along immediately, and also that his friend from California was thrilled to learn that the professor's protege was going to consider applying for admission to Pepperdine.

"Herman would like nothing better than to offer any assistance he can to guide you toward matriculation at his institution. He has heard enough about your musical talent from me to convince himself that you would be a great asset to the school, and he hopes you will take advantage of his knowledge of

California in general and Pepperdine in particular as often as you wish. He has enclosed a note to that effect inside the school catalog, complete with his telephone number."

"Gosh, Professor Ludwig, I certainly appreciate all the trouble you have gone to to help me out. And your friend, too."

The professor merely nodded, then continued, "Christopher, it has occurred to me that you may feel that I am putting pressure on you to force you in the direction of Pepperdine, and I certainly don't want to do so. After all, I have only my friend Herman's enthusiastic description to go by, so please keep that in mind. If you were to tell me tomorrow that you had decided on another school entirely, it would not upset me at all. I hope you understand that."

"Oh, no, Professor. I know that you are just trying to help. California is attractive to me at this point, but I am really just shopping. You have done so much for me, I know that anything you offer is with the best of intentions. I am anxious to see the catalog and to learn all that I can about Pepperdine. Maybe I can talk Dad or Mom into letting me take a trip out there to look it over."

"Yes," replied Professor Ludwig, 'that would be an excellent idea. Perhaps it would serve the purpose better if one or both of them could accompany you. An enthusiastic verbal report on the school and its surroundings from one so young might strike them as suspect, whereas what they see for themselves would make it considerably easier for them to arrive at a decision."

Christopher laughed. "As usual, your advice makes very good sense, Professor. If I'm still seriously considering Pepperdine after I read the catalog and see what else I can turn up about it around here, that's just what I'll suggest."

Christopher studied the Pepperdine catalog thoroughly. It revealed nothing to discourage him; in fact he loved what he read, so at the first opportunity he spoke to his mother about his discussion with Professor Ludwig.

"Do you really think that you would be happy to be so far from home?" she asked. "Don't you think it might be more comfortable for you around New England where you are familiar with the surroundings and the people, and where you could drop home conveniently?"

"No, not the way I've figured it," he replied. "I want to be able to give my whole attention to my music, and of course, to whatever related studies are required. If I'm too near home or to people I know and have to socialize with, I feel it will be too distracting, and from what I read and hear, there's no better place to relax when you do have a little time off than that part of California."

Libby paused to weigh the situation. Chris had consistently shown an unusual degree of dedication and dependability. Was there any reason to believe that he would be less deserving of trust and confidence in his selection of a college? No, she decided, there was none, and now was the perfect time to reassure him of her total support in the preparation for his future. If ever a mother had had a boy who brought her great pride and happiness, it was she, and Chris was the boy.

"Dear Chris," she said, leaning forward in her chair and taking his hand in hers, "I know how very much your wonderful music means to you, and how completely you give yourself to it. I understand how you feel about wanting to pursue it to the exclusion of nearly everything else, and yet I am amazed and delighted at how thoughtful you always manage to be toward me and the rest of the family. You are a marvelous person, Chris, and I hope you will always be as you are today. Your father is away so much and is so involved in business even when he is here that he misses out on a lot of the joy that I get from your music, but he is enthusiastically behind you and follows your progress eagerly. I know that I can speak for him as well as myself in saying that you have our blessing to pick out the school you want. It would certainly appear to be a good idea to take a trip out there to look things over, though, before committing yourself."

Chris nodded vigorously. "Oh definitely—I wouldn't want to be too quick about it. Who knows? I might be turned off completely when I see the place."

"Yes," said his mother, "you must look it over carefully and try to get more information about the school from people who are from the area or who have attended it. Do you think you can find someone dependable to go out there with you? I wouldn't like the idea of your making such a trip alone."

"Well, actually, I was hoping that maybe either you or Dad could find the time to take the trip with me." He peered hard into his mother's eyes and then added, "But I'm afraid I can see that that's not going to fly—right?"

Libby nodded her head slowly. "I'd love to go, dear, but you know that my time is pretty well spoken for right here. I'm sure that you can make other arrangements that would probably be more fun, anyway."

"I don't agree for a minute, Mother. But I do know how busy you are, and Dad's a total loss with that schedule of his. I'll give it some thought and see if I can come up with any possibilities. You can do the same, Mother—you have a lot of contacts with the local ladies. Maybe some of them would have a suggestion."

And so they left it at that for the moment.

A couple of days later, Libby walked to the west wing and peeked in at the door of the conservatory. There was Chris at the keyboard, coaxing a quietly beautiful melody from the depths of the instrument. She waited quietly until he came to the end of the piece.

"May I disturb you for a minute, dear?" she asked.

"Any time, Mother, you know that."

He turned toward her. She could not help noticing that as he turned away from the keyboard, he ran his hand gently, lovingly along the mahogany above the keys. "How he loves that instrument," she thought.

She sat down on the edge of a chair.

"About our discussion the other day, dear—about the school—I just came back from a luncheon meeting with my Middlebury reunion committee, and in the course of our chit-chat, I mentioned that you were giving some thought to attending Pepperdine, and guess what?"

"I'll bite—what?" Chris asked, grinning.

"Marion Compton from Middletown says she knows quite a bit about the school. Her husband's brother-in-law came from out around Malibu and he sings the school's praises. He thinks it is destined to be one of the great California institutions, and he has a lot of respect for its art program. She says that he travels back and forth quite often to visit his mother and a sister, I believe, who are still living out there, and while she didn't want to speak for him, she said she's sure he'd be tickled pink to have you accompany him the next time he goes. What would you think of that?"

"Gosh, it sounds like a great solution, doesn't it? How would we find out if she's right?"

Libby laughed. "Give me a little credit, dear. Do you think I was going to let an opening like that slip by? I have the man's name—it is Jonathan Baldwin. He lives at 493 Hillcrest in Middletown, and his number is right here." She handed Chris a piece of paper. "She says you should call him right away, as she is pretty sure he will be going out there again shortly."

Chris and Libby both stood up. He stepped forward and gave her a hug.

"Thanks a lot, Mom. I'll follow up on this right away."

Mr. Baldwin was, indeed, planning a visit to the west coast within the month and was very pleased at the thought of having a young traveling companion. The trip was undertaken and Baldwin went out of his way to be helpful to Chris. He not only insisted that the boy stay with him at his sister's home, but he also personally conducted Chris to and through the university and around the surrounding area. By the time they had spent four days together, Chris had accumulated a wealth of information about the academic, cultural and social life of Pepperdine and the Malibu area. The nearly magical unreality of bustling Los Angeles and its satellite communities—Santa Monica, Redondo Beach, and of course the glamorous Hollywood and Beverly Hills, had an almost irresistible appeal to the artistic temperament of the young man, and he realized that no other place would quite measure up as a potential residence for the next four years.

Chris returned home bursting with excitement. His mother had never seen him quite so enthusiastic about anything, other than his music, of course.

"It's definitely the place for me, Mother! I just can't describe it adequately. The school is great, and the ocean and the sun and the feeling of youthfulness and vitality are unbelievable! Mr. Baldwin and Professor Ludwig's friend, Professor Gottfried, arranged a sort of impromptu interview with the Dean. They insisted that I give them a short private concert, which I did, reluctantly. I guess I should have been grateful. I must have been in unusually good form that evening, because I've never received such compliments! Of course, they couldn't very well tell me I was 'in' if I wanted to be, but they didn't leave much doubt that they were ready to recommend me. They even arranged to furnish me with information about a couple of big scholarships they feel that I would have an excellent chance of getting. It's sort of sad in a way, isn't it?"

Libby looked bewildered. "How do you mean—sad? It sounds pretty wonderful to me."

Chris shook his head. "No—not that what they said was sad. What I mean is that it looks as though I can get in easily and probably get pretty much of a free ride, while there are lots of kids who can't afford the education who could use that scholarship help. I'm sure you and Dad were expecting to pay my way, weren't you?"

"Yes, of course." She mulled it over for a few moments. "Tell you what, dear—why don't you go ahead and make your application to the university, but forget about applying for the scholarships. That way, perhaps some of those young people you referred to will turn out to receive the assistance after all. And, although it makes me feel a bit underhanded, we'll forget to mention your oversight to your father. This is a case of 'what he doesn't know won't hurt him'—except financially, that is, and he can well afford it!"

They chuckled conspiratorially.

Chris was readily accepted by Pepperdine and was welcomed into its artistic community, his musical reputation having preceded him. In his calm and practical way, he found his niche in the life of the institution, developed a circle of friends, and settled into the routine of practice, eat, sleep, study and practice some more.

He did take jaunts with friends to the beaches, the mountains or the clubs. He attended an occasional one of the uninterrupted stream of parties, also, although he had a mind of his own—he was not one to follow blindly the more reckless of the young studs on some of their escapades. If something sounded like fun and relaxation for a short time, he enjoyed going along, but he did not hesitate to excuse himself from any outing which he suspected might become dangerous or ridiculously juvenile. The fact that he had purchased a dependable used car assured him of always being in demand, but he was able to pick and choose his companions and the events that interested him without alienating anyone. Naturally, his love of music took him and some of his acquaintances in the arts program to many concerts which featured leading artists.

His first year at Pepperdine started in the fall of 1964. He felt like an entrenched "Angelino" by August 1965 when the race riots occurred in the Watts section of Los Angeles. During his junior year, the revolutionizing music of The Beatles, The Rolling Stones and other similar groups, and the undercurrent of resentment and rebellion against the Vietnam War, so prevalent on the west coast, resulted in what came to be called the "Summer of Love" in San Francisco. Thousands of young people decided to simply drop out of the mainstream and live an unfettered life of love, music and drugs, much to the disgust and consternation of the establishment. Some of Chris' friends eagerly joined in the movement, but he recognized it as an excuse for a long, pointless fling with no acceptance of responsibility. He simply ignored it.

During his last year at Pepperdine, Chris was the center of a great deal of attention and respect. His talent at the piano had outstripped that of his contemporaries, so he was constantly being lionized by art patrons and offered opportunities to appear with celebrated musicians up and down the coast. Over a period of several months, he was welcomed as guest artist with virtually every symphony orchestra in California, and offers to join a number of them poured in. Because he loved contemporary popular music almost as much as classical, he occasionally accepted an invitation to play with a dance band or Pops orchestra.

When the 1967 Christmas break approached, Chris called home to ask Libby if it would be all right to bring a friend home with him. Of course, his mother was happy to approve.

"Is this friend a male or a female, dear?" she asked with a chuckle.

"A male, Mother. Terry Stanton. You know—the one I've been rooming with this year. You've heard me mention him before. He's a fellow musician, and we've become quite close."

"Oh, yes. I remember. Isn't he the one who is such an outstanding violinist? You told me he had received offers to study further in Europe—Vienna, wasn't it?"

"That's right. He's really quite sensational. We'll give you a few duets while we're home."

"That will be wonderful, dear. We'll undoubtedly have lots of guests around here from time to time over the holidays. What a special treat that would be for them!"

"Okay, Mom. We'll work out a couple of short programs. No charge, of course!" and he laughed.

Chapter 38
Susan

Chris' sister, Susan, completed her high school education at Newvale High in June 1967. Her record was excellent—she managed to maintain honor marks without working very hard. It was not that she disliked studying particularly, it was just that she was involved in so many other activities that she often had to zip through her assignments. To her, life was fun. Susan was always among the first asked to participate in any activity. She played on sports teams, sang with the chorus, worked on the school paper, belonged to the camera club and the outing club, served on most of the party and dance committees, and still found time to assist Libby at hostessing for the steady stream of guests who visited Henderson Mountain.

Libby had prevailed upon Susan to make a couple of visits with her to her alma mater, Middlebury College, with the unstated but fairly obvious purpose of interesting her in attending when the time came. Libby realized after the second such effort that the school did not have the same appeal for her daughter that it had had for her. This made her feel a little blue, but she had no intention of trying to influence Susan to apply there against her will.

On the other hand, when Susan visited Smith College in Northampton, Massachusetts, with one of her friends and the friend's mother, she was immediately won over. She enthusiastically obtained and completed an entrance application and was promptly accepted for enrollment. Then, Susan wondered if her mother was upset.

"Gee, Mom—I hope you don't feel bad about my choosing Smith over Middlebury. I guess the right thing to do would have been to talk it over with you more thoroughly before I made the actual application."

"Don't worry a bit about it, Sue," Libby said. "You must have some of my blood in you—I knew where I wanted to go as soon as I saw it, and you apparently did the same. The fact that your preference in colleges is different than mine only points out your independence, which doesn't call for an apology."

So, in the fall of 1967, Susan entered Smith College. She proceeded to continue, uninterrupted, the same successful program mix of studies and extracurricular activities which she had pursued in Newvale High. Her good looks, vitality, intelligence and friendly attitude, again made her a very popular student. Smith was a women's college, and as such was a mecca for young men, primarily those from the other colleges which abounded in the eastern Massachusetts area. Under the sponsorship of the school, dances and parties were held, and male students were invited to attend. Just before Thanksgiving in 1967, a mixer was held with men from MIT in Cambridge. Susan danced with one fellow and then another. During a break between dances, as she chatted with a couple of the girls, she became aware of someone standing just off to her left, apparently wanting to get her attention. It was a tall, slender young man, and when she looked at him, he bowed slightly and smiled. When she smiled back, the gentleman stepped closer and said, somewhat hesitantly, "Good evening. I wondered if I might ask you for a dance?"

Susan laughed softly and replied, "I think you might—when will I know whether you will?"

The young man seemed somewhat taken aback. A puzzled frown puckered his forehead.

"Pardon?" he asked.

Susan realized that she had made a mistake. His accent and the formality of his approach should have warned her that he was not a local fellow, but she was still in the process of absorbing and interpreting the sometimes rather broad Massachusetts version of English and had not immediately recognized the difference.

"I'm sorry," she said. "That was silly of me. Yes, I'd like to dance. My name is Susan Hacker."

"Maitland—Spenser Maitland. Er—that is my name, I mean."

He smiled again and presented his arm in the formal British fashion. She slipped her hand in the crook of his elbow and they stepped to the dance floor, as the band resumed playing.

This fellow appealed to Susan. Although she was sure she had never seen him before, something about him seemed strangely familiar. They started dancing, and she was pleased to find that he was quite graceful and relaxed, yet guided them around and among the other dancers with firm confidence.

"So, you're at MIT, Spenser?" Susan asked.

"Yes, I am."

"What is your major?" she continued.

"Actually, I am in the graduate program," Spenser replied.

"Oh, really?" she said, impressed. "Where were you before?"

Almost sheepishly, he said, "I have been fortunate enough to have received a fellowship in science. I—I am from England, you see. Took my degree in chemistry at St. Timothy's College early last summer and was notified in August that I had received the grant to attend MIT. I am thrilled about it and extremely grateful—it is a marvelous school and a great opportunity for me."

"That's wonderful!" Susan exclaimed. "What, exactly, are you studying?"

"My field of interest is nuclear energy, so I rather cross the line between the physics and the chemistry disciplines, I suppose. I find it most exciting—it has such endless possibilities, you see."

"I'm sure it does," she laughed, and added, "that sort of thing is so far over my head that I wouldn't even be able to discuss it intelligently. I think it's terrific that there are people like you who have the capacity and the interest to understand such subjects."

Spenser responded, "If one has an interest, the subject generally unfolds quite readily—the difficulty is in *having to* study things for which one has no curiosity. I am certain that I would find it impossible to master—oh, say, accounting, for example."

"Yes," said Susan, "there is logic in that. Fortunately, or unfortunately, depending on your point of view, I expect to take only the run-of-the-mill liberal arts course. If something piques my interest in the next year or so, I can select it as my major at that time. If not, I think I can be quite satisfied with the social sciences and plenty of English Lit. Actually, I enjoy school and usually find myself fairly well absorbed with whatever I am studying at the moment, so I try to learn as much as possible, even if I'm not aiming in any particular direction. That way, I feel that I'm not just wasting Daddy's money. Does that make any sense to you, or is it just typical girlish rambling?"

"No, no—it seems quite a justifiable approach. I can think of nothing to discredit the concept of random learning, and as you say, plenty of time to select a major later, if you wish."

They danced in a relaxed and happy mood. "He's a good dancer," she thought, "and he seems quite normal, for a 'brain', which he obviously is."

"What a remarkably attractive girl," mused Spenser to himself. "I must see what I can do about exploiting this contact."

"Would you care for some refreshment, Miss Hacker?"

"Please—'Susan,' or better yet, 'Sue.' Yes, I think there is some punch round here somewhere—unless you would prefer something a little more bracing."

He hesitated a moment. "Why not a sip of punch now, and a stroll to a pub a bit later? I am very much enjoying the dancing and conversing with you, but the throat is a trifle dry. What say?"

Susan was elated that he apparently felt an attraction similar to her own. Her usual openness allowed her to accept the offer without a thought of being concerned that her willingness might be misinterpreted.

"That sounds like a very good plan to me. The music is really good and you are an excellent dancer. We seem to do pretty well together, don't we?"

"Indeed we do, and that is, for me, a pleasant surprise. I am not renowned for my virtuosity at the ball, so to speak!"

They strolled off to find the punch bowl, and they continued to dance and to talk until the band stopped playing and the party ended. Not being ready to leave each other, they sought out a cozy bar and sat sipping beer and continuing their conversation until they realized that it was getting late. Spenser dropped her off at her dormitory after making a date to visit her soon. It took him until 4 a.m. to get back to Cambridge.

Over the next three weeks, Susan and Spenser saw a lot of each other, despite the fact that he had to negotiate the distance of about 100 miles which separated their schools.

They found they had similar tastes. Several times, Susan laughed at some quip or facial expression of Spenser's because it seemed so familiar.

"You remind me so much of my brother, Spenser," she told him. "I can't wait for you to meet him. My folks, too, or course. By the way—I have a surprise for you."

"And what might that be?" he asked.

"I've told my mother that you are a poor, stranded foreigner who has no place to spend the Christmas holidays, and she insists that you come home with me! What do you think of that?"

Spenser's face showed his astonishment, because they had not previously discussed the matter.

"I hardly think that that would be fair," he said. "I would not want to place a burden on your family."

Susan could not suppress a loud laugh. "I really don't believe that one more will put too much strain on the budget. You haven't seen it, of course, but our place is rather—uh—large. Huge, would be a more accurate description. You see, my father is—I guess you would describe him as an 'entrepreneur.' He built this monstrously large home, and he is constantly inviting business contacts and various dignitaries from anywhere and everywhere to stay for anything from a day to a week. He darts in and out like a jet plane. Sometimes, we go weeks without laying eyes on him. All we get are wires from Vienna or Lisbon or Sidney or Lima, and when he is home he often spends ten or twelve hours or more at a time, holed up in his office, out of reach and out of touch with the rest of us. But then when he has one of his rare moments of relaxation he can be very thoughtful and charming. Mother has always adored him, and he her, I believe, even though he has for many years been so consumed by his business interests that he has virtually ignored her for months on end. While I'm at it, I might as well tell you about the rest of the clan, if it won't bore you too much."

"By all means, continue. I am fascinated. I'd no idea you had such an interesting home life."

"Well, Mother is, by any standard, a doll. She has all the good qualities—so many that I could never hope to emulate her. She's pretty and smart and pleasant and just so—so *good* that everyone loves her. She puts up with Dad's crazy schedule without complaint and runs that huge household and makes arrangement for all the guests, including the unexpected ones, without ever appearing exasperated, or even ruffled. How she does it, I just don't know. If you don't fall in love with her when you meet her, I'll be very much surprised."

"She certainly sounds a remarkable person," Spenser said, nodding.

"The only remaining member of the immediate family is my big brother, Chris. He's another paragon. He inherited my mother's placid nature and quiet talent, but he must have, hidden inside somewhere, a supply of that—that doggedness—a determination to be the very best—which made my father so successful, because he is the most amazing musician you have ever heard. I must have mentioned that he is finishing college this year at Pepperdine University in California, and he literally has people standing in line begging him to come with them. He is a classical pianist and any number of American and European orchestras have made him offers. He will be home for the holidays, too, so you'll get to hear what he can do. You'll be amazed and delighted. I get chills listening to him."

Spenser had been listening very carefully and when Susan paused, he shook his head slowly.

"I don't know whether I should accept your generous offer, Susan, dear. I shall certainly not measure up in such exciting company. I am sure I shall be quite intimidated and shall probably squawk and gurgle like a strangled chicken in their presence!"

"Don't be silly, Spense—the awe will be in the other direction when I introduce you as a budding nuclear scientist. Anyway, Mom and Chris are very plain and easy to know, and Dad is too, if you can get him to light long enough to rev down a little. Believe me, you'll love it." She moved closer and looked coyly up at him. "Besides, you'd better get to know the family if your intentions are as honorable as you assure me they are!"

He slipped his arm around her and pulled her close.

"You know I'm mad about you, dear Sue. Don't tease me. Despite the short time we have known each other, I am sure there is no one for me but you. I do so want to meet your family and let them know that we are formulating plans for the future. If you are sure that the holiday visit is appropriate, I shall be thrilled to accept the invitation."

She reached up, put her arms around his neck, and pulled his head down. She kissed him, hard.

"Just try to get out of it!" she said, threateningly, but with a big grin.

Chapter 39
Christmas Preparations

In mid-December 1967, Hack had a few days at home between foreign trips. Once he had arranged his material and satisfied himself that he could relax for a while, he left his office and went in search of Libby. At the moment, there were no guests in the great house and the empty rooms and halls seemed somehow oppressive. Here and there he glimpsed a member of the household staff, but they did not alleviate the sense of vacancy. He was so accustomed to being in the middle of frantic activity that he was feeling more and more alone and uncomfortable when finally he located his wife in the greenhouse, scissors in gloved hands, selecting and snipping off roses to brighten up a room.

He stepped into the warm and humid atmosphere of the greenhouse, saying, "Ah, this is where you're hiding, Lib! I've been looking for you all over the place. You don't appreciate how big this house is until you set out to find someone."

Libby was happy to see him. "Well, well. You decided to come out of your lair, did you?"

"Yes," he replied. "Believe it or not, I think I actually have things pretty well caught up at the moment. It looked as though I was going to have to leave by Wednesday to meet some German bankers and go with them to Copenhagen. There's an interesting cartel being formed, and I definitely want to be in on it, but I just received word this morning that there has been a change in plans and we won't be able to get together until after the first of the year."

"Good," said Libby. "Then there's no reason why you can't take a little time off and celebrate the holidays here for a change. I've heard from the kids, and they'll both be here for several days over Christmas. They'll be thrilled to learn that you will be in residence."

Hack took a minute to digest that suggestion. Why not do just that? He had certainly been on the go long enough to deserve a nice long break. It had been so long since he and Lib and the kids had spent some time together that he almost had trouble remembering what his offspring looked like.

"By God, Lib, that's just what I'm going to do. I'll call my service and tell them I won't be available until January 2nd. Old Hack is going to get reacquainted with his beautiful wife and his grown-up kids!"

He grabbed her arms and started dancing her around in a circle.

"Christopher! Stop it!" she cried. "Can't you see that I have scissors in my hand?" But she was laughing as she said it.

This was the most kittenish she had seen her husband in years, and she wanted to enjoy it while it lasted.

"Do you know when they will arrive?"

"Susan and her boyfriend will come down late on the twenty-second."

"Boyfriend?"

"Yes. She has met some young fellow from MIT and is quite gone on him, from what little she has told me. She begged to have him here for the holiday, her reason being that he is from out of the country and has no place to go. I didn't press her too much—you know that she has always had good judgement for a young girl. Any way, we'll find out all about him when they arrive."

Hack nodded.

"Okay. How about Chris? Is he bringing his girlfriend?"

Libby shook her head.

"No, he's bringing his roommate, Terry Stanton, and they are coming in to Laguardia on Saturday, the twenty-third. Terry's another musical prodigy, like Chris, only his instrument is the violin. Chris promises that they will perform for us and any guests who may show up. Won't that be wonderful!"

"Hey," said Hack, "that does sound like some concert! I'm going to enjoy it. I've been away so much—I can't remember the last time I sat down and really listened to Chris play something all the way through. Considering the tremendous talent he has, I guess I should be ashamed, but you know the sort of schedule I've been on for the past few years. Do you think Chris understands that the problem isn't lack of interest?"

Libby immediately replied, "Of course he does, Christopher. He's a pretty perceptive fellow, you know. He's terribly wrapped up in his music, but he always knows what is going on outside the music world, too. Both he and Susan have very sharp minds. We've been very fortunate to have such children."

"You're absolutely right, Lib, and I'm going to do my best to show my appreciation for them while they're home." He walked over to her and patted her on the fanny. "And for you, too, you doll."

They embraced and just stood, glued together and gently rocking back and forth, for a long time, love flowing from each to the other. It was the closest they had been in many years. It was the closest they would ever be.

Chapter 40
Revelation

Once Hack had his mind made up that he was going to spend the holidays at home with the family, he decided to make sure that it would be the most memorable Christmas season they had ever known. In typical fashion, he insisted that Libby go to great lengths to bedeck the mansion with special decorations and to plan and provide for sensational food. He had been exposed to some very exotic fare in his journeys around the globe, and he worked hard at dredging these specialties up from his memory. He then put several of his employees to work tracking down ethnic restaurants from which each dish might be ordered, or its recipe obtained, and from which delivery to Mount Hacker could be guaranteed by his deadline. Between his efforts and those of his wife, little was left to be done by the time the children arrived.

Friday, December 22, 1967, was cold but clear. By eight o'clock in the evening, the air over Newvale was crisp and the stars were beginning to shine brightly. A twenty-foot Christmas tree glittered with blinking colored lights at the top of the rise in front of the main entrance, and the entire long winding drive from the road up the hill to the mansion was outlined with huge candles, the flames on which flickered and sputtered, but managed to remain lighted. In each window, across the front of the house and down both wings, a tiny white light glowed, while the tall columns guarding the front of the building and the brick wall behind them were bathed in light from a number of flood lamps at ground level.

As the limousine which Susan had hired to bring Spenser and her from Massachusetts turned through the gates in the high wall, the beautiful panorama leapt out at them. Spenser gulped, in spite of himself.

"My word!" he gasped. "My bloody word!"

Even Susan was somewhat awed. "Well, they've really outdone themselves this year!" she exclaimed. "It is beautiful, though, isn't it, dear?" she added.

Spenser was still trying to regain his composure. "Do you mean to say that this is your *home*, Susan?"

With an embarrassed laugh, she said, "Yes,—I'm afraid so."

"My word!" he repeated. "Had you told me it was the state capitol, I would have believed you! I—I'm just unable to cope with it, all at once. You really should have prepared me rather better, Susan. My word!"

They were delivered to the front entrance, and Susan grasped Spenser's hand and ran him up the steps. She pulled the bell handle and very shortly, the door swung open, at the hand of Mary Chaplin, the housekeeper. She beamed at Susan and in her charmingly quiet way said, "Welcome home, dear."

She stepped quickly aside as Libby rushed forward to greet her daughter. She was clad in a very pretty dress of a deep, rich red, and with a tiny matching bow of ribbon set into the graying hair on either side of her head. Spenser inadvertently sucked in his breath once again, stunned by beauty that he would scarcely have expected in a middle-aged woman.

"Mother! cried Susan. She flung her arms about her and kissed her soundly on the cheek.

"You look so pretty—but then, you always do. How do you expect a daughter to impress her man when you are around!"

She towed the young man forward.

"Mother, this is Spenser Maitland. Spenser, my dear mother, Libby Hacker!"

"Delighted to know you, Mrs. Hacker."

"And I am delighted to know you, too, Spenser."

To herself, she said, "What a nice looking young fellow. He looks familiar, somehow—around the eyes, I think. Yes,—he has eyes a lot like Christopher's." Then, she resumed, "Well, why don't we go right into the library and give you people a nice warming drink. Susan's Dad is in there, waiting for us. He promised to have a nice fire going and drinks ready.

Libby gestured to indicate the direction, then led the way; the two young people followed behind, hand in hand. Spenser's eyes noted the rich carpeting, expensive looking furniture and the tastefully elegant hangings. The library was only three doors down from the foyer, on the west wing of the building. Libby opened the door, stepped inside, and held it open for them. Hack, who had been poking the fire logs when the door opened, straightened up and turned toward them.

"He looks just as one would imagine the tycoon," Spenser thought. "With the fire behind him and the wall of books, one might take him for the man in the magazine liquor advertisements."

Susan dropped Spenser's hand and ran forward to give her father a quick hug and a peck on the cheek. Then, she stepped back and introduced her young man.

"Daddy, this is Spenser Maitland. Spenser, my father, Christopher Hacker."

The two men extended their hands.

"A great pleasure to meet you, sir," said Spenser.

"And I am very happy to meet you, too, Spenser. I trust you two had a nice ride down from Massachusetts. No snow up there yet, is there?"

"No, sir, not yet. They've been promising it, but nothing to date."

Hack determined their preferences in drinks and prepared them. Small talk about the weather and the trip down from school filled the time until they were all settled into comfortable chairs, drinks in hand.

"Well, Spenser, tell us all about yourself. I've been away much of the time since Susan left for Smith, so I'm not up-to-date on her friends. I understand you are studying at MIT, correct?"

Spenser acknowledged this to be true.

"And how did you come to choose that excellent but reputedly very difficult school?" Hack continued.

"Well, sir, my home is in England. While attending St. Timothy's College in Brighton, I applied for a fellowship in science which was offered by MIT, and I was fortunate enough to receive it. I have a great interest in the developing field of nuclear energy, and was given to understand that this is an excellent school at which to pursue it. Frankly, I was shocked to find myself selected. Delighted, but shocked."

Hack was impressed.

"That is wonderful, " he said. "You and your family should be very proud. Is you father a scientist, too?"

"In a modest way, I suppose. He is a pharmacist and has his own apothecary shop in Winchester."

A slight chill ran up Hack's back and tiny mental warning lights blinked on and off. "Spenser? Winchester? Quite a coincidence. But certainly only that. Come on, Hack—stop flinching at shadows. This young fellow's name is Maitland, whereas Sally's son was known as Spenser Finch; that information was given by Mrs. Finch in that damned letter she wrote, remember?" He could feel the pulse in his temple throbbing and a prickling sensation on the skin of his arms. But his will was too strong to permit such weak suggestions to rule him. He shrugged, mentally, and changed the subject.

"Well, Spenser, I'm involved in a number of different enterprises both here and in several other countries but I recognize my limitations—I know nothing about nuclear energy except that I respect it a great deal and fear it somewhat. My interests run more to manufacturing, but I'm sure that sooner or later the two fields will cross, and when they do, I may come looking for a bright young fellow like you."

Susan felt this was her opening to acquaint her father with the relationship she hoped to build with Spenser.

"Dad," she said, blushing a bit and dropping her eyes, "if our plans work out as we hope they will, perhaps you won't have far to look."

Hack eyed her, trying to be certain that he understood the message she was sending.

"Do you want to explain that to me, Sue?" he asked.

Susan reached for the hand of her embarrassed guest. She gazed adoringly into his eyes, then turned back to her father, saying, "We are in love, Daddy. I've never met anyone to whom I was so attracted, and Spenser assures me that he feels the same toward me. We aren't going to rush into marriage while we are still in school, but we do plan to be engaged and later, married."

Hack absorbed the news without any outward sign of concern.

He forced a smile and asked, "Has your mother been in on this secret without telling me?" He turned toward his wife and said, with mock concern, "You wouldn't do that to me, Libby, would you?"

Both Libby and Susan started to protest, but Susan won out, saying, "No, no, Dad—we haven't had a chance to speak to Mom, and besides, we preferred to let you both know at the same time."

Then Libby added, "They haven't spoken to me about this before, Christopher, but I won't deny that, as a woman, I was beginning to suspect that this was more than an ordinary friendship. And let me add, I think it is wonderful. I feel that I know Spenser quite well, even though we have just met face to face, because Susan has been telling me a lot about him in her letters and by telephone." With a smile, she added, "And, I swear, he has Chris' eyes!"

Another bell rang in Hack's mind. He hesitated as long as he could without seeming to be disappointed with the news. Then he rose and extended his hand to Spenser, who jumped quickly to his feet and accepted it, with a large smile.

"Congratulations, Spenser. You couldn't have picked a finer girl!"

"Thank you, sir—I quite agree!"

Hack turned to Susan and held out his arms. She rushed to them and buried her face in his chest. After a long moment, she raised her happy face to her father for a kiss.

"Congratulations to you, too, dear. At least on the basis of first impressions, it appears you have shown excellent taste."

"Oh, Dad—you can't imagine how much it means to me that you and Mother approve! This is going to be just the happiest Christmas ever! And I can't wait to have Spenser meet Chris! I just know they will hit it off."

The group resumed their seats and fell into a more relaxed and easy exchange. The youngsters were feeling very pleased and comfortable in their newly announced relationship, but try as he would to forget the little suggestions of a possible problem, Hack was suffering recurrent pangs of doubt and suspicion. He freshened the drinks, but drained his own. He replaced it with a new one and emptied that within a short time. Uncharacteristically, he poured himself a third, after receiving polite refusals from the others. Libby watched with surprise, but smilingly attributed the unusual imbibing to the disclosure by Susan of her intentions.

Hack continued to hide his nervousness as best he could through dinner, but he was edgy. As soon as he could gracefully do so, he repaired to his office on a pretext of having to send a wire. Actually, he just wanted to be alone long enough to think through this disturbing similarity in backgrounds between Susan's young man and the boy Sally had had. He tried to convince himself that it was strictly coincidence. After all, Spenser was probably a very common name in England—not like John, or Robert, or Thomas, but common, all the same. And Winchester was a pretty large city—probably several hundred Spensers there. But, in the back of his mind there was a gnawing insistence that there was something else—some other clue, that he was overlooking. He tried hard to dredge it up, but nothing came forward. Eventually, Hack realized that it was not his nature to wait and wonder. When he suspected a potential problem in business, he went right after it and made sure that it was straightened out immediately. "Let's get this out of the way right now, so I don't have it bothering me," he decided. "I'm sure it's just nonsense, but there's only one way to get it out of my mind once and for all."

He left the office and went looking for the young Englishman. He found Libby sipping coffee in the library, alone.

"Where are the kids, Lib?"

"Oh," she answered, "I had Mary show Spenser to his room and when he returned, he and Sue came in here to have coffee with me, but I could see that they were more interested in being alone together, so I suggested that Susan give Spenser the ten-cent tour. They seemed relieved and started right out. I don't know in which direction they went." She could not resist adding, with a smile, "Their announcement must have struck you rather hard, didn't it, Christopher? I can't remember when I last saw you have three drinks in the space of an hour. It flustered you, didn't it?"

It surely did, he thought, but not for the reason you think. To Libby, he said, "Frankly, yes. He does seem like a very nice young man, if you go for the veddy, veddy proper British type, but it was sort of a bolt out of the blue. A man doesn't have his only daughter tell him she's engaged to some stranger every day. I'd like to talk to him in private for a little while when he's not busy. That's why I'm looking for them."

Libby permitted a slight frown to crease her forehead.

"Do you really think you should so soon, dear? Wouldn't it be better to let them have a couple of days to just rattle around and get acquainted with everybody? Chris should be here by tomorrow afternoon with his guest. They'll want to spend time together sorting out what they have in common. I think it would be more friendly and more hospitable to wait until after Christmas to have any serious discussions. Don't you agree, dear?"

Hack bristled. "Libby, you should know by now that I'm not the 'wait until tomorrow' type. I want to have a nice intimate chat with young Spenser, and I'll be uncomfortable all weekend if I don't get it over with now. I'm not going to bite him; I just feel that I want to know more about him so that I can be somewhat more relaxed about what Sue is planning—or can send him packing, if that is indicated."

Libby shrugged and sighed. "Do it your way, Christopher—you always have. Please, though, try to be gentle with him—I think he is pretty uneasy with us, as it is."

Hack didn't respond as he left the room to resume his search for the young couple. He finally located them, arm in arm, looking over the indoor swimming pool.

"Oh, there you are, kids. Maybe Spenser would enjoy a nice warm swim before bedtime, Sue. I find that it helps me sleep better than the warm milk treatment."

"That seems a fine idea, sir. I may just take advantage of it."

Hack walked around the pool with them, answering Spenser's questions about the operation of the filtering system, control of the humidity and mechanism of the vacuum cleaner. As soon as a proper lull in the conversation permitted it, he casually addressed the young man.

"By the way, Spenser, when you have a few free moments, I'd like to sit down with you and have a nice little chat, without any ladies interfering," he said, squeezing Susan's arm playfully.

"Certainly. I'd be happy to, sir."

"I don't mean to take him away from you, Sue, but there must be times when you have woman things to do, and you can turn him over to me then, okay?"

Susan knew her father well enough to understand that what he really meant was 'right now.' She was concerned as to what he could find so pressing to talk to Spenser about, but she kept it well hidden.

"Sure, Dad. As a matter of fact, I have to go straighten out some of my clothes that I'll want over the holidays, and I might as well do it now." She rose up on her toes and kissed Spenser lightly. "See you at breakfast, dear," and she walked off, leaving the two men standing uncomfortably.

"If you've had the tour, why don't we take a walk over to my office where we can lean back and relax?" Hack proposed.

"That sounds fine to me, sir."

They started walking and managed to complete the trip without feeling the need to converse. When they arrived at Hack's office, he opened the door and said, pointing, "Why don't you take that leather chair on the left and I'll sit opposite you. Do you smoke, or would you care for any refreshment, Spenser?"

"No, thank you, sir. I'm quite comfortable."

Hack sat down, leaned back in the deep chair and crossed his legs.

"Well, now. It is nice to have you young people here for a while. You've no idea how much it brightens up the place."

"Glad you feel that way, sir. I am rather awed at the size and beauty of your marvelous home. I wasn't really prepared for anything so splendid."

"Yes, well, I have worked hard to give my family the best that I can provide, and in all honesty, I am quite proud of it. I hope you don't find it ostentatious."

"Not at all, sir. Ostentation occurs when there is an effort made to impress others. After meeting you and Mrs. Hacker, I know that you are not that sort of people."

"Good. The reason I wanted to sit down with you, Spenser, is that I'm very interested in learning more about you and your family. Susan may have told you that I spent some time in your country as an American soldier during the war."

"Yes, she has mentioned it, Mr. Hacker."

"As luck would have it, I was stationed temporarily at the air base just outside of Winchester, and then transferred to a Signal Corps unit attached to an infantry division down at Sherborne. While I was at the air base, I made several friends in and around Winchester. I found it to be an attractive town, and the people tried hard to make our stay there as pleasant as possible, under the circumstances."

Spenser seemed quite interested. "Perhaps you met my father. Wouldn't that be exciting!"

"Was he in the service? Would he have been around there in the latter part of 1943 and early 1944? That's when I was there."

"Probably so, sir—he would probably have been around there, that is. I imagine he was just finishing up his schooling. He entered the service late because of it, and never did get assigned overseas."

"I see."

Spenser fidgeted a bit. He colored slightly and scraped his foot nervously back and forth on the rug, before adding, "In all candor, sir, the man I refer to as 'father' is actually my stepfather. I shouldn't want our relationship to be based on any inaccurate information. You see, my actual father was killed in the war. I was raised for the first few years by my mother and grandparents. It wasn't until I reached age seven that Mum married Mr. Maitland. He insisted on adopting me and giving me his name, which was very good of him, I'm sure."

Hack could feel the hairs on the back of his neck stiffening and sweat popping out on his body. Suddenly, he knew what the clue was that he had been missing—it was the eyes, as Libby had mentioned. This fellow's eyes were so much like Chris'! The coincidences were beginning to pile up. He felt that he had to ask the next question or he would explode, but when he tried to form it, his mouth felt dry and his heart increased its pounding.

Spenser noticed a sudden change in Mr. Hacker's appearance. He seemed almost to be swelling up, somehow. His face had taken on a dark red hue, and his voice quavered as he stammered out, "Wha—what.....was your father's—your *real* father's name?"

Spenser edged forward in his chair, worried now. "Are you quite well, sir?" he asked with trepidation.

Hack rasped out, "Damn it! Answer the question! What was your real father's name?

Dreading the reply he felt certain he would get, he gripped the arms of his chair so hard that his forearms trembled.

"Why—it was Abernathy."

Hack's appearance worsened. The hammers were beating hard in his head, and his throat was constricted so that he could barely squeeze out the other two words he needed to say to have his worst fears confirmed.

"First name?" he grated.

Then, as Spenser said the name, he involuntarily mouthed it along with him, "Richard."

Hack collapsed like a tent in a gale. As he sagged against the back of his chair, Spenser leaped forward to help him, but Hack waved him off.

"Just get me a drink of water, please," he whispered, then changed his mind and said, "No—there's brandy on the bar against the wall. Get me a shot."

Spenser sprang to the bar, splashed brandy into a glass and quickly handed it to his stricken host. Hack took a large swallow, coughed, and straightened up. He still looked terrible, but Spenser's fear that he might die, subsided. Not knowing what to do next, he asked, hesitantly, "Shall I call for Mrs. Hacker—or a doctor, perhaps?"

"No! Just sit down and wait a minute. I've got to ask you a couple more questions."

Gradually, as the potent liquor made its presence felt, Hack grew somewhat calmer, but he was still obviously very uncomfortable. Spenser found himself completely at a loss to understand what had caused the sudden transformation from genial host to apoplectic tyrant.

After making poor Spenser wait through what seemed another eternity of silent apprehension, Hack slowly pulled himself up to his feet and took a few hesitant steps. Once he appeared to have satisfied himself that he was able to control his movements, he looked straight into the bewildered young man's eyes and said, very low and very slowly, "Stop me if there is anything incorrect in what I am about to say. Your name now is Spenser Maitland—Spenser *Joseph* Maitland, perhaps?"

Surprised at this knowledge, Spenser could only nod.

"Your grandparents' name, I believe, was Finch?"

Receiving no contradiction, he continued.

"Your mother's name is Sally, and the address at which she lived with her parents was 10 Robin Lane, off Damien Road in Winchester—right?"

Spenser's mouth dropped open.

"RIGHT?" Hack virtually shouted, leaning toward him.

Spenser recovered sufficiently to nod weakly and reply, "Right, sir."

Hack shrank visibly from this acknowledgment, like a man who has just received a death sentence. He bent his head and shook it slowly from side to side.

"Damn!" he said softly—"Goddamn!!"

He moved laboriously to his desk and pushed a button. Soon, a female voice came over the intercom, "Yes, Mr. Hacker?"

"Mary, will you please find both Mrs. Hacker and Susan and ask them to come to my office?"

"Certainly, Mr. Hacker."

"And, Mary—"

"Yes, sir?"

"*Right away!*"

He dropped wearily into the large leather chair behind the desk. Without looking up, he said, "I think perhaps you had better get yourself a glass of brandy, Spenser."

"I—I'm not much for liquor, sir."

"I'm not, either, dammit, but I want you to have a shot of brandy ready, just the same."

Spenser rose, and dutifully, hand shaking slightly, poured some brandy into a glass. He returned to his chair and faced his host.

Thoughts were racing this way and that through Hack's head. That impossibly far-fetched moment which he had confidently expected and fervently hoped would never come, had arrived. How could fate have played such a rotten trick on him? He had been completely sure that there was no way that the sordid little story of his brief passionate encounter with Sally, and the product of it, could ever be revealed. What possible circumstances could ever arise which would make him admit that it had happened, he had thought? Even if the story reached his family in some weird way, all he would ever have to do would be to deny it. Even if another letter came, bearing further evidence, and even if it fell into his wife's hands, he knew he was clever enough to talk his way around it and if worst came to worst, he had lawyers who could put the thing quietly to rest.

But this nightmare that had just unfolded wasn't going to go away. In his wildest dreams he couldn't have come up with this crazy scenario. Once the shattering truth of the matter had been accepted, he realized he had no alternative but to bare the whole story to all of the principals. Even if it destroyed his marriage, he couldn't let the innocently incestuous relationship of these youngsters continue for another minute. No matter how hard it would be for the rest of the family to take, he had to reveal the fact that Spenser was his child, before he and Susan made a horrifying mistake.

Spenser continued to sit quite still, not knowing what to expect. Hack remained quiet, trying to gather strength for what he knew had to come next.

The office door swung open and a happy Libby and Susan entered, laughing over some shared secret. But the chilly atmosphere in the office immediately became apparent to them, and they peered at the two men questioningly.

"Please help the girls to chairs, Spenser," Hack instructed, but the courteous young man had already started to do so.

In an effort to ease the tension, Susan said, "What sort of plot have you two been hatching?"

But it did not have the desired effect.

Hack sighed deeply, and started. "Please, Sue, try to listen carefully to what I am about to say, and try to understand that it is gospel truth—no one is trying to be in the least funny. I'm terribly sorry, but it is so unbelievable you would think I was making all of this up, if I didn't warn you first. And, Spenser, you'd better pour a little brandy for the ladies before I start."

When they both timidly protested, Hack said, "Pour it!"

As Spenser did so, Hack took another deep breath, and began.

Chapter 41
Hack's Tale

"I've got to tell you people a brief story about something that happened during the war. I'll try to make it short, but certain details have to be covered, even though you may find them very shocking.

"I was wounded in North Africa, was sent back to Casablanca for treatment, and from there to England, where I was assigned temporarily to an Air Force signal unit just outside of Winchester. While I was at the air base in England, as I mentioned to Spenser before, I met some very nice English people. I don't believe I ever met his stepfather, Mr. Maitland, but I did meet his mother, Sally Finch."

Gasps of astonishment escaped the two women.

"She danced with me at a social given for servicemen, and we hit it off so well that we eventually became very close friends. Her betrothed, Richard Abernathy, was serving with Montgomery, and my darling Libby was going to college back here in America. Spenser's mom and I spent lots of time comparing notes on the news we received from our true loves and dreaming about what we would do when the war was over and we could be with them again. I spent many happy hours enjoying the hospitality of his very fine grandparents, the Finches, at their cottage on Robin Lane."

Hack looked directly at Spenser.

"Everything was fine until your mother received the tragic news that Richard had been killed in action. At about the same time, I was transferred into the infantry and started staging for the invasion of France. Your mother was so devastated by Richard's death that her parents didn't dare tell her about my situation, for she had depended on me for support, as I had, her. For weeks, she would talk to no one, see no one—not even me. When she finally recovered somewhat, to the extent that she agreed to let me visit her, my time to ship out was imminent. She didn't yet know that I was about to leave. We went for a ride to a deserted area which we liked and where we had often walked and talked. I felt that I had to tell her that this might be my last visit, but when I did so, it made her very angry. She was just beginning to get over the loss of her lover and now she was about to lose her friend and confidante. I was about to be sent into God only knew what terrible danger and didn't know what my chances were of ever seeing Libby again. We were both about as low as you can get. In a moment of rebellion against the unfairness and the utter frustration of our situation, we abandoned our principles and made love, recklessly. It wasn't very romantic—it was as though we were getting back at the cruel system which had brought us to that moment. Until then, I'm sure we had never thought of each other romantically at all. Neither of us expected anything like that—we didn't plan it—it simply happened. And that was the only time."

Spenser was listening intently, scarcely believing what he was hearing, and fearing what was coming next. Susan also sat transfixed, like a small child listening to a fairy tale. But Libby was the one who was hardest hit. Already, her husband had contradicted vows which he had repeatedly made to her and which she had accepted at face value. Who knew where the rest of this story might lead? The sensation of departure from reality which had haunted her more and more during periods of mental stress as the years slid by, now came rushing over her in an irresistible tide of proportions she had not previously experienced. Something had to block out these searing words from the man at the desk. He was telling some crazy tale which surely had no connection with her or her family. They were the Hackers, and they had no such problems. Before long, he would finish telling this story and they would return to their normal pursuits. In the meantime, she could see clearly only straight ahead, as though peering through a tunnel, to where the narrator was continuing his tale. What he was saying was as unintelligible to her as Swahili. She would listen, but only as a disinterested party.

Hack continued. "Shortly thereafter, I left with the invasion force, and never saw or heard from Sally again. It wasn't until I was a married man with a family that I received a letter from your grandmother, Spenser, telling me that Sally had become pregnant as a result of our momentary indiscretion. That was when I first learned that there was such a person as Spenser Joseph Finch. That's what they called you at that time. I was shocked and disgusted. There was no way that I could acknowledge you—no way that I could justify your existence in the eyes of my family, who were all convinced that I was the soul of propriety and honor. So I simply destroyed the letter and went on with life in the normal way. What a mistake that has proved to have been!"

Everyone sat silent, dreading further revelations. Then, totally crestfallen, shoulders bowed, eyes staring into the distance, Spenser asked, weakly, "Are you...are you saying, then, that you are—that I am....Your son?!"

Hack looked at the floor, then raised his eyes to his wife, his daughter, then back to Spenser. He nodded slowly.

"Yes, Spenser—I'm afraid you are. I know what a blow it must be for you—for all of you—but once I suspected what the situation was, I had to follow it through and prove or disprove it once and for all. Can you imagine what a disaster it would have been if you and Susan had carried out your intentions!"

Spenser's shoulders drooped even more at the mention of Susan's name. He forced himself to look at her, and what he saw made his heart ache. She was staring at him as though he were a stranger—not a lover, not a brother, but a stranger. And now this sudden upheaval of their lives struck him similarly. How can one, in the twinkling of an eye, convert one's devotion for another from the passion of a lover to the passive affection of a sibling? Through the turmoil in the minds of both, and in the light of this new knowledge, there emerged a rude sensation of uncleanness—aversion, actually—at the thought of their former joyous intimacy. It was sickening. Unable to control herself any longer, Susan leaped up and dashed, screaming, from the room.

Hack had never know that it was possible to feel as miserable as he did now. He had admitted to an almost innocent affair from many years ago, and by having done so, had promised to tear into shreds his family and the life which they had enjoyed. Not really knowing what to say or do, but accepting the fact that it was up to him to conclude the matter, Hack moved forward and put his arm around the younger man's shoulders.

"Sue's tough, Spenser. She will handle it all right, once she gets over the initial shock. And I know you will, too. Like it or not, there's no question but that you are my son. You'll just have to find the strength you need to cope with that fact."

Hack then turned to Libby, who had made no sound and had not moved from her chair. She exhibited no grief, no upset, nothing. She simply sat and stared straight ahead at the vacant chair where her husband had sat while delivering his cataclysmic message. Of course, it was not anyone she knew about whom that man had been talking—just some pitiable strangers in a story. She let a sad little smile of compassion turn up the corners of her mouth. She did not hear Hack speaking to her. He tried, puzzled at first, to get her attention and to tell her how sorry he was—sorry that he had been living a lie, and sorrier still that he had been placed in a position which left him no alternative but to confess. When she did not respond, he thought perhaps she was so angry that she was refusing to speak to him, but gradually he came to realize that he simply was not getting through to her. Nothing was, in fact, getting through to her. She was in shock. Hack reached for the brandy again and forced a little into Libby's mouth. The harshness of the raw liquor in her throat caused her to gag and then to cough, but it did break through the aberrant mental defenses which had been thrown up, at least enough for her to dimly recognize her husband.

"Wha—wh—!" she stammered, staring at him.

"Lib—Lib, darling—what's the matter?"

He was frightened by what he saw in her eyes. He knew that she had had some slight trouble a few times in the past, but he had given it no serious thought. She had not even needed a doctor's attention—she just drew herself into a shell for brief periods and went off by herself. Now, she really seemed to have been separated from her surroundings. She appeared bewildered and lost.

"Libby—let's go to our room and rest for a little while. It's been a tough evening. If I can possibly make it up to you somehow, I will, darling."

For the first time in his life, he felt small and useless—almost dirty. But his inherent toughness and pride slowly pushed such feelings out of his mind. He put his arm around Libby and guided her from the office, while the other shocked witness to the whole drama, Spenser, stood helplessly and watched.

Down the long hallways and to their suite he led her. She still had not recovered her senses fully, but had started crying softly. As tenderly and solicitously as he could, he removed her outer clothing and tucked her into bed. Then, he undressed, showered, put on his pajamas and bathrobe and moved to a chair in the adjoining sitting room from which he could see her. He sat for a couple of hours, thinking, thinking and monitoring his wife's behavior. She had gone immediately to sleep and gave no indication of rousing, so he finally removed his robe and climbed into the huge bed beside her.

For a long time, he lay awake, staring into the darkness while alternating waves of guilt and bitter resentment rolled over him until he, too, fell asleep.

Chapter 42
Final Stroke

The next day, all of the parties to the fateful meeting took pains to avoid each other. To each of them, the shock was still too great to tolerate facing any of the others.

Hack, the agent of all their misery, arose early. He remembered immediately the details of last night's debacle. He silently checked to be sure that Libby was sleeping peacefully, then shaved, showered, dressed and walked into the sitting room. He picked up the intercom phone and called the garage and instructed the employee who answered to bring the Chevrolet station wagon around to the kitchen entrance and leave it there with the motor running. Then he went to the kitchen himself, drank a cup of coffee and ate a roll and went out to the car.

The day was cloudy and the air was clammy. He was thankful that the man had turned the car's heater on, making the interior quite cozy. He drove for a while without concentrating on anything in particular. He just admired the neat, pleasant village which had been the hub of his existence. No matter where he had roamed, to Africa and Europe while in the service or to all corners of the world on business in recent years, this was the place that gave it all meaning—this was the haven to which he always subconsciously ached to return.

Hack had loved growing up in Newvale. The friends and neighbors here were much closer than any he had acquired in his travels. Here, his triumphs were far sweeter because he could display them before the appreciative eyes of people who understood him and his family. They knew where he came from and how he had dedicated himself to being a success, right from the beginning. There were still many people who remembered him as a boy, hustling around his route, delivering papers from a bag so big and heavy that it nearly dragged on the ground. Some people remembered his struggling to push a lawnmower, the handle of which was nearly as high as his chin. And although he had been guilty of neglecting it in recent years, he had created a beautiful family for the townspeople to admire and respect. He had married the lovely Libby, certainly the pick of the Newvale crop of their generation, and together they had produced a handsome and talented son and a smart, pretty and popular daughter. And he saw to it that his family wanted for nothing, absolutely nothing!

But what had he done now? He had well-nigh ruined everything with his confession of last night. It was not as though he had had any choice in the matter—to have let the relationship between Susan and Spenser go any further would have been to court disaster. Once he learned that they were blood relatives there was only one course to follow, and he had firmly followed it, regardless of the consequences. But with this dreadful knowledge came huge new problems. Now that he acknowledged Spenser as his son, the status of Chris and Susan changed substantially. As the earliest born, Spenser emerged as his number one son—his primary heir unless otherwise designated by him. How was he to settle this mess? What would be Chris' reaction when he discovered that he had an older brother? And how long would it take poor Sue to adjust to this transformation of her concept of Spenser? Would she ever? And, of course, Spenser's feelings had to be considered, too, although at this point, Hack could not think of him as his child with the same degree of concern and affection that he had for Chris and Sue.

And how about the mothers? My God—how will Libby be able to face this situation! Instead of Spenser becoming her son-in-law, as she had happily anticipated, the man now emerges as an unwanted stepson! But it will be Sally whose status will change most dramatically in Libby's mind. Instead of a nice young member of a thoughtful English family who had tried to make her husband's life a little more pleasant as he prepared to face Armageddon, Sally will now seem as an evil seductress who had shared a guilty secret with her husband for all these years. And how about Sally's husband, Maitland? Was he aware of the fact that Spenser's father was a wealthy American ex-GI, not a heroic Britisher who had died fighting for his country? When he learned the true story, would he feel that his wife had hoodwinked him with the tale about Abernathy in order to cover up a sordid affair?

"Good God!" he said. "Is there no end to this can of worms?"

He rode along for several miles, twisting and turning the car from one back road to another—roads he had explored thoroughly so long ago, most of them repositories of memories of youthful adventures. The thoughts concerning his confession kept tumbling about in his head— each one a problem, but gradually his unwavering faith in himself, his indomitable self-satisfaction, permitted him to rationalize all of the negatives until, finally he said, "Hey—wait a minute! I've made a clean breast of everything. I've done my part. Now it's up to the rest to decide how to go about living with it. The only thing I have to do right now is to be sure that I am the one to break the news to Chris."

Chris' plane was scheduled to arrive in New York at 2:00 p.m., and Chris and his friend were to take a limousine from the airport which should get them home around 4:00 p.m. He would tell Libby to tell Chris nothing, but to send him straight to the conservatory where he would be waiting for him. He thought it might be easier, somehow, if Chris was near his beloved piano when he received the bad news. With this in mind, he relaxed and drove back toward town. As the tension in the muscles of his stomach eased, he suddenly felt extremely hungry. He pulled in at the local diner, parked and ran up the steps. Inside, the proprietor, "Fat Cassie" Donovan, one of his old classmates, glanced up from the grill he was tending and greeted him with a look of pleasant surprise.

"How the hell are ya, Hack!" he asked, with a big friendly grin.

"Fine, Cass, fine," Hack replied.

"We don't get to see you here very often. Still chasin' around the world on business?"

"Yeah, most of the time. Thought it was time for me to spend a couple of weeks with the family before they forget what I look like."

"Well, damn! It's good to see ya, old buddy. What can I get for you?"

Hack tilted his head back and made a production of sniffing.

"Do I smell that good country sausage, Cass?"

"Sure do. How about a big helping of sausages and buckwheat pancakes? Only take a couple of minutes."

"Okay," Hack agreed, smiling broadly. "Let's do it!"

Cass poured him a cup of steaming coffee which Hack sipped at eagerly. It tasted great. The odor of frying bacon drifted into his nostrils and made him even hungrier. When Cass set the food in front of him, he attacked it like a starving man, relishing the tasty mixture of hot pancakes, sausage and maple syrup. He allowed the pleasure of the hot breakfast to push his troubles from his mind temporarily. When he had finished the food and a second cup of coffee, he slid off the stool, smacked his lips appreciatively and said,

"Man—that was really great, Cass. Haven't eaten a breakfast like that in a long time!"

Donovan beamed. He had always admired Hack, and this little visit reassured him that all the sensational success the man had experienced had not made him feel he was too good to associate with old friends of lesser affluence.

"Drop in again before you take off on your next trip."

"Count on it, Cass. Merry Christmas."

He paid the cashier and left.

With the hot food resting comfortably against his ribs, he felt more capable of facing his family again. He particularly wanted to find out how well Libby had recovered. But first, there was one more thing he felt he had to do. He drove back home and pulled up at the garage. Before he had time to get out of the car, the nearest door opened and a man in coveralls stepped out, wiping his hands on a rag.

"Back already, Mr. Hacker?" he asked.

"Yes, but not to stay. Bring the Jeep out, will you please, Harry?"

"Sure thing," the man replied as he turned and trotted back inside the building. In a few moments he drove out with the small, rugged vehicle.

"It's all gassed up and ready to go."

"Good. I won't be gone long—just want to drive up to the back of the property and didn't want to risk scratching up the station wagon."

"Fine, sir. Just leave it at the house when you're finished, and we'll pick it up."

Hack climbed in, revved the engine, slipped it into low gear and left. He drove around behind the garage and picked up the service roadway which wound up the rise and disappeared eventually in the woods. The Jeep climbed steadily until it reached the tree line near the top of the hill. Looking to his right, Hack could see a stand of cedars a couple of hundred yards away. He turned and headed for them, bouncing along on the rough, frozen ground. When he reached the cedars, he pulled the Jeep up close, turned off the motor and got out. He walked into the cedars until he was hidden, then found a spot where he could peer out between the branches and look back down the hill. There was his estate, spread out before him. There was the huge house, the six-bay garage, the barns, the swimming pool, the flower gardens and summerhouse and the tennis courts. Separated from these by a long, high hedge of hemlock, against which ran a white rail fence, was the line of stables and the supporting buildings. Even now, when most outdoor activity was shut down for the winter, there were members of the staff in evidence here and there. It was his, all his! It was really impressive, and it represented a pile of money. It was the certification of his success. And it was bigger than the Jay's, or the Lamson's, or the Borgeson's, and it was on a higher elevation than any of them! He chuckled as he thought, "The only thing I overlooked was a throne room!"

Hack was perfectly aware of what he was doing. The symbolism of the hideaway in the cedars was a terrific touch, he thought, smiling. He recognized that this little safari was entirely ego driven, but he was not embarrassed or ashamed to admit it to himself. Hell, this was what he had set out to accomplish, and by God, he had done it! He could buy and sell the people he used to think of as the super rich. That was the balm that could soothe any hurt.

After a while, the bitter cold began to gnaw at him. Reluctantly, he went back to the Jeep and drove slowly down the hill.

Hack was sure that Libby would be up by now. He walked into the house, and started toward their suite in the west wing. Shortly, he encountered Mary hustling along a hallway with a tray.

"Good morning, Mary. Is that tray for Libby, by any chance?"

"Yes, sir, it is."

"And she is in the suite? She's up and about and seems all right?"

Mary nodded and said, "Yes, she is. I've just fixed her this light breakfast."

"Fine. Let me take it, please."

He took the tray from her hands and walked away.

Mary, obviously crestfallen, watched him as he went. She had looked forward to delivering the food to Libby, whom she adored, and who almost never requested this kind of service. She had lovingly prepared the tray herself, warming the muffin, putting on two small compotes with a choice of marmalade or strawberry preserve, and filling the delicate small teapot with piping hot tea at the last minute—tea brewed to the exact strength the mistress preferred. And across the napkin, she had laid a small pink rose, for which she had made a special trip to the greenhouse, and from the stem of which she had carefully removed all thorns. Why had Mr. Hacker deprived her of the happiness she would have experienced by seeing Libby's appreciation? Deflated now, she returned somberly to her regular duties.

Hack entered the suite with his dual burdens of food and guilt. He was very relieved to see that Libby was sitting at a small table, dressed in robe and slippers, and apparently quite normal. However, he did not have to look too closely to see that she appeared very unhappy.

"Good morning, dear," he offered. "I intercepted Mary in the hallway, bringing you this nice little breakfast." He placed it carefully in front of her on the table.

"Thank you," she said, tonelessly.

Hack let the tense atmosphere hold for a short time, hoping that Libby would say something to ease it, but nothing was forthcoming. Finally, he decided it was up to him.

"Lib, I realize what a shock you had last night. I'd rather have cut off my right arm than to have done that to you. You've no idea how heartsick it made me to admit what happened so long ago, which I had put out of my mind completely. But this absolutely crazy—this almost impossible—development, left me no choice—no choice at all. I simply couldn't risk having anything further happen between Sue and Spenser. You do understand, don't you, darling?"

He stepped to her side and slid his arm across her shoulders, but she involuntarily shrank from his touch, so he stepped back, humiliated. Libby continued to sit silently for so long that Hack was beginning to wonder whether she had reentered that scary detached state which had claimed her the previous evening. But eventually, she slowly lifted her eyes to his and said, "Yes, Christopher, I understand. I understand why you were forced to reveal your guilty secret. At first, I simply couldn't accept what I was hearing, but after a while I came to grips with it. What I cannot understand is why you never told me before. All these years I have been thrilled and proud to believe that you truly meant it when you told me I was the only one. Now this—this nightmare comes to life! What do you think that did to my faith in you! What reason have I to believe that this was your only secret affair? Do you really expect me to just forgive and forget? How many other unacknowledged children might you have—or how many other girls may you have slept with? How can I ever trust you again?"

Libby's voice had been slowly rising as she spoke, and, with it, the color in her cheeks. Hack was not accustomed to this kind of spirited assault from her. She had always remained cool and sensible, whatever the provocation, but now she was filled with anger and bitterness. As he listened to her attack, resentment started rising within him. Hadn't he explained to her that he had not been involved with any other women—just that one time with Sally? Now here she was, practically accusing him of having had a lurid past and of having left the path behind him sprinkled with little bastards! His pride would not permit him to accept such a browbeating meekly.

"Wait just a damned minute, Lib! Don't start pretending to believe that I'm some sort of roue who's been chasing around with all kinds of women. Sally was the only one—the *only* one—that I ever had anything to do with, except you! And I explained how that happened. It was nothing either of us planned. You've never been in a situation like we were in at that time, so it's pretty damned unfair of you to judge us. My biggest mistake was in deciding to cover up the news of Spenser's birth, but when I got that letter from Mrs. Finch, telling me about it, my first reaction was, 'My God, what will Libby think!' I just didn't see how I could explain it to you in a way that wouldn't put a lot of strain on our marriage. And then I thought, 'Hell, there's no way she's ever going to know about it unless I tell her.' So I just pretended to answer the letter and then destroyed it."

Libby blanched. In the back of her mind, she had wondered how he could have ferreted out the relationship with Spenser so rapidly—that was part of the reason why the whole story had floored her so. One minute she was being introduced to a nice young student from England who was showing serious interest in marrying their daughter, and the next, she was being called in to listen to an earthshaking confession by her trusted husband, acknowledging that he had sired the boy! So that letter from England which she had delivered to Christopher eighteen years ago was not the innocent little message of friendship that he had pretended it to be. In her semicomatose condition the previous evening, Hack's reference to Mrs. Finch's letter hadn't registered at all. Now it became clear that it had actually brought him the news that he had fathered a child about whom he had not known. How smoothly he had glossed that over! Pretended to tell her what the letter said, and read her his reply—only it wasn't what it said, and it wasn't his reply—he had just fed her a fairy tale and she had swallowed it whole!

That eerie feeling started stealthily creeping over her again, but with a great effort of will, she forced it away. She would not succumb to that frightening sensation—she was too angry with her husband to let anything interfere with what she wanted to say.

"I would never have believed you capable of such duplicity! How could you have told me such lies with a straight face! Poor Chris. Little does he know what he is walking into! How are you going to break the news to him?"

Hack shrugged his shoulders.

"I'll just meet him in the conservatory and lay it out for him, straight. There's no point in beating around the bush. He's certainly man enough to take it—Hell, it won't be half as hard for him as it was for poor Sue. Maybe he'll take a swing at me and that'll be the end of it. When he arrives, be sure that he is sent to me in the conservatory before anyone else gets a chance to speak to him."

Libby bristled again. "NO, Christopher! I'm his mother and I have a right to be there when he learns about this. When he arrives, we'll both be in there waiting for him."

Once more, Hack shrugged. "Okay, if that's what you want. We'd better have someone posted to intercept him when he pulls up. I'll call Harry at the garage and tell him to watch for the limo and to tell Chris he is to come straight to the conservatory. Well, I suppose we'd better have his guest come, too, or the poor guy will wonder what the Hell is going on. When we've been introduced, I'll ask that Terry—that was his name, wasn't it?—be shown to his room and given a chance to relax while we go over a rather pressing family matter with Chris."

Libby offered no objection, so he left her in the bedroom and went to his office, where he could busy himself until it was time for his son to arrive.

Chapter 43
The Piano

At five minutes before four, Hack arrived at the conservatory, only to find that Libby had preceded him. Neither could think, readily, of anything to say, but, fortunately, they had not long to wait in silence.

The door opened and in stepped Chris; his friend, looking embarrassed, trailing behind.

"Hi, Mom!—Hi, Dad! How are you?" he asked, beaming.

Involuntarily, his gaze swept from them to the elegant grand piano, waiting patiently for the caress of his hands, then quickly back to them. He hugged his mother and patted his father on the shoulder.

"You've been hearing about Terry through my letters and phone calls for months. Well—ta da!! Now you get to meet him, in the flesh! Mom and Dad, this is Terry Stanton—Terry, my folks."

They all smiled and exchanged handshakes and "How-de-dos."

The young men's glowing California suntans seemed somehow out of place in the brisk cold of the New England December.

"So," offered Hack, "did you fellows have a good flight?"

They assured him that they had.

"Are you hungry or thirsty, or would you prefer to wait until later?"

They both indicated that later would be fine.

"Well, Chris, if Terry won't think we're terribly rude, we have a little family matter to discuss that just won't wait. We thought perhaps he would like a chance to relax before dinner anyway, so if it is all right, we will just have Mary show him to his room and you can pick him up later. Maybe he would like a nice swim to shake the dust off, so to speak."

Turning to Terry, he said, "We normally have better manners than this, Terry, but you know how it is with families."

"No problem, Mr. Hacker. The swim sounds like a great idea. I'll be perfectly happy fending for myself from now until dinner, as long as someone points me in the right direction."

"Well, fine. Mary will show the way and will be glad to help you to anything you need."

Hack stepped to the narrow tapestry bell pull and tugged it twice. It was Mary's code. She appeared within a few moments, as though she had anticipated the summons, and as she stepped into the room, Libby smiled and said, "Terry, this is our old friend and housekeeper, Mary Chaplin. Mary, this is Chris' friend, Terry Stanton. Please see that he is comfortably settled in the brown room, and that he is provided with anything he may want or need between now and dinner."

Mary and Terry exchanged smiles and nods and Mary said, "Certainly, Mrs. Hacker," in her polite way of addressing Libby in front of guests or strangers. Then, turning to Terry, she said, "Just follow me, please, sir."

They turned to leave, but suddenly, Chris said, hesitantly, "Ahh—Mary—just a minute, please."

"Yes, sir?"

His face reddened through the tan.

"Please show Terry to my suite, and have our things sent there, too. We just dropped everything in the foyer when we came in."

Mary looked a bit confused. She cast a quick glance at Libby, who, after a brief hesitation, gave an almost imperceptible shrug, then nodded assent.

Once the two had left the room, Chris looked first at his mother and then at his father. He laughed, self-consciously.

Libby was nonplussed.

"I don't follow your reasoning, Chris, dear. You always seem so happy to get back to your own little private nest, and I thought Terry would enjoy the view from the brown room. Why double up when there is so much idle space?"

An awkward silence ensued, during which Chris colored even more. He looked rapidly back and forth at his parents, who gave no evidence of understanding the inference of his instructions to Mary. Finally, he took a deep breath and said, "We would prefer to be together, Mother."

Still seeing no sign of comprehension, he plowed on. "You see, some time ago, Terry and I realized that we had become—ah—much more than roommates."

Noting that the querulous expression remained on his mother's face, he blurted out in embarrassed frustration, "Do I have to draw you a picture!"

After one more deep breath, he continued, as matter-of-factly as possible, "We sleep together. This seemed like the appropriate time to let you folks know. I thought it fairer to wait until I came home, rather than to try to discuss it on the phone or by mail. We're counting on your being able to understand."

His glance flickered between his parents again, revealing a tense combination of hope and apprehension.

Hack turned white. The stillness in the large room seemed emphasized and magnified. Libby could feel her problem returning with a rush. She staggered to a chair and fell into the seat.

Chris' words, though, had now broken through his father's mental defenses with the force of an exploding bomb. Thoughts raced through Hack's mind—No! God, no! Tell me I didn't hear that! Not Chris—not my son!

Slowly, deliberately, looking him straight in the eye, Hack half whispered, "I think I must have misunderstood you, Chris. Would you repeat what you just said, please!"

"Oh, Lord!" Chris thought, "I can see that he's going to be difficult." Then, aloud, he said, "What I said, Dad, was that Terry and I are not just friends—we're—well—we're—lovers!"

His father cringed at the use of the word.

"We're hoping you'll respect our feelings and not make a big, unpleasant scene about it," Chris continued. Then, turning a concerned eye toward the chair into which Libby had collapsed.

"What's wrong, Mom?"

To his father, he asked, "Is she all right, Dad?"

Then, as his concern over his mother's strange reaction grew, he asked her, "Are you okay, Mom?"

There was no response from Libby, but Hack took two quick steps which placed him between her and her son. His eyes were reduced to slits and there was nothing but icy sarcasm in his voice, as he said, "Oh, sure, Chris—your mother is fine—absolutely fine! Why wouldn't she be? She just learned last night that her daughter was making plans to marry her own half-brother—whom neither of them knew existed, incidentally—and before that shock wears off, you come sashaying in and announce that you've gone queer! How could a little thing like that upset her?"

Chris stood, mute, his bewilderment balancing his resentment.

Hack proceeded, his whole being now exuding venomous disgust.

"That's what we wanted to talk to you about—the fact that this young Englishman, Spenser, whom Susan fell in love with, believe it or not, turns out to be my illegitimate son by a girl I met while over there in the army! The *only* time in ,my life, by the way, that I ever cheated on your mother! That's about the wildest, craziest, most incredible goddam coincidence anyone ever heard of! When I managed to uncover that mess and made myself accept the facts, I was absolutely sick at having to break the news to your mother and sister. But, you know something? Not nearly as sick as you make me! You not only announce that you're a fairy—you actually seem to be *proud* of it! Well, buster, you can go somewhere else and practice your perversion—not in my house! You're not welcome around here! Don't even unpack—go pick up the other fruitcake and make tracks the hell out of here as fast as you can! And don't ever come back! As of right now, you're no longer any son of mine! Get out, before I break your goddam neck!"

With every passing second, the rage within Hack was increasing. Jesus Christ! This was the last straw! His immediate instinct was to belt the filthy young bastard right in the mouth, but even in this violent state, he drew the line at physically abusing his own biological son, disowned or not. As the rancor inside him mounted, he cast about for some means of venting his fury. His eyes, darting here and there, suddenly came to rest on the beautiful piano. That was it! That piano represented the most important thing in Chris' life—Yes!—he would take his vengeance there! An incident from his past flashed briefly through his mind—a segment involving another homosexual and a heavy mop bucket. As he sought an appropriate weapon, he spied, standing at the side of one of the large windows, a three-foot tall brass urn, holding a dried arrangement. He dashed across the room, and with the superhuman strength generated by his anger, he bent and lifted the massive object high above his head and made straight for the piano.

Instantly, Chris realized what his father was about to do. With a strangled cry, he leaped forward to intercept him and save his beloved instrument. He threw his arms forward, desperately hoping to push the heavy piano out of the way, but by the time his hands made contact with the keyboard, the urn was already descending, and it came crashing down. Amidst a cacophonous jangle of musical notes and splintering ivory and mahogany, Chris' shriek of agony and disbelief filled the atmosphere of the room as his wonderfully skilled hands absorbed the mangling blow.

Partially roused by Hack's shouting and subsequent actions, Libby's tortured mind dimly grasped the situation—he had told her wonderful Chris that he was to leave immediately and never come back! And then she had observed him as he dashed to the urn, brought it back and smashed it down on the piano. But what was that terrible scream? She did not realize that the blow designed to destroy Chris' precious piano had accidentally crushed his beautiful hands—the hands which meant everything to the boy! It was not until he turned frantically toward her, arms hanging limply down, utter consternation and horror etched upon his face, that what had happened registered on her confused mind. Instinctively, she took a few steps in his direction, but then her inner defenses took over and she lost consciousness.

Faithful Mary had been summoned and had seen to it that her mistress was transported to the bedroom, and she had then ordered everyone else out. She gently eased Libby into sleeping attire and into bed. Mary remained in a chair beside her for a couple of hours, until she was satisfied that her charge was in no danger. Libby's even breathing indicated that there was nothing physically wrong, and she was sure that sleep was the best medicine she could have. Mary had been told that young Chris had met with an accident and had been rushed off to the hospital. As far as she knew, the shock of the mishap was the only cause of Libby's semiconscious state.

Once all the excitement of Chris' accident and Libby's swoon had subsided, a subdued Hack took stock.. He was angry and he was shocked, but he was still firmly in control. He saw to it that adequately vague explanations were sent to at least temporarily mollify the other interested parties scattered around the mansion—Susan, Spenser, and Terry. When this was done, he went to his office where he could be alone to think everything out without distractions. Obviously, there were a number of critical decisions to be made very soon, if the shambles into which his family had been thrown was to be rectified. Well, he had handled tough problems before, and, by God, he would handle this one, too. He closed the office door behind him, poured a large glass of brandy, and embarked on a torturous brain session, sipping at the strong liquor as he alternately paced the floor and sat uneasily in the big leather chair behind his desk. This was going to take some time.

Three hours later, Libby awakened. Mary had left the room in darkness when she tiptoed out, except for a dim glow from a baseboard-mounted night light. When her eyes first opened, Libby was disoriented. Why was she here? How had she gotten here? The last she recalled was greeting Chris and his friend.—- Then, suddenly, she remembered. Oh, my God! she thought. Something terrible has happened to Chris! She struggled to dispel the cobwebs which hung before her, making indistinct the picture of what had befallen him. Her natural impulses insisted that she fight her way through this maze and get at the truth, and gradually, relentlessly, she did. Chris' beautiful, talented hands had been smashed beneath the crushing blow of the huge urn. Had it really happened, or was this more of the dream world which she had been dropping in and out of lately? No—this was no bad dream—it had really happened! How could anything so tragic have occurred? How could her son be suddenly shorn of the flesh and blood instruments so vital to the flowering of his gift? And who had wielded that horrible agent of destruction? Could it really have been Christopher, himself—the boy's own father! There was no denying it. Large beads of perspiration stood out on her forehead and nausea assailed her, but she was able to fight it back. Gradually, insidiously, a new concept of her husband was beginning to form in her beleaguered brain. Who was this man, really? Was he simply Christopher Hacker, husband, lover, father, breadwinner, war hero, model citizen—or was he, perhaps, some sort of demon, masquerading in these roles? Wasn't it Christopher, the chameleon-like character, who had been ruling all of their destinies right along? It was Christopher who had sired Spenser and had thereby caused their daughter, Susan, to find herself in a terrible, nightmarish, potentially incestuous relationship. What had started out to be a wonderful, joyous family holiday had turned into a hideous farce. And who was at the bottom of it all? Christopher! Not the admirable Christopher who had strived so hard all his life for success. Not the attentive Christopher who had pretended to faithfully squire and protect her through their early years. Not the seemingly heroic Christopher who had interrupted his young life to serve his country by shedding his blood on foreign battlefields. Not the hot-blooded, amorous Christopher who had returned to marry her and raise a family. Nor was he the clever but crafty Christopher who had built an amazing business empire while still a young man. No! None of these! Here was a different man altogether. Here was a man who always got what he wanted. Here was a man who used whatever means necessary to achieve his ends, whether in sports, or love, or business. And here was a man, or demon in male form, who, in the short space of twenty-four hours had destroyed her faith in him, ruined, in a singularly sickening manner, his daughter's romance, as well as that of his newly acknowledged elder son, and violently wrenched away his other son's reason for living! The trauma of it all deepened, as this new and horrible picture of the man took shape. What would be his next perfidious act! The miasma, in and out of which she had been flitting in recent hours, descended upon her with a vengeance.

Suddenly, through her mental shroud, she perceived dimly what she must do. This agent of the devil who had been wreaking havoc among his supposedly beloved family, while actually simply carrying out his evil purpose, had to be stopped!

Chapter 44
The Answer

Like an automaton, Libby rose slowly from her bed. She lifted her robe from the chair across which it had been laid, slipped her arms into it, and tied the belt at her waist. She marched slowly and deliberately to the sliding doors of the long closet, slid one open and stepped inside. Turning to her right, she stepped carefully up on the edge of the lowest of a series of shelves which ran from floor to ceiling across the end of the storage space. Gripping the top shelf tightly with her left hand, she groped with her right beneath the blankets piled there. In a moment, the hand came away, and in it was the Luger pistol which Hack had taught her how to shoot so long ago. She stepped down, turned, and left the room.

Next, she slid the heavy weapon under her pillow, then headed for the door to the hallway. Once in the hall, she turned right and marched along until she reached a small, seldom used room, too restricted in size to serve as a bedroom, which had become a catchall for the temporary storage of anything which needed to be removed from underfoot. She entered and moved to an old chest of drawers standing near a corner of the room. She bent and slid open the bottom drawer, reached into its far right-hand corner, beneath a jumble of odds and ends of linen and clothing, and brought out a box of .9mm ammunition. She poured a few cartridges into her hand, closed the box and restored it to its hiding place. She dropped the bullets into the pocket of her robe, closed the drawer, then returned to her bedroom.

Once there, she retrieved the Luger from under the pillow, snapped the clip out, slid the cartridges into it against the resistance of the spring, and when they were all in place, snapped the clip back into the gun. Oddly, even in her detached state, or perhaps because of it, she had remembered the drill exactly as Hack had taught it to her so many years before. Finally, she snapped off the safety, and in order to conceal the large weapon, slid the barrel up the generous right sleeve of her robe, letting the grip rest in her cupped hand. When she stood in a normally erect position with her right hand hanging down at her side, the sleeve of the robe covered virtually all of the pistol. One would have had to look very closely to discover it.

Her preparations completed, she left the bedroom and like a sleep walker, homed in on the east wing and her husband's office, where instinct told her he was most likely to be found. As luck would have it, she met no one in the course of the few minutes it took her to cover the distance. When she arrived at the office, the door was closed. She turned the knob with her left hand, pushed the door open, stepped inside and leaned back against the door to close it. There sat the devil she must destroy.

Hack looked up in surprise.

"Libby, darling—what are you doing here? Are you all right? I thought you were sleeping."

As he finished speaking, it became obvious to him that she was as impervious to his questions as though she were stone deaf. She stepped mechanically to a position immediately in front of the desk and slid the pistol out of her sleeve. With no sign of emotion, she raised the Luger in both hands, as he had instructed her, and pointed it at him.

Incredulity and then terror gripped Hack as he realized what was about to happen. He started to rise, ducking to one side in an effort to move out of the line of fire, as he shouted, "No, Lib, no!"

But before he had time to say or do more, like a programmed robot, she squeezed the trigger, then peered straight ahead as he was hurled back against his chair and sagged to the floor. Her original aim had been at his forehead, but his quick movement caused her to swing the pistol and the slug tore into his right temple.

In his last split second of life, there flashed before his eyes a vision of a German Major, laughing fiendishly.

❖ ❖ ❖

Faithful Mary, who had peeked routinely into Libby's quarters and was shocked to find her missing, came scurrying down the long hallway seeking her and was within a few feet of the office door when the report of the Luger ruptured the quietness of the wing. Hesitating only a moment as she tried to make sense of the totally foreign noise, she opened the door cautiously and nearly fell to the floor as she took in the horrible scene. There stood her beloved mistress, the hand with the smoking gun hanging at her side, and as she stepped quickly to her, she saw that slumped on the floor, unmistakably dead, was Mr. Hacker. That Libby had killed him was beyond any question, though Mary had no idea why. Mary's loyalty to Libby was, however, unqualified. Whatever she did was automatically justifiable. After a panicky moment, it dawned on Mary that she must do whatever necessary to protect the mistress she loved so dearly, and she must do it very quickly. Time enough for explanations later. A deadly purposefulness washed all other thoughts from her mind, and she swung into action as though covering up a murder were a routine part of her duties.

"Darling Mrs. Hacker—Libby! Whatever happened?" Then, soothingly, "Don't be alarmed, dear."

She had seen enough television mysteries to know the importance of fingerprints and some of the methods used to prevent smudging them. With crafty efficiency, she picked a long pencil from the desk, slid it into the barrel of the Luger and coaxed Libby's hand away from it. The weapon was very heavy and for a moment she feared that she would not be able to hold it by the few inches of protruding pencil, but necessity lent her the strength. Touching only the pencil, she bent and placed the handgrip of the weapon in the dead fingers of its owner. With a shudder, she closed Hack's hand, with the index finger in firing position in front of the trigger. Then she slid the pencil free and dropped it back on the desk. Already, she could hear running footsteps pounding down the hallway. She stepped back to Libby's side and put a strong arm around her.

"Come, dear," she said softly.

She steered her charge quickly toward the back stairs that would take them to the second floor. By the time they had exited, she could hear people rapping on the front door of the office, concerned for its occupants but hesitant to enter the master's private sanctum without permission. Now, Mary thought, if they could just be lucky enough to find no one in the upper hallway, she might be able to spirit Libby back to her room before anyone saw them. Luck was with them. Urging the oblivious Libby along—practically dragging her at times, Mary managed to gain the room without being observed. She slipped off Libby's robe and eased her into bed, then she collapsed into a chair as sweat poured from her and an uncontrollable trembling set in.

When the spasm subsided, she stroked Libby's hair and said, "Time to rest now, dear. You've had a bad dream but now you can sleep peacefully. Mary is here. Close your eyes."

Like an obedient child, Libby did so and was asleep almost immediately.

Mary knew that she must make her way back to the office the long way, but she would have to hurry if she was to prevent people wondering what had taken her so long to respond to the commotion which had, of course, arisen soon after the gunshot. Although the mansion was huge and people were scattered throughout its various parts, it did not take long for word of the disaster to spread and for everyone to come running. Most of the early arrivals were staff people.

"Who is it? What was that—a shot?"

"It's Mr. Hacker! He's dead!"

"My God! What happened?"

"The boss? I don't believe it!"

"Holy Christ! It is him! Who shot him?"

But, by now, those who had crowded in close to the body could see the blood and the fingers clutching the butt of the gun.

"Jesus! He killed himself!"

"Did anyone call a doctor?"

"Doctor! Hell—he won't need any doctor!"

"Well, how about the police—did anyone call them?"

By this time, both Sue and Spenser, who had been silently trying to recover from the previous night's revelation in their respective quarters when the shot occurred, had responded to the shouting and running and had followed the traffic to the east wing and the office. Spenser arrived a moment ahead of her and took in the tragic scene. He could plainly see that Mr. Hacker was quite dead. Instinctively, he turned to find her and put a protective arm around her.

"Sue—I'm not sure you want to see this."

"Wha—wha—what is wrong?"

She tried craning her neck to see around Spenser and the others who were blocking her view, but he held her back.

"It's your father, Sue. I'm afraid he has been shot."

Then to himself, ironically, "Your father? *Our* father, I suppose I should say."

Susan gasped and wilted in his arms. "This will kill her altogether," Spenser thought. But suddenly she straightened up.

"How bad is it—can you tell?" she asked.

"As bad as it gets, I fear. There certainly is no sign of life."

Her knees buckled once more, but she righted herself. "Could anything worse happen?" she thought. "Why is the world suddenly falling apart?"

Someone had to try to restore some order before the authorities arrived. Someone had to ask those assembled to step back away from the victim and to avoid disturbing anything. Someone needed to cover the body. Someone, in other words, had to take charge. With quiet efficiency, Spenser found himself fulfilling that role. He asked that all but the family members please leave the room, specifically excepting Mary, who had slipped back in unnoticed.

"Where is Mrs. Hacker?" he asked her in a low voice.

"She is in her bed, sound asleep. I really don't believe we should disturb her until it is absolutely necessary—she appears to be quite exhausted. She may be coming down with something."

Spenser nodded, thinking to himself, that it was last night's news that had exhausted her. He then asked Mary to bring something to cover Mr. Hacker. He picked up the phone and called both a doctor and the police.

These duties finished, he sat down on a sofa facing away from the body. Gently, he pulled the softly sobbing Susan down beside him and held her while they awaited the arrival of the police.

Chapter 45
Transition

It took the police a surprisingly short time to do all of the investigating which appeared necessary. There was nothing in the way of evidence to indicate anything other than a suicide. Routine examination showed that the gun was Mr. Hacker's and that the only prints on it were those of himself and his wife, both of whom were known to have shot it before. As the questioning gradually but steadily uncovered the terribly upsetting sequence of events of the previous twenty-four hours, the police became firmly convinced that suicide was the only logical answer. The revelation of the story of Spenser and what it had done to Mrs. Hacker and the daughter, and the ensuing maiming by Mr. Hacker's own hand, of his gifted son, was more than enough provocation, they believed, to put a proud, envied man over the edge.

The account of Mrs. Hacker's apparent nervous breakdown and complete incapacity following those tragic events would have ruled her out in any case, especially since the housekeeper, Mrs. Chaplin, had stated that the lady had been confined to her bed at the time of the shooting and constantly watched over by herself.

Perhaps, had the police not been anxious to clear the case up in deference to the reputation of the family, and had the circumstances, as revealed, not made suicide perfectly plausible, there might have been more forensic investigation. Those telltale fingerprints told the story—only the victim and his wife had handled the weapon, and she was solidly alibied not only by her condition at the time, but also by the testimony of the dignified and honorable housekeeper who was attending her. No paraffin test of anyone in the house at the time was deemed necessary, and there were some obvious powder burns around the wound. The only detail which bothered the inspector in charge was the absence of a suicide note. There was almost always a note.

"Why didn't he leave a note?" he asked his assisting sergeant. "They usually do."

"Think it was a spur of the moment thing? Presumably, Hacker must have kept the weapon in his desk, as so many are inclined to do. Maybe he just sat there feeling really lousy and suddenly decided to knock himself off—you think?"

"To tell you the truth, Inspector, I think that's compatible with Mr. Hacker's personality. He was so damned sure of himself and sort of gave the impression that he didn't give that much of a damn about others. I can see him making up his mind to do it and just going ahead with it and to hell with everybody."

The officials were willing, with varying degrees of reluctance, to accept this explanation. Everyone's first question was, why would the ultra-successful and healthy Hacker, with so much going for him, have had any reason to kill himself? It was the last thing that anyone who knew him would have expected, but that was because the circumstances which could obviously have triggered such action had developed so quickly. Only the family and a few discrete police officials knew the details of the shocking events which had led up to the tragedy. Eventually, therefore, the most popular assumption by townspeople and Hack's far-flung cortege of business acquaintances was that he had learned that he was harboring symptoms of some lethal health condition.

The days following the shocking violent death of the master of the mansion on Henderson Mountain were totally unlike those which had preceded it. Instead of a happy, lively place, with guests and staff constantly bustling about, the house reflected a somber air as the greatly reduced traffic slowed its pace to a monotonous crawl. The formerly spirited atmosphere, filled with the voices and laughter of busy, confident people was now hushed and businesslike. It was very apparent how integral to the well-being of the mansion and its occupants, the mistress, Mrs. Hacker, had been. Calm, efficient, reasonable and always pleasant, she had set the tone of the household and her absence made the place seem even emptier than it was. Ever since the shooting she had been confined to a sanatorium, totally unable to communicate and totally unaware of what had happened.

Chapter 46
Aftermath

Once things began to settle down following the double-barreled tragedy at Henderson Mountain, Sue came to the uncomfortable realization that she was the sole member of the Newvale family of Christopher Drummond Hacker who was still capable of functioning. This allowed Susan only two choices of action; she could fall apart completely, leaving everything in the hands of her father's attorneys, or she could take charge. She quickly decided that she had too much pride and too much of her father's drive and determination to accept the first solution, so she took a few deep breaths and plunged into a task which would have been a challenge to almost anyone. The paternal grandparents, John and Melody, were now permanent residents of Florida in John's retirement. Both the distance from Newvale and their now less than robust health, dictated that it was better that they stay there until the immediate crises were over. Susan was fortunate in that Mary stepped forward and completely assumed the role of housekeeper, which she had formerly shared with Libby, and performed so well that Susan could turn her attention elsewhere.

After discussing her mother's and brother's conditions with their respective doctors, she went over the arrangements for her father's funeral. Despite the renown of C. D. Hacker, she was emphatic in her decision that it be a private ceremony, without even close friends or associates in attendance. There would be time later for a memorial service; for now, she could not consider coping with anything like that. She, along with Spenser, had had to deal with the police investigation, of course. Within a day or two of the tragedy, phone calls and telegrams were pouring in, and there was a long line of cars backed up along the road leading to the Hacker mansion. Fortunately, Sue had instructed the guards at the entrance gate to let in no one without official credentials.

Much to her amazement and her everlasting gratitude, it was Spenser who made the difference, offering to handle any part of the huge problem of sorting out what had to be done. With heartfelt thanks, she set him to work as her lieutenant, deciding which details had to have her personal attention and which he could handle. There were panicky calls from a number of prominent business associates, seeking assurance that their particular deals would not be affected negatively by the sudden demise of the legendary Mr. Hacker. An avalanche of cards, letters, wires and cablegrams threatened to bury the little office complex where Spenser had set up headquarters.

Fortunately, Hack had maintained a working relationship as well as a friendship with Jonathan Cartwright, III, second generation representative of the old Newvale law partnership of Bridestead and Cartwright. Jonathan became a very important consultant to Sue and Spenser in their efforts to maintain a semblance of order to the complex ventures of C. D. Hacker. He realized that Hack had relied on him more for things of a personal nature than for counsel on his worldwide operations, but he was invaluable for his appraisal of the legal angles involved in handling specific situations as they arose.

Once the pace began to slacken, Cartwright told Sue that he would like to do a quick review of her father's will. It was obvious that there could be no formal reading until such time as Chris, and hopefully, Libby, were recovered sufficiently to participate, but he felt that he could and should do everything possible to reassure Sue that everything had been well planned by her father to cope with all exigencies. This information did have the desired effect of letting her know that they would eventually be able to straighten everything out.

One decision Sue had had to make immediately—she had to take a leave of absence from school which she had only begun a few months before. Because Spenser was in graduate school, he had the flexibility to render assistance for at least a few months without it interfering seriously with his schedule. Because Sue and Spenser were so busy with Hack's work, they found themselves able to push the shocking devastation of their love affair into the background, though vestiges of their former intense feelings had not completely subsided. Between them, they made an efficient team, and time slid by almost unnoticed as they became more and more deeply involved in the operation of Hacker Enterprises.

Chapter 47
Storm

The large gray stone sanatorium, sitting regally on its somewhat elevated grounds, gave the impression of having been in place a long, long time, even though it appeared to be in perfect repair. Not a spot on the wooden casements, doors, cornices nor any of the other trim showed the slightest need of painting. Neither moss nor ivy corrupted the crisp, square lines of the masonry and granite structure, and the heavy red roof tiles appeared capable of successfully withstanding another century of buffeting by nature. Handsome trees and artistically trimmed shrubs and hedges were strategically located around the building, the extensive and well-tended lawns, and lined the long, white pebble drive.

The whole place reeked of money and, indeed, the majority of the institution's clientele consisted of the pitiful wreckage of wealthy families who had proved better equipped to cope with the problems of industry, politics and commerce than with those of their innermost beings.

Outside, above the hills to the north and west, hazy clouds had been assembling for some time, darkening steadily, until they blotted out much daylight. A pinkish incandescence outlined the scalloped edges of the clouds, and angry looking rolls of gray within them signaled the tumultuous birth of the powerful winds which would soon erupt.

At ground level, whatever breeze there had been was suddenly stilled. Every leaf on every tree hung lifelessly, birds abruptly ceased their saucy conversations, hushed by the unfamiliar and uncomfortable drop in pressure, and were nowhere in evidence. The unmoving air had an oppressive feel and in the eerie silence, all living things waited expectantly, apprehensively.

Some of those inside the huge old building sensed the ominous approach of the storm. Members of the staff moved quickly and silently, seeing that windows and doors were shut and that those inmates given to panic under any threatening or unusual circumstances were ushered into inner rooms and halls, where the peal of thunder and flash of lightning would be camouflaged to a degree. Those who either took pleasure in such disturbances as welcome breaks in their monotonous existence, or took no notice whatsoever of external occurrences, were allowed to remain in their accustomed chairs, beds or other sanctums.

Away from the windows, near an undecorated corner in the walls of the Common Room, on a plain but comfortable chair, sat a middle-aged woman dressed in a neat and pretty flowered robe. Her feet were slippered and although she wore no makeup, her elegantly coifed silver hair gave evidence of having recently received the attention of a professional beautician, as did her fingernails. Even after three and one half years of inactivity in the asylum, she still retained the figure of a much younger person, and her facial features were still attractive—except for the eyes. It took only a quick glance at those eyes to see that they were merely windows on an empty mind. The irises were still a rich brown, and the whites were clear and healthy, but obviously little or nothing which they observed registered on the brain behind them. She sat with her arms crossed tightly under her breasts, feet squarely on the floor, and head tilted slightly forward so that the focus of those vacant eyes was steadily on the pattern of the carpeted floor. None of the traffic about the large room, none of the familiar noises of a busy facility, not even the occasionally wild or silly or weird or horrible babblings of some of the other inmates seemed to make the slightest impression on her. She was as effectively removed from the proceedings of the establishment as though she were in another place and time.

Outside, the first physical evidence of the gathering tempest appeared in the form of some large and widely separated raindrops. Gradually they increased in tempo and volume and the wind began to rise, the skies became darker still.

Cra-a-a-c-k, boom, rumble—the first loud roll of thunder announced the arrival of the storm. The lightning which had fathered it was still too far away to be readily noticed inside the heavily walled building.

Rapidly now, the elements combined and intensified until they produced a furious medley of sound, light and action, all seemingly bent on destroying the fortress-like edifice and all of its occupants. Lightning so bright that it lit up every crack and cranny in the big room came repeatedly—so often that there almost seemed to be no break between attacks, and it was accompanied by the roaring thunder, which made even the staunch and rugged old structure tremble and groan. Torrents of water raced down the sides of the building, streaming across the windows in such volume that nothing whatever was visible outside. The violence of the storm was such that many of the occupants, including even a number of the staff members, lost their composure and cowered, whimpering, against the inside walls.

It was unquestionably one of the worst thunderstorms which had visited the Newvale area in many years, and it seemed that it had sought out the old asylum as the focal point of its evil passion. The power and fury built in intensity minute after minute, like a steadily accelerating artillery barrage. Finally, in what appeared to be an all-out attempt to level the place, the storm paused momentarily, poised above the great tiled roof, and then unleashed its most spectacular exhibition of light and sound. Although previous displays of thunder and lightning had been remarkable, the ultimate B-o-o-o-m was almost beyond description. Sparked by the deafening fortissimo of the battering storm, sudden frenzied activity erupted at the chair of the heretofore silent lady. The blank, staring eyes lost their vacuity and filled instead with a look of terror. Responding to what, in her twisted mind, she took to be the terribly amplified report of the Luger, the murderous power of which she seemed once again to feel leaping in her hand, she flew up from the chair with a soul-searing scream, hands pressed tightly against her ears. The listless body was suddenly transformed into a mass of energy. Legs pumping rapidly, she made for the heavy oak door that gave access to a courtyard at the immediate rear of the building. Before any of the stunned staff could interfere, she plunged through the door, down the steps and out into the teeming rain.

"Christopher! Oh, Christopher!" she screamed, at a decibel level calculated to compete with nature's loudest efforts. As she stood fully exposed to the storm, another violent shaft of lightning momentarily flooded the courtyard with its brilliance. By now, an attendant noticed that one of the inmates was in grave danger. He raced for the door and out into the courtyard and, without breaking stride, scooped the lady up in this strong arms and dashed back to the safety of the building. She had at first started to kick and struggle, but suddenly went limp in his grasp. Fearing the worst, the attendant shouted for a doctor and rushed his inert burden into the nearest bedroom, where he deposited her on the bed. Since everyone's attention had been drawn to this noisy and lively drama, word had reached one of the doctors within seconds. He dashed for the room where pointing fingers indicated the patient had been taken. Much to the relief of the attendant who had rescued her, it took only a very short examination to convince the physician that the patient had suffered little real physical harm.

"It's all right, Donald," he said to the man, "Mrs. Hacker will be fine. Please take her to her room. Just lay her on her bed and stay with her for a few minutes while I collect my bag. I'll be right there."

When the doctor reached Libby's room, he was astonished to find her sitting on the edge of the bed, apparently fairly alert, but obviously quite bewildered.

"Well, Mrs. Hacker, how are we doing?" he asked, pulling out his stethoscope and starting to apply it to her chest.

As he continued his examination, Libby asked, "Where am I, Doctor? Is this a hospital? What happened—was I in an accident? Where is my family? Do they know I'm here? And why are my clothes wet?"

"Now, now—just relax while I finish checking you over. Yes, this is a hospital and your family knows you are here. You were involved in a, well—an accident, and you have been virtually unconscious for quite some time. I'm sure that your son and daughter will be here soon and will be delighted to find that you have regained your senses. They are being notified right now."

"But—but—I don't understand! When—what—"

"Please, Mrs. Hacker," said the doctor, patting her hand gently. "The sudden return of your senses is a wonderful thing—the thing we have all been hoping and waiting for—but you cannot expect to clear everything up in a matter of seconds. What I would like to have you do right now is to take a nap. I'm going to give you something to make you sleepy, and probably when you wake up, some of your family will be here. Will you do that for me?"

His manner was so soothing that Libby found herself relaxing, and she allowed him to give her a shot which began almost immediately to make her drowsy, despite the disordered hodge-podge of thoughts tumbling about in her head. In a matter of minutes, she was asleep.

❖ ❖ ❖

Christopher, on the mend physically but still learning to cope with the terrible truth that his days as a concert pianist were behind him, was the first to learn that his mother seemed to have made a sudden great leap toward recovery. Happily engrossed in composing a complex piano piece in his beloved music room, he received the call from the sanatorium. The doctor told him briefly that something about the storm seemed to have shocked his mother back to reality, at least temporarily, and suggested that he and Susan should come to see her at once.

"There is no guarantee that this is a permanent situation, but at least for the moment it looks most encouraging," the doctor explained.

"Believe me, Doctor, we'll be there right away," Chris responded.

Fortunately, Susan was in her father's old office, dealing with a complicated business situation which she had inherited following her father's death. Christopher phoned her, his voice almost hysterical.

"Sue! Sue—the best news! Doctor Vegada just called to say that Mother has made a sudden recovery of her senses! It may be only temporary, but he says for us to get over there right away! Whatever you're doing, drop it and meet me out front. I'm calling for a car right now."

He hung up without waiting for an answer, and called the garage on the intercom, telling them to get a car—any car—to the front door as fast as possible.

Chapter 48
Conclusion

After allowing Mrs. Hacker to sleep for a while, Dr. Vegada had staff people awaken her and dress her and put her into a comfortable chair in a small conference room. He conversed with her for a while in order to appraise the state of her mental health. She appeared to be in control of her senses, but was very confused as to her reason for being in the hospital. He preferred to wait until the family members arrived before giving her any real explanation.

Presently, the door was opened by an attendant and Libby's children hurried in.

"Mother!" Sue cried, rushing to her arms. Chris was right behind her and threw his arms around both women, all three of them crying happily.

"Oh, Sue!, Chris! How wonderful to see you."

Then she asked, "Has the doctor given you any explanation of what is going on? He has been very pleasant to me, but hasn't told me why I am here, or how long I have been here, or anything. What happened? And where is your father? Off on one of his trips, I suppose."

Momentarily, there was a marked silence, then the doctor spoke, after a meaningful glance at Susan.

"Let's all sit down and be comfortable."

Once they had taken seats, he asked, "Mrs. Hacker, don't you remember anything at all about the circumstances that caused you to be here?"

"No, Doctor, I certainly don't. But I am getting a definite feeling that you are reluctant to supply the answers." Pressing forward, increasing alarm becoming apparent in her voice, "Something terrible happened, didn't it? What was it? Tell me! Please, please, tell me! Sue—Chris—what is going on?"

The doctor leaned close to Libby and put his hand on her shoulder.

"Mrs. Hacker, do you think you are strong enough to handle some bad news?"

She hesitated, then asked, "How bad?"

He judged from her expression that it would be all right to continue. "It has to do with Mr. Hacker."

Libby gave a noticeable shudder. "He—he's had an accident—a bad accident?" she asked, tremulously.

"In a manner of speaking, yes. A very bad one, Mrs. Hacker."

Libby trembled, but seemed in control of herself. She swallowed hard. "Fatal?"

The doctor took her hand and nodded. "Yes. It happened quite some time ago, Mrs. Hacker, and the shock of it caused a very serious reaction. Your mind couldn't quite cope with it, and you went into a catatonic state from which you just emerged this morning. Apparently the violence of the storm we had, triggered something in your brain that brought you back to reality."

Libby accepted this terrible news without more than a shudder. "Poor Christopher! My poor, poor Christopher! How did it happen? Was it an auto accident?"

"I think it would be better if we just stopped discussing it temporarily, Mrs. Hacker. There will be plenty of time to go over the whole story when you have had a chance to return to a more or less normal routine. We want to see you continue the great improvement you have shown, and dwelling on unhappy subjects is not good therapy."

"Even so, Doctor, I have to know how it happened. I am sure I can handle it. Just tell me what happened, at least."

Her appearance was better than the doctor would have expected, and he could see that she was not going to accept any further delay.

"Very well," he said. Turning to Susan, he raised his eyebrows in a gesture indicating his doubts. Susan took the cue.

"Mother," she said, soothingly, "let me sit next to you." She sat down on the arm of her mother's chair and put an arm around her shoulders.

"Mother, you're going to find this very hard to believe, but Daddy—well—there is no easy way to put it—he—committed suicide!"

The shock of this announcement almost lifted Libby off the seat, and caused the doctor to fear that he had made a foolish decision. Too late now to revoke it. He mentally crossed his fingers as the words registered.

"What!?" she cried.

Susan held her even closer, and Chris came over and hugged her, too.

"I know it is hard to imagine, but that is what it was," Sue explained.

"But—he would never do that! Whatever could have caused him to—to—do away with himself?"

Susan glanced rapidly back and forth at the doctor and her brother.

"Don't you remember what Daddy told us when we were getting together for Christmas? About—about Spenser, Mom? Don't you remember that?"

Suddenly, the bad news came flooding back to Libby. Christopher had uncovered the story of Spenser's background and his own involvement in it, and had presented it to the family as an unwanted and totally unexpected Christmas gift! Unbelievably, he had admitted to having sired the nice young Englishman to whom their daughter had become engaged!

"Oh, my God! Yes—I do remember now. Oh, poor Sue! Poor, poor Sue!"

She grasped her daughter's hand and squeezed it hard, then pressed it against her cheek.

"I'm used to it now, Mother," Sue assured her. "It's been over three years—almost four, really. Everyone has adjusted nicely to the situation. In fact, Spenser gave me all sorts of help in straightening out Daddy's affairs and has only recently been able to resume his studies. You remember the accident to Chris' hands?"

Another shock wave passed over Libby, but the old problem of slipping away from reality did not arise. Yes, she remembered that horrible episode in the conservatory—remembered her husband's violent rage at Chris' announcement of his homosexuality, coming hard on the heels of the shattering confession of Christopher's having fathered Spenser. But now, she was able to consider these disasters at face value and as something to be dealt with, not as completely unacceptable fairytales. Her mind felt clear and totally operable. Four years? How could so much time have elapsed without her knowing anything about what was going on? She had to find the strength to face the memory of Chris' injury and other shocks which she had been dealt. She summoned what it would take from deep inside, squared her jaw and drew back her shoulders.

"Chris, darling—how are your beautiful hands? Have you recovered? Can you play?"

Chris looked at her and sighed.

"Mother, my hands have mended as much as they are ever going to; the doctors tell me I can do just about anything with them now—except to play concert piano. I play, and very well, too, but there just isn't the mobility necessary to do justice to the more complex pieces."

As the tears welled up in Libby's eyes and her lip trembled, he hastened to add, "Don't worry about me. I am perfectly happy, Mom, really. My new loves are composing and arranging. I'm into music as much as ever—more, actually. And I'm starting to be in demand for those talents. Probably much better off than I would have been over the long haul as just a pianist."

How brave of him, and how wonderfully practical, Libby thought proudly. Whatever social problems Chris might have, he was a beautiful person with great strength of character.

The doctor had carefully monitored these exchanges and was pleased with the way Mrs. Hacker was handling everything. She seemed able to cope with the revelations and he felt that that was paramount in importance.

The conversation among the family members continued for some time, and finally, Dr. Vegada said, "It appears that you are making miraculous strides toward a complete recovery, Mrs. Hacker, but I want you to stay here for another week so that we can do a thorough evaluation of your condition. If all indications continue positive, you can be released to return home, which I am sure is the best news you could hope to get."

Libby brightened. "Oh, my—it certainly is. But what I need most right now is the comfort and love of my children. Turning to Sue, she asked, "Isn't there some way that you could stay with me—at least for a day or two? It would mean so much to me, and you will be able to fill in all the empty spaces that are already starting to crop up in my mind about this whole terrible nightmare."

Susan looked at the doctor and said, "Mother is absolutely right. I can arrange to stay with her for however long it is necessary, assuming that you can accommodate me. As long as I have access to a telephone, I'll be able to take care of business from here, temporarily. And Chris, you can probably drop in for a while every day, can't you?"

"I sure can—and will."

"Will that work out, Doctor?"

"No reason why not. I'll have a few changes made in your mother's room and you should be perfectly comfortable for a few days. I am sure it will be excellent therapy for you, Mrs. Hacker, to be able to get some answers direct from Susan and Chris as they come to mind."

❖ ❖ ❖

The week went by rapidly. Hour after hour it seemed that Libby came up with something else that she needed or wanted to know concerning the course of events during the past many months. Susan explained to her how she and Spenser had gradually adjusted to their abruptly altered relationship and how much of a rock of dependability and assistance he had been in handling Hack's business obligations. After a couple of years, the pressures had finally subsided to the point where Spenser could resume his studies—he would not consider leaving her sooner, even when she insisted that she could get along and hated to see him wasting his valuable time there when it should be spent in pursuing knowledge in his special field. Libby asked how Spenser had been able to explain the situation to his family.

"Well," Susan told her, "with typical British taciturnity, he had never mentioned me to them—preferring, I guess, to wait until we were married. Then, when everything came apart, he decided it best to *never* tell! He thought it might be as much of a strain on his family as it was on ours, if they knew the details. He simply told them he had found a position which he liked and which would make him a modest amount of money, although it would delay completion of his education. Finally, when he was convinced that his presence in Newvale was no longer essential, he made arrangements to return to MIT, after settling some questions as to whether or not his fellowship money was still available."

Fortunately, they ruled in his favor, although Susan had assured him that any financial problems were simply to be referred to her.

By then, Chris had endured a whole series of operations and hundreds of hours of therapy and was resigned to the fact that he was never going to be the artist he once had been. He was building a new life and did not need the mothering which Sue had lavished on him during the first few desperate months. He lived in his old suite in the mansion and spent many hours every day in his beloved music room with its beautiful new piano. He volunteered nothing about his love life, and Susan did not ask. All she knew or cared was that he was an affectionate and wonderful brother whom she dearly loved. Chris had not, as yet, considered returning to Pepperdine to complete his senior year, although he always said that he planned to do so.

Soon after she took over the reins, Susan, in consultation with lawyer Cartwright, and with the approval of Chris, had made the decision that as soon as her father's current deals were concluded, the actual operation of Hacker Enterprises as a viable vehicle of commerce would end. The corporation would be continued indefinitely, but would eventually be transformed into a foundation underwriting charitable, philosophical and educational endeavors. It would take several years for this to become a reality, because the plan was to transfer the ownership of a number of the subordinate businesses to those who had been managing them. A few segments, particularly those where Hack had been indispensable, would simply be phased out and converted into cash.

Because she had been so busy with the business, she had had no time to socialize. The scar left by the revelation of Spenser's parentage would doubtless have immunized her against romantic entanglements for some time. By the time of Libby's recovery, Sue still had not developed an interest in other men. Furthermore, she wanted to get back to her schooling. The thought of returning to Smith was not appealing; her tenure there was a happier time. She now knew that she had a definite interest in and talent for business, so she arranged to attend the nearby branch of UConn, with the intention of studying business administration.

Returning home was the best medicine for Libby. She took over the reins of running the mansion a little at a time. Mary, who had been managing the household very well during Libby's absence, was overjoyed at having Libby back. She had no regrets at being slowly relegated to the background. The secret of the actual drama of Mr. Hacker's death was sealed up inside her so securely that nothing and nobody could ever pry it loose. Libby saw to it that Mary, who was beginning to show signs of age, had plenty of light duties but no large responsibilities. On the one occasion when she asked Mary about what had happened the day that Hack died, the answer was matter-of-fact. She had heard shouts and people hurrying through the corridors, and when she left Libby's bedside to go to Mr. Hacker's office, she had learned of his suicide. Mr. Maitland had asked her to bring something to cover the body, which she had done. When the police interviewed her, she could only tell them that at the time of the shooting, she had been in with Mrs. Hacker, who was ill and in bed. From time to time, the subject of Hack's suicide crept into Libby's mind, try as she might to forget it. From the first time she heard of it, it had puzzled her. She simply could not get it out of her mind that Christopher seemed like the last person she ever met who would choose suicide as a way out of his problems. He had shot himself, they said. That, in itself, seemed extremely odd to her. What would he have used for a weapon? She had never asked, but now she made up her mind to do so. The next time she saw Susan, she brought the subject up.

"Susan, I want you to tell me more about your father's suicide. No one has ever given me any information about it, except to say that he shot himself."

"Oh, Mother—do you think it is good for you to discuss that? Isn't it better to just try to forget it?"

"Well, Sue, I really think I should know more about it than I do. For instance, if he shot himself, where did he get the gun?"

"Why, he used that old pistol he brought home from the war."

"The Luger?"

"Yes—I'm sure that's what they called it. It was the one he brought home from Germany."

"But—well, I guess that's the only hand gun he ever had. Yes, I suppose it must have been that one. But I still can't make myself believe he did it. It's so unlike him. And why no suicide note? Wouldn't he have wanted to tell us why—to say goodbye, at least?"

"Well, Mom, the police considered everything and were satisfied that that was it. They are the experts, after all. Can't we switch to a more pleasant subject?"

At the end of the day, Libby sat quietly musing in her suite. Something about the information Sue had given her sat uncomfortably on her conscience. She remembered the time years ago when Christopher had taken her out to the gravel bank and taught her how to shoot the Luger. She had told him that she hated guns and wanted nothing to do with them, but he had insisted that she should know how to use one in case she ever needed to defend herself. After she had passed his test, he told her that he wanted to keep the gun handy for use in case of an emergency. To satisfy him, she had agreed, but it was understood that the gun would be kept in one place and the ammunition in another and that only the two of them would know where to find them. When they moved into the mansion, it was weeks before all of their household goods, old and new, were distributed about the place. Christopher was far too busy with his work to participate in such minor details, so Libby inherited the responsibility for every facet of the move. In the confusion, it was some time before the Luger, and later, the ammunition, came to the surface. When it appeared, she had hidden the gun under some blankets on a shelf in the closet in their suite. When the box of bullets turned up, she had stashed it down the hall in an old chest of drawers, but she had never remembered to tell Christopher where either the weapon or the ammunition were hidden, and his mind was far too full of mergers and licensing and buyouts and other business coups to ever think of such trivial matters.

…Wait a minute—what was she saying?

She had never remembered to tell him where they were hidden !!!

Suddenly, as the meaning of this struck her, her legs went weak and watery. Beads of sweat popped out on her upper lip. She staggered to a chair and flopped into it, sobbing. Now, she knew for sure that Christopher's death was no suicide, and furthermore, *she knew who had killed him !!*

But, again—did that make any sense?—if that were really the case—if she had, indeed, in her deranged condition, salvaged the weapon and the ammunition and gone to the office and shot him, as it appeared she most certainly must have done, how had the gun gotten into his hand and how had she escaped detection, or even suspicion? In her condition at the time of the tragedy, she surely would not have been crafty enough to plan, let alone carry out, any such cover-up. Who then? Who?—and why??

As she sat, frantically casting about for answers, there was a soft knock on her door. After a moment, it slowly opened and Mary's saintly gray head appeared, her face bearing an adoring smile.

"Can I do anything else for you Libby, dear—anything at all?"